Typhoon Ace

TYPHOON ACE

RUSSELL SULLMAN

LUME BOOKS

LUME BOOKS

Published in 2020 by Lume Books
30 Great Guildford Street,
Borough, SE1 0HS

ISBN 978-1-83901-216-7

Typeset using Atomik ePublisher from Easypress Technologies

www.lumebooks.co.uk

Acknowledgements

I want to express my heartfelt gratitude to all the amazing folks at Lume Books, and in particular to the incredible Alice Rees, who somehow filtered out a novel from the reams of burbling where Typhoon Ace was hiding inside, and to the wonderful James Faktor and Rebecca Souster.

And lots of love and thanks to my family. You lift me up, and your decorative additions to my study are appreciated (though I'm still not sure where exactly to put half a dozen rather feral-looking Barbies, the battered collection of cars and Transformers, or the broken Henry vacuum cleaner!)

Prologue

The faint shapes of the two fighter-bombers appeared suddenly as if by magic, coming in low from the distant haze of a clear morning sky. Shadowy, almost imperceptible cruciform shapes, swiftly gaining form as they dropped even lower, racing in at high speed towards the coast, low, dangerously low over the waves, almost touching the sea, lustrous shapes dancing over their shadows on the glittering whitecaps beneath.

None of the onlookers at the shore noticed them for some moments; all eyes still focussed anxiously on the first tight formation of six raiders, now beyond the range of the coastal guns, far to the south and out over the water, heading back for the sanctuary of their airbase in France.

The six enemy fighter-bombers had appeared without warning, attacking unexpectedly at treetop height from an inland approach, strafing the town centre before bombing the army training camp, whilst the alert and waiting eyes of the defences had all been looking out to sea.

The air raid siren still wailed mournfully, and dirty banks of smoke drifted slowly from where the bombs had fallen, the sound of the sudden explosions leaving behind a legacy in the shrill peal of ambulance and fire service bells and the cries of the wounded.

By the time the first of the defenders noticed them, the oncoming pair of little raiders had already eaten up more than two-thirds of the five miles separating the point in the haze at which they had emerged from the heart of the harbour.

Desperately, gun barrels trained towards the departed fighter-bombers were spun around and dropped, bringing them to bear on the new formation.

7

A small naval minesweeper, little more than a modified trawler, was tethered securely and comfortably beside a tightly packed knot of shabby and hard-worked fishing vessels. Sailors in various stages of dress were already streaming back onto the open deck. The gun-layers too, having relaxed as the first formation passed swiftly out of range and disappeared into the haze, scrambling frantically now to bring to bear the First World War-vintage four-inch gun mounted on the foredeck.

The harbour AA defences beat them to it, and the sky around the little deadly shapes was abruptly stained by an eruption of lethal fiery blooms. But the raiders merely dipped ever lower, terrifyingly lower, almost brushing the sea as they approached. Plumes of spray rose from their slipstream, and then their cannon began to sparkle prettily, and shells churned the water before tearing viciously through metal and wood and flesh on the little minelayer, bowling over the gunners in a cloud of splinters and blood.

A small, dark cylinder suddenly dropped from beneath the leading aircraft and the lightened enemy jumped upwards, even as the minelayer shuddered and shook from the raiders' blistering machine gun and cannon fire.

The bomb hit the water, slowing and skipping back upwards atop a shimmering wave, glistening over the ship, perilously close to the tailplane of the number two raider, then crashed down again against the side of the dock, exploding ferociously.

The effect of the bomb on the dockside was deadly and devastating. But even as the harbour wall shattered and splintered into a rapidly-expanding and lethal storm of metal, stone and concrete shards, the reflected blast impulse and the overpressure of the explosion blasted up and back and outwards from the dock wall, the foremost force of the detonation slamming brutally against the hull of the little minesweeper, tearing and crushing a destructive path violently through the little warship's hull.

The shockwave and blast damage boiled harshly over nearby ships, but the diminutive minesweeper suffered most from the 500kg of explosive.

Hull ruptured and ripped apart in that instant of sudden, cruel destruction, its luckless crew of dead and dying men having been thrown mercilessly into the raging water, the sundered remnants of the minesweeper quickly slipped beneath the violent maelstrom of torn water.

A swelling storm of pressure and whirling stone shards swept over the nearby trawlers, tearing at crews and onlookers with bloody injury and death.

As his stricken ship sank, the mortally injured naval lieutenant coughed out his last tortured breath. He had no time to grieve the death of his beloved first command and felt only bitter anger for the enemy, his last sight before the light went being that of the two raiders in close formation, tightly sweeping back towards the sanctuary of what lay beyond the open sea.

Within moments, the danger from the AA was past and the death and destruction they had wrought showed only as a dark and hazy cloud in the beautifully clear blue sky, arching over the remote faded streak of the enemy coastline behind.

*

Peter laughed shakily with burgeoning relief, his heart still racing with excitement and terror.

After a sleepless night, and all the agonizing of earlier that morning, in the hours before this first mission, the act of actually attacking the enemy harbour and dropping his bomb had been easier than he had feared.

In the end, after barrelling through that vicious gauntlet of defence, the opposition had turned out to be more bark than bite, the nerve-shattering rattle of shrapnel and the hoarse bark of the AA bursts being ultimately ineffectual.

Yet despite this, the run-in under fire had required all of his self-control to hold course as they raced into the teeth of the defences.

His leader had shown no such fears, and sank the little warship with singular expertise, placing his bomb perfectly to maximise its effect.

Peter's own bomb had not been quite so efficiently placed, skidding across the waterfront before exploding to create a scene of bloody chaos. He had not seen the impact, but as they turned tightly back the way they had come, he momentarily caught sight of the blazing, blackened vehicles burning amidst a glittering sprawl of splintered glass and torn metal, the adjacent shopfronts sagging and burning, debris and bodies scattered haphazardly like broken toys beneath a swiftly rising shroud of dirty smoke.

I did that. Me.

He had killed the enemy, many of the enemy, and Peter felt the flaring glow of euphoria at having struck a successful blow and having survived a successful raid. His home town had been bombed the previous week, and he had returned the favour and brought death to the perpetrators.

The oily streaks and stains on his canopy and the harsh stink of acrid cordite and smoke in his mouth and nose were proof of his successful delivery of the fight.

The raid was done. Scores of the enemy were dead at his hands and those of his compatriots.

He had survived, and having done so, found himself a veteran.

*

High above them, in the vast, endless dome of the intensely bright blue sky, beyond and behind and unnoticed by the pair of fleeing raiders, two more shapes plummeted earthwards in vengeful pursuit.

The eyes of the man behind the canopy of the leading fighter were hard and pitiless, his teeth clamped in cold fury beneath his oxygen mask.

His section had failed to intercept the earlier formation of six raiders, and his rage demanded blood.

One finger impatiently tapped the gun button on the spade grip of his control column, as the distance to the escaping raiders narrowed, his seething soul eager to wreak brutal vengeance for the deaths of all those who lay blown apart or maimed beneath the miasma on the horizon.

The enemy aircraft were so low that the slipstream from their racing propellers created white furrows in the surface of the sea, hazy plumes and whorls of spray swirling away behind them.

They were just a quarter of a mile ahead of the pursuers now, and tiny droplets from the enemy's slipstream spray mixed immiscibly with the black blobs of oil thrown back by the hard-pressed Rotol propeller, onto his windscreen.

The airframe was vibrating madly around him with the speed he had gained in the dive, and now he corrected, the column stiff in his hands, expertly pulling the fighter's nose up and throttling back to lay on just the right amount of deflection, settling into position just above and behind the racing enemy fighters, skimming and wallowing in the turbulence of their slipstream and spray, throttles forward just a little against the stall.

Almost there …

His thumb caressed the gun button.

Try a long range shot, or close the distance?

And then the enemy formation split apart, their grey exhaust trails thickening as they opened their throttles, and his target, the formation leader, was curling into a steep banking turn to starboard, his wingman turning a little less violently to port.

Squadron Leader 'Granny' Smith turned as hard as he could after his target, but the enemy pilot had overdone it in his desperation to protect his young charge and face his foe, the sharpness and speed of his turn edging on a stall, but he was too low, and the starboard wingtip of his little fighter dropped slightly – ever so slightly, but just enough to cut a curving white furrow of spume in the surface of the water.

The FW 190A teetered for a moment, a dark and malevolent shape seeming almost to stand still in front of him against the bright water, already doomed, and Smith kicked rudder and pulled back hard on the stick into a climbing turn. "Break, break!" he called to his wingman, opening the throttles to gain safety and avoid the enemy aircraft as it cartwheeled into the sea, one moment a sleek and potent weapon of war, the next an expanding storm of shredded metal fragments, plastics, rubber and gobbets of flesh.

The fighter's fuel tanks split open then, and the growing blur of wreckage was enveloped in a meteoric ball of vivid orange fire that rolled and hit the water hard, creating a burgeoning circle of boiling water. Fragments formed shining crystal feathers of spray around the rising waterspout made by the fallen fighter.

11

A bloom of fiery satisfaction flowered within Smith, but he stamped on it, for there was at least another of the enemy close by.

Another one to kill.

He levelled off and sought the other FW 190, but there was only the haze over an empty sea, thicker now and blending sea and sky into a single blank emptiness.

The other Hawker Typhoon clung faithfully alongside him. Good old Brat, the boy had stuck to him like a limpet.

"Did you see where the other one went, Blue Two?"

His wingman's voice was apologetic. "No, Blue Leader, sorry, he disappeared into the haze."

Smith cursed, looking back at the pitifully small fragments burning on the surface of the sea, all that was left of the enemy aircraft.

"At least we got one, and that without firing a shot. A half each, Brat, I fancy. I'll treat you to a mug of tea and a bun when we get back. Wish we'd got 'em both, though."

Chapter 1

He gazed with disinterested eyes at her sagging, grey and cheerless curves, and sighed.

Her name was Gladys, and she was a barrage balloon. For some reason, unlike her sisters nearby, she was tethered closer to mother earth than was normal, like some recalcitrant child harnessed to a nervous parent.

Harry Rose turned away from the window, with its rather unprepossessing view of Gladys basking sullenly against the leaden sky, and sighed again.

The view of his desk was just as uninviting, the shabby tower of crumpled requisition and request forms, inexplicably larger each morning no matter how late he had worked the previous day, unmoved by his despondency.

His eyes drifted from the unseemly pile to the framed photograph perched precariously on the edge of his desk, and his wife's eyes gazed back at him from the picture, warmly.

He smiled at it wistfully. Dearest Moll, my beloved, I miss you so very much...

His eyes lingered longingly on her face for a moment, the sweet smile he loved so much, before moving to the infant in her arms. The little boy's laughing face and the bright, shining eyes showed delight at his father's antics, caught for eternity at the moment the photograph was taken.

Rose's heart was hollow, and gaping with love and loneliness and gloom.

Danny. My sweet Danny, my darling little chap, how I wish I could hold you in my arms right now, smell your baby fragrance, and kiss your sweet head...

Another overwhelming wave of loneliness washed over him, and he reached for the frame and clasped it to his chest.

But his family were hundreds of miles away, staying with Moll's mother in a little village near Lake Windermere, far safer from the enemy than he was here in London.

And here he was, flying a bloody desk and shining his backside on an Air Ministry chair.

He replaced the picture frame carefully on his desk, placing it beside the small metal model of an Mk1 Bristol Beaufighter, presented to him by the groundcrews of B Flight at RAF Dimple Heath. It was a twin to the one received by Chalky the day they left for the final time.

He smiled fondly at the memory.

BANG! The door to his office was kicked inwards and Rose jumped in shock as it slammed open. For a moment he saw a tall, lean officer framed in the open doorway before the door, rebounding from the wall, slammed back into its frame.

The door was opened again, this time more gently, to show the officer, a squadron leader, rubbing his nose gingerly. "Ouch, by dose," he muttered crossly, behind a gloved hand.

"Granny!" Rose exclaimed with delight, and rushed forwards, his hand outstretched.

Squadron Leader Daniel 'Granny' Smith, DSO, DFC, DFM and bar, MiD, CdeG, OWVM, RAF, let go of his nose, and reached out and took Rose's hand, and they shook warmly like the old friends they were.

"Wotcher, Flash, thought I'd pop in and see you."

Rose laughed with pleasure. "Really?"

Granny shook his head and smiled back at him. "No, not really. I'd heard that the Chief WAAF had caught her knickers in a typewriter and was in urgent need of expert attention. And who better to provide gentle ministrations?"

He laughed at Rose's expression and shook his head. "Just pulling your leg, Flash. Of course I'm here to see you, you daft mug. Why else would I set foot in a place like this?" He shivered theatrically. "Too many brasshats in one place for my liking."

He looked around Rose's little office. "I see you've carved out your kingdom, here, Flash, me old fart. Ain't you going to ask me to sit down, then?"

"Oh my goodness, of course! Sorry, Granny. It's just so good to see you! What a wonderful surprise!"

Strangely, Rose felt tears in his eyes, and he pointed at the visitor's chair in front of his desk.

"Take a pew. I can't believe you're here. I heard you'd got back from North Africa recently. That's quite a tan you're sporting!"

"Glad you like it. Dark and mysterious. Bloody irresistible I am, totty are finding me beguilingly alluring! They can't get enough of it!" Granny settled himself comfortably onto Rose's chair behind the broad desk.

Rose cocked an eyebrow in amusement, then sat down on the visitor's chair that he had just indicated, in front of his own desk.

"I can imagine. No changes there, then. I almost didn't recognise you. And it's not just the tan. There's not a single smear of oil or grease on your uniform. And your shoes are positively gleaming! You look like an RAF officer! Turned over a new leaf?"

Granny snorted. "You cheeky beggar! Not likely! By the time we'd stopped Rommel, our kites were falling apart and our kit was just scruffy rags. They issued us new uniforms when we were pulled back from the Blue. That's what we called the western desert, dunno why. Think the Aussies had something to do with it. Anyway, the desert was big, chum, damned enormous, and bloody empty, like an endless sea that went on forever, and Jerry seemed to be everywhere. It's a miracle, but somehow I never got shot down, not once, thank God, even though Jerry kept trying!"

Granny scratched his neck, and Rose noticed the pink, recently-healed scars made by shrapnel.

"The squadron had Hurricanes when I first got out there, but they weren't like the ones we flew at Foxton, these kites were properly clapped-out. Couldn't even out-turn a blinking Zeppelin. It could just about hold its own against the Italians, but no chance against a 109. The lads were just waiting for their turn to die, morale was shattered, absolutely rock bottom.

I think the CO I was taking over from had gone bananas by then, poor cove. If I'd been fighting the way he had, I'd have probably gone bloody doolally an' all."

Rose thought to himself, just like we were, back in 1940, outnumbered and overwhelmed, getting back up there, day after day, wondering if it was our turn next, half hoping it would be, just so it would stop… We didn't go crazy, though.

But then he felt ashamed of himself.

Had the previous CO fought the massed Nazi air fleets over the fields and towns of Britain before having to do the same all over again in the desert? Who knew what the poor bloke had suffered?

Granny and I are the lucky ones…

Smith ran a finger gently over the wing of the shining model Beaufighter. "Luckily, we re-equipped with Kittyhawks a couple of weeks later. Snappy little jobs, better than the Hurribags but still surpassed by Jerry, but having them gave us a fighting chance at least against fat Hermann's lads. We were used primarily as escorts for the bombers, but half the time the bastards got through anyway."

He smiled grimly, and Rose noticed the fresh lines around his friend's mouth. "We were totally outclassed by Jerry. Same old story. Sound familiar?"

Rose nodded silently, memories of the shadows of massed fleets of Luftwaffe aircraft crossing the British countryside still strong.

Warming to his theme, Granny leaned forward over the desk and planted both elbows on it. "We kept a couple of Hurricane Mk IICs on strength, though. You know the ones, Flash, those cannon-armed jobbies. You've knocked a few down with cannon in your Beaufighter, so you know what a mess of Jerry they can make. Thought I'd fly one and see what it was like, on an intruder mission. I'd heard Dick Smith got a couple while flying an IIC during the Battle of Britain."

He shook his head in disgust. "Well! The damn thing had all the flying characteristics of a lamb chop, the blasted drop tanks didn't help at all, and I got bounced by a couple of 109s west of Mersa Matruh. The first one was right up my arse, so flaps and wheels down quick as you like and trim set, so she slid across like a randy cow on ice, and he shot past like the cork out of a bottle of champers, not that there was much of that out in the Blue. Thought I'd drop my tanks and give him a couple of rounds of 20 mm, and the ruddy recoil slowed me right down, I was going so slow I could've landed!"

He barked out a sharp-edged laugh. "The cannon shells missed Fritz completely but scared him shitless so he scarpered, and the other one had to avoid flying into one of my bouncing drop tanks and then, misjudging my speed, almost crashed into the back of me, so he flew off bloody sharpish after his leader." Granny grinned humourlessly, remembering how his hands had twitched uncontrollably for an hour after. "Shame, I was itching for a fight!"

Then, his good humour disappeared. "Good thing one of the 109 pilots wasn't old Hans-Joachim Marseille, I'd have been properly buggered if he'd been there! The Jerry pilots in the desert were the cream, and keen as mustard, and he was one of the best. No wonder they called him the Star of Africa. We all respected him."

Granny bit his lip. "I lost a lot of decent lads out there in the Blue, Flash, fighting out there was a fucking nightmare. Just miles and miles of endless emptiness and blinding blue sky that never seemed to end. Sandstorms that buggered everything up, no bloody landmarks, scorpions, and flies. Oh God, the flies!"

He closed his eyes for a moment in disgusted recollection. "Bastard things were all over everything. We got used to them crawling all over us, all over your food, in the crack of your arse, behind your balls, all over everything, until you almost didn't notice 'em. Used to cover the food. I must've eaten thousands of the horrible little blighters."

He noticed the jug of water on Rose's desk. "Mind if I have a drink, Flash?"

Rose passed him the jug and water. "Of course. Not like you to ask, old chap."

"Hm, well, out there in the desert, a man's ration of water was like gold. Sometimes you only had a pint and a half to get you through the day." He poured himself a glassful, eyes on the clear stream of water. "You'd brush your teeth, wash your face, armpits, the old man and balls and feet, then what was left was for drinking." He held up the glass to the light.

"Wasn't enough to wash your arse properly, we stank like baboons." Granny's speculative stare made Rose think for one horrifying moment that his friend was about to perform his ablutions beside the waste paper bin, but thankfully, Granny put the glass to his lips and drank it. "Mm, lovely!"

Putting the empty glass down, he snatched at the topmost form on the pile in front of him. "Hm, *somebody* needs a lot of braces and socks."

He balled up the form and cheerfully threw it at Rose, who caught it deftly and tried straightening it back out again.

"Granny," he scolded, "that's an official RAF communication, they could charge you with treason or something for doing that!"

Granny blew a raspberry. "Well, balls to them. I'd like to see some of them desk wallahs back in Cairo swallow bully beef and fly stew every day!" He held up his hands, palms outwards, and grinned apologetically. "Not that any of them were like you, of course, my old china. These were the bastards who spent all bloody day in some nice cool office dozing and jawing, and all bloody night down the Ezbekieh Quarter catching the pox."

Rose, hating that he might be thought of as a desk wallah, particularly by someone like Granny, said nothing.

Granny picked up the picture frame. "Ah, Flash junior. Bless the little soul. I'm glad to see the little man looks like his mammy." He chuckled. "Cripes! Just think if he'd got your looks, gorblimey, luvaduck!"

Rose, who rather fancied that his little Daniel was the spitting image of himself as a child, felt mildly put out, but he smiled good naturedly. "Your kind words are appreciated, Granny. But, tell me, why do they call the desert the Blue?"

"Fucked if I know, pal." Granny shrugged and put down the frame before picking up the little Beaufighter. "Nice. What's the story about this, Flash?"

"Did a night fighter tour of ops on Beaufighters back in '41, while you were out there lazing in the sun, Granny. Not the nippiest of kites after flying a Hurribag, but powerful, and packed a bit of a punch. I was teamed up with a young lad, Chalky White, as my RO, and we got a handful of victories at night. The squadron ground crews made that for me in the workshop and presented us with one each when we'd completed our tour."

"RO?"

"Stands for radio observer," Rose said, feeling rather superior.

Granny nodded. "Ah, he was your radar operator."

Rose was surprised. "Oh. I thought it was all hush-hush. You know all about the air intercept radar, then?"

"Your dear old Granny knows everything, my old son. You should know that. So where is this Chalky White now? Is he waiting for you to go back on ops?"

"No, poor lad, he broke his leg on a motorbike. He's not fit enough for aircrew anymore, Cat B3, poor sod, so he's assistant adjutant for a Coastal Command squadron in Cornwall. I'm glad, because he more than earned his DFC and DFM, and his wife has one on the way. I'd like to see the lad enjoy peacetime."

Rose smiled at the memory of White's proud, shining face as he shared news of the impending arrival with Molly and Rose. They had visited him in the hospital, laid up with his leg in plaster and Mandy at his side, and Rose recalled her relief, poorly hidden, at the news that Chalky would be unable to fly operationally again.

"He's a good kid, done his bit, done more than enough, I reckon," Rose added fondly.

He's not the only one, thought Granny sadly, looking at his friend with affection. "Picked up a bit of fruit salad, too?" He lounged back comfortably.

Rose looked down at his chest self-consciously. "The Bar to the DFC was for some successful interceptions, but I feel a bit of a fraud wearing the DSO." He nodded at Smith's ribbons. "I'll bet you earned yours, out there in the desert, but what Chalky and I did was probably unnecessary."

Rose wondered what, if anything, he should tell Granny. They had all been sworn to secrecy, the Nazi attempt to seize a functional air intercept set having come so close to success.

Don't be daft, he thought, *Granny's no Nazi spy, and he pretty much knows everything that goes on in the RAF, anyway.*

"Chalky and I shot down a Beaufighter pinched by a pair of Nazis masquerading as Norwegian air force crew. The thing is, the wretched thing was doomed, wouldn't have got to enemy territory, Molly and an airfield defence corporal put some well-aimed shots into an engine, and the kite was well alight when we found it out over the sea. It was a foregone conclusion. We just hastened the end."

He looked down at the little red and blue ribbon on his chest. "Molly should be wearing this."

Granny grunted. "We heard rumours of a WAAF officer chasing after an enemy plane on a motorbike with sidecar and blasting away at it with a Tommy gun. Didn't know it was Molly, but it sounds just like the sort of thing she would do. She was daft enough to marry you, after all, eh?"

Rose laughed. "She damaged the engines on the rogue Beaufighter, with the help of an army corporal from the airfield security section; they were really responsible for foiling Jerry." He grasped his wedding ring absent-mindedly, twisting it around his finger as he gazed at her photograph. "She's amazing. If it had been me, I'd have probably just sat there like a pudding whilst the Nazis made good their escape."

"You and Chalky made sure of it though, dintcha? I did also hear tell that you and he notched up a pretty decent score, too. Ten all told? Sounds like you earned that DSO, my old son."

Then, Granny sat up straight. "OK, notwithstanding the chief WAAF's need for my tender care of her nether regions, I do have an ulterior motive for coming to see you. I can see you're jolly useful here, old cock, and that you're having the time of your life, but I need you."

Rose, his mood lifted by Granny's presence, leaned forward. "Oh?"

"They've given me Excalibur Squadron, and we're outfitted with Hawker Typhoons. I'm to be Arthur and I want you to be one of my knights – C Flight commander, in fact." He wagged a finger. "But you'll have to get familiarised with the Typhoon first, get some hours in, OK old man?"

Fly again with Granny? How could he say no? But… Hawker Typhoons?

Excitement and trepidation in equal measure flared bright and powerful in his chest, but Rose already knew what his answer would be. There could be no other.

"That sounds great, Granny, but the old man insists we do a six-month tour as temporary staff officers. I've still got three months left to do."

Granny tapped his nose and winked. "Don't worry about that, my old son, it's all in hand."

As if on cue, there was a tap on Rose's door and he turned in his chair, but before he could utter a word, Granny bellowed deafeningly, "Come!"

To Rose's horror, the senior WAAF admin officer, Squadron Officer Harvey-Lewis stepped in. Known for her unbending attention to detail and severe efficiency, Harvey-Lewis ran her department capably, albeit with a rod of iron.

Now, she eyed Rose coldly as he scrambled to his feet. "Flight Lieutenant Rose? I have some new orders for you, and a travel warrant. You have a week's leave before your posting, so kindly make sure that you put things in order before you leave."

She passed him the paperwork and he took it with astonishment. "I must also take this opportunity to thank you for your industriousness and good behaviour. The C-in-C will see you at 1500 hours tomorrow, please be there on time. I'll send down your replacement this afternoon so you can familiarise them with their duties. I do hope you have a good leave, and I wish you well for the future." She blinked, then added, "I hope you stay safe and well."

Her eyes moved then to Granny, still lounging on Rose's chair with a slight smile.

"Granny. Six pm?"

Granny nodded. "Mm, lovely, see you then, Babs." And to Rose's incredulity, he winked salaciously at Harvey-Lewis.

Dear heavens, *Babs*? Rose thought, and then, Oh, good Lord! Is she actually smiling?

21

With a final nod, the WAAF left the room, and Rose stared after her, before disbelievingly turning back to his friend, his papers still clutched in one hand.

Granny smiled complacently at his speechless young protégé and, pulling a packet of cigarettes from his pocket, he crossed his feet comfortably on Rose's desk. "What did I tell you, Flash? Bloody irresistible, I am!"

Chapter 2

Sydney Camm, the exceptional designer of the Hawker Hurricane, also designed the Hawker Typhoon, the prototype of which first flew in early 1940.

It was a powerful beast with a great deal of promise, but was plagued from the very beginning with problems that caused the deaths of pilots during testing and then on operations. Issues included the tail inexplicably coming off in flight, a very poor engine life coupled with a litany of failures in the Napier Sabre power unit, the cockpit routinely filling with carbon monoxide due to inadequate seals, necessitating the constant use of the oxygen mask from start-up to switching off, and the mid-flight opening of the peculiarly-designed cockpit door arrangement. Elevator flutter and compressibility effects also had to be resolved.

It didn't help that the Typhoon was sometimes mistaken for a not-so-friendly fighter by Allied air forces, resulting in a number being shot down in error, with the loss of some pilots.

Problems continued long into operational use and the new fighter was almost withdrawn, but senior frontline pilots, including Roland 'Bee' Beamont and Desmond Scott, recognised the Typhoon for the thorough-bred she was, and appreciating her exemplary performance as a low-level interceptor, intervened and fought to keep the aircraft in the vanguard.

With the Spitfire V faring poorly against rampaging FW 190 fighter-bombers, an alternative was urgently needed…

*

The Hillman lurched to a stop. "Here we are then, sir, P for Popsie."

Rose looked speculatively through the windscreen at the Hawker Typhoon before them. "Right, OK, thanks for the lift."

The leading airman peered morosely at the clouds above. "Sir. Lovely weather for it."

"Hm, yes." Rose let himself out of the RAF Hillman, clutching his flying helmet and parachute pack with suddenly sweaty palms, despite the frigid air of the morning, and stared up at the sturdy aircraft in awe for a moment, trying to recall Granny's advice.

P for Popsie squatted on the tarmac hardstanding, more than seven tons of powerful Hawker Typhoon, huge and solid and unyielding, close to twice the weight of his dear old P-Peter, the graceful Hawker Hurricane in which he had first found success against the Luftwaffe in 1940, completely different, and yet it was obvious even to the most casual of onlookers that the two shared a common background and heritage.

The members of the ground crew, bulky in their protection against the cold, watched him approach with interest, two of them, either side of the air intake, clutching fire extinguishers in the event of a fire at engine start-up. The cold weather wouldn't help things.

Earlier, looking alert and fresh despite a delightfully vigorous night with Babs, Granny had been succinct.

"The kite's a beauty, Flash, my old lad, a real thoroughbred, but she's a lot more potent than you might expect at first. There's bags of power hidden beneath that cowling, so don't go bananas up there. Take it slowly, because she can be quite a handful." Granny grinned. "Like a few girls I know. And like them, she's a lot of fun to be with! Anyway, treat her with respect. She's no kitten."

Granny rapped the table sharply with the bowl of his unlit pipe to emphasise the point, the grin gone, dark eyes serious and his voice low.

"Start off gentle, old cock, get to know her first. No need to push it, make sure you have plenty of height, start at, say, about 12,000, and begin with gentle manoeuvres, then go from there, but gradually, OK? Slowly, slowly, catch the donkey, or some such bollocks."

Rose had shaken his head. "It's not the first time I've flown a new kite, honestly, and you're flapping on like my granny." He smirked smugly at his friend, pleased with his riposte, and feeling rather clever.

Granny grinned affectionately at him again and shook his head. "You are a daft bastard, Flash." The grin faded and he became serious once more. "I thought I knew better the first time, too, thought I'd seen it all, but I soon learnt better. Almost splattered myself across a muddy farmyard like strawberry jam on a crumpet."

Talk of jam and crumpet reminded Granny of a particularly memorable breakfast in bed with a second officer WRNS in Gibraltar, and he smiled fondly at the memory before shaking it away.

He waved his pipe reprovingly at Rose. "Didn't do my pants any favours at all. Don't rely on what you think you know, the Tiffie is different, a whole new kind of kite compared with what you've flown before. She's bigger and heavier. Mind my wise words, you cheeky bugger. No power dives at first, gentle turns, plenty of height."

Rose hummed noncommittally. "Oh, I don't know about that, Granny. I told you about my tour on Beaufighters last year. My dear old D-Dog was quite big and heavy, and she was pretty powerful, too. I think I can handle your little kite."

"Well, this one's a lot faster than your dear old Dog, Flash, you soppy tart. She goes like the fucking wind. You will not believe the horsepower she packs."

The Typhoon had substantially thick cranked wings, level with the top of Rose's head, and each of them housed a twinned pair of devastatingly potent 20 mm Hispano cannon. Her undercarriage was set wide apart, just like that of her older sister, the Hurricane, promising the same characteristics of stability, steadfastness and strength.

The underside of P-Popsie's wings and fuselage was adorned with a series of black and white stripes, to assist in aircraft recognition from the ground. Too many Typhoons, mistaken for FW 190s, had been inexcusably lost in friendly fire incidents.

"So, Flash, Like the dear old Hurricane, the Tiffie has a wider track and sturdier undercarriage, so she's more stable in take-off and landing than, say, a Spit." Granny sighed dreamily. "I always like the ones with a bit of a gap between their legs…"

Rose rolled his eyes. "For goodness' sake! Don't you ever think about anything else, Granny?"

Granny looked surprised. "Course I do, you daft bugger."

"Go on, then, what else d'you think about?" Rose raised his eyebrows enquiringly. "Surprise me."

Granny scratched his neck. "Well, erm…" He took a long sip from his mug of tea and played with the crust of his toast. "Um…"

Rose groaned in exasperation. "Flipping heck! I can hear the cogs grinding, and smoke's pouring out of your ears. I'd like to get to try out your blinking Typhoon sometime this morning, so, if you've any more useful tips, now's the time."

"Oh, is that so? Well, I must say that I think I liked you a lot more when you were a wet-behind-the-ears, newly fledged pilot officer, you cheeky wanker." Granny's lips drooped sorrowfully, and he shook his head. "You used to hang on to each word I said. Now look at you, a couple of shiny gongs on your manly breast and a pair of rings on your sleeve, unwarranted I might add, and suddenly you know it all." He sniffed reproachfully.

Rose laughed and dipped his head in a derisive bow. "OK, sorry I spoke, O wise and knowledgeable one. Please pardon the impertinence."

Granny's eyes twinkled. "That's better, you little blighter. And don't call my Tiffie 'blinking', she's a lady and deserves a bit of respect. And her name's Popsie, P-Popsie."

Rose rolled his eyes again, but silently he thought, Popsie? Hm, that's original.

"OK, OK, I'm sorry, Tiffie, er, Popsie."

"Much better. Right, well… God help us, but I think you're about ready for a go on her, but remember what I said. In a nutshell, she's strong, so be firm, don't be too adventurous, at least not until you've an idea what she can do. Just like a real Popsie, you need to know what she'll do, and more importantly, what she won't. Be a gentleman, stay within her limits, OK?" He winked at Rose. "Plenty of height. Loads of rudder to hold her steady on take-off. And don't you dare bend her, or I'll bend your ruddy neck!"

*

"Flight Lieutenant Rose, sir?"

The ground crew corporal's face was pinched with the cold, and his quiet, respectful voice intruded into Rose's musings. But his eyes said, come on, mate, what you waiting for?

Annoyed with himself for standing and gawping at the Typhoon like some novice, Rose answered brusquely, "Yes."

Like the other members of the ground crew, the corporal was wrapped up well against the weather. His face was respectful, but inwardly he sighed. Luvaduck! Here we go, another bloody tyrant. Bloody officers.

"Sorry for staring, corporal, I was just appreciating her lines."

Mollified, the corporal returned Rose's smile. "That's alright, sir, she's worth ogling, she's a bit of a looker, ain't she?"

And actually, she was, truly. Relative to the delicate elegance of a Spitfire or a Hurricane, Popsie might be bigger, heavier and bulkier, but she was also beautiful.

Beautiful in a strong, reliable and stylishly powerful way. From the tip of the sky blue airscrew spinner and the massive black three-bladed Rotol propeller, 14 feet in diameter, to her retractable tail wheel, she reassuringly exuded power and dependability.

But still, his heart pumped hard and his nerves skittered at the thought of flying this massive fighter.

Rose slowly walked around the huge aircraft, noting the scratches, stains and patches where the paint had been worn away, the black and white stripes on the undersides of her gull wings and fuselage, the huge, potent cannons, the way the dull light shone on her camouflaged flanks and surfaces. He checked the surfaces that should move actually did so, and that the surfaces that ought not to, didn't.

"Here, sir." The corporal indicated the retractable step at the base of the starboard wing. A rigger jumped onto the wing, took Rose's parachute and placed it into the pilot's bucket-seat.

"Cheers, Corporal." Rose clambered gingerly onto the wing, taking care to place his feet carefully into the flap-covered recesses set into it, before stepping into the cockpit of the fighter, stopping for just a moment to gaze with interest at the novel cockpit arrangement.

He nestled comfortably into the surprisingly roomy cockpit, which was much larger than that of a Hawker Hurricane, the rigger helping him with both the seat harness and that of his parachute, and then his intercom leads. Then he tucked his dog-eared picture of Molly, which had flown with him operationally, both in Hurricanes and Beaufighters, carefully into place on the control panel, before checking the controls that Granny had familiarised him with.

The controls, column and spade grip were very like his dear old Hurricane, but with additional side consoles on either side of his thighs, creating a strange sense of déjà vu.

Already he could feel the butterflies settling, the apprehension and excitement rising inside him.

OK, attach the oxygen hose, turn the knob and check the flow, make sure the gauge is visible before you seal the cockpit.

Time to get her going.

Rose took a deep breath, sweat prickling his forehead already, and nodded to the extinguisher-wielding airmen outside as the rigger closed the door.

One last squeeze of the little teddy bear tucked carefully in his pocket.

Help me, Lord God…

*

For a first effort, Rose's Napier Sabre start-up was successful and surprisingly smooth, and he felt quite pleased with himself. The airmen clutching the extinguishers looked rather relieved, too. Following Granny's instructions,

Rose had anxiously delivered the requisite number of strokes to pump the correct amount of trigger mixture into the engine cylinders.

The sharp report of the 'shotgun' Coffman starter made him jump and gasp, and suddenly, with a bright sheet of flame that shot back from the exhausts on either side of him, and a thick spurting cloud of dirty grey-brown smoke and dust, the Sabre engine turned over and roared into life, then settled into its normal strident rumble. At least it no longer emitted that high-pitched whine, which the test pilots had found irritating.

Cockpit checks repeated, just to check the oxygen was flowing nicely, and he carefully guided her onto the runway, all set to go, zigzagging all the way and with the assistance of the airmen.

Full rudder trim? Elevator neutral, rudder port. Set.

Mixture, rich, OK.

Prop? Full fine pitch.

Fuel load, looks good, pressure off, tank cock off.

Flaps ten degrees down, no more.

Supercharger to moderate, and open the radiator flap.

Boost pressure set and check revs – 1600 revs? That'll do nicely.

Ready. Full throttle, God, heart is racing, she's so loud, even after sitting between two Pegasus engines in dear old D-Dog, she's loud… The vibration coursed through his body, brakes released, and suddenly pressure thrusting him hard back into his seat, hard, to compensate for the powerful torque further as she pulled to the right, more left rudder, more still, but not too much more (else you'll swing and ground loop).

Uh-oh, she's swinging, compensate… easy… that's better. That's it, hold her there…

Steady. Less than a foot of clearance with the runway beneath the shining propeller disc, so maintain a slightly tail-down attitude.

The huge nose in front of his cockpit dipped as the tail came up, and he steadied her, fearful the tips of the massive propeller would clip the rushing ground before them.

Dear God! She was like a rocket, lifting already, altimeter winding up, lift flaps gently, not too fast or you'll probably sink… he held her steady, firmly grasping the spade-grip, and then he was completely airborne, the ground falling away.

Correct rudder tab and undercarriage up, pressing the brake to stop the wheels and reduce the tremor in the airframe as the wheels tucked up comfily into the wings.

Flaps up, close the air intake. Oh, bloody hell, the vibration! The power of the liquid-cooled Napier Sabre coursing through him like a liquid torrent of energy.

She was powerful, but he could also feel the strength of her structure; the feeling of dependable security he had once felt in his Hurricane was now flowing warmly through him again.

OK, quick couple of circuits of the airfield, oops, speed building and curving outwards, back, throttle back and then re-join the circuit, just practice landing her, keep the speed up though, else she'll lose height too fast. Cor! This cockpit's like a blinking hothouse!

The landing was good and feeling more confident now, Rose took off again, confident and grateful for his previous experience in the Beaufighter. If he had transitioned directly to Typhoons from the Hurricane, he might have felt the significant generational difference between the two exceptional Hawker fighter aircraft, the forceful torque to the right and the power might have been more than he could handle.

OK, those're the formalities over with, he thought, now let's try some more complex moves, Popsie, old girl. With plenty of height in hand, as Granny kept on wittering about, just in case…

On his way to an altitude of 14,000 feet – 2,000 over Granny's recommendation, just to be on the safe side – Rose was already enthralled by this incredible machine of war, and he understood Granny's love for the aeroplane.

She was the new trump card for Fighter Command, and the Luftwaffe would need to change their tactics quickly to counteract Popsie and her sisters.

To begin with, he started a series of gentle turns, then steepened them, before initiating a succession of straight and turning stalls from a mixture of both high and low speeds.

Hm. She was heavy; her weight dragged her down and she fell further than he was used to before he could return her to stable flight, but she was reasonably easy to recover. And the weight was not an issue. Flying a Beaufighter in combat had prepared him physically and mentally.

She was responsive enough, and if he was honest with himself, he might call her a delight, but the added speed meant one had to adapt and be a wee bit more cautious with the stick.

*

He actually felt some regret later, when he brought P-Popsie back in to land. The glorious euphoria of his flight, the smoothness coupled with such power, his hesitation and apprehension dismissed by her strength and silkiness, lingered in his memory.

Popsie, you are a beauty! What a kite!

Turn to starboard into the circuit, cut the speed gradually, flaps down, set trim, prop in fine and loosen the door latches, just in case... 145 mph, reduce speed gently, 130 mph, dropping sweetly, OK, stick back to allow her to settle, slight bit of throttle to hold the power, wheels kissing, hold her straight, old chap...

At dispersals, he switched off, detached his leads and, with the help of the fitter, stepped from the cockpit onto the wing, surprised to find that he was soaked in sweat.

"Good flight, sir?" The airman's face was pale with cold, eyes tired. Poor sod, working in this cold for goodness knows how long, probably couldn't care less.

"Like a dream, thanks."

He stepped down and touched her wing, almost caressingly. I can see how Granny was seduced by you; you're lovely, wish you were mine.

Before the flight, he had still been unsure about his decision to go back, but now everything had changed... He nodded to himself, the metal smooth and cool, pleasurable even, beneath his fingertips.

With a wizard kite like this, I'm ready.

31

Chapter 3

"Now that's what I call spectacular!"

Couldn't agree more, thought Rose as he leaned against a rock, trying to get his breath back and surreptitiously eyeing his wife's rather lovely behind.

If he hadn't been following that incredible bottom, it was likely he would not have managed to reach the summit of the Old Man of Coniston. Even the baggy climber's trousers she wore did not diminish the view Rose was currently enjoying.

His homecoming had been joyous, with Molly's parents seeming as happy to see him as their daughter, whilst his son chuckled and cooed and bounced with pleasure at his arrival – or so he believed.

Molly had held him tightly, pressing herself against him, much to his pleasure. She had been less than thrilled, however, when she later unpacked the 'Pilot's Notes for Typhoon 1A and 1B Aircraft' from his case.

Now, Molly took a deep breath of the cold air and sighed in contentment. "Did you know that this is the inspiration for the mountain the Swallows and Amazons climb in Ransome's *Swallowdale*? After I read the book, I badgered Daddy for weeks until he brought me here, I just had to see it!"

"Oh," Rose replied weakly, trying to think of something intelligent to say. "Erm, you mean, Katmandu?"

"No, you silly man, Kanchenjunga. My goodness! Katmandu? Did you actually go to school?" She turned to look at him in surprise.

"Well, a chap can't remember everything," he muttered defensively. "I haven't got a memory as good as yours."

"Never mind, my darling, I find myself drawn to stupid but handsome men, so you'll do, at least for now. Don't worry, I still love you."

She noticed his eyes had wandered again. "Harry, are you looking at my bottom?" She indicated the view before them with one sweep of her shapely hand. "Even with all this natural wonder to enjoy?"

"Certainly not, can't think of a thing I'd like to look at less. Your bottom isn't the only wonder of the world, there are others, y'know."

Like your breasts of course, or your deliciously soft vulva…

"I saw quite enough of your bottom this morning, thank you," he declared haughtily, then hurriedly added, "Not that I'm complaining, of course."

Molly gave him a disbelieving look. "Mm, alright, if you say so. Come and hold my hand, then. Give me a cuddle. I've always loved this prominence; you can see so much."

"Yes, ma'am."

Leering at Molly's bottom had created a not inconsiderable prominence of his own, and Rose slouched forwards resignedly, gas mask container positioned strategically in front of his groin to hide his erection, lest the group of middle-aged women standing some distance away should see it. Luckily he had had the foresight to bring along his walking stick, should his weaker, once wounded leg create issues in the climb upwards. Now, he leaned on the stick gratefully.

"Look, Harry, can you honestly say you've seen anything like it? Go on, take a really good look." She scolded him gently, taking his hand in hers.

The sight of those valleys and mountains when I looked up from between your legs this morning was far nicer, he thought grumpily, but said instead, "No, my love, quite breath-taking."

Just like that blinking climb to get up here, he thought but didn't quite say.

"You can see so much, Harry, look. Luckily for us, it's such a wonderfully clear day today, so we can actually see quite a lot of the Lake District, look, Morecambe Bay, those are the Pennines, and see, there? That, just there? The smudge in the distance? No, you wonderful, silly man, *there*, on the horizon? That's the Isle of Man! Isn't it simply amazing?"

He looked at her profile, her hair windswept beneath the scarf, face pale from the cold except for the pink tip of her nose, soft and delectable lips smiling with pleasure and wonder at the vista before them, and marvelled at his exceptional good fortune in being married to such a woman. Intelligent, very well read, brave as a lion, sophisticated and elegant, and, dear God, incredibly, exquisitely beautiful.

She pointed again. "And there, Harry, look, just down there, that's Dow Crag."

Rose stared at the grey-black fell and nodded with what he felt was hopefully just the right amount of enthusiasm. "Impressive, it must be quite something to climb its face."

Her eyes shone. "I thought so too, my love. Everybody should see these sights. When he's old enough for the climb up here, we'll bring Danny."

She bit her lip as she said it. *Please, God, look after my Harry now he's returning to operations again, give us the chance to return here together as a family, when there's peace.*

Rose saw those beautiful eyes glisten. *I will kiss her,* he thought, *hold her tight to me amongst this rugged beauty, press my aching hardness against her…*

"I say there! Hallo there!"

They turned in surprise, to see that the group of lady walkers had joined them.

"Please pardon the intrusion, my dears." The speaker was a woman in her sixties, dressed sensibly in tweeds with her grey hair secured firmly beneath a tartan scarf, bright brown eyes filled with interest and sympathy. "We noticed that your young man's been injured."

"Injured…?" Molly echoed in surprise.

"Oh yes! We couldn't help but notice how your young man was bent over his walking stick when he joined you. I hope you'll forgive us, but we wanted to thank you for protecting us, and for getting injured in so doing." The others nodded and bustled excitedly on either side of her.

A blushing Rose turned towards her, and looking down, Molly noticed the bulge in his trousers. He bent to hide it, slipping his gas mask case further in front of it, and she giggled.

"You will have to excuse my husband, ladies, he's awfully shy and a touch tongue-tied. But I'm very proud of him."

Molly simpered gleefully at Rose. "You see, he's a fighter pilot, a very brave and good one, and he's seen plenty of action and been awarded lots of medals, a DSO, the DFC and bar, and an AFC for saving the life of his instructor. I love him loads, and he's my hero."

They were agog, twittering with excitement at the news, and Rose, disconcerted, blushed anew under their attention.

"Oh, how wonderful! A hero in our midst! Have you killed many of the beastly Hun? Will you take tea with us down in Coniston? Do say yes!"

Rose glowered at Molly as she took his hand and gushed, "Come on, Harry, my darling, let's go back down with these ladies for a nice cup of tea, a piece of cake and a little chinwag, shall we?"

Rose hobbled back down the fell, his erection subsiding as the ladies jostled around him, almost making him lose his balance more than once in their eagerness to help.

Molly's enjoying this, he fumed, all thoughts of a lingering kiss and fondle banished from his mind as he leaned on his stick more heavily, for the benefit of their new travelling companions.

*

The little boy's eyes were closing, the sweet face peaceful in his father's arms.

"So, it's Hawker Typhoons?"

"Yes, my darling," Rose whispered, eyes on his son. "Wonderful fighter, it's the answer to Jerry's Focke-Wulfs. Fast, strong and packs a punch and a half. Granny says it's ideal as a low-level interceptor."

"You remember Daphne from Foxton? Awful girl, curly brown hair, green eyes, laugh like a drain, danced with you at our wedding. Don't pretend you don't remember, you brute, I saw her hand clutching your bum."

"No, dear," protested Rose weakly, remembering the pleasant sensation of Daphne's hands. "The only one clutching my bottom that night was you."

Molly sniffed. "Liar. Well, anyway, she's at Bentley Priory now, and she says that there's been a lot of talk about problems with the Typhoon. The brass had some plans for it and Desmond Scott told them they were talking a load of tripe." She grinned, playfully. "Except he didn't use the word 'tripe'."

"Oh, any problems have been ironed out, sweetheart," Rose replied airily, "why do you think Des spoke up for it? And why d'you think Granny wants me to fly them with him? If there were problems with them, he wouldn't have asked me, would he? Not his godson's father."

She looked thoughtful and relieved. "Do you think so, Harry?"

"Of course I do, my tiny tasty pudding. Besides, with you sprightly old dears of the WVS patriotically knitting balaclavas for the troops, the rest of us have to do our bit, too. If Hitler saw you all with your knitting needles unsheathed, he'd probably wet himself in terror."

Molly looked affronted. "We don't knit balaclavas, you monstrous fiend, and who are you calling an old dear?"

The little boy's eyes were closed, his breathing peaceful, and she gently took him from Rose. "Give me my son, you dreadful beast!" she breathed.

Reluctantly, he let her take the little one.

Looking at him coquettishly from beneath lowered lashes, she murmured, "Get into bed, Mister Rose, and don't you dare go to sleep!"

He smirked and patted her bottom salaciously. "Yes, ma'am!"

*

At last, Danny was asleep and tucked up cosily in his crib, and Rose held back the covers so Molly could join him in bed.

"My hero," she breathed and kissed him lightly on the lips.

"You didn't have to lay it on so thick, my love. The way those old girls were going on, you'd have thought I'd taken on the bloody Luftwaffe all on my own! And all this 'he's a special operations pilot', all the 'hush-hush' nonsense!" he whispered, one eye on the crib.

"Sometimes, Harry Rose, you can be such an old woman! They adored you! If I hadn't kept my hands on you, they would have been all over you.

36

Did you see the little one with the jade hairclip? She would have had you there and then on the table if she could have!"

"I have had enough of old dears for one day," he grumbled. "Oh, and what is it, anyway, about you and old men?"

She sat up in outrage. "What on earth are you wittering about, Harry? Me and old men? What old men, you cheeky swine?"

"Shh, dear! Well you know, the Old Man of Storr, the Old Man of Coniston." Rose spoke sheepishly. "Every time we visit the blessed places you endlessly wax lyrical about, either we get chased off by ghosts and ghoulies, or I get carried back down the hill by a monstrous crowd of old girls! I don't know about the one with the hairclip, but the old dear with the deerstalker would have shagged the arse off me if you weren't there!"

"I thought you fighter boys were used to being mobbed by totty," she said slyly. "In fact, I rather had the impression all you boys welcomed female attention."

"It would've been alright if I'd been eighty years old," he protested, "and I wouldn't have minded that much if they all looked like you, but those old darlings didn't!"

"I thought you liked the older woman," she said, innocently.

He leaned towards her. "*One* older woman." He reached up and cupped her breast in one hand, feeling the hardness of her nipple through the nightdress, revelling in the firm, warm pliancy against his hand. "One with the most extraordinarily amazing tits!"

"You dirty, horrid man!" she giggled, wriggling beneath the quilt beside him, one smooth thigh sliding across his groin, and ankles interlocking as she turned to lie against him.

Molly kissed him again, her tongue flicking softly against his teeth, the palm of her hand on his flat stomach, and leaned into his embrace as he responded to her passion with his own.

Danny cooed in his sleep and they froze, alarmed, before sitting up and staring towards the crib. But the little boy continued to sleep, and they smiled at each other in relief. She kissed him quickly. "Wait a minute, grouchy boy, let me pull the screen across."

As Molly pulled the folding screen to, between the crib and their bed, Rose crossed his arms behind his head and enjoyed the sight. She saw him staring and shook her head. "You stay where you are, Harry. It's quite alright, don't get up, I can manage!"

"Well done, dear, you do it so well, you're simply amazing," he simpered.

The screen now blocking the view of their bed from Danny's crib, she grinned evilly, undid her nightie and let it drop. There she was standing naked before him, achingly beautiful in the soft light, like a raven-haired Aphrodite risen from the sea. The sight always made him catch his breath, and his eyes ran over her body in frank admiration. He marvelled again at how soon she had regained her figure after giving birth to Danny.

She stretched languorously, and he gawked as the light danced silkily across her lightly tanned skin. One finger to her lips, Molly threw back the covers, climbed onto the bed and grasped his pyjama bottoms. "We shan't be needing those anymore," she whispered, and pulling them off him, tossed them into a heap onto the floor.

Rose held his breath as she leaned over and grasped him, hot kisses against his skin, her tongue soft and breath warm.

He closed his eyes with enjoyment and gasped quietly at the incredible sensations she elicited.

And then, still holding him, Molly clambered up to sit astride him, and her gasp echoed his as he gently entered the warmth, his heart dancing with the thrill of their embrace.

The girl bent over him, breasts lightly grazing his chest and her thick raven tresses a curtain around their faces, the scent of her body and the hot sweetness of her breath, her dark eyes like pools of profound longing.

"Harry, my darling, dearest man, I love you with all my heart." Grasping his shoulders, she kissed him tenderly. "Now, you naughty boy, hold on to your hat and get ready for the ride of your life!"

Chapter 4

"Toffee Red Leader from Toffee Red Two, shall we practise a bounce, sir?"

The calm, gruff voice came from Rose's wingman, Flight Sergeant Raymond 'Hairy' Cox, a grizzled pre-war regular and veteran of the battles in 1940 over France and Britain. Cox was one of the lucky ones, with a hard-earned DFM and bar to show for three years at war; stocky, with steady eyes and grey already showing in his bushy thatch of brown hair, quiet and impassive and eminently dependable.

Granny had paired them to ensure Rose was properly 'worked up' for operations in the Typhoon.

Behind them, as the altimeter wound upwards, the sprawl of Poole, its nascent layer of barrage balloons, and the wide harbour, greyed in the haze as they raced southeast over Poole Bay.

Above them was cloud in an even, unbroken and dirty layer. Rose was slipping back into the old patterns: methodical search of the sky, check the mirror, a quick sweeping glance at the instruments (he wasn't quite sure he trusted this big powerful beast quite yet), and then repeat. And again.

"Sounds like a good idea, Red Two. Shall I bounce you, Hairy, or…"

"I'll bounce you, sir, see if we can't shake off the cobwebs."

Cheeky bugger! God, it was hot in the cockpit, sweat already dampening his battledress, pooling at his crotch uncomfortably and rolling down his sides and the back of his legs.

"Righto, off you go, then, old son…"

Cox's Typhoon dropped its nose and swept away downwards towards the sea, and despite Rose's best efforts to follow its progress, soon disappeared into the haze.

He'll come after me from through the cloud behind, he can't bounce me from the sun, so I'll stay below the cloud cover. Well below, enough to give me plenty of time to respond, but I'd best keep a good lookout just in case the bugger tries to fool me and climbs back up through the haze and tries to catch me from the side or below…

Gentle aileron turns, gentle rolls to better survey all around, nothing so far, don't forget the mirror, instruments, OK? Yes.

Instruments, oxygen flow fine, sides and back, below? No, nothing. Check the mirror and behind…

As if on cue, as his eyes flicked to his mirror, the other Typhoon appeared at his five o'clock, diving like a wraith, losing substance as it headed down towards the sea and to the mist that hung below.

His eyes followed it down, watching as it drew closer, counting down the distance, until, when it was less than a quarter of a mile away, he kicked right rudder and threw her into a starboard turn, pushing forward the throttles – carefully, please, tailplane, don't fall off! – turning into the other Typhoon, already knowing that something was wrong as more shapes emerged from the clouds from behind the first, even as the first now slid past and below, Rose just catching sight for a split second of a surprised face looking back at his own…

That was no Typhoon!

Black spinner, black and green camouflage with bright yellow panels, sleek but somehow stubby with a small tailplane and big radial engine, the black Crosses and swastika awfully familiar…

Bloody hell! A Focke-Wulf 190!

As indeed were the second, third and fourth fighters that had emerged from the cloud above.

His heart lurched painfully and buttocks clenched with sudden tension. "Oh, shit…"

He was caught in the middle of a tip-and-run raid on Poole. And no bloody warning from Blackgang, the radar based on the Isle of White! What the hell…?

Rose fumbled with the safeties even as the second and third enemy fighters slipped past his Typhoon, ailerons and rudder already working as they sought to turn after their unexpected foe. Only the fourth had enough time to loose off a burst of fire, but this was hurriedly and poorly aimed and came nowhere near him.

You're definitely not an ace, at least! An ace would have been faster on the trigger, and a far better shot, he thought gratefully, turning more steeply after them.

The first enemy fighter had continued straight down towards Poole, whilst his wingmen, having jettisoned their bombs, were turning hard after Rose, vortices whipping off the wingtips with their violent manoeuvres.

Damn it, if I go after the first, the others will get me…

"Red Two, get back here immediately, we've got company!" He panted beneath his oxygen mask, arms straining with his powerful mount as an ovoid blob of oil from the engine flew back and away behind.

"Ops from Toffee Red Leader, be advised there is a raid on Poole."

Stay calm. Calm…

Already the second fighter was closing in from a wide turn behind, and he knew that with the odds so badly against him, there was little chance unless he turned, and kept turning so that they had to turn too, and try and lose height at the same time, even though at 12,000 feet his Tiffie would still shine.

Come on, T-Tommy!

"Ops to Toffee Red Leader, your last garbled, but please be advised of possible trade in the vicinity of Poole."

Now you tell me!

The fourth FW 190, the formation tail-ender, passed in front, too far away, but Rose straightened out for just a moment to fire a quick, hopeful burst from his cannon, quickly nipping back into his turn.

In his first contacts with the enemy, when flying the Hurricane in 1940 and then the Beaufighter in 1941, Rose had been successful – and very lucky – on each occasion, destroying an Me 110 and a Heinkel 111 respectively. But this time it was not to be, as his hastily-aimed burst of cannon fire did not connect with, or even come close to, the fourth Focke-Wulf, and he cursed through straining lips.

Pull back the stick further into the turn, watch your airspeed, a touch of flap to help tighten it – for the one behind him was on his tail now, and he grimaced as the forces pulled at him. The sight of the sparkling guns on the shape in his rear-view mirror and the accompanying zip-zip-zip gave harsh encouragement to go even tighter.

Come on, Hairy, where the bloody hell are you?

The glittering enemy fire could not reach him, for the enemy fighter could not squeeze his turn tightly enough to achieve a position where Rose was in his sights.

The other two FW 190s had climbed and were turning back to come down into a slashing pass, but their position was poor, and the angle of their dive unhelpful, and so they sped past without even firing, knowing that in shooting they were more likely to hit their compatriot than his opponent's Typhoon.

Oil flew back from the bellowing Napier Sabre, some of it splashing and smearing thinly on Rose's windscreen, but the slipstream whipped most of it away.

Instruments, good girl, Tommy, all OK, mirror, clear. Phew! I'm melting… This cockpit feels like a blinking greenhouse in summer…

His arms and legs were aching now, face slippery with sweat, heart thumping, mouth parched, and the temptation was great to break out of the turn and chase after the others. But he knew to follow after the two FW 190s would allow the one behind the opportunity he needed to finish this deadly game of ring-a-roses.

He didn't even have enough breath left to call out again for his wingman on the R/T. His world was a spinning torture of blurry pursuit, although his pursuer was slowly losing ground, now almost at the opposite end of the wide turning circle within which the two pilots gasped and strained.

Glance again at the mirror, clear. Thank God... but where are the others...?

The enemy pair were above again, light catching their wings and canopies as they twirled down, but with the approach still tricky and their colleague not far from the danger of their guns, they once more slipped past without firing, formation ragged with frustration.

They had dropped below 10,000 feet, and he looked up through the Perspex window of his canopy to catch sight of his opponent.

And he was catching his hunter. He was slowly closing within the circle they shared. It was true, just as Granny had promised, the Typhoon could out-turn the Focke-Wulf at low level!

I just need to keep up the pressure...

NO!

He was dimly aware of a flash of bright light in the distant harbour, followed almost immediately by a second, this one above the harbour, as the enemy leader first hit his target, and then in turn, was swatted from the sky by the anti-aircraft defences, just too late, dropping like a blazing meteor into the harbour, leaving a dirty cloud of oily smoke hanging low above the packed shipping. One vessel was already alight.

Rose felt sick, knowing that men and women had just died or been maimed horribly in that faraway flash of light – and he had been unable to save them.

I failed them...

The enemy pair were climbing again, this time rolling into a turning circle wider than his, anticlockwise to his clockwise. They would try and gun him down as they passed in opposite directions, his Tiffie's four Hispanos against their combined guns – except there were now, somehow, three of them, a third closing behind the first two... but the newcomer was another Typhoon!

His gunsights were almost on his erstwhile pursuer, and he could see the German pilot glancing back at him fearfully.

Press the button lightly to fire a speculative half-second burst... but it curved away uselessly below.

Not quite there, but almost.

He risked another fleeting glance at the others. *Where are they?*

But now there was only one FW 190, diving hard to the east, whilst the other was a falling, broken, vividly burning thing, spinning out of control and dragging a comet's tail of fire, disintegrating as it plummeted. Twirling, twisting smoke marked its passing, as the Typhoon of his wingman was curving smoothly upwards to help him.

Rose's chest was tight around his lungs, but he felt like shouting for his deliverance. Thank God, oh thank you, my merciful God…

Looking forward again, he saw the FW 190 easing into his gunsight, and he fired a two-second burst, the Tiffie shaking and slowing from the recoil, wobbling right on the edge, and he had to catch and hold her before she stalled.

A twinkling of hits and a single puff of grey smoke, lost in the slipstream. A frayed piece of the enemy's rudder broke off, whirling wildly back, disappearing behind and below him, and the FW 190 twitched into a half roll to dive away, straight down.

Slick with sweat, Rose opened up his turn to follow his opponent as Cox re-joined his wing, but once he had taken his eyes off the FW 190, he lost sight of it.

Damn it, where did you go?

"Red Two, am I glad you're back! Did you see where mine went?"

"Low level, Leader, pulling out now, two o'clock low."

Rose strained but couldn't see anything.

"I can't see him. Take the lead and let's try and catch him."

"Red Leader, Spitfires at four o'clock high." Cox has amazing eyesight, thought Rose, the incoming shapes being barely visible to him.

A couple of squadrons of Griffon powered Mark XIIs with the newer 'universal wing' were based along the south coast for low-level patrols, in addition to the Hawker Typhoon squadrons.

"OK, Hairy, I see them."

"I think it would be best to get out of it, Red Leader, it'll be a long stern chase if we go after Jerry, and the Spitfire bods aren't all that good at telling the difference between the Tiffie and FW 190s. They can take over the patrol until the readiness pair get here. They'll be on their way already. I'll call Ops to tell the Spit lads to expect them. And I don't think Jerry will try again today. They shot their bolt. " The usually phlegmatic Cox sounded rather pleased with himself, as well he should be. It wasn't every day one gets to shoot down an FW 190.

The fight had lasted less than four minutes, but Rose was exhausted and slick with sweat. He considered their next move for a moment. There was no reason to push his luck. The enemy kite would be lost in the haze by now, but even if it were still visible, with the 190's head start and just a 30 mph advantage over the 190's top speed, they would only catch up with the enemy fighter-bomber as it was crossing the French coast.

He didn't fancy playing with the Flak batteries that awaited them, neither did he want an overeager Spitfire pilot chasing after them and peppering him in the backside with his cannon. He'd had quite enough, in those frenzied moments of the fight.

Rose was unhappy that his 190 had escaped, but saw the sense in Cox's advice, and sighed. You've done enough, time to go home and get a nice cup of tea inside you.

His enemy had been lucky, but then again, so had he. In a dogfight in which he had been surprised and badly outnumbered, Rose had managed to hold his own, even taking a chunk out of the enemy, and he could at least claim a 'damaged' from his first ever skirmish with the Focke-Wulf scourge.

Sometimes, mere survival is sufficient.

"Hm, fair enough. They do say discretion is the better part of valour and all that, so lead the way home, Hairy."

The flight sergeant was remorseful as they turned away from the Spitfires and headed for RAF Little Sillo. "Sorry for being late for the party, sir, I was setting myself up for the bounce, wanted to catch you unawares. Didn't expect to see you mixing it up with Jerry when I came down again, but I was set up nicely, and you seemed to have things in hand."

"I'm glad you came when you did, Hairy. I think they were going to try out a different approach against me. Well done on yours, though. I'll confirm it, of course, I saw it go down. But then, so did most of Poole!"

They flew home at a respectful distance from Poole's anti-aircraft zone and saw that the burning ship, a small merchantman, was sinking. The thick plume of smoke was visible behind them long after Poole itself had faded into the distance. They knew beneath that funereal column many lay dead or dying, mangled obscenely, flayed and torn by the bomb they – no, *he* – had been unable to stop.

Of the downed enemy formation leader's FW 190, there was nothing left.

*

Granny was waiting for them at dispersals when they got back to RAF Little Sillo.

Excalibur Squadron had been reassigned from Manston to a smaller airfield in Dorset during Rose's leave. The Manston anti-aircraft gunners tasked with airfield defence were not especially particular about who they shot at, or perhaps were just incapable of differentiating between the Hawker Typhoon and enemy aircraft.

Even in the air, more than once Manston Spitfires had engaged Manston Typhoons, with unfortunate and fatal results for the Typhoon pilots.

Granny decided that it was quite enough for his boys to be shot at by the enemy, and he didn't think much of the idea that their countrymen should be having a go at them, too. He hastily arranged an appointment with the AOC, 10 Group, resulting in the immediate transfer of Excalibur Squadron to a new home in Dorset.

Similarly, to protect other Typhoon units, 56, 266 and 609 Squadrons were sent to RAF Matlaske, RAF Warmwell and RAF Biggin Hill respectively.

Rose was pleased to step out from the steamy cockpit and stretched gratefully before removing his gloves and jumping down. The cool air and solid ground beneath his feet were a blessed relief.

His fitter noticed that the cannon had been fired and now asked excitedly, "Any luck, sir?"

"Mixed it up with some FW 190s over Poole Bay. Only managed a damaged though, Jimmy, I'm afraid, sorry I couldn't get you one confirmed." Thoughts of the enemy's escape still rankled, since of the two, Poole had suffered the more terrible harm.

"A damaged! Well done, sir! It's a long flight back to Hunland, maybe he'll end up in the drink anyway!" The fitter handed Rose a ragged cloth. "Towel, sir. More importantly, you brought Tommy back safe to us." The groundcrews formed deep bonds with their aircraft, toiling for hours by day and night to keep them airworthy, and felt it keenly when one did not return.

Rose was touched by his consideration, even though the cloth looked none too clean, but he shrugged mentally and wiped his slippery face and hair, trying not to let Jimmy see his shaking hands.

I need a long soak.

"Thanks, Jimmy. Here's to the next time, eh?" His legs were trembling, and he leaned against the side of T-Tommy. The cloud had partially cleared, and now he closed his eyes and turned his face to the sky.

On the far side of the field, the Immediate Readiness pair sat in their cockpits, and already two more Typhoons were being prepared for fifteen-minute readiness.

Granny grasped the stained barrel of one cannon and shook his head. "When I told you two to practise a bit of fighter training, I didn't mean that you should shoot at each other, too!"

Rose laughed, but that laugh was high-pitched, and the tremulous sound made him flinch with embarrassment.

But nobody seemed to notice.

"I just heard that you lucky blighters actually intercepted a raid without Ventnor guidance, and you nabbed a Hun to boot! You jammy beggars!" Granny's face relaxed. "The senior defence officer for the Poole area has just been on the blower, singing the praises of a pair of Tiffie pilots who interrupted a raid before it really began. He said you lads got one and drove another into the AA defences. They took some damage, but nonetheless, they're over the moon, promised a good time for all concerned next time you're in Poole, and asking if you can please do it again tomorrow."

Cox joined them, parachute pack over his shoulder, wet thatch of hair flattened by his flying helmet. "We were unbelievably lucky, that's all, sir. Right place, right time."

Rose nodded in agreement, wiping his face with Jimmy's 'towel'. "Right place, right time for Hairy, but it was the wrong place, wrong time for me. It was just luck we happened to be there. Hairy was about to practice bounce me when they appeared from nowhere. Three of them decided to play tag with me and dropped their bombs over the sea. No early warning, and a rather belated advisory from Ventnor control. Something went wrong, but at least we messed up the raid, and Hairy got one."

"And you damaged another."

Granny scratched his chin reflectively. "Well, if you held three FW 190s at bay while Hairy was off picking daisies, and managed to stop most of 'em from dropping their bombs on Poole, you must have been doing something right. Old Mata Hari will be pleased, I'll give you a lift to see him. He'll be champing at the bit to get all the details." He waved an imperious hand to his waiting driver. "Taxi! Come on then, Flash, I'll stand you and Hairy a mug of tea and a bun first. You've both earned it. Mati the Spy will have to wait a few minutes."

Chapter 5

Excalibur Squadron's role at this stage of the war was to act as anti-raider patrol and interception (known also as 'anti-Rhubarb patrols') in response to the Luftwaffe's tip and run campaign, and its assigned patrol line was Weymouth–Milford Haven, with an additional remit to cover the English Riviera, should the need arise. The latter was unlikely, as the Luftwaffe conducted few raids that far westwards.

As Granny confided to his flight commanders, "Those of your lads hoping for plenty of action will be sorely disappointed. We're unlucky to be so far west, raids will be few and far between so there's going to be a lot of tedium, but at least it'll allow us to get our new boys experienced, operationally. And I'm sure the poor old civvies living on the coast aren't complaining – the fewer the raids, the better for them."

Patrolling was a monotonous business. Granny having decided that each pair of pilots would remain together operationally until they knew each other better than they knew themselves, the sections of Typhoon pairs would take off at low level and stay there. No flying high, where raiders incoming could be warned that they lurked.

Once at the coast, they flew in line abreast at low level to five to ten miles out, where the Ventnor RDF station (known by the codename Blackgang) could pick them up, but the more distant and less precise German Wurzburg and Freyas could not.

The normal rule for squadrons closest to the enemy coast was to fly at around 50 feet – or even less – above the waves whilst on patrol, a harrowing business even at the best of times. The further away from France, the higher the patrol could be.

Understanding the concerns of his pilots, Granny ordered the patrol height to be higher, 80 feet or more. Thus, the Isle of Wight at least partially shielded them from the prying tendrils of German radar. The stations on the Cherbourg peninsula and in Brittany were close, but the height flown on patrol meant that contact, if established, was intermittent.

They waited for the enemy in line abreast, under orders of strict radio silence, flying along the patrol lines with minimal revs and a lean mixture, to save their fuel for as long as possible in case of a fight or emergency.

The squadron's patrol lines were demarcated by small dark blue or grey-black buoys, but these were smaller than those in use by the fishing fleet and could be hard to see, particularly in bad light or poor weather. Sometimes the blessed things disappeared altogether.

However, the Excalibur pilots soon devised their own points of reference and knew their patrol lines well enough not to need the buoys, although they remained useful when the haze was significant – which was often.

And of course, a day when visibility was limited would also most likely be the day when the boys of the Luftwaffe appeared.

The ongoing problems with the frustratingly complex Napier Sabre H-24 piston engine added further unease when flying low out at sea, a significant distance from land. It was hard enough having one pair of tired eyes expected to check the controls, sky and one's mirror all at once, without also having to have one ear constantly straining to pick up any untoward change in the thunder of the engine. Hence Granny's allowance of a patrol height of 80 feet or so, although in the event of engine failure, how useful would the extra few feet be? At least it gave them some room for movement whilst actually on patrol.

Line abreast in a loose formation at a reasonable height was marginally easier on a flyer's heart – no unnecessary risks for Granny's boys with close formation flying or turning at low level whilst keeping one's eyes on the controls, the sky, the surface of the sea and on one's fellow Tiffie flyer all at once. They were worth too much, each man was too valuable, to risk pointlessly.

Furthermore, with his mysterious network of connections, Granny also managed to wangle two experienced engineering officers – flying officers Wilkins and Evans – and arranged regular visits for the squadron's fitters and flight mechanics to the Napier factory, to better understand the problematic engine.

Nonetheless, despite the regular care and efficient maintenance, engine reliability remained a concern for pilots, until the problems were finally resolved by the English Electric Company.

With three flights, Excalibur maintained a section of two Typhoons on patrol at all times of the day, with another pair at Immediate Readiness, ready to respond in the event of attack within two minutes of receiving the alert. An additional two were at fifteen minutes' readiness. Whilst on Immediate Readiness, the pilots would be sitting in the cockpit, engines warm and ready to go.

When weather conditions made flying impossible, the pilots would talk to the operations room from their parked Typhoons at dispersals, pretending that Excalibur's patrols were up, just in case one of the Luftwaffe's daredevils fancied a raid despite the atrocious conditions.

It was the preferred practice of the enemy to raid when the conditions least favoured the defenders, so the likelihood of an attack was greatest at the beginning or the end of the day when the light was poor, or when there was haze or even mist, and in the rain when the sea and sky began to merge and visibility was greatly reduced.

The pilots usually each flew two or three flights a day, air tests in addition to patrols. Given Rose's experience as a night fighter, Granny chose him and Cox to fly as many of the dawn or dusk patrols whenever possible – although so far, they had nothing to show for it.

Maintaining patrols in such conditions increased the wear on both man and machine, and the hard-worked men and women supporting them. There seemed to be no respite for the groundcrews, who often worked in the cold, throughout the night, as every hour in flight required many hours of maintenance afterwards.

But, at least the living and working conditions at RAF Little Sillo were as comfortable as was possible anywhere in wartime Britain. The little aerodrome was a satellite airfield of the main RAF base at Exeter, and lay a quarter of a mile south and uphill of the village of Little Sillo – with its indispensable tavern, the Ramrod Inn, better known by those at the airfield as 'the Twitchy Stick'. It was twenty-five miles north-east of Exeter and 175 miles from the distant delights of London's nightlife.

Surrounded by stubbled fields of harvested wheat and barley, hosting winter crops of turnips and beet, the airbase comprised three grassy runways between 1,650 and 1,250 yards in length, located within a generally rectangular boundary road. Off that road were multiple single and double fighter pens and hard standings, with the indispensable windsocks at the north-western and south-eastern corners of the boundary.

The firing butts were to the east, workshops to the west, and hangars north and south of the boundary road. The watchtower – with its great, taped-up glass windows – the boxy water tower and offices, messes, billets, and other airfield buildings were set well back and situated south of the grassy expanse. It was as different from the tented desert landing grounds and the dusty tents of Granny's previous Desert Air Force command as it was possible to be.

Officially, this was an airfield in which the station commander should have been a wing commander, but Granny was the senior RAF officer at Little Sillo, ably assisted by a highly capable team comprising an adjutant (Flight Lieutenant Donald 'Uncle' Nugent), intelligence officer (Flight Lieutenant Joe 'Mata Hari' Mason) and the WAAF senior admin officer (Flight Officer Belinda 'Belle' Bolt).

This capable trio handled most of the everyday administrative and technical requirements of running a fighter airfield and its resident fighter squadron, also assisting in the station commander's duties. This left the commanding officer of Excalibur Squadron, the only squadron based there – Squadron Leader Daniel 'Granny' Smith, DSO, DFC, DFM and bar,

MiD, Croix de Guerre avec Palme, Order Wojskowy Virtuti Militari, RAF, veteran of the Battle of France, the Battle of Britain and of the Western Desert Campaign – more time to lead the men into battle.

This, then, was RAF Little Sillo, Hawker Typhoon fighter interceptor airfield – and Granny Smith's dominion.

Chapter 6

The phone on the makeshift table rang clangorously, and Peter, half asleep in the cheerily striped deckchair (purloined from the charming beach of Équihen-Plage as a trophy of war) amongst the group of pilots beside the watch office, stiffened and sat up, heart thumping, the month-old dog-eared copy of *Der Adler* falling unheeded to the ground.

The late afternoon sun shone bleakly through a thin sheet of whitish-grey cloud as he waited with the pilots of Calais-Marck aerodrome's Alarmstart Rotte – the readiness section.

He wondered bleakly, how can I get onto the mission? My beautiful machine is broken…

His Focke-Wulf had developed an oil leak on an air test, and the ground crew, known colloquially as the Schwarze Manner for the black colour of their overalls, were working on his aircraft as he waited. Anxiously, Peter wondered if his Staffelkapitan (squadron commander) Braun would still use him as his Rottenfleiger (wingman).

The basic Luftwaffe Jabo (shortened from Jagdbomber, or fighter-bomber) combat formation was that of a section or the Rotte, a pair of fighters comprising a section leader, the Rottenfuhrer, and his wingman, the Rottenflieger.

Peter knew how very lucky he was to have survived his first mission some weeks ago, and the subsequent bounce in which his section leader had sacrificed himself to save him, turning back into the Typhoon attack to cover Peter's escape, was a sacrifice he keenly felt. The subsequent missions had hardened him, and given him at least a modicum of confidence for the confusion that was air combat and raiding Britain.

He felt like a veteran now, and got to his feet and surreptitiously examined his reflection as Braun spoke on the portable phone. Peter liked what he saw: medium height, tanned and lean from his time in the Hitler Jugend and then pilot training, fresh faced in his flying gear, orange-brown flying suit and bright yellow life preserver creased and frayed, the dark brown leather flying jacket and his black flying boots scuffed and worn. He liked the image of what he had become.

Luckily, neither his CO nor the Gruppenkommandeur (wing commander) insisted that Peter wore an immaculate uniform when on flight duties, unlike some of the senior officers in other Jagdgeschwaders.

He was fortunate to have been made the Staffelkapitan's regular wingman, with just ten operations flown altogether. Perhaps it was to do with the way he faithfully clung to his assigned Rottenfuhrer's wing, like a limpet, or the way he hammered the Spitfire that slipped in behind his section leader's 190, without noticing Peter in his covering position behind and to one side.

His Staffelfuhrer put down the phone and shouted out to Peter. "Hey, lazybones! The big cheeses want us to conduct a Störangriff on the south coast. Coming?"

A nuisance raid! Peter stamped to attention. "Jawohl, Herr Oberleutnant! But my 190 is having work done for an oil leak. What should I do, shall I check?"

His CO patted Peter's shoulder, kindly. "Don't worry, Peter, we'll take a couple of Bulges for the raid." Braun used the familiar term for the Messerschmitt Bf 109G6, although other officers, more unkindly, termed them 'Boils'.

The bulge in the G6's cowling allowed increased space for the workings of the heavier machine guns, but the loss in airspeed was greatly compensated for in firepower, and Peter thought it worthwhile.

Peter felt the thrill of excitement course through him. "Target, sir?"

"Anything that looks like it needs its arse given a damn good slap, should be back just before dusk. Chichester, maybe? My father was held in the POW camp there. Give them his warmest regards, eh? Come on, Peter, take-off in ten, and don't forget to take a piss before you climb aboard."

*

The sun was lower than Peter had anticipated when they finally took off and clearing the coast quickly, they adopted the Rotte standard with his Bf109G about half a kilometre behind and to one side of his leader's.

The sunlight, reflecting towards them through a thickening haze to port, blinded them and made it difficult to read their instruments, let alone make out any enemy aircraft that may be lurking above. This is stupid, Peter thought, we're attacking at a disadvantage. I hope we're low enough to evade the enemy patrols.

A haze lay low over the water and dulled the sharpness of the light, which obscured the horizon and made judging their height over the water difficult. Accordingly, Braun kept the formation a little higher than normal, so to Peter, his Staffelkapitän's sleek fighter shone like a shining orange-silver dart ahead and to starboard.

It took them twenty minutes of eye-watering flight, constantly half expecting to be attacked from the radiance, before the moody slate grey coastline appeared, washed out in the glare. At their low level Peter could not see much. Neither, it seemed, could Braun, because he began a sweeping turn to port, probably to approach the coastline with the sun behind and to one side.

What is the old man doing? Peter thought, we're completely exposed, and we'll never see enemy fighters but for the sun…

Peter had fallen behind, and as he hurriedly began a delayed turn after Braun, something fell out of the blazing sky ahead, closely followed by a second thing. With excitement, he realised the objects were Spitfires, shadows in the light, curving swiftly after Braun, and he turned his own 109 tighter, then tighter still, his approach partially hidden by the brightness of the lowering sun.

56

"Leader, Achtung! Achtung! Spitfires behind! Spitfires behind!"

His heart was racing with excitement as Braun's Messerschmitt pulled up suddenly and soared skywards in response to his warning, using the speed advantage in the climb to get out of the way whilst the Spitfires, sticking close together, reacted immediately, raising their own noses to skid after Braun.

Peter pulled after them, climbing fast, admiring the beautifully clean lines of the two RAF fighters, the smoothness of their formation, how the sun caught and flashed bronze and gold against brown and green camouflaged surfaces, rounded Perspex and elliptical wings, until the range had closed and he pulled back harder to allow for deflection, ranging on the trailing Spitfire. He could see now it was a cannon-armed Vb model and pressed the firing button for a one-second ranging burst.

His cannon and machine guns thumped out a curtain of hot metal that passed just behind the Spitfire wingman, climbing ever steeper as he fought to keep up with his leader. Braun, climbing almost vertically now, drew further ahead of his labouring pursuers.

Peter cursed and, pulling back harder on the control stick, held the nose steady and hit the button once again, and once more his guns punched out, deafening over the raucous snarl of his Daimler Benz, and he felt his aircraft slow with the recoil. He fought to hold the ruinous destruction of his guns onto the soaring RAF fighter and saw the first rounds dance across and brutally kiss the Spitfire's shapely tail, chewing it into torn and curved wreckage, the rudder and elevators shattering, the stabilisers folding back and torn away in a shower of gleaming, twisting metal fragments, glowing like falling petals in the light from the setting sun, as the Spitfire writhed beneath the destructive onslaught.

Its rear end shorn off completely, what was left of the Spitfire's fuselage spun slowly to starboard, the damaged fighter sliding and falling away in an uncontrollable yaw, the engine's torque initiating an axial spin, and for a moment Peter saw the pilot struggling desperately with his canopy, like an insect trapped within a jar beneath the pitiless sun.

I got you, damn me, I got you! Elation bloomed inside him like a warm flower opening.

But then he was chasing after the enemy leader, no time to see what had become of his first victim as he pursued his second.

The leading Spitfire had pulled around into a tight descending turn, and Braun was turning, half rolling, having temporarily gained enough distance from his pursuer even as Peter was destroying the enemy Rottenflieger, and now he came straight down.

Knowing he had the advantage in the turning fight and unable to turn into the Spitfire, Peter hurriedly pulled up his nose and raced upwards at full throttle to get out of range of the RAF fighter's cannon with his speed advantage.

Lining up on the Spitfire as best he could, Braun slashed past the turning fighter and pulled up to climb again. "Pah! I couldn't bring my guns to bear on him. Peter, have a go."

"Ja, Herr Hauptmann." And timing his descent carefully, Peter pushed her back downwards again, careful, careful, he should be just… there!

He pressed down convulsively on the firing button and waited for the Spitfire to pass through the destructive fingers of slashing metal reaching for it, then gaped as the Spitfire continued to turn smoothly, his bullets and shells arcing uselessly away behind and to one side.

With just the right amount of deflection and a perfect approach, he might have been successful. But trying to make gunfire occupy the same spot at the same time as an enemy fighter is made immeasurably harder when said enemy fighter is turning tightly, and one slashes past at a tangent to the turning circle, wherein the turning circle's angle of rotation is not even in the perpendicular – all whilst trying not to hit the enemy aircraft with one's own aircraft!

Trying to hit such a target in a three-dimensional arena with the nuisance effects of gravity, haze, low sun and the sea terrifyingly close, created a solution that favoured the Spitfire. Only the greatest of Luftwaffe pilots might have succeeded, and unfortunately, whilst Braun was good, and Peter improving in leaps and bounds, neither was yet amongst the greatest.

"Come, Peter, let's hit him together. Perhaps flying in formation we can create a wider area of destruction for him to fly through."

"Ja, Herr Hauptmann," wheezed Peter, turning towards his Staffelkapitan. His lungs and body ached and he was bathed in sweat.

They formed up and turned towards the flitting, turning shape of the Spitfire, faint above the haze and water, the light dimming with the oncoming dusk and night.

The enemy fighter had been turning towards them, so they could catch him as he was on the outbound part of the circle. As they approached, he suddenly levelled off, pulled up his nose and let loose a stream of glowing tracer. Luckily for them, the Spitfire pilot too, was exhausted, and he aimed on the run, so the tracer arced past, but too low to hurt them.

"Verdammte Hölle!" Braun laughed as they levelled off and began to climb again. But Peter could only feel the fear that had washed over him like a freezing wave as the radiant bullets and shells sped towards them.

"This fuckers' got the balls of an ox!" Braun laughed again, but Peter felt the tension in his voice.

Peter strained his neck around and saw the Spitfire disappearing into the haze, glowing pink and yellow as the sun touched the horizon. "He's gone!"

"Let him go. He was good, Peter, but at least you got his wingman. He was done for, no doubt about it, that was some damn fine shooting. Thank you for saving my hide! I'm getting too old... no more Störangriff just before dusk in future, I think. The fucking light was chronic, my head is aching and I need a drink. Let's get home, I promised I'd get you back before dark – wouldn't want you to turn into a pumpkin or turnip or something, would we?" He laughed again.

Despite the strain of the mission, elation bloomed in Peter's heart once more. I got one! RLM didn't confirm my claim for that Spitfire a week ago, but Braun will confirm this one, he saw it all.

The two sleek fighters merged with the approaching darkness, the Rottenfuhrer swallowing dryly, faithfully trailed by his ecstatic young

Rottenflieger, who, had he been born with a tail, would have been wagging it furiously.

*

As soon as they landed, Peter was hauled triumphantly from the cockpit by his Schwarze Manner, then carried on the shoulders of his fellow pilots to the officers' mess, where he was toasted by the Kommandeur.

With his previous experience, the earlier 'damaged' and now a confirmed victory, he was eligible for the Eisernze Kreuz II, the Iron Cross, second class. And so it was in an impromptu ceremony, having drunk more than a few glasses of good champagne, a slightly unsteady but proudly beaming Unterfeldwebel Peter Stark received the EKII from his Gruppenkommandeur, Major Claus Schenk.

Peter was still in his flying gear, so Schenk cut a very small hole in the brown cowhide jacket to attach the decoration. The cross hung, shining brightly, from a red, white and black ribbon.

Later, with yet another glass of champagne to hand, Peter looked down proudly at his medal with a sense of achievement and satisfaction, trying hard to focus his tired eyes upon it as they threatened to close.

I am a veteran, and I now have the proof for all to see. An accomplished soldier of the Fatherland. What would they think now, down Wilde Buschstraße? The little lad with the weak chest and knobbly knees had developed into a lean and muscled aerial warrior, a defender of the Reich.

That'll show 'em…

*

Braun smiled as he looked down on the battle-stained and worn out young man sprawled and snoring on the easy chair.

You're a fine young wolf, Peter, and with luck, you'll go far, but you think a little too much. I'll tell you about your promotion to Feldwebel in the morning. All you have to do now is keep your wits about you and your eyes open.

He took the young flyer's glass and placed it on a table. It would be a shame to spill such fine champagne.

I'm getting jaded, Peter. If it weren't for you, I fear I'd have died today. Thank you.

Chapter 7

Rose yawned, jaw stretching wide, tired eyes still searching the flaring firmament around them.

The lacklustre sky was laced with fleecy cloud, tinted orange on its undersides by the searing orb settling on the horizon westwards, which also burnished the rough waters below with copper.

Two hours of patrol nearly over, it was almost time to go home as night slowly spread towards Dorset.

A glance at Cox's Typhoon, a watchful dark shape hunched beneath the canopy; like Rose it probed for the enemy. What a bind it was, to fly for hours so low and silently in formation, constantly vigilant. The buggers haven't raided Exeter since May, doesn't look like they will again. Probably a huge waste of time…

But, for the sake of those under their protection, they had to continue defensive patrols.

Rose's eyes were gritty and he felt cross. There had been a raid on Portsmouth earlier that day, and the boys from 266 at Warmwell had got two of the raiding FW 190s.

Lucky blighters. Nothing for us. Again.

But then there was that quiet little voice in the back of his mind. Be careful what you wish for…

He glanced west as the sun sank. Due to flying at low level, salt from the spray had formed uneven, delicate patches on the Perspex, and the golden rays refracted faintly through them. Beware the Hun in the sun. But there would not be any lurking out here, so far westwards and low down, he thought. Soon be time to turn again, one last circuit, and then home for dinner before the light fades to nothing.

Suddenly: "Toffee Red Leader from Toffee Red Two, formation of aircraft at 10 o'clock, low."

Level? Level with us? Cripes, they're a bit low! Rose stared hard in the direction Cox had indicated but saw nothing. "I can't see them."

Just then, something glinted in the distance. Apprehension and excitement flared in equal measure.

Be careful what you wish for.

"OK, I see them. Red Two, safeties off, we'll lose a little height, but we'll turn into them when they get closer."

Don't want to catch the sun and warn them we're here, if they haven't seen us yet, and we're maybe a little lower than they are at the moment. Hopefully, any reflections from our propeller discs and leading edges will blend into the glittering waves.

"Anyway, they might be Coastal Command kites."

"Maybe." Cox sounded unconvinced.

A formation of dots swiftly appeared from the ashen sky, tiny black specks lower than he had expected – a lot lower – and Rose turned into them, adjusting the gunsight, checking the safeties again and increasing the throttle as they closed. He felt the cold clutch of fear grasp his heart. If they're 109s or 190s, things are going to get bloody dangerous…

"They're Heinkels! Five, no, six of them, in line astern."

Dear Lord, that man has phenomenal eyesight! But Heinkels? Why not fighter-bombers, as usual? Is there an escort? He peered above the little group of bombers but saw nothing.

"Two, any sign of fighter cover?"

"None, Leader, they're on their lonesome, poor lambs!" Cox replied, gleefully.

They must have thought to exploit any gaps in cover during the switch over between daylight and night fighter patrols…

Glance around, instruments, mirror, all clear – right then…

"Close up, Two. Head on attack, give the leader a squirt, then split up, I'll break to starboard."

Fill your lungs with oxygen, here goes!

And then they were climbing, the Napier Sabres in full boost thundering defiantly as the distance closed further. He saw the leading Heinkel 111 twitch anxiously, as they suddenly appeared from the dark murk of the sea below and ahead of it, wide elliptical wings and tail unmistakable, dancing in the gunsight as he lined up and pushed down hard on the firing button.

Fire ripped out from his cannon in a fleeting one-second burst, the recoil brutal, slowing his Typhoon. Press the button for another short burst…

Rose saw, in an instant, the lead bomber loom before him, a bright sparkle of small explosions tearing the starboard Junkers Jumo 211 engine into ruin. A flash of flame, vivid in the half-light, the nose glasshouse exploding and collapsing into a bright cloud of ephemeral glittering fragments, catching the light like fireflies – and already the bomber was rearing up, instead of falling as he had hoped, and he pushed forward the stick, kicking hard right rudder desperately as the bomber's outline expanded suddenly before him.

"Break, Two, break!" he yelled into the radio transmitter.

The Heinkel 111 was climbing out of control, the tailplane seeming to fill his windscreen for one heart-stopping instant – and then he was past, somehow, passing beneath and to starboard, miraculously avoiding the head-on collision which had seemed inevitable by the thinnest of whiskers.

The Typhoon shuddered and bucked as it passed through the enemy bomber's slipstream, and he fought to hold her in a banking turn, his heart thumping so hard he could feel his chest wall shudder.

How did we not hit each other? Still lucky…

"Hairy?" he asked breathlessly, now turning in a wide circle, looking back.

Oh, sweet God, please let Hairy be alright…

Behind him, Rose saw the formation split apart wildly like a startled flock of pigeons, and there was no return fire from the shocked and confused gunners as he curved around out of range. He allowed himself a second to stare in awe at the bomber his cannon had ravaged.

There was a flash of gold, but not the flicker of an explosion, just the dying light briefly illuminating the port windows and gunner's canopy, glowing for an instant on the shining olive green fuselage, the hateful black cross on its side plain against the sea below.

But now the stricken Heinkel was losing airspeed, driven only by the undamaged port engine, and it ceased climbing, hanging for a moment as it stalled, the thin trail of smoke from its torn engine kinking as it slipped down into a sideways flat spin to starboard, before slamming hard into the dark water below. The ascending waterspout and attendant cloud of shattered debris rose convulsively to briefly mark the crash site and the final resting place for its crew of five.

Gone in a few shocking seconds. Preparing to bomb one minute – excited and fearful, perhaps – but dead the next.

One down, only five more to go…

And there, praise be to God, was the other Typhoon, turning to port.

"I'm OK, Flash. Blimey, that was close!" Cox sounded as shaken as Rose felt, but already both of them were turning after the remaining bombers, now raggedly reforming into two separate formations. "You definitely got that one! I hit the second in line!"

The sky was darker now, there was not a moment to waste.

"Hairy, engage the starboard formation, I'll take the ones to port."

How is my voice not shaking?

He swallowed to moisten his mouth, but it didn't help. "Control, incoming raid, Heinkel bombers, ten miles south of Exeter. One destroyed, engaging remaining five. Please advise Moonglow Control."

Moonglow was the ground control intercept station controller for the sector's night fighters. With night approaching, Rose feared the enemy may escape. Night fighters would have a better than evens chance of catching them.

Oh, Chalky, I could really do with you right now, pal…

"Received Toffee Red Leader, will advise Moonglow of raiders, well done." The girl's voice was calm, a professional, as were they all, bless them, and now it softened. "Best of luck."

Cox's formation had turned away, heading eastwards towards Weymouth, and his wingman closed with them, the flicker of his cannon answered first by the wicked bright orange streak of return fire from the Heinkels before the tail-end member of the bomber formation suddenly disappeared within an angrily expanding sun. A bright ball of billowing yellow flame, dissipating into itself as a guttering ruin, all that was left of the bandit, spiralled down in a steepening arc amidst a trailing shower of burning fragments, the sudden blaze and the last of the sun's rays weakly lighting the underside of Cox's Typhoon. The black and white identification stripes shone starkly and momentarily as he banked after the other bombers.

"Good show, Hairy!" Two down…

Full throttle, engine spitting and snarling like a caged animal, airframe bucking in the air currents as he cranked after them, closing with the two Heinkels fleeing together in the port formation, closing to 1,000 yards, another one-second burst, ten-degree deflection from the port quarter, acrid stench filling the cockpit, fuselage vibrating crazily in time with the cannon, a single white flash on the trailing Heinkel's empennage, no other apparent effect on the enemy.

Damn it! Too far, get closer…

The heavily-laden bandits were racing hard for the coast at more than 200 miles an hour, drawing closer abreast for the added comfort of mutual support.

Closing the distance to 500 yards, and approaching from dead astern of the one to port, Rose emptied a two-second burst into it, no deflection, ignoring the curve of smoking orange balls that seemed to reach for him from his target, vivid in the failing light, terrifying as they drew closer, faster and faster, before falling away uselessly.

Whilst the German gunner's return fire may have been ineffectual, Rose's cannon shells were not. Flashes flickered brightly on the dark shape. A puff of white smoke, a second, much larger, and then a thicker plume of dark greyish brown curling back, tasting bitter in his dry and aching throat, a cloud of devastation shot through with flames.

Remembering the violent way in which Cox's bomber had just blown up under fire, Rose reduced throttle and fell back, even as he fired another two-second burst into the smoke and flames. A flurry of twinkling hits blossomed like short-lived and malevolent white flowers on the half-obscured shape, and the bomber shed pieces of itself as it suddenly curved downwards, falling into an uncontrolled dive.

Breaking away, and climbing into a wide turn to port lest it explode beneath him, Rose knew that the Heinkel was finished, plunging downwards, even as a shape detached from it, a parachute trailing behind.

He left the doomed bomber and its solitary survivor as he continued the frantic pursuit.

Three down, but where's the last one...? Throttle back, right back, don't overshoot...

The night had now overtaken the day; the sky was empty blue darkness and the sun merely a golden afterglow, lighting the horizon's edge in the west.

Staring like an idiot at the blazing bomber had affected his ability to search the mounting darkness. He was soaking wet beneath his battledress and fancied the painful thump of his heart was louder than the clatter of his Hispanos.

The sky was empty. Oh no, I've lost it! The realisation brought an agony of anger and guilt. In the darkness, he could see nothing. Oh Chalky, if there were ever a moment that I needed you, this is it.

His eyes were drawn once more to the fuel gauge.

Damn it! It's too low. I should be on my way home already! But I can't go home yet...

An idea lit in his mind. "Ops, this is Toffee Red Leader, scratch another Heinkel, but I'm afraid I've lost the last one. I could do with a bit of help. Can you ask Moonglow if they have anything?"

"Well done, Toffee Red Leader. Please wait and we'll check."

Was there an undercurrent of warmth in that serene voice? She sounded nice, and for a moment he wondered what the girl looked like – and then felt guilty at his thoughts. They all sounded nice. When one was sharing the cold airspace with just an enemy kite for company, they were the warm sound of home.

A glance at Molly's photo, her face indistinct in the shadowed cockpit. Sorry, my darling, wasn't thinking impure thoughts, honest, but I must admit I wish I were with you right now, and that you had just stepped out of your underclothes…

"Toffee Red Leader from Ops?"

Thoughts of a seductive and very naked Molly and the things he wanted to do were banished into the shadows with her photograph. Just for now.

"Toffee Red Leader to Ops, please go ahead."

Check controls, oxygen gauge, quick sweep of the sky, can't see a thing. God, it's hot in this blessed cockpit…

"Moonglow knows of you, Toffee Red Leader," she said guardedly – and was there just the faintest touch of curiosity there? "And advises that your bandit is at angels six and a heading of zero-eight-five, range three miles."

Rose grinned savagely as a bolt of ice shot down his spine. There's still a chance!

Already he was hauling his powerful machine into a turn to starboard, Exeter a target no longer. But the Heinkel, heading eastwards, could now potentially bomb Sidmouth, Weymouth or Bournemouth.

"Ops, is it possible for you to patch me in with Moonglow, please?"

If only Ops could give me the frequency over the radio transmitter, but then, of course, Jerry would know it too…

There was a fumbling, then a sharp burst of static that left his ears ringing. "Hello, Toffee Red Leader, are you receiving?" A different voice, lower, softer, strangely familiar.

His tired eyes continued to search the darkness fruitlessly, pulling the Typhoon to an altitude of 6.000 feet. I could sleep for a week …

"Receiving, Moonglow."

"You are approaching slightly below bandit, recommend you maintain current angels, you are only two miles behind, change heading to zero-nine-five."

"Understood, Moonglow. Would you please advise me at 2,000 yards?"

Over the next few minutes, one eye on his fuel gauge, correcting his course minutely according to the slight alterations given to him by Moonglow, Rose worried that he would not see the bandit through the smoke and oil-smeared windscreen. And all the while he anxiously looked for bomb blasts on buildings below, which would signify his failure.

"Toffee Red Leader, you are roughly 2,000 yards directly behind Bandit, same course, and slightly below, it's all up to you now. Good luck!"

He'll be doing 200mph with a bombload, I'm doing twice that, at this speed you'll be up his arse lickety-split, better reduce throttle, use your peripheral vision, calm, calm, match his speed, no fuel to spare for this nonsense!

Relax, let him show himself to you…

But nothing materialised from the darkness, no fleeting shape, no exhausts glowing in the dark.

Nothing, just an empty vastness of dull nothingness.

His eyes strained… there?

No.

With the exhaust stacks of his Sabre flaming on either side, he was unable to use his hard earned skills in peripheral nocturnal detection.

Shit and blast!

His clothes clung to him, sweat rolling down his body, skin stinging beneath his oxygen mask.

I can't see a bloody thing!

Panic stabbed through Rose like a thin splinter of ice, and he eased the oxygen mask against his sweating face.

Now what? Lord God, what now? What can I do?

How can I find him?

Sweat rolled down his back and his eyes stung with the effort.

Oh, my Lord, don't desert me now!

Think, *think*. He's in front of you…

Only one thing for it. Last chance…

Rose pulled back on the stick 20 degrees, pushed hard on the firing button and the control stick at the same time as ruddering side to side, pitching his Typhoon's nose back down, his cannon ripping out a ragged, divergent zig-zagging swathe of shells. The effect of the recoil slowed the Typhoon, drastically reducing his speed by some 40mph.

Almost instantly, as the nose pitched past five degrees from the horizontal and a little to starboard, there was a single white flash. Bullseye! It had gone in a second as the nose continued to dip, but a line of blazing tracer slashed back at him like a suicidal stream of deadly fireflies from the emptiness before him.

Instinctively, heart in his mouth, Rose hauled the nose of his hard worked and faithful Typhoon back up to roughly centre his gunsight onto the source of the tracer (Cripes, it's getting a bit close!), keeping his thumb hard on the firing button for a viciously long burst of cannon fire. Might as well use it all up, probably won't get a second chance…

Zip-zip-zip-zip-zip, the sound of his enemy's reply, reaching out for him in the darkness. The radiance of the tracer lit up his cockpit, and he saw for a moment her face, dark in the stuttering crimson radiance, but the line of fire was just slightly too high – thank God! – and cleaved the air above the speeding fighter without causing any damage.

Get him, get him, get him! *Empty your bloody cannons into him!*

No time to think, just the desperation of his clamouring heart and the thunder of his guns, and then the tracer stopped. A bunched constellation of stars flaring suddenly in the void, a plume of white smoke lit from within, and a second, curling back towards him, and then the Heinkel was outlined in a halo of flame, both engines alight, rolling to starboard, debris and tongues of oily flame peeling back from the dark silhouette, the extending flicker drawing out behind the enemy bomber like a fierce cometary tail, even as the starboard wing outboard of the engine bent back and broke off, lazily turning over and over as it disappeared behind them.

His heart thrilled with the success, even as his guns clattered silent, the empty breech blocks chattering impotently. But they had done what needed to be done.

His eyes turned from the plunging, rolling bomber even as the bomb load detonated, the all-consuming eye-searing bubble of furiously boiling light and heat enveloping the broken Heinkel, bathing the countryside below like a flashbulb with its sudden destruction, a flying machine and five men one moment, a shower of burning hot shrapnel and ashes the next.

Then the heat and compression waves reached him with the dull *bu-BOOM!* Like a sullen crash of thunder, audible even over the raging growl of his Napier Sabre, and he kept her nose pointing into it, fighting through the hot, tempestuous air, holding her steady until the waves had passed him by.

Glancing anxiously once more at his instruments, Rose saw that he had lost height during the chase and shoot-down; he was now down to 4,000 feet.

Still no danger to him at this altitude from the high ground here, but there was no more time; if he didn't get down soon, he would have nothing left in the tanks.

I don't fancy my chances flying a glider with an air scoop on the nose and weighing over 11,000lbs at night. Where's the closest landing ground? RAF Warmwell, probably.

Already turning onto a course he thought would get him to Warmwell, he keyed his radio transmitter: "Scratch another Heinkel, Ops, and thank you very much indeed for the invaluable help. That one's yours, I fancy. Could you give me a course, please?"

Chapter 8

As he cut the engine, and the great propeller before him finally slowed and creaked to a stop, Rose felt a surge of emotion.

Safe and sound, thank you, dear God!

It had been close, closer than he had ever been. Closer even than he had deserved. The fuel gauge read zero as he made his approach to Warmwell, and would not stir from that position, no matter how smartly he tapped it.

T-Tommy had brought him through one of the hairiest flights he had experienced. It was incredible the kite had behaved so well, despite having flown through debris at least twice and been strained to the limits, before getting him to Warmwell and finally landing on fumes.

The night air felt like ice after the heat of the cockpit, delightfully crisp against his skin, and he wiped his face with his sleeve, even as the duty crew van shot up and disgorged a gaggle of ground crew.

Luckily, RAF Warmwell was a fighter airfield operating Hawker Typhoons, too. They'd have him rearmed, refuelled and made ready sharpish – although Rose had had more than enough for the night.

I'll fly back to Little Sillo as soon as it's light, he thought, eyes on one of the resident fighter squadron's aircraft in the next hardstanding, the letters ZH of 266 squadron bright on its fuselage. The other Typhoon's engine tarpaulin had slipped off, and he could see she was one of those which had been painted white from the propeller to halfway along its exhaust stack as and aid to identification.

The night duty ground crew's NCO trotted up to him and saluted, and Rose saw the professional interest in his eyes as he surveyed the weary young flight lieutenant, muscles trembling, breathing heavily and steaming in the cool air like an exhausted dray horse, standing silently beside the battered and stained Typhoon.

"Welcome to Warmwell, sir. I'm Sergeant Williams, senior ground crew duty NCO. Any problems we should know about with the kite?"

Rose returned the salute, his arm feeling heavy as lead. "Harry Rose, Excalibur Squadron, Sergeant Williams. No, she's OK, but if you could just go over the airframe, have a look at the Sabre, and rearm and refuel her, I'd be grateful."

The sergeant stared at the line of ribbons beneath Rose's Mae West, then turned back to 'Tommy', victory markings conspicuously absent on its oily and smoke soiled fuselage. Hm. One of the Little Sillo mob, and a veteran, too, going by those medals, though he looks a bit young to be flying a Tiffie, Williams thought. A DSO and two DFCs? Just like dear ol' Paddy Green, the CO of 266 Squadron. And those cannons have been fired, but I see no swastikas on her side.

"Any luck, sir?" Williams asked respectfully. Now that he was closer, he saw the lines around the boy's eyes and mouth, the calm brown eyes that returned his gaze despite the strain and exhaustion they reflected.

A veteran, then, after all. But, after three years of war, ain't we all?

Rose wiped his face with his sleeve again, blinking, his smeared face settling into a grave smile. "Three Heinkels, Sergeant Williams."

Disbelief turned to astonishment and then to delight. The sergeant and his crew perked up, grins lighting their faces. Bloody Hell! Three! Three kills in one trip! Good God!

"Oh, well done, sir! Bloody good news! May I shake your hand?"

Rose, self-conscious, held out his hand, aware of the tremor in his voice. "With pleasure."

"I'll take you to the officers' mess, sir, see if we can't sort out some nice hot grub for you."

"I'd best have a chat with my CO on the blower first, sergeant, tell him where I am, though Ops should have done that already. Is your CO around?"

Williams shook his head. "Sorry, sir. I'm afraid most of the squadron are out for a jar or two and a knees-up, but the MO and the padre are usually there 'til late, I'm told, playing chess. In the meantime, let's get you some food, and we'll get your kite ready for…?"

"I'll make my way back at first light if that'll suit."

The sergeant seemed to bounce on his toes. "She'll be ready, sir. I'd ask the lads to put your three up on her side, but I think your own boys would like to do that. We'll sort you out a bed at dispersals after. If you'll follow me, I'll drive you, sir."

Rose nodded to the men checking 'Tommy'. "Look after her, please lads, she's had a rough night."

Not turned into a martinet yet, the sergeant thought as he opened the door of the crew van for Rose. But it's only a matter of time, they all do. Shame, seems a nice lad…

As he stepped around to the driver's side, Williams waved a finger sternly at his men. "I'll be back in a flash, lads, so no slacking! And I've got my eye on you, yes you, Jonesy! No crafty fags, else I'll tan your gormless hide!"

*

Familiar with pre-dawn take-offs for patrol, Rose arrived back at Little Sillo the following morning with the sun still on the horizon. Cox's fighter was standing beside the watch office.

Granny had already told him, on the telephone the previous night, that Cox had returned safely. But seeing the evidence of his wingman's survival was something else, and the sight of Cox's faithful 'J-Jenny' brought tears of relief to his eyes.

Good old Hairy!

He landed and taxied straight to dispersals, parking his stained 'Tommy' near the Typhoons on fifteen-minute readiness, and immediately Jimmy scrambled up and opened the door to help him out.

Jimmy's face was split by the biggest grin Rose had ever seen. "I heard what you done, Mr Rose, I never heard of three at the same time, an' Mr Cox got two. The CO's over the moon!"

Rose's smile faltered. *If Hairy got two, That means one escaped, damn it!*

Jimmy chortled. "Leastaways, that's what we thought! The adjutant got a phone call an hour ago, sir. Mr Cox lost the last Heinkel at low level in the night, but it came down on the South Downs. You and Mr Cox done it! Saved all them people!"

We got them all!

None had escaped, and Rose was filled to brimming with fierce and unadulterated elation. Miraculously, they had managed to prevent death and destruction in Exeter again and, directly or indirectly, caused the loss of all the enemy bombers.

Just as Jimmy had been awaiting his return since before dawn on an English airfield, there may still be ground crews on an airfield in occupied France, waiting for their aircraft to return, even though there was no hope left at all in the early sunlight of the new day.

And whilst those Luftwaffe ground crews were coming to terms with their losses, here at Little Sillo, the defending force had successfully returned home, safe and whole.

Thank you, Lord God, for your mercy in saving our lives, and of those who are entrusted to us. For putting us where we needed to be, Thank you, Lord.

He clapped Jimmy on the back. "No, Jimmy my old son, *we* did it. Mr Cox and I couldn't have done a damn thing if it wasn't for you chaps!" Rose raised his voice to include the rest of the men checking over the aircraft. "Thank you, lads, you gave us exactly what we needed, as you always do. These kills belong to you! Bloody good job! Well done! Keep it up!"

Already, the hulking shape of Big Dave, one of Rose's armourers, could be seen daintily painting a swastika on the side of 'T-Tommy', the can of paint resembling a thimble in his huge hand. Three swastikas on her side would give the boys a boost, be some kind of recompense for the thankless hours of work at all hours maintaining these kites, despite the heavy demands of their defensive role. Big Dave began painting the second swastika, and Rose turned away.

The last time he had got three, it was with Chalky on his last tour, and one of those 'kills' had worn RAF markings and been a stablemate of his own beloved D-Dog. That desperate night time pursuit in the skies seemingly crowded with enemy night fighters, to find the stolen Beaufighter and shoot it down, still made him sweat. They had come so close to losing the invaluable AI technology to the enemy.

At least these three enemy aircraft had flown under their true colours.

His hand stole down to his pocket, and he squeezed the little teddy bear he kept there. She's still looking after me, Moll.

Thank you, my God, for your mercy. For keeping alive the beating heart that adores Molly so.

He stood in the sunlight for a moment, in the blessing of a new morning, a slight unwashed figure in rumpled clothing, savouring the easy warmth in his heart and on his skin.

In his mind was the memory of sunrise with B Flight, RAF Dimple Heath's band of brothers, and their customary standing together in grateful silence to celebrate the dawn after a night of operations, in gratitude for their survival.

There was much to be grateful for.

Lord my God, thank you.

Chapter 9

Dinner had been better than usual. Granny continued to amaze – how on earth had he managed to get an RAF cook who had once been a chef at The Savoy in London? Had the man no limits? Now, Rose was sitting comfortably in the mess, pleasantly full, wondering what Cox was doing. It was hard to believe that together they had accounted for six Heinkels the previous evening.

How can I convince Hairy to accept a commission? He should be here with us, we all share operational time, we should spend our non-operational time together, too. Should be able to have a natter in the same mess, damn it!

Granny would be landing soon, having taken the pre-dusk patrol duty in their stead. On his return in the early hours of that morning, Granny had removed Rose and Cox from the flying roster for the day and told them to take the day off.

However, there had been a telephone call from 10 Group. The AOC, Air Vice Marshal William Forster Dickson, wanted to see the men who had singlehandedly prevented an attack, and probably saved hundreds of lives.

It would have been the first attack against Exeter since the Blitz of April–May 1942, when almost half of the city's medieval centre had been reduced to ruins. The cathedral survived, but German radio had gleefully claimed to have destroyed the 'Jewel of the West'.

More than 150 people died in the April–May 1942 Blitz, and many hundreds were injured. But this time, the Luftwaffe had been unable to add to that total.

Granny had met the AOC before, first at Hawkinge before the war and then again when the AOC accompanied Leigh-Mallory on a trip to the Western Desert some months earlier. The young and outspoken Halton 'brat' that Dickson remembered from Hawkinge had become a decorated squadron leader in a tattered and dusty uniform by their second meeting, with sand-reddened eyes and a mouth tight from lack of sleep and the loss of too many of his young flyers. This was evidence of the pure quality and unbreakable spirit of the graduates of RAF Halton.

Dickson, recalling that weary but unbroken figure in the desert, had telephoned Granny personally just after Rose's return from Warmwell, and after proffering his warmest congratulations, demanded that Granny send his 'brave boys' to RAF Box, Rudloe Manor, 10 Group's operations centre, so that he could congratulate them personally and hear their account.

The recently-promoted air vice-marshal listened with great interest over tea and sandwiches, and the two pilots learned the Heinkel that crashed in the South Downs had suffered damage from 20 mm Hispano cannon, this being instrumental in its loss.

Cox had winged it in the fading light with the last of his ammunition, causing just enough harm to render the Heinkel useless, and its jettisoned bombs blasted only empty fields before it crashed. It looked as if Cox would be allowed it as a third victory credit, and there had been mutterings from the AOC of a 'mention' for them both.

Cox, having already received a mention in dispatches earlier in 1941, grumbled after the audience with Dickson that it was "…nice of him to suggest it, but the little leaf keeps falling off when I get into punch-ups."

Rose's thoughts were interrupted by the two men who piled onto the settee opposite, and he smiled in greeting.

"Wotcher Flash! We heard Red Douglas just got back."

Rose stared doubtfully at the new arrivals. "What? He's back? Already?" He was intrigued. "Hell! I thought they'd have kept him in for another night, at least."

The previous day, Red Douglas from A Flight somehow successfully ditched his Typhoon just offshore, having lost oil pressure. Miraculously, he was still alive, and his squadron mates were eager to discover how Red had managed the feat when many Tiffie pilots had not survived such a manoeuvre. One day, they too might be in that position, and first-hand knowledge could prove extremely useful.

"If it was me, I'd have buggered off pretty sharpish to the Big Smoke for a week. I've got a girl waiting." Flying Officer Sid Brown was 28, dark haired and thickset, a pre-war regular who fought in France and returned minus his Hurricane via Dunkirk, then fought again over Britain when, like Rose, he was injured.

A native of Canning Town, Brown had experienced the agony of seeing that neighbourhood bombed, day after day, by the Luftwaffe in 1940, and lost both his parents during the Blitz. He wore a DFM and a couple of pre-war service ribbons and had seven confirmed victories to his name, including an FW 190 caught west off Weymouth.

Brown's companion was Flying Officer Jacko Briggs, who was quite unlike his friend. Tall and wiry, at the beginning of the war he was a sergeant pilot in the RAFVR, and he too had survived the merciless cauldron of fighting in the aerial contests over Britain, and the later forays into enemy-occupied territory. The DFM beneath his wings was evidence of his skill and luck. He, too, was highly experienced, having earned six victories to date. Despite his taciturn manner, he seemed to have the most astonishing luck with members of the opposite sex.

Brown and Briggs were the leaders of Rose's blue and yellow sections, and Rose was thankful to have such highly experienced veterans in his flight. The two were inseparable on the ground.

"Are you boys going to stop for coffee and biscuits?" Rose asked his companions, as a white-coated mess waiter approached with a tray.

"Naw, Flash, we'll be off as soon as we've seen Red. Jacko wants to try his luck with Mavis at the Ramrod."

Jacko nodded sadly, rubbing the puckered skin on the back of his hands, testament to a rapid and lucky escape from a burning Spitfire over Kent in 1940.

"Oh?" Rose vaguely remembered a friendly face beneath red curls. "She seems a nice girl."

"Jacko thinks he's in with a chance, Flash. But to be honest, she'd have to be blind or desperate to accept his advances. He's got no chance."

Jacko sniffed with disdain and took one of Rose's biscuits. "Well, she's neither. But we'll see, won't we?

Rose watched as the folds in Jacko's tunic caught the cascading crumbs of his biscuit.

"Red!" Sid stood up quickly to wave, knocking the little table. Rose's coffee slopped onto the saucer holding the biscuits. Jacko hastily retrieved them, and holding the plate, popped another into his mouth.

The man they'd been waiting for, Red Douglas, had just walked in and now made his way towards the little group, sporting a bandaged head, split upper lip, bruised cheek, splinted nose and two black eyes.

"Hello, chaps!"

"Flipping heck, Red!" breathed Sid, eyes wide. "What the crap happened to you? Did Lily from Piccadilly catch you?" Jacko grinned.

"Ditching a Tiffie in the drink, Sid, that's what!" Red saw Rose's cup and picked it up. "Cor! Talking of the drink, I'm absolutely gasping, I could do with a coffee, ta very much!"

Through a mouthful of crumbs that signified the end of Rose's last biscuit, Jacko spoke up. "How'd you do it?"

To Rose's consternation, Red Douglas took a large swig of his coffee. "Mm, lovely. I needed that!" He ran his tongue over his split lip. "Ouch! That stings like a bastard. Anyway, I was tootling along on patrol with Jeff when the bloody engine cut out, just cut out, and I shat myself!" He rubbed the seat of his trousers, a nondescript working sailor's pair, and looked sheepish. "Too low to bail out. Poor old M for Maud was at 100 feet, so fuel cock and switches off, checked her straps, released the door latches and jettisoned them and the hood, so I could scarper as soon as possible. So there I was, losing height, and as soon as I was just a few feet above the waves, I pulled back a touch, to try and keep the nose up so I didn't scoop up a ton of water, and instead the tail began to skim the water, slowing me down gradually, smooth as you like. There was hardly any swell, it was pretty flat, thank God, and luckily the prop had stopped with one blade pointing straight down, so that helped, too, because the planing water supported the wings a bit. It was all I could do to keep the nose up while trying to keep her floating just above the briny, but I thought, come on Red, keep it up for just a few seconds more 'til poor old Maud has slowed right down."

He took another sip from Rose's coffee, and the cup tinkled against the saucer from the almost imperceptible tremor in his hands.

"So there I was, skating along the water, just like Cecilia Colledge on the ice, but a little rougher and jerkier, easing down the flaps a little bit with the handpump, airspeed dropping off nice as you like, and the prop blade at the front was curving back and it sounded like it was gradually crushing and closing off the radiator scoop intake. I thought to myself, nothing to it! Piece of piss! I even released my straps and detached the R/T plug, so I could leg it sharpish as soon as she'd stopped. But just as soon as I was down to about 60 or 70 mph, the fuselage suddenly cracked behind me, or the tail fell off, I'm not sure which – probably because of the stress from the nose up angle – and she just reared up for a moment, I was looking at the sky, and I thought I was going to do one of Cecilia's layback spins, when the nose came back down again right way up, and she slapped down hard against the drink. I once saw her skate, did you know that, lads? You know, Cecilia. No, Jacko, not M-Maud, you soppy twit. Most graceful thing I ever saw, Cecilia, that is, fucking gorgeous she is, I tell you. Bloody amazing ice skater." Red faltered. "Um, where was I?"

"Maud had just slapped back down onto the sea," prompted Rose.

Red touched the side of his nose gingerly. "Oh yeah. Anyway, she hit so hard I bashed my noggin on the gunsight, should've kept my straps tight, and the next thing I know, I'm being pulled from the water by the crew of an MCS high-speed launch who'd been nearby, and no sign of poor old Maud. Can't remember a blessed thing about getting out of her, not a thing."

He picked at the bandage gently. "Lucky me – right place, right time to ditch, I guess. I think I passed out again after they poured about a gallon of rum into me. I didn't wake up until I was in the back of an ambulance on the way to the hospital. They must have thought they'd killed me when they poured the rum down my neck, what with the head injury as well. Anyway, I'm right as rain now, but I reckon all my gear is still on the bloody launch."

"You're a lucky blighter, Red!"

"Not lucky, Sid, just good!"

Sid laughed. "Join us for a pint down the Twitchy Stick? Jacko fancies his chances with Mavis, poor sod. God loves a trier, I guess."

Jacko bared his teeth in what Rose supposed was meant to be a smile.

"No, but thanks, chaps. Thought I'd have some grub and call it a night, see if I can't get a warrant off Belle to bring back a new Tiffie for Granny tomorrow." He smiled, wincing, and dabbed at his split lip as he finished off the last of Rose's coffee. "After all, I did lose the last one, so I need to replace it!"

Rose nodded, placing a hand on his shoulder. "Capital idea, Red, eat something then get a good night's kip. Quite an experience you've had, there. Have a word with Granny and Belle in the morning. I'm sure they'll want to know all about the ditching, and I daresay Granny will want you to recount it to the rest of the boys."

Red put down the empty cup and saucer. "My stomach thinks my throat's been cut, haven't eaten anything since lunchtime, what's for dinner tonight?"

As if to emphasise his words, Red's stomach rumbled loudly.

Sid slapped his lips. "Nice bit of soup and a stew, not half bad, was it, Jacko?"

Jacko grunted in agreement, and Rose smiled inwardly, wondering what the chef would think to having his rather fine consommé and the delightfully rich and satisfying goulash described as 'soup and stew.'

"I'm glad you're back, Red, we'll see you later, yeah?" Sid looked at his wristwatch. "See you later, Flash. Come on, Jacko, tits and totty wait for no man."

Red nodded at Jacko as he turned to go. "Best of luck, boyo, you'll need it! Just don't talk her to death, OK?" He sniggered at his own joke. "Cheerio, Flash, I need some grub. See you back here later maybe?"

Rose stared ruefully at his empty cup and tray as Sid and Jacko headed one way and Red the other, then looked across the almost empty room, to see if he could catch the waiter's eye again.

I could do with a coffee, and a biscuit or two to go with it would be quite nice…

Chapter 10

Rose watched a squall dawdle across the grey horizon towards them, the unyielding shadows beneath the dull clouds merging with the sea as a silent warning of the coming downpour.

That's all I need.

If it comes our way, I'll call it a day, and take Hairy home. Jerry won't fly in all that clag, he thought, nobody will be able to see a bloody thing.

Cloud was down to around 2,000 feet or so, and the spindrifts flying off the waves below were testament to the force of the wind.

Is this my fate? Flying up and down, hour after hour, waiting for action and bored out of my brains? Seems to have become something I do. Firstly on Beaufighters, stooging around at high altitude, hour after hour, waiting to be called to action by the GCI. Now, well over a year later, the story's much the same. Stooging around in a Tiffie at low level for hour after hour, waiting to be called by Ops or Blackgang. At least now it's by day and only for a couple of hours or so.

He mused upon which of these was the most boring, quartering the sky efficiently, watching for the slightest movement in his peripheral vision, just as Granny had taught him when they had both been pilot officers, one highly experienced and the other not at all, in that hot summer of 1940.

Despite the bitter cold of the season, he was sweating, the belt buckle, harness and parachute pack digging into his sides and backside, his shirt sticking to his back. It would only take seconds for a speck to become an enemy aircraft, and there would usually be little time to react.

Typical. Whilst I used to freeze my arse off in dear old D-Dog's cockpit, now I swelter like a hothouse vegetable inside T-Tommy's.

What a bind…

"Toffee Red Leader, please steer zero-two-five, bogey at angels two, range ten miles."

A bogey? So, an unidentified contact. They don't know what they're looking at…

"Safeties off, Hairy." He pushed the throttles forward.

Already, he could imagine the Immediate Readiness of Typhoons being prepared to replace them if required, though with the bad weather front moving in from the south-west, they would likely be recalled if they were scrambled.

"Off, Leader." Good man, keep it short.

He could feel the excitement coursing through him. As Rose scoured the skies around and ahead keenly, Cox called out, "Two to Toffee Red Leader, single bogey, one o'clock, level."

Rose shook his head. A moment or two of concentration and he too caught the glint of light sparkling from Perspex or metal. Then, a second fleeting flash that helped give him a bearing for the incoming bogey.

That bloody man. Wish I had his eyesight!

But the fact that there was just one immediately put him on edge. Why *one*? This situation bore the hallmarks of a bounce. But with low cloud, setting one up would be a lot harder, albeit not impossible, and very difficult to carry out.

Fearing a trap, he redoubled his scrutiny of the surrounding airspace, but nothing sinister lurked, waiting to bounce them as they investigated the lone contact.

With the tailwind, they closed rapidly on the unknown aircraft. It seemed to catch the light, glittering like a precious stone, and again Rose agonized that this seemed like a target that drew the eyes – but drew them from *what*?

Disquiet nibbled at his spine, muscles tense and hard. Things could go haywire in short order, but the adrenaline coursing through his system sharpened his sensations.

However, as always, he felt completely unprepared for what might be coming.

Drawing closer, they could see that it was a large aircraft, Rose glancing ever more frequently at it between his all-around checks. It still looked like a silvery, vaguely cruciform blob to him, but gradually it clarified, and he thought he could make out twin tails.

"Dornier, d'you think, Two?" An anti-shipping sortie, perhaps?

"Don't think so, Leader, four engines, heavy fuselage."

To the east, he could just make out the faint outline of the Isle of Wight, ghostly and distant in the haze. The sight of land was reassuring, as it always was when he was flying on patrol, the threat of engine failure a spectre that lurked in their minds.

The shape was strange to him. "Hairy, ever seen one of these?"

Rose took the Typhoons into a wide, sweeping turn, circling until they were on a parallel course at a safe distance from the bogey.

"Leader, bogey has USAAF markings, I think it's a Yank, it's a friendly. I think it's one of their B-24s. They look a bit like a Wellington, but with four engines, and two rudders instead of one."

I'd best advise control. "Ops, bogey is a friendly, repeat, friendly."

Rose inspected the American bomber. It had a deep, heavyset fuselage, a broad twin tail, and impossibly thin wings mounting two radial engines each. It made him think of a bumblebee. Like the insect, it seemed bizarre that such a bulky aeroplane could fly.

"Well if it's a Yank, it's way off course, I'm going to get a bit closer, Hairy. Maintain current separation, and provide cover for us, old chap. I'm going to be concentrating on him, so keep an eye out for me."

He needn't have asked: Cox was an outstanding number two, which was likely why Granny had assigned him to Rose in the first place, and by rights should be leading his own section. But Rose felt wary of the moody sky.

"Received, Leader."

The bomber was bristling with guns, and Rose's skin bristled in sympathy at the sight of them. Flipping heck, the thing's armed like a fortress!

Cautiously, he eased closer to the bomber, the silvery fuselage bright against the muted sea, watching lest one of those evil-looking machine guns swung his way. But the guns on the side appeared unmanned, whilst those of the rear turret pointed up into the sky. He thought he could see a figure hunched unmoving in the shadowed rear turret, but it was hard to be sure.

Closer up, he could see that the airframe was grimy with the stain of war; long smears and streaks of grey-black soot from the wicked blossom of anti-aircraft fire. And the B24 bore not just stains, but battle damage, too. There were rents and tears and holes in the airframe, a neat line of bullet holes diagonally stretching from the nose to the tail, and as he drew closer, he saw the panels of the cockpit had been blown out, the blackened steel a twisted and scorched mess.

There was no indication of life within.

Where the top turret ought to have been was just a tarnished hole, the edges torn and pointed, the turret itself completely gone. The bomber had clearly run the gauntlet of German fire and had not gone unscathed.

Yet, despite the extensive flak damage, the engines continued to run perfectly, the clear, shining discs of the propellers carrying it to an unknown future.

On its current heading, the bomber would drone onwards into the Atlantic, at least for as long as its fuel lasted, and Rose searched anxiously for a crewman looking back to him. Someone he could guide to safety.

They're heading out into the expanses of the Atlantic. I need to get them to change their heading… but how? The cockpit looks like a charnel house. Is it even *possible* to change its heading? Or to fly it?

He contemplated the bumbling bomber unhappily, wondering what he could do next when to his astonishment, a face appeared at the open port of the waist machine gun position. The face stared at him, wide-open eyes startling in a bizarrely painted face – until he realised that the glossy redness was not paint.

The man now gazing at him intently had been born and raised on the other side of the Atlantic, crossed it to fight in this bloody awful war, and his long journey had led him to this place, this moment, to be here now, alone with Rose.

Rose gaped with horror at the face, and the expressionless eyes looked back at him, silently. Rose tapped his helmet, indicating to the bloodied crewman that he should contact him via his radio transmitter, but there was no reaction. He tapped again, but there was still nothing from the man at the open port.

A streetwise kid from a grey metropolitan expanse, or one whose memories of home were of the endless flat farmlands of the South? Was there a girl, or aged parents, or – God help us all – eager-faced children patiently waiting for him beyond the sea?

With much luck and not a little skill, Red had survived a ditching against the odds, but how could one ditch a behemoth like this battered B-24?

Dear God. What can I do to help him? How do I get him to understand that he needs to use his parachute? How can I tell him that his kite is on a journey to oblivion?

From her photograph, Molly smiled beautifully, shyly, but there was no help for him there.

He looked back at the big bomber, despairing.

Oh my God, Moll, what do I do? What can I do to save this boy?

The crewman stared at him for a moment longer, then the eyes blinked and the face turned away, disappearing below the edge of the open port.

He must know already. There was nowhere for him to go, after all. But he could bail out, surely?

Rose stared at the empty space where the boy had been, completely at a loss. It was as if there had never been anyone there.

Had there actually been someone there a moment earlier, or had he imagined the flayed face and the staring eyes?

Was it all in my mind? Am I imagining things?

Or was this lost aircraft haunted, doomed to carry the souls of its crew ever onwards?

"Toffee Red Leader, rough weather ahead." Cox's voice aroused him from the silent world of the battle-torn bomber.

The heavy squall Rose had noticed earlier yawned hungrily before them, a driving cascade into which they were heading, and he baulked at the thought of flying into and through it.

That way led only to disaster.

There's nothing I can do to help, he thought, hating himself for thinking it, but knowing the wicked reality of his helplessness. Which made it no easier to shake the feeling of shame.

With a heavy heart and a last guilty glance at the empty port on the side of the bomber, Rose pulled T-Tommy into a long, sweeping climb back towards Cox.

Together, they watched the bomber continue on its journey, with no sign of life, no deviation from its course, a shard of unflinching metal gradually growing more distant… and then it entered the squall, a shape that quickly faded and lost definition, ghostlike, until it became so faint they lost sight of it altogether.

Ours will be the last eyes to see that bomber, and that poor lost boy, thought Rose. We'll continue one last leg east, and then we'll call it a day. Conditions will be too poor shortly for Jerry to attack this far west.

And I've had more than enough.

I need to go back to the laughter and warmth and companionship of my friends, gathered around the smoky red-black stove at dispersals, to the banter and the sweet tea.

Rose thought of the boy, forever joined to him in those few seconds, now amidst the torrential storm of water, heading out into the Atlantic with his dead comrades, towards a home that he would never see again, could never reach.

Despite the warmth of the cockpit, Rose shivered again, the growing void inside his chest heavy for the American boy lost forever in the squall, and also for those on both sides of the Atlantic who would one day learn of his loss and have to live with just his memory for the rest of their lives.

Chapter 11

Just before dawn at dispersals.

Almost six o'clock, still dark outside, and Rose rubbed his smooth cheeks, the splash of icy water before he shaved the only thing that could awaken him properly.

Thank goodness Granny insisted that his boys must be all in bed by 11.00 pm at the latest, no exceptions. No late-night drinking jamborees with subsequent hangovers, or late nights with the girlfriend for the boys on patrol duty the following day. Their operations were wearing enough without additional pain from the excesses of a knees-up the night before.

Granny, the perennial master of high jinks, was strict with his boys and girls; nothing must interfere with their focus, their responsibilities were too great. They were the first line of defence, and his squadron would not be found wanting. He did not deny himself all pleasures however, for Rose had once seen a slightly dishevelled and bleary-eyed Belle tottering with exhaustion from Granny's quarters, early one morning.

Now, as the very faintest flush of early morning light just kissed the eastern horizon, he brushed past the blackout curtain and stepped out onto the concrete, leaving behind him Cox clad in his flying kit, slurping a cup of tea and hunched beside the smoking and glowing stove inside.

Rose could hear the sound of the ever-reliable 'erks' making the final adjustments to their fighters; a sniff, a hollow cough, the sound of metal on metal, a whispered curse.

He would step back inside, into the warmth, in a moment, but for now, he would let the breeze play easily over him, bringing the blended scent of the English countryside and a fighter airfield to his nostrils, enjoy the wonderful feeling of open space, soon to be curtailed when he stepped into and was sealed inside the cockpit of his Tiffie.

It was cold but dry. The Meteorological Branch had confirmed a low cloud base, less than 2,000 feet, with a little gusting from the south-east, and light rain possible in an hour or so. Not dirty enough for the raiders – or just perhaps dirty enough.

The new day would soon be upon them, but for now Rose and his fellow knight of Excalibur Squadron would still need their torches in the dark to safely reach slumbering chargers.

Right-oh, then, suppose I'd best get my gear and pull old Hairy out of his tea.

Once more he thought of Molly and wondered what she was doing at that moment. Was she asleep, perhaps dreaming of him, or was she awake, suckling little Danny, and thinking of him? The thought of his conceit made him smile for a moment. *Oh, Moll, my precious darling…*

Sighing, he checked his pockets, feeling for the little pink bear and her photograph, for they were his most important operational items. Without them, he could not fly.

I love you, Moll, wish I were with you and held by you…

*

Getting onto the grass runway and the take-off were almost automatic, and before he knew it, they were approaching the coast, the dawn already breaking at this altitude, while the earth below remained draped in night.

They climbed through the cloud to check above, but, as usual, there was nothing there, the fluffy blanket stretching from one horizon to the other, the sky empty and no enemy aircraft crawling across it towards them.

Down again, through the fleece and over the coast, dark irregularity against darker smoothness but features just becoming visible. They droned westwards six miles offshore, closer to the coast than normal, but they would gradually move outwards if necessary, as the light improved.

Quarter the sky and sea, aileron to clear behind, check mirror, glance at the control panel and check the gunsight.

Hairy flying a quarter of a mile abreast of him, dark, hunched figure going through the same motions.

Quarter the sky and sea, aileron to clear behind, check mirror, glance at the control panel and check the gunsight.

Molly smiling at him, her photograph tucked near his left knee behind the undercarriage handpump, and he wished he could feel her warmth against him.

Quarter the sky and sea, aileron to clear behind, check mirror, glance at the control panel and check the gunsight.

The memory of her lips on his, her hot skin sticking against his, her sweet scent mingling with the heavier musk of his sweat, her grasp of him tight and soft and wet…

Quarter the sky and sea, aileron to clear behind, check mirror, glance at the control panel and check the gunsight.

The Isle of Wight visible as a smudge ahead and to port of them now, Weymouth to one side, a darkened sprawl to the northwest of the Isle, but it was much lighter now, with more to see, the darkness slowly draining away from the world below, light filling the skies now.

Quarter the sky and sea, aileron to clear behind, check mirror, glance at the control panel and check the—

"Toffee Red Two to Leader, bandits at 11 o'clock, low."

He saw them then, slivers of metal, eight of them in line astern formation, so low over the sea that he wondered if they were Light Coastal Forces units on the water at first, turning towards the coast now.

"I see 'em, Hairy, full throttle, Buster!" The Sabre thundered harder as he pushed the boost.

And then, "Ops to Toffee Red Leader, bandits bearing two-eight-zero, angels zero…!"

Even as Ops blasted out over the radio transmitter, Rose and Cox were turning after them, the distance between them closing into battle formation as the bandits began to climb.

The Tiffies on Immediate Readiness will be rolling into their take-off runs, but for the moment, it's just us. Eight against two. Shit.

Fear thrilled in a series of breaking waves of heat and cold through him, and his heart and buttocks clenched agonisingly.

The rev counter showed almost 4,000, and his heart clenched hard again. Tommy, please don't let me down…

"Toffee Red Leader to Ops. Received, am engaging…"

They had been seen, thick smoke trails leaping back suddenly from exhausts, and the last four of the formation broke away and formed up into two pairs, one pair turning tightly to starboard and the other to port to come back at them, the small shapes of their bombs detaching and falling into the water below to detonate harmlessly in growing white spouts. The leading quartet of fighters continued on, towards the town.

Damn it! So much for a successful bounce…

"Two, take the pair to port, I'll take the ones to starboard."

"OK, Leader." Cox's voice strained as he pulled J-Jenny after the two bandits, and Rose saw that the enemy were FW 190s, sleek and short, exhausts pumping out dark smoke thickly even as their BMW radial engines dragged them powerfully around.

Check mirror, nothing. Blobs of oil slewed back from his propeller and spotted the Perspex, driven back and along as he climbed, feeling his body pushed back hard into his seat.

Reduce throttle to an almost-stall, flaps, and half roll off the top, eyes on the enemy pair, nothing in the mirror, slice back down after them full throttle again, dropping in just behind their port quarter, the enemy wingman looking back at him through the Perspex, eyes wide in fearful disbelief.

Rudder and aileron, lead for deflection and push down hard on the firing button, breath tight in his parched throat and sucking hard at the oxygen as his Tiffie slowed from recoil, *ugh*, cordite tasting bitter in his mouth and throat and vision straining, greying as his shells reached out for the enemy.

Hold her steady, steady, keep her out of the stall…

A two-second burst of cannon, flash, flash, flash as his shells sparkled harsh against the enemy fighter, and it twisted, white smoke streaming back from the engine – coolant? The long canopy sliding away to expose the struggling pilot, suddenly dipping a wing, stalling and falling away below, an oil-stained belly and empty bomb rack showing for an instant before it was gone, behind him.

Leave it. No time for him, he's out of the fight, get the leader…

Distant shapes incoming high above the land and just below the grim cloud, was it the boys at readiness?

Come on then! Quick, lads, get on with it, get stuck in! more than enough to go around! He felt hysterical laughter bubbling in his tightening chest as he chased after the 190 element leader.

"Gotcha!" A squawk of triumph as Cox accounted for one of the Focke-Wulfs that he had been pursuing. Well done, Hairy, now get the other …

Ack-ack was flickering above the town now, a brighter, larger spark in the grey-brown sprawl showing where a bomb burst in the middle of the town, lighting up the streets and the undersides of the barrage balloons, and he tucked in after the enemy leader, his heart thrashing like a sledge-hammer against his ribcage.

He was gasping, muscles straining, alive with the terrifying and exhilarating thrill of peril.

The FW 190 was jinking, and he feinted after it, throttling back to remain with it, punching out a short burst, 30 degrees of deflection from 150 yards, which did not connect. And then the enemy pilot, knowing there was no future in this one-sided contest that could only end in one way if he didn't change the dynamic, his mirror showing Rose's Typhoon huge behind him, wrenched his trim little fighter into a sudden, steep climb, up, up, and then began his stall turn to try and face the Tiffie. But Rose was too close to allow its completion.

With minimal deflection, the range closed between the British and German fighters. Rose gave the enemy aircraft a quick burst, his shells splashing against and into the cowling and starboard wing root of the FW 190, which twitched beneath the chaos of exploding metal and began to flounder.

A thick cloud of white boiled backwards from the German fighter's engine, and its propeller disc wavered and then began to windmill, a plume of dust or tiny flakes of paint forming a dirty plume that combined with the expanding plume of coolant.

A glance at the sky around, one for the mirror. Nothing. Thank God.

The FW190 rolled to starboard, the propeller whirling uselessly, and Rose delivered a two-second burst with no deflection. A streamer of white flame licked back from the starboard wing where it joined with the fuselage, intense and awful, lengthening to stretch past the neat little tail of his enemy, searing the paintwork and making him squint and throttle back to open the distance between the FW 190 and his T-Tommy again.

Spurts of a dark liquid gushed behind in a dirty torrent, mingling with the glycol and dusty banner which unfurled behind the stricken Focke-Wulf like some awful tapestry. There was a vicious explosion and the starboard wing slowly folded back and broke off, gyrating wildly past the Typhoon, coming nowhere close to Rose but still giving him an almighty scare.

All semblance of flight ceased, and the FW 190 rolled slowly about its axis, the flame now enveloping the entire rear of the aircraft. Fierce exultation gripped Rose and he felt like shouting it aloud as he saw the enemy curve downwards.

Fuck me! I took on two, and got at least one! I got my first FW 190! The much-vaunted FW 190 isn't unbeatable! And the other will be a damaged, at the very least!

Something burst in the BMW radial engine, and pieces of the aircraft broke away as if trying to escape the conflagration that now rendered the trim aeroplane a fiercely eye-searing ball of intense flame, falling to earth in a strangely jerky fashion, at the head of a curling column of oily black smoke that led straight down.

I don't know about the first, but there's no doubt about that one. Hope the gun camera shows what I just saw.

Nothing in the mirror, no immediate danger in the suddenly empty sky around him.

Not a classical bounce, but we were in the right place at the right time. I got an FW 190!

Dear God, thank you for keeping me safe.

Despite the burning ache of his strained muscles and the rigidity of his spine, he felt vibrantly alive. He looked for the first 190, but it was nowhere to be seen. In the distance, scattered pieces of wreckage burned on the surface of the sea – all that was left of Hairy's kill? Please God, let it not be all that's left of Hairy – whilst a pall of dark red and brown smoke hung still and heavy over the town's centre.

Their defence had not been watertight, but it had at least stopped half the attackers from bombing, and precious lives had been saved.

But it wasn't enough, and the exultation drained from him as he thought of the dead and injured civilians beneath the cloud over the town, and he turned his beautiful machine towards the east, well clear of the town's AA zone and balloon barrage.

Where are you, Hairy? And more importantly, where are the other 190s?

The debris of his 'kill' impacted the sea, small pieces feathering the sea for a moment, the ball of fire raising a water spout to swirl and glisten momentarily amidst the falling spray, the rippling, expanding circle of disturbed water marking the Focke-Wulf's end, and he enjoyed the sight for a moment, wondering where the boys from readiness were.

"Break! Flash, break, BREAK!" Cox was screaming into the radio transmitter.

Hairy? What…?

Then, several things happened, all at once.

Instinctively, Rose pushed forward hard on the control column, pushing Tommy down and already kicking the rudder bar to roll, his eyes too long from his mirror after his victory, now catching the fearful sight of a bright red spinner close behind him. There was the sudden crash of impacts,

CHUNK-CHUNK-CHUNK-CHUNK followed by a staccato BANG as his fighter was hit multiple times, the shuddering of the airframe and jerking of the control column under the onslaught matching the terrified hammering of his racing heart.

A line of holes appeared, as if by magic, along one wing – ragged and shiny, miraculously missing the wing fuel tanks inboard of the cannon and making the fighter buck and wallow as if in pain. But T-Tommy's Sabre continued to roar powerfully and without hesitation, while several somethings slammed hard against the nose and fuselage of the Tiffie, one punching the rear wall of the armour plate behind him, smacking hard against his seat and he cringed, vision fading for an instant, hunching behind the shield it formed, breath catching in his throat as tracer lanced bright close above the cockpit, but slashing away as he dived, his assailant's shadow passing over him.

If he could, he would have viciously kicked himself.

Idiot, he raged, you fucking idiot! You're going to die today, you daft bastard, pootling about watching your kill go down like some greenhorn novice. You bloody rank amateur! You stupid, stupid, silly shit!

Poor Tommy's engine was still turning, but the rhythm seemed uneven, irregular, somehow rougher and wrong. And he was still hurtling down, pressure pushing him hard back into his seat, and he despaired at the harsh stresses pulling on Tommy's tail, even with the 20 alloy fishplates holding it in position, but he had to pull out, for he was too low. Already he could feel the yaw to port, and Rose gently corrected with the rudder trim tabs.

Faint heart never won fair maiden, he thought, and let the wounded Typhoon roll – once, twice, until the wings were level with the horizon, rudder and hold her there – and pulled back, with a silent prayer that the damage to Tommy's fuselage would not cause her to break apart, his muscles straining as the sea filled his windscreen, seeming to rush towards him, the nose rising, rising, but oh God, so slowly!

With a crick-BANG! that made him jump, a panel beneath the starboard exhaust stack crumpled back and tore off, and a thin rivulet of glycol began to stream and boil from the Sabre, down the starboard side of his fighter, dense and white.

The Sabre continued to growl powerfully, but he worried, for he knew things were badly wrong.

Muscles hardened from hauling a huge, heavy Bristol Beaufighter around the sky were prepared for this, and, as his vision began to grey, the horizon finally appeared before the nose, then dropped away as Tommy screamed upwards again, less than 100 feet above the choppy grey waters, and he saw his attackers for the first time, just below the cloud base, Cox's Typhoon circling threateningly behind them. But they were no danger to him now, and there was something about the way that they flew that reminded him of shamefaced schoolboys.

Spitfires! Bloody Spitfires! More than likely from Exeter! Not the readiness boys, after all, fucking hell!

He levelled off and clicked to 'send' on the radio transmitter. "Hairy, I need to get back, she's been damaged by those turds in the Spits, and I want to get her on the ground ASAP."

No reply.

He tried again, but with the same result.

Balls! They must have wrecked my radio set! I can't talk to anyone.

The oil pressure gauge was dropping rapidly, but luckily the inflammable glycol was still just a thin, bubbling stream, so he had a little time before he lost all the coolant.

I need to get the sea behind me, I don't fancy ditching.

And then: How am I still alive?

Cox had saved him, that desperate warning cry to which he had reacted automatically, had rendered a killing burst merely damaging, saving his life.

I owe you a pint, Hairy, old chap.

Milliseconds, the difference between life and death…

He pocketed Molly's picture, passed a hand fleetingly over the lump in his pocket formed by the little pink bear, Thank you…

That little voice in his head, wait until you're on safe ground before being thankful…

He pulled the Typhoon into a gentle climb towards the nearby coastline, feeling the strange vibration in her airframe, making the doors rattle noisily in their frames. He would not get Tommy back to Little Sillo, but he would settle for being back over dry land, and as close to the airfield as he could get.

He licked his painfully dry and cracked lips, face tight with tension.

God, what I wouldn't do for a cold drink right now…

The recommended procedure in this kind of situation would be to bail out, not try to land, but he and Tommy had flown umpteen hours together on patrol, and together they had accounted for four German aircraft – including an FW 190! And anyway, his ground crew had put so much elbow grease in looking after her, he *had* to try and get her down in one piece.

He would stay with her. I'm not going to abandon you, old girl, let's see if we can't get both of us back safely.

The Immediate Readiness kites must be on station by now, he thought with relief, so any follow-up raids will have to face them, and I need to concentrate on getting Tommy down safe.

He found he was rocking gently in his straps as if that might help get them to safety, and perhaps it did. For after a few breathless minutes, the coastline passed beneath them and they were over Dorset once more, and mercifully the ack-ack did not engage him, whilst the idiots in the Spitfires had slunk off to wherever they had come from.

Cox protectively settled into position half a mile behind and to starboard, covering him.

Dear God, help me, please…

Chapter 12

There was a sudden clattering sound beneath the engine cowling, a harsh grinding, and then a single sharp BANG and the engine cut out altogether, Rose's heart stopping for a tortuous moment in sympathy.

One last blob of black oil flew back to smear itself against the windscreen, spreading sullenly in the slipstream, and giving the vibrant checkerboard panorama of fields below a dulled grey tinge.

Quickly he switched off, checking the fuel cock twice.

The action reminded him of Molly, always checking, getting up at night just to make sure, for the umpteenth time, that the gas stove was off.

He could feel an upswell of panic building, and he crushed it, brutally. Behave yourself…

The huge gleaming disc of the propeller faltered, slowed, and with a last weary sigh, stopped, and there was just the moan of the air as it whistled over the torn surfaces of the aircraft, the sound of Cox's Sabre muted and distant.

Dear God, I need you, please don't abandon me.

They were at 500 feet now, and he knew that he needed to set her down soon, for Tommy was no glider, and now without hydraulics, she was even more of a handful.

At least the scorching heat, which had been coming back from the overheated engine into the cockpit, had lessened considerably.

Propeller speed control as far back as it would go to improve the glide length available to him, and he pushed the nose down slightly to maintain his airspeed, well above the stall, eyes searching for a suitable landing ground – a field in regular use without trees on the approach, not necessarily a large grassy one, for it wouldn't do to impale Tommy (or himself, God forbid) on anti-glider obstructions. These had sprouted in locations deemed to be potential enemy glider landing grounds.

It was unlikely that he would encounter any part of the Taunton Stop Line, but the thought of being riddled with fire from a machine gun emplacement manned by a lot of bored but keen and enthusiastic soldiers, or piling Tommy up against an anti-landing obstacle, or even into a ditch, was unattractive, to say the least.

Luckily, the area considered to be most useful for glider landings – gliders being a mode of attack at which the Nazis had already shown themselves highly capable – were large open areas within ten miles of the coast, so it ought to be safe once he had flown inland beyond that.

And I must have flown at least that already, so there must be very little risk in landing in an obstacle-ridden field now… please God.

And of course, without power, he would be unable to lower his wheels. There were no hydraulics or brakes available now. He could lower the undercarriage using the handpump on the control panel, but the only way to ensure it actually locked into position would be to throw Tommy into a series of skidding manoeuvres, which would be suicidal without an engine.

Thank goodness those murderous sods in the Spits have cleared off…

Even as his roving eyes searched desperately – for there was little choice without an engine and at this height – his thoughts returned to Molly, and the evening they had spent together beneath a tarpaulin thrown over a concrete post that formed part of the anti-tank defence of a railway line near Dimple Heath. The summer night sky was awesome, and although Rose did not share Molly's love for the great outdoors, the time spent with her as she identified the planets, stars and constellations (was there anything that amazing girl didn't know?) had been idyllic.

He checked his pocket, feeling for her photograph, and pushed it deeper into his pocket.

Dear God, give me many more such magical nights.

He held the column steady with his knees, crossed arms and pulled the levers inwards and down quickly – so that his elbows banged against the cockpit's 'car doors' at the same time to dislodge and jettison them. Pain shot sharply up his arms and into his shoulders as his elbows jolted, and with a muted clatter the doors fell away, the hood panel above automatically coming off with them, a whistling torrent of air flowing cold and turbulent into the suddenly exposed cockpit, clutching and cooling him, turning his sweat-sodden clothes icy cold, his breathing shallow and eyes wide behind his goggles.

He hunched against the chilly blast of the slipstream, elbows and shoulders still throbbing.

Disconnect leads, have to pull twice as the radio transmitter plug wants to remain coupled with its socket.

There! Ahead of his Typhoon, beside a road and to one side of a forest, was a lovely long meadow. No field of crops that might anger the Ministry (or a burly farmer), but a turned field ready for planting, which would – hopefully – cushion him and absorb the shock of his unpowered, wheels-up landing.

OK. I'll only get one go at this. Check straps are tight enough and seat down, check fuel cock again, umm, yes, it's off.

200 feet, the whistle of the air over her surfaces and through the bullet holes and rents in her airframe, the frenzied drubbing of his heart making his ribs ache, mouth dry with trepidation, holding the control column steady – it wouldn't do at all to drop a wing at this point of the proceedings – with trembling hands making gentle adjustments, close enough now, the hedgerow bordering his chosen landing ground passing just beneath his nose... pull up slightly, maintain 200 indicated airspeed, hand pump the flaps down a bit, then push forwards smoothly – careful – nose pointing down, and as he lost height, pulling the stick back again to flare out... Oh God! I don't think it's long enough...

Just before he pulled back, he saw a 30 cwt truck on the road beneath, the pale faces of shocked soldiers staring back up at him.

Heart beating raggedly like a kettledrum. Easy now...

The Typhoon, wallowing and shuddering, dropped the last few feet into the field with her nose up, the stick wobbling in his gloved hands as she began to stall.

T-Tommy's tail just missed the field's hedgerow border and bit into the soft earth. As soon as he felt the contact, he pushed the stick forward – but not too hard, just enough to push her down and engage Tommy's nose with the ground, careful, just a kiss. The tight straps hauled back painfully on his shoulders and chest and waist as the heavy fighter suddenly slowed, tailplane lifting, tipping him forwards, and the two lower propeller blades bent and curled back with a metallic screech, forming curved makeshift ploughs that cast the soft soil back like brown curtains over Tommy's wings, cowling and back into the open cockpit. The straps held him, but his backside bounced painfully against the rubber dinghy beneath, barely cushioned by the parachute.

With a sharp Cr-a-a-ack-CRUNCH! the radiator air intake collapsed and Tommy settled lower, the tail lifting again (Oh God, don't flip over, don't flip over), and he pulled back on the stick idiotically, as if he could prevent her from flipping, half expecting fragments of the intake to shoot up through his seat and parachute and impale his clenched buttocks, crying out involuntarily with fear as his chin banged down hard onto his chest and the straps held him firmly.

Just as he was sure she would flip, the tail came down again, and stayed down, the weight of the loose earth skimming and flowing over the wing surfaces, stabilising and settling the fighter, the sound of rending metal loud and terrifying.

A small stone hit him on the head; it was no more than a pebble, more shocking than painful, but Rose took a sharp breath and grunted with fear, convulsively ducking further down behind the edge of the cockpit, as far down as the straps would allow, and folding his arms protectively over his head.

Showers of dust and stones and loose earth pelted him as T-Tommy skimmed and raced across the field, shaking and lurching and staggering amidst a rising plume of disturbed dirt, rocks and pebbles ricocheting from her airframe like dense sleet, marking her way with a deep and uneven furrow in the once beautifully level ground.

The vicious ride seemed to go on forever, the Sutton harness miraculously not breaking despite the violent forces throwing him this way and that, and he cringed from the forceful contact he expected at any moment with the hedgerows and trees at the far end of the field… but then he felt Tommy slow, beginning to curve into a ground loop as one wingtip dug in and the speed dropped.

Tommy wheeled through one full ground loop, pushing him sideways against his straps, then began a second, but finally slithered to a halt facing back the way she had come.

He raised his head gingerly to survey the ravaged field in disbelief, seeing it dotted here and there with shreds and pieces torn from Tommy as she'd slithered across it.

Rose gasped with relief. Dear God, I made it! I can't believe it, I did it!

Knowing that a crashed aircraft is not the safest place to be and that they have a worrisome tendency to blow up without warning, Rose gave the control panel a last cursory glance, pulled off his oxygen mask and his safety harness and clambered awkwardly from Tommy's cockpit, earth and dust cascading from the folds in his clothing. In doing so he slipped off the wing, which was half submerged beneath the mounded soil, landing jarringly on his backside.

Clawing himself back onto his feet, backside smarting and the smell of fresh earth and hot metal filling his nostrils, Rose half ran, half stumbled through the rut his Tiffie had delved until he was at what he thought must be a safe distance from poor T-Tommy. Then, he turned to look back, gasping with the effort and shrugging off his parachute as he did so.

Wonderful, trusty, faithful Tommy! They'd fought and won together, and she had kept him safe throughout. But in doing so one last time, she had paid the price.

Poor Tommy. It was a heart-breaking sight. She was facing him in a very sorry condition, pieces torn off and propeller blades bent back like curved liquorice, battle damage as nothing against the rents and tears in her, bespattered with long streamers of earth and encrusted black oil, her rudder missing. She looked awful, but he hoped fervently that she could be made airworthy again.

But she had remained true to him, and he had survived because of her toughness. He remembered the first time he had seen her, and now look at her! The sight made him want to cry. Then, relief splashed over him like iced water on bare skin, and he began to feel the reaction setting in.

He should have been jubilant in his survival, but he merely felt exhausted. So exhausted that he could have lain down and gone to sleep. But he had survived, and there was so very much to be grateful for. Danny still had a father, and Molly had not been widowed by those fools in the Spitfires.

And he'd be able to shoot a line now to match that of Red Douglas!

Dear God, thank you, thank you for your glorious mercy. For sparing me and for the precious gift of my life.

He checked that he still had the little bear and Molly's picture in his pockets, then turned his tired and stained face upwards to the heavens. His body was trembling now in reaction, but the relief had ushered the wraith of fear back into the shadows.

A throbbing, deafening roar grew and swept over him as Cox flew low above the field, one hand raised in salute behind the car door of his cockpit.

Rose waved back, feeling a surge of deep affection and gratitude to his faithful wingman. Thank God for Hairy Cox, whose warning had saved Rose's life, and who had stayed with him throughout this trial, ensuring his safety against aerial threats from both sides.

Rose could see a group of soldiers running towards him now, fanning out, presumably from the army truck he had seen earlier on the road. With a bit of luck, perhaps he could ask for a sentry to guard poor T-Tommy's wreck until the recovery team arrived, and cadge a ride to their base.

Their officer, a stick-like second lieutenant (Oh good, I outrank him) wheezed up to him, and pulling out his Webley revolver, shouted, "Hande hoch, Fritz! Fur siederkreigist, um, over."

An outraged Rose looked at him in disgust.

He had been shot down (almost) by Spitfires, and now this! Didn't *anyone* in the country know what a ruddy Typhoon looked like, for goodness' sake?

Rose shook his head angrily, body bruised and battered by the rough landing, feeling creased and sticky and exhausted, and he spat dirt from his mouth. "Fuck off, you silly bloody chump! Who d'you think I am, the ruddy Red Baron? Can't you see the blessed RAF roundels on my kite?"

To be fair, if he had turned and looked, he would have noticed that Tommy's markings were obscured beneath a coat of stains, oil and sticky earth.

The young officer stared at the dirt-coated and oil-splattered, sweat-sodden figure with a waxy, muddy face and trembling hands, that stood before him, and the excitement dropped from his face. He blushed.

"Oh, I say! I'm sorry! I thought you were a Jerry!" The young lieutenant sounded rather disappointed, but thankfully he re-holstered his sidearm and ordered his men to shoulder their rifles.

With scorn saturating his voice, Rose swept a trembling arm, which felt as if it weighed a ton. back to indicate poor T-Tommy, "What did you think that is, genius, a fucking Stuka?"

Chapter 13

It was a veteran of both the Peninsular War and Waterloo, an infantry corporal, who in 1818, on return from the wars with plenty of back pay and a pack full of war booty, established The Ramrod Inn in the village of Little Sillo. The weather-beaten sign hanging outside still showed a redcoat with his musket in one hand and a ramrod in the other.

Mounted on a wall beside the bar, behind cracked glass, was the veteran's uniform. The red had faded to a weak pink, the thick stripes of his rank greyed with age, but the red and blue fabric – discoloured now – and tarnished discs of the Waterloo Medal and the Military General Service Medal still sat proud on its breast.

A hero's uniform, and more importantly, the uniform of a survivor.

The redcoat had survived the fiercest and bloodiest of battles in Spain, France and Belgium, and then more than thirty years of peace until the issue of the MGSM to all living veterans of the Peninsular War had been authorised.

Gazing with interest through the dusty and yellowed glass, Rose could just about read the names of forgotten battles on the MGSM's clasps. *Vittoria, Nivelle, Nive, Orthes, Toulouse.*

The soldier who had earned and worn these medals had been to all of those places, had seen unimaginable horrors and had been one of the lucky ones, surviving to return to this tranquil place.

Had that lucky veteran found the serenity of a real peace after battle, Rose wondered. Had he found all that he had craved and dreamed of when campaigning in Spain and France? Did he awaken in the night to remember the faces of those who had not been so fortunate?

Or did he yearn once more, in the wee quiet hours before dawn as he lay warm and safe in bed with his wife comfortably beside him, for the comradeship and the exhilaration of battle?

Whatever the truth, the soldier had survived, and surely, in the end, after the cries of the wounded, the thick stench of blood and the choking bitter gun smoke, that must have been enough. To awaken each morning to the sound of birdsong and the breeze, not to be rudely roused by the rustle of musketry or the barking cough of cannons.

To know permanent and enduring salvation from danger, injury and death.

Rose closed his eyes and, standing at the open window, savoured the fragrance of the inn's gardens. He felt the niggling bite of the ever-present disquiet in the shadows of his mind, and he held out his hand.

Rock steady, Thank God…

Lord, grant me such mercy as this unknown soldier found. Let me see the peace and grow old with my Molly and our family…

"You haven't fallen asleep already, have you, Flash, you daft sod?"

Rose opened his eyes and looked at his CO. "Oh, hello Granny! I was just thinking about what it might be like when the war is over."

Granny grinned crookedly and pulled a packet of tobacco from his pocket, the half-pint glass of bitter ale in his other hand slopping dangerously.

"Move your dozy bones, you silly tart. There's someone here who wants to see you."

Rose's forehead furrowed in confusion. "What? Who?"

A match flared and Granny puffed ferociously at his pipe. "Get off your shiny arse and find out!"

He blew smoke in Rose's face, took another deep pull from the pipe, and coughed violently.

The landlord beamed. "Go on, Granny, cough it up! It might be a gold watch!"

Granny ignored him. "Oh, my Gawd! What do they put into that tobacco?" He wheezed, waving the pipe at Rose. "Well? What are you waiting for? Fat Hermann to come marching down the High Street?" He waved a hand imperiously. "Come on then!"

Wiping his streaming eyes and trying not to sneeze, Rose got to his feet. Mention of Hermann Göring reminded him of a member of Excalibur squadron during the Battle of Britain. A large black tomcat, which Excalibur had adopted – or been adopted by – at the beginning of the war had been named Hermann by the squadron. He had travelled up to Wick with Granny when he was given command of a Spitfire squadron in the winter of 1940, but unlike Granny, Hermann the Tom had not returned, opting to remain north with a persuasively slinky Scottish tabby, rather than return to RAF service in the south.

Lucky little beggar, Rose thought affectionately. Hermann was better off out of it. But Rose missed him, nonetheless. Having the big furry bugger on one's lap for an hour always helped ease agitation and stress.

He forced a smile. "Anyone I know, Granny?"

"She seems to know *you*, you cheeky swine." He stared at Rose's smile. "Are you alright, me old spanner? You look a bit constipated." Granny coughed again. "Cripes, this tobacco's a bit grim! That old stinker Stan would love it. I'll have to send it to him."

Making a disgusted face, he emptied his pipe into an almost empty glass at a table. The owner of the glass was too busy to notice the faint blue flame burning atop the dregs, drunkenly leering as he was at the barmaid, Mavis.

"Got any gaspers, Flash?"

Rose rolled his eyes with exasperation. "Honestly, Granny! You know I don't smoke!"

His friend let out a sigh and looked sorrowful. "Bloody choir boys in my RAF! Proper gets on my tits!"

They joined the gaggle of pilots standing at the bar. Rose hadn't realised, until then, that a pair of WAAF officers stood amongst them.

One was Belinda 'Belle' Bolt, Little Sillo's senior WAAF, the other he had never met.

Granny spent a lot of his off-duty time exclusively with Belle, and Rose was certain they were seeing each other. That was unusual for Granny, who normally cut a charming swathe through any airfield's WAAFs. "They all deserve a chance, see?" he was fond of saying.

One WAAF at a time was very unusual behaviour for his friend.

Perhaps it was because he was the CO, and felt that his usual behaviour might be prejudicial to service discipline – which undoubtedly it would – but Rose rather thought it was Belle's beauty that kept him interested.

Belle was a tall, willowy girl in her mid-twenties – around Molly's age, but where Molly was dark and exotic, Belle was a typical English rose, with flaxen braids and pale skin, high cheekbones, blue-green eyes and a full and sensuous mouth that seemed always to be smiling.

Recently, Rose had noticed her staring thoughtfully at him, but this expression turned into a soft smile whenever she knew he'd noticed her looking.

My Gawd. I hope she's not interested in me like *that*! Molly and Granny will be fighting over the scissors to emasculate me!

But where Belle was tall, her WAAF friend was small and petite, no more than 5 feet tall and in stockings. Her posture was that of a ballerina – Rose had spent rather a lot of time looking at ballerinas over the last two years, but only because Molly adored the ballet, of course – and she was a flight officer, a two-ringer equal in rank to himself. Her shoulder-length dark blonde hair was swept back neatly over her small ears, large tawny eyes dancing bright beneath her fringe.

The girl was rather attractive and those eyes seemed to draw him in. He shifted uncomfortably beneath the intensity of their interest.

"Hello!"

Rose didn't recognise her, but he smiled back, conscious of the watching eyes of his CO and squadron mates. "Hello. I'm 'Flash' Rose, how do you do?"

Her head tilted, merriment in those eyes as she shifted in position. Like a ballerina, her movement was smooth and graceful. "You don't remember me, do you?"

What? Not wanting to seem rude, he held his tongue, thinking furiously. She seemed to know him – but who on earth was she? Rose was certain they had never met before.

One doesn't forget very lovely girls that easily, even when one is married to a gloriously rare beauty like Molly.

She put one small and shapely hand on her chest, and he noticed a wedding band. "Go on! Have a guess where we met!"

"Erm…" Granny was smirking, and Rose pointedly ignored him. Sod off, Granny. "At the Air Ministry?"

She shook her head, sadly. "And it was only a few weeks ago, too!"

Met a few weeks ago? The girl was speaking in riddles!

"I'm disappointed! I think you've forgotten me!"

Some of the younger pilots were looking bored, and they began drifting away or talking amongst themselves. One sat down at the decrepit piano and began to plink at the keys.

Rose fidgeted. "If you could give me a clue … ?"

She held him with her eyes, golden-flecked brown, framed by long dark lashes. She was awfully pretty. He tried not to stare at her.

For goodness' sake, don't stare, old man, she'll just think you're another randy stoat in air force blue with designs on getting her knickers off.

"We met one night, and after a short conversation, it ended with an absolutely wizard bang!"

What? WHAT? He gaped. Granny grinned at Belle, and she looked strangely satisfied.

The girl smiled playfully. "Oh, your face! I'm sorry, I'm teasing! Alright then, I'll tell you, then. I was Moonglow the night you shot down those Heinkels!" She held out her hand. " Flight Officer Charlotte Flynn, known as Moonglow by my pilots, Charlie to my friends. I hope you'll be among them?"

Ah.

He took her small hand carefully; it fitted nicely into his, soft and warm like a delicate bird. "Harry Rose! How do you do? And, yes, I'd be honoured to be your friend, Charlie, and I owe you a very large drink. If you hadn't guided me onto that last one, he'd have scarpered off into the night. I only got him because of you." He nodded, seeing again the sudden shocking glare as the bomber exploded like a huge firecracker, the falling, burning debris. "Moonglow and luck, a magical mixture!"

She saw the young man's face relax. "I knew you would get him because you're rather used to catching them at night, aren't you?"

He was surprised. "How did you know that? As far as I can recall, we've never met!" He thought for a moment. "Wait, Ops told me at the time of the interception that you knew *of* me. What does that mean? Did you? Know me, I mean. Have we met before, Charlie?"

If I can forget a very pretty girl like this one, maybe I do need a rest after all.

She smiled. "Buy me another drink, and I'll tell you!" Inside, she was surprised at how like her beloved John he was, and she felt the awful empty feeling in her stomach again, and a wave of misery washed over her.

Granny screeched, "Better watch him, Charlie, he's married!" He placed his pipe into his pocket and crabbed his way onto the pianist's stool, pushing the young pilot already sitting there onto the floor. "They're the worst!"

She laughed, holding up her left hand to wiggle her wedding band at him. "Granny, you naughty man, you might not have noticed, but he's not the only one!"

"Just don't kiss him, he'll be all over you like a rash if you do!" He raised his glass and blew her a cheerful raspberry.

Seated at a table in the corner, they watched Granny as he began to crash and thump at the piano and sing some awful song that would have made a merchant seaman blush. Rose felt discomfited, but the girl seemed unconcerned, foot tapping unevenly to Granny's discordant beat.

She leaned forward to speak into his ear, and he was uncomfortably aware of her nearness, her scent fighting for supremacy over the cigarette smoke and beer.

"Such a nice man, but goodness he *always* seems to be on heat, or does that only apply to cats? What is it when a tomcat is always chasing after the females?"

What on earth…? "Um, I'm not sure… "

"*Horny*, that's the word!" she said triumphantly, then her brow creased. "Er, at least, I *think* it is."

Oh my Lord… Rose was mortified and indignant for his friend, knowing there was some truth in her words, but overwhelmed by the girl's bright and rather forthright manner.

"Um, so, uh… Charlie, you were going to tell me how you know of me?"

She put her drink down carefully and leaned towards him conspiratorially. "David Morrow," she said and stared at him triumphantly.

"David?" he murmured in surprise. Morrow and Rose had completed the Beaufighter night fighting training course together as a crew, and then Morrow had been 'requisitioned for the duration' from Rose's crew and sent somewhere very hush-hush, straight onto special duties.

Luckily for Rose, 'Chalky' White and he were crewed up to become RAF Dimple Heath's highest-scoring night fighter crew from B Flight.

Morrow, as a GCI Station CO, later wangled an operational flight with Rose, managing to claim a 'damaged' for them together after a successful interception, whilst a fretful Chalky White waited on the ground.

"Wing Commander Morrow was also my postgraduate tutor at university. He asked a group of us to serve in… " Charlie lowered her voice, leaning closer to whisper into his ear, "RDF."

Despite the appalling noise that Granny and the others were making, Rose looked around them to ensure no-one was listening, very conscious of her closeness, feeling both guilt and pleasure, wanting to lean back but not doing so.

"David was always talking about you, always using you as his ideal example of what a night fighter pilot should be like. He said that your daytime fighting experience made you better suited to hunting the enemy by night." She took a sip, looked at him over the rim of her glass. "I think all of us who were taught by him in special duties got to know about you. I think he's got a soft spot for you."

David mentions me in his training? Rose was embarrassed by the delight he felt. Oh dear, I think I'm getting a bit conceited.

"He'd always begin by giving an account of your record, or he'd say, 'In this situation, Flash Rose would do this,' or 'In that situation, Flash Rose would do that.'" Charlie nodded shyly at Rose's decorations and smiled fondly at the memory of her mentor. "And his motto is *'Bona illa, bona noctis,'* which, as you know, roughly translates as: 'Good by day, good by night'. So, if you'll forgive me, it was actually quite an extraordinary experience to direct *that* Flash Rose in an interception. And very gratifying to know that I helped when you were on your own up there."

Rose was grateful for the dim light, hiding as it did his pleasure and gratified blush.

He cleared his throat. "Oh dear, I'll have to have a word with him, Charlie. He's made me into something I'm not."

"I think he might be right, Flash. You showed that you could intercept and shoot down a Hun with GCI alone. I think there might be an opportunity to define new tactics… "

There was a commotion at the piano and Granny jumped up, howling and slapping at his smoking pocket. Clearly, he had not completely emptied the pipe of hot ashes before he put it back.

The barmaid, Mavis, rushed out with a pitcher of water and flung it onto Granny, who screeched loudly. "Argh! Jesus, Mave! That's bloody cold. I'll probably end up with pneumonia, now!"

Mavis waved the pitcher as if she was going to hit him on the head with it. "I've just saved your silly arse, Granny! A word of thanks wouldn't go amiss."

Granny huffed as Belle helped him shrug off his tunic. "Thank you, Mavis!" he grated out ungraciously.

Mavis retired back behind the bar, muttering darkly to herself.

The landlord, Dennis, peered over the counter. "Oi, Granny! Can I 'ave yer coat?"

Granny looked coldly at him. "Get stuffed! This is HM property, Den; if I gave it to you, Winston would put me up against a wall and have me shot! Be bloody *treason* if I gave it to you, you cheeky wanker."

Ignoring Granny's manner, Dennis held out his hands. "Aw, come on, Granny, it's ruined, you can't wear that! And it would look proper handsome in a glass case next to the redcoat, wouldn't it? You know you want to! Go on, please?"

Granny looked doubtfully at the jacket, with its pocket scorched dark, frayed and now drenched.

"I could claim it as being damaged as a result of enemy action, Danny," Belle said quietly and laid a hand on his shoulder.

Dennis could see him wavering. "I'll chuck in three bottles of whisky an' all."

Granny stuck out his hand to shake. "Give all my boys" – he smiled apologetically to Belle – "and girls a pint on the house as well, and it's a deal. But good stuff, no watered-down wee-wee, mind."

Dennis grasped his hand eagerly. "You're on!" Then he had a thought. "Can I have yer medals, too? Just for the display?"

Granny pulled his hand away and stuck up two fingers. "And the rest! Piss off, Den!"

Dennis cackled and grabbed for his trophy. "Oh well, you don't get if you don't ask, eh?"

"And sometimes you don't get even if you do ask, you daft mug!" Granny roared. "Now get me another drink before I knock you bloody sparko!"

Charlie laughed, a bright and pleasant sound, and Rose turned to look at her, surprised to see her staring at him, something strangely intense in her eyes.

She leaned forward to make herself heard over the noise, and he felt the pleasure of her closeness, the way their knees touched, and was ashamed for feeling it. "He means a lot to you, Flash, doesn't he?"

He pushed his hair back and she thought again of how much like John he was, even the shy smile and the reticence. Like John, this boy had become proficient in the art of war, but not necessarily in that of life, for his eyes were still gentle and kind despite the weariness on his face.

She felt a powerful urge to hug him, and it was so strong she almost did, just managing to control herself in time. What on earth would he think?

"More than I can say," he said simply, looking back as Granny settled himself once more behind the piano and the caterwauling began anew. It sounded like 'O'Reilly's Daughter', but Granny's voice was ululating so abominably and the words were so garbled, Rose could not be sure. "If it wasn't for him, I'd not be here today. I would have been long dead, back in the summer of 1940. He taught me how to fight, how to try and survive. How to live. Saved me when I had lost hope. There's no-one else like him."

And when I thought I had lost Molly; he found her and took me to where she lay, injured and bleeding. He knew how much we needed each other. No words exist that could explain how much he means to me. And when the Spits almost shot me down, he was going straight to Exeter to beat the hell out the offending pilots, and Belle had to lock herself in his office with him to talk sense into him.

He could feel emotion welling inside him, so he turned back to the girl, aware of her proximity, enjoying the scent she was wearing – and he wished that it was Molly so that he could draw her to him and kiss her and feel the peace that only she gave him.

"Tell me about yourself, Charlie. Is your chap in the RAF, too?"

Her face changed, a shadow fell across it, and he cursed himself for his insensitivity.

Oh, Lord! What if he's dead? You idiot!

She sighed. "Yes, he was, is. John flew Short Stirlings. He was – is – a flight lieutenant with the Pathfinders."

The Pathfinder Force was an RAF formation, initially of five squadrons, formed in the summer of 1942 in light of critical findings in the 1941 Butt Report on RAF bombing, and was the target marking element for the main bomber force.

Charlie pursed her lips. "John did a tour on Wellingtons, and he was due a well-deserved rest in March. I told him to take it, but his flight commander invited John to join him with the new force, and off he went, straight on to his second tour. He was shot down on the way back from Kassel in August, and I didn't know for ages if he was even alive. We only heard from the

Red Cross over a week later." A sob escaped her and, uncomfortably, Rose reached over and squeezed her hand. She smiled wanly at him and put her other hand on top of his.

I shouldn't have done that. She'll feel the tremor in my hand, and realise that I'm not as special as she seems to think I am.

But a little voice whispered, it doesn't matter. Why should it? Nothing matters except for what Molly thinks...

"He bailed out OK, but lost his left foot, dislocated one hip and broke both his legs. He's a POW in a hospital in Denmark, and there's talk of repatriation when he's recovered from his wounds. Though they say he may never walk again." Her voice was bitter. "He stayed over the target because the primary marker had been shot down, so he guided in the main force of bombers. John was instrumental in the raid being a success, and he received an immediate DSO for his actions, to add to the DFC from his first tour, and I'm sure he'd be proud, but what good is that to me? I don't want his medals – I want him."

The bright and cheery façade had slipped and he saw the deep hurt and despair in her eyes.

What do I say to that? Words are so useless sometimes.

"I'm so sorry, Charlie..."

"Why did he do it, Flash?" she asked him, her face suddenly bleak, voice brittle with anger and regret. "Why go back to it after he'd already done a full tour of thirty ops? He'd done his bit, beaten the odds. He had done enough, surely? Was I not enough to stop him from going back out onto another tour?" She sniffed. "Wasn't I enough for him?" Her eyes were huge in her face. "Aren't you too scared to go back?"

What a thing to ask a chap! Who isn't scared? Only the bloody daft and the liars, that's who.

He considered giving her the standard line, but the misery in her eyes made him candid. "Oh, Charlie, of course we're scared, we wouldn't be human if we weren't, but you have to overcome it. When I'm sitting in the cockpit, my rigger and fitter keep chatting so much it helps take my mind off it. They do what they can to make it easier. Sometimes, you

117

feel so sick before take-off you don't think you can fly, but as soon as you're up, it seems to fade. It's hard to sit back and rest when you know others are continuing the fight. You feel guilty, knowing that they are and you're not. I know you'll think I'm crazy – I could have stayed in a cushy number, but when Granny asked me to join Excalibur, I jumped at the chance. My wife, Molly, hated it, but she didn't say anything because she knew that I had to go. Duty takes us from the ones we want to be with, and it can't be ignored. I love Molly so much, much more than I can say, but I had to go when he asked. There's no other choice. But when we go back, it's not just for those very special people of ours whom we love, but for everyone in this country, to keep them safe best we can, not hide, no matter how much we might really want to." He squeezed her hand gently again. "Molly is the only thing that keeps me from going bananas; flying and fighting is no picnic, you know that better than most, Charlie. John *couldn't* say no when he knew his friends were going back. He felt he could go because he knows he has your love and your support. When you know you're fighting for what you love, what you hold most precious, you can do it. That's what makes it just about bearable and gives one the strength. You're his anchor, you know. He knew that no matter how awful it was, he could come back to you and everything would be alright." He smiled reassuringly. "John will be dreaming of being with you this minute. I'll bet he can't stop thinking of you."

Her eyelashes were moist, but she didn't cry. "I know, Flash, I know. I just want him back, you know? I love him so much. He's such a sweet, kind man. I feel so lonely without him. I miss him." Charlie let go of his hand, although she found she didn't want to, and smiled wanly. "Sorry for holding your hand so hard. Hope I haven't broken anything!"

His hand did smart from where she had gripped it so hard, but he forced himself not to rub it in front of her. "Glad to be of service, ma'am!"

"Thank you for letting me yammer on, Flash, I didn't mean to bend your ear, but you remind me of him, and I felt so very lonely for a moment. Your wife is a lucky woman, I think. I can see how much you

118

love her." The bright mask was back on again, the moment of weakness overcome.

"Oh, I do, Charlie, with all my heart, Molly means everything to me. But I must say, I think you are a smashing girl, and I'll bet John is absolutely mad about you."

God! How patronising I sound!

She nodded. "We were very happy, and I know we will be again, given half a chance. If they repatriate him, there'll be no more ops and I can think about looking after him." She sighed. "I dream about it all the time, Flash."

"Keep dreaming, Charlie, it's just a matter of time before it's real. He'll be back before you know it. You've made the sacrifices, but you have a lot to look forward to. Be patient, it won't be long. Winter is here, but the summer's not far off."

"Thank you, Flash, you're really kind." She hesitated. "I enjoy talking to you, Flash, would you like to meet up again? For a show, or perhaps dinner? I'd like to thank you for being so kind and thoughtful, for understanding. A girl needs a man's ear to bend every so often." Charlie grinned irreverently. "And you aren't like the others. I feel safe with you. Isn't that strange?" She smiled wryly. "They all expect you to drop your knickers in gratitude if they take you out, and I'm not like that."

Well, she's not a terribly shy girl…

Rose vacillated. "Er, I'm not sure we should, Charlie. I'd love to, but it might not be a good idea."

She looked disappointed but nodded with understanding, and he was sorry he had refused. She had only suggested dinner, after all, not an orgy. Surely Molly wouldn't mind…

Are you sure about that?

"I'm sorry you think that, but alright, Flash. If that's how you feel, fair enough. I hope you change your mind, though. You're so like John, thoughtful and kind, I'd love your friendship. It would be nice to be able to go out for a meal or a drink or see a show without being expected to deliver the goods in a haystack or some damp air raid shelter at the end of the evening, so to speak. We could be a pair of chums enjoying the occasional evening in each other's company."

I'm not sure the missus would quite see it that way, dearie…

She looked across the room, as if searching for a face in the singing throng. "I do miss him, so, Flash. It's very lonely, being in love with someone you can't be with."

Tell me about it, Rose thought to himself, thinking longingly of his family.

Belle made her way to them, and now she indicated that Charlie should join her. "Come on, Charlie, I'm heading back to Little Sillo, Danny's going to make his own way back, God help us, with Flash and the boys. I'll drop you off at the train station on the way." She beamed warmly at Rose. "So, was this Flash Rose character all you thought he was? Or was the legend greater than the man?" Her eyes danced with amusement as she teased him.

He liked Bolt and returned her easy smile.

Charlie got up and checked her gas mask container. "Turns out he's exactly the chap I thought he'd be, Belinda. The legend befits the man, it's been a pleasure, Flash, I can see why David likes you so much." Quickly she bent down and kissed Rose lightly on the cheek.

Thank goodness Molly's not here to see that! I'd have got belted, good and proper!

"Thank you for kindness and honesty, Flash." Charlie's cheeks were pink, and she smiled at him shyly. "I need to ask your opinion on some ideas I have, Flash, but it's not the right place to discuss it here, so we'll meet again soon. You will have dinner with me, Flash, you'll see! Cheerio! Au revoir!" And with a little wave, the girl joined her smiling friend and they left.

He raised his hand to his cheek, still feeling her soft lips and the way her hair had brushed against his face. He thought of Molly and felt irrationally guilty, for he hadn't done anything to betray her. But the feeling remained, as did the memory of Charlie's soft kiss.

Then he caught Granny's eye, and his smirking friend raised his pint glass in salute and blew him a kiss, receiving a scowl from Rose in return.

Uh-oh, this could mean trouble. Big trouble. I'd better watch my step, or I'm going to get my lights punched out by a highly decorated and very gorgeous ex-WAAF squadron officer!

Chapter 14

It was a miserable morning when they arrived on their patrol line, the faded early light reluctant to illuminate the morose day, with low, heavy cloud and light rain. The sea below thrashed into a white-tipped and frothing chaos.

The wind continued to push against them, pushing them perfidiously towards France, and Rose pulled the section up to 200 feet, visible to German radar, but at least their altitude would be difficult to judge with the enemy equipment's limitations. There was too much turbulence lower down.

Taking them higher also increased their field of vision, providing a wider range of coverage, and of course it was Cox who spotted something through his rain-spattered Perspex.

"Red Two to Leader, object to starboard, on the surface, two o'clock low, about one mile."

"I see it, Hairy." Rose peered through the gloom at the twisting shape, automatically opening the range with caution. "Is it a ship?"

"I think so, Leader, though they're having a bloody rough time of it."

"Is it one of ours?"

"Cripes! There's about another 100 metres of it ahead! It's an E-boat, Flash, and I think it's being towed!"

As Rose caught sight of the second enemy torpedo boat ahead of the first, there was a sudden rising surge of water at its stern and it curved around towards them, slipping the tow from its helpless companion.

They were well within range of the enemy gun and lights sparkled brightly on the low grey shape as the crew opened fire on the Typhoons, a line of bright dots leaping up towards them. But they were already racing away and down, and as the tracer arced over him, Rose pulled up and broke to starboard. The unsettled surface of the water also made it difficult for the enemy gunners to track them accurately.

"Flash, give the stopped one a squirt, I'll keep his pal busy."

"OK, Hairy, be careful, those sods pack a punch and a half!"

"You too, chum!"

He pushed forward a little on the stick, fearful of the turbulence of the wind and the nearness of the water.

God, we're so low! Any lower and we'll be underwater!

But in losing height to evade the AA, he also lost sight of the enemy gunboat on the uneasy swell, and he pulled back the stick gently to climb again and turned his head to search.

There was a crossing of bright tracer in the murk some distance to the west. "Hairy, are you OK?"

Cox was breathing hard. "Almost bought it just now, this bastard's a tough nut with sharp teeth!"

Rose caught sight of the enemy again, a shining metal splinter tossed on the duller waves. "Leave it, Hairy, let's get this one. I might lose sight of it in the mist."

The E-boat, one of three unadvisedly searching with little sense – and even less luck – for Allied merchant shipping inshore in calmer seas earlier that morning, had been treated roughly in a close action brawl with Royal Navy Fairmile MTBs from the Weymouth Flotilla, losing one companion but escaping in the pre-dawn darkness and a sudden heavy squall of protective rain.

The port side rudder had been twisted in towards the main central rudder by a shell bursting close to her stern in the dying moments of the battle, and then a broken fuel line had starved the big engines in its stern, and the Schnellboot found herself adrift. She was still dangerously close to the English coast, and with dawn lightening the sky, had been found by her flotilla-mates, and after some difficulty in the rough sea, been taken in tow.

But their misfortune had not ended there.

Just as they had managed to get underway, two RAF fighters had appeared from the haze, and hoping that the Typhoons might miss them on the heaving grey canvas, the E-boats held their fire with the aim of going unnoticed.

But as the aircraft turned, they knew that luck had again deserted them, and their companion boat hurriedly slipped the towline and turned in a desperate ploy to protect them.

Below decks, the engineer was trying to jury rig repairs to the fuel line, but on a boat tossing and turning it was an almost impossible task.

Approaching from the stern, Rose ruddered side to side as he tried to hold the gunsight on the wildly rolling vessel, the fighter trembling and thrown about by the wind and effects of the rough water so close below.

Terrified to be so low, yet equally unwilling to expose himself to the flashing muzzles of the enemy guns, he held his finger off the red Bakelite firing button until he was close enough, the E-boat looming large amidst the waves, tracer racing to lace the air before him. Then he stabbed the button, kept it down, churning the water into an avenue of spouting eruptions ahead his new Typhoon, S-Sugar, keeping the button down as the air above and around sparkled and fizzed and glittered with enemy ack-ack, his cannon shells climbing up and across the stern of the low sleek shape, ripping away chunks of metal and flesh in a devastating instant of tearing destruction and rippling flashes, permanently ending the unfortunate engineer's attempt to reattach the fuel line, one of the lines of defensive tracer stopping suddenly as his shells tore through the gun position. And then he was over, head down, finger off the button, guts like liquid ice as an erratic necklace of red glowing tracer sliced over his wing. A shallow furrow opened on the surface of the roundel of his port wing as the last of the tracer rounds whipped off a two-inch deep length of the surface.

He hadn't felt the moment of impact, but he could feel that something wasn't as it had been before, the slight tremor just detectable in the control column.

Head down, keep going for a count of twenty, shallow climb, keep her high enough to clear the wave tips, look back as you bring her round in a sweeping curve, one eye open for the dangerous and undamaged enemy boat lurking nearby.

A mushroom of light and fire and smoke blooming above the upper works of the big Schnellboot, flinging fragments of men and boat into the air, outlining the shape of Cox's Typhoon before it as he hurtled towards Rose following his own attack, looking as if he were going to fly into the sea for a heart-stopping moment as the explosion clutched at him, before recovering control to lift the nose back up, etching the image of the wobbling Typhoon outlined by the blast behind it onto Rose's startled eyes.

There was no need for another attack as a second explosion punctuated the E-boat's end, broken in two from the ferocity of the 20 mm hurricane of highly explosive cannon shells, the two separate sections rapidly tipped up like a last, contemptuous V sign of defiance from the dying enemy. That symbol was well alight, the blaze quickly extinguished by the icy depths as the remnants sank, leaving behind burning debris and a thin smudge of whipped oily black smoke as evidence of their demise.

Rose wiped his greasy forehead and gulped down a mouthful of oxygen.

That last burst from the E-Boat could have done for me, so close to chopping away my wingtip…

"Great shooting, Hairy!"

Cox's voice was terse over the R/T. "Nah, he was burning before my run-in, Flash. I reckon you did for him. The pressure wave from the explosion almost upended me into the drink, though!"

"Thought J-Jenny looked a bit wobbly, Hairy! The E-boat blew up quite spectacularly after your strafing run! I think that one belongs to you, old chap."

"We'll share it, old man. Half of an E-boat will do very nicely, thanks very much."

"OK, if you're sure. Sounds good to me. Did you see where the other one went?"

"He disappeared into a bank of sea mist; I lost him, I'm afraid. Got in a few licks, though. He'll be long gone to Auntie Adolf by now, I should think."

Rose felt robbed as well as relieved. "OK, we won't waste fuel searching. He gets to live for another day."

As do we, hopefully.

"We were lucky enough to stumble across the blighter in the first place. Shall we carry on with the patrol, or do you want to get your kite checked?"

"Mine feels OK, actually, Flash. Do me a once-over, and I'll return the favour."

They had been lucky, the only damage a shallow furrow on the upper surface of Rose's port wing, whilst there was a pattern of holes from shrapnel across Cox's rudder and tailplanes.

Sometimes, the damage that does for you doesn't look too bad, so Rose gave Ops a bearing for the site of the sinking, in case ASR decided to look for survivors, before asking for and receiving permission for them both to return for a check of their airframes and to rearm.

The readiness section would take their place, so their lines would remain patrolled as they headed for home.

Whilst the lads were swarming over and checking their kites, he could check over some of his paperwork, for a flight commander's work is never done.

*

In his previous ranks of pilot officer and flying officer, Rose had had little responsibility or duties additional to those of flying. His job back then had been to fly and fight as required, and look after those he fought and flew with.

Ah, those were the days!

As a flight lieutenant and flight commander, however, he found things very different indeed. Rose was responsible for more aircrew, groundcrew and equipment than ever before.

As well as his normal flying duties, he was answerable for more than thirty members of groundcrew: fitters, riggers, armourers and mechanics, all of whom were supervised by a flight sergeant.

They were responsible for the repair, care and maintenance of the six Typhoons and one spare allocated to C Flight, with 'his' flight office being in C Flight's hangar, south of the boundary road.

For work that could not be performed by the flight's groundcrew, there was access to the central engineering section, overseen by the two engineer officers. Normally, fighter squadrons had one engineer officer each, but this was Granny's squadron, and with aeroplanes that had initially come with a variety of troubling issues, he did his best to safeguard his pilots as much as possible. Consequently, accidents and fatalities were rare for Excalibur Squadron.

Rose's position reminded him of the tireless and unending efforts of the groundcrews; it also gave him insight into their lives.

Caring for the Typhoons never stopped, and whilst he had always known that for every hour flown, the groundcrews spent many more ensuring their charge was ready for the next flight, he had never truly appreciated what was involved until now, having dealt with it first-hand.

Making an unserviceable aircraft serviceable required a great deal of exhausting and back-breaking work, often throughout the day and night. With a patrol roster starting at dawn and ending at dusk, the groundcrews began early and finished late, servicing, maintaining and repairing each aircraft, before checking and inspecting each Typhoon again in order to declare it airworthy.

Whether it was changing an engine, repairing a battle-damaged fuselage or using rags to wipe the airframe and windscreen clear of oil stains and dirt, the work did not stop. With little thanks and virtually no official recognition, the men and women of the RAF groundcrews kept the defenders flying.

He was constantly amazed by how they could take apart a Typhoon and put it back together. On more than one occasion, Rose watched with admiration as a team of fitters and mechanics removed a Sabre to replace it, carefully craning the old one out before dropping in and fitting its replacement, routinely completing the unbelievably complex task in under eleven hours.

One did not fly a kite unless absolutely necessary, due to the degree of care needed to maintain the airworthiness and operational serviceability.

Every day most, if not all, of the squadron's aeroplanes were flown on air tests, ensuring everything worked as it should – for there are no second chances when jousting to the death with the enemy. The pilots often returned from such tests with at least one concern requiring attention.

It was widely known that a serviceable aircraft, if left alone for just an hour or two, might develop an issue that could make it unserviceable, requiring further work, thanks to the gremlins that lived discreetly on every airfield, tinkering with things that they shouldn't when no one was looking.

For the groundcrews and their flight sergeant, safety was all. They developed emotional bonds with 'their' aircraft. They were the true unsung heroes and heroines of the RAF, and Rose admired and respected them immensely and did his best to ensure their wellbeing.

And he came to hate the flight office telephone. Hate it with absolute loathing.

The bloody thing never seemed to stop ringing, calling for attention like a chick demanding constant feeding, and, combined with the constant clatter of metal against metal, the heavy thump of cannon being tested in the firing butts and the raucous and ear-splitting din of Sabres being tested, Rose was certain the damnable thing would eventually drive him stark staring bonkers.

And on top of all this, he had other responsibilities, in particular keeping a protective and caring eye on the pilots of his flight.

Life was definitely not what it had been at RAF Foxton or at RAF Dimple Heath.

And Molly's absence was a gaping void in his life, robbing him of the peaceful sanctuary that he found in her arms, her gentle interaction and loving consideration, and of the deliverance and affirmation of his manhood found in the physical release of their intimacy.

Despite Granny's company and the camaraderie of his fellows, he daily felt the despair of loneliness.

With his day job, satisfying the constant needs of operations and liaising with other departments to ensure the optimal performance of C Flight, in conjunction with his operational flying, Rose was kept busy enough.

And when he finally fell into bed each night, it was with an exhaustion that promised a deep and dreamless sleep, his only escape from the vague and unsettling background feelings of disquiet and foreboding that had become his constant companions when awake.

Chapter 15

It was darker than it should have been at seven in the morning, with mist and rain and low cloud blocking out the sun, conditions that would have made any normal-minded soul take one look and then stick their heads back beneath the covers.

So, it was a surprise to the nesting seabirds when the two sections of Focke-Wulfs whistled out of the tearing wind and rain at 500 feet, blasting past St Aldhelm's Head like thunder given physical form.

Had the eight Luftwaffe aviators known how very close they were to the research centre of Leeson House, and what incredible discoveries were being achieved there, they would have immediately banked hard and turned onto a heading to attack and obliterate what was likely one of the country's foremost centres of radar research and development.

As it was, the clandestine establishment remained shrouded and unknown to German intelligence, so the FW 190s streaked past like blurred grey wraiths in the half-light, the formation splitting into four Rottes to hit their individual targets.

The weather conditions were appalling, but the men in the little bomb-laden Jabos were experienced, and their run-in to landfall had not been direct, but involved doglegging back from the west to confuse the defenders, passing close to the little Observer Corps station and turning onto the headings for their targets now to the east, nestled south of the New Forest.

Already, the phone lines were buzzing and the warnings were going out to AA Command, but there were no RAF duty patrols due to the weather.

With a cloud base of 600–800 feet and low lying areas of mist and fog, interception by the aerial defenders would have been almost impossible, and extremely hazardous.

*

The eight FW 190As from Peter's Staffel had formed up over the airfield following some knee-trembling moments during take-off and headed for the English Channel at low level in a loose formation, two Schwarm in line astern, each comprised two Rotte, the four fighters of each Schwarm about 200 metres abreast of one another.

A pair of Bf 109s, without bombs, joined them, to provide an escort until they reached the enemy coast, after which they would split off into a frei Jagd (free hunting) of their own against any targets of opportunity.

They sped out across the water, fighting the wind to remain on course, the lead Schwarm half a kilometre ahead of the second, with the two 109s a kilometre to starboard. With the conditions as they were, Peter wished that they were able to put on their navigation lights to better see the other fighters.

Passing the Isle of Wight, they began a wide, sweeping curve to starboard back towards the land, the 109s falling back to follow them in.

He had fretfully checked again that his flare pistol, eight flare cartridges and water-colouring dye pouch were either tucked in carefully or securely attached to his flying suit. God forbid that he crash-landed in the water, the dinghy would – hopefully – keep him out of the freezing sea, but the dye would provide a spreading vivid yellow circle to mark the spot for the searching eyes of his countrymen.

But the sea looked a churlish, tempestuous dark grey mess today, and he prayed he would not have to try out his dinghy.

His pockets were already filled with the two blue packets of Hildebrand's Scho-Ka-Kola high caffeine milk chocolate, the little crunchy oat and honey biscuits, and the essential Pervitin tablets. These were methamphetamine, known as 'pilot's salt' by the flyers.

His Luger pistol and two spare clips of ammunition were tucked into his flying boots. The boots were from an RAF Hurribomber pilot shot down and injured during one of the raids the RAF called a 'circus'. Cigarettes in fair exchange for the fur-lined boots, and they were proving extremely comfortable and useful.

Satisfied, at least for a minute or two, that he had everything he needed, Peter stared moodily out through the smeared windscreen at the approaching headland of St Aldhelm's Head, powering over at full throttle and wary of possible windshear and the updraft, the brooding battlements of Corfe Castle an ancient grey shadow shrouded to near obscurity in the mist.

He would much rather have flown in one of the 109s, but the Gruppenkommandeur, Major Schenk, had decided that he wanted to go for a frei Jagd and had taken Braun as his Rottenflieger.

This meant of course that Peter had to fly with Leutnant von Lutz. Von Lutz was a steifes hals schwein,(stiff necked pig) but unfortunately also a competent combat pilot. He treated all other ranks, both aircrew and ground crew, as his inferiors, ordering them about as if they were servants at his Schloss.

Blutiges schwein.

But at least the Pig was behaving himself for the moment.

Peter's stomach rumbled, and he thought longingly of the soft yellow omelettes and the crisp buttered toast of breakfast. If only he had been able to overcome his early morning nerves enough to eat them.

The Rottes separated, and von Lutz led him towards the grey mass of shipping in Poole harbour, huddled beneath a forest of barrage balloons, glistening like a silver-grey layer of cloud in the murk.

The 109s had already fallen behind, to follow up with a strafing run on that verdammt RAF tracking station on the Isle of Wight.

They dropped as close to the sea as they dared, flak streaming out towards them desultorily from Brownsea Island and from the land, but even though it buffeted them and shrapnel pattered against them, none of it connected.

Thank God the Tommies haven't placed any of their Maunsell forts here!

Now the harbour loomed before them, and they turned further past the side of the town and towards the naval anchorage beyond. Von Lutz, sensible to the difficulty of attacking into the teeth of the naval base's defences, both active and passive, turned them further to where a battered large freighter of about 3,000 gross metric tonnes was slowly steaming to a sheltered anchorage. The sudden foaming disturbance of water at her stern showed her captain's sudden order for evasive action.

Whether or not the ship was armed was unclear, for there was no defensive fire from it as the two Jabos closed the distance. Drawing together, they released their bombs and zoomed over the masts of the helpless vessel. The Pig broke away to port, Peter to starboard.

As soon as he released, he realised with a sick feeling that the bomb had not fallen from the rack, but, even as he broke away, the problem was resolved – there was a sudden jolt and it arced away to explode uselessly on the water, behind the ship.

As if in admonishment, a solitary arc of coloured tracer lifted off from the shore, a string of light cutting through the mist, but it was too far and it fell away hopelessly.

There was a flash and, looking back over his shoulder, Peter saw to his chagrin that von Lutz's bomb had hit the side of the freighter, which was now burning amidships and listing slightly to one side.

"Ha! Better luck next time, Feldwebel!" The condescending tone of the Pig's voice made Peter bristle, but he managed to be gracious as they closed up together, heading north away from the defences of the naval anchorage and the town.

"Well done, Herr Leutnant. Good hit. That ship is finished, looks like it's going down already."

Ja, well done, you arrogant pig. My bloody bomb caught on the racks. If it hadn't, you'd have been congratulating me, or rather you'd try but the words would have choked in your stiff neck.

There was no reply from his Rottenfuhrer, and they continued north in silence before turning again onto a westerly course, to overfly the New Forest in a wide circle to be well clear of the main AA defences of the area.

As he continued to watch for enemy fighters, Peter saw the ship was heeling over to one side and was well alight now, a fiery beacon in the mist, topped by a pillar of smoke pushed to one side in the gusty grey of the day.

The next leg was back eastwards, low over the New Forest, von Lutz opting to take them across the gap to the South Downs, looking for targets of opportunity north of Southampton on the way.

The cloud base had dropped and they roared along just above the rolling layers of fog. Peter wondered anxiously if there were any army units encamped within the forest below, half expecting a burst of machine gun bullets to lance up through the floor of the cockpit and pierce his cringing body.

What had seemed a good idea earlier appeared much less so, now.

The fog was thinner here, revealing the tops of the trees blurring past beneath the two fighters. And then, the leafy green floor flowing beneath was behind them and Southampton lay to starboard in the rain and mist, barely visible.

To Peter's surprise, the Pig turned his 190 tightly onto one wingtip, vortices streaming in the cold air as he pulled towards the dull expanse of the naval town.

Scheisse! What the fuck is he doing?

The South Downs were their escape route, east-south-east along the carpet of trees and they would arrive neatly at the coast between Brighton and Worthing, a lovely easy route to the English Channel and back across to France.

Instead, with this new route, they were going to have to brave the air defence zone of Southampton.

He considered leaving the Pig to his own devices, but it wasn't something he could do, even with someone like bloody von Lutz. His place was with his Rottenfuhrer.

"Herr Leutnant?" With a sigh of exasperation and irritation, Peter turned hard after the rapidly disappearing shape of his leader.

"Herr Leutnant? He called again. "The fog's too thick, we'll not be able to see anything! And the defences are too heavy! We have no bombs!"

"Scared, Unteroffizier?"

Peter didn't answer.

Screw you, Herr Leutnant. Of course I'm scared. Why aren't you? What the fuck is wrong with you? What are you trying to prove? And to whom? Only an idiot would not be scared of attacking a heavily defended target like a major naval port. And only an idiot would attack such a target where mist and low cloud obscured so much. The barrage balloon cables indicated where the targets might be, but only an *absolute* idiot would even consider weaving between the balloon cables and firing relatively blind.

I can't do it, it's crazy! Damn you, Herr Leutnant. I'm not following you in there…

Shaking his head in frustration, Peter turned away from the forest of cables beneath their hidden balloons, and even as he turned, he saw von Lutz turning away too, firing at the base of the first of the cables. If he was lucky, he'd hit something, but there was no way of knowing what. Clearly, the thought of flying between the cables didn't attract him much, either.

There was a flash deep in the fog, just for a second, and a dirty ball of rolling fire, bright and awful, rose through the carpet of fog. The Pig had hit something vital with his random burst of fire – or perhaps it was not so random.

"Ha! That gas holder was full!"

That man has had all the luck on this damned raid, thought Peter, sourly.

Even as he thought it, dirty brown puffballs of smoke erupted all around von Lutz, buffeting the 190 as he turned back to join Peter.

"Continue, Feldwebel, we've served the Reich sufficiently. I think I've earned my schnapps."

"Yes, sir."

I notice you only said that *you* had earned a drink, you arrogant…

Peter suddenly noted a faint thread streaming behind his leader's fighter. "Herr Leutnant, you have a smoke trail, is all in order?"

"My engine is overheating." Von Lutz's voice betrayed his unease. Had those flak bursts finished the Pig's run of luck?

"Sir, let's try and gain some height if you can get over the English Channel…?"

"No, the revs are off the dial, I'm going to have to put her down… "

A thin tongue of flame licked back along the fuselage from the vertical cooling slit in the fighter's cowling, and the exhausts began to issue darker smoke as the engine strained.

"But we don't know what's down there, sir, please, let's gain some height, see if it's possible to glide her out beyond the coast, there may be a chance… "

The flame had lengthened, extending beyond the 190's rudder, dirty brown smoke streaming back thickly, mixing with the exhaust smoke to mark the death knell of von Lutz's BMW 801D-2 engine.

"Herr Leutnant? Bail out! While you still have height, bail out! Please, sir."

"My luck has been good so far, Feldwebel, I'll chance it on the ground."

Von Lutz's propeller windmilled and stopped.

"But sir, the South Downs are below us, look, I can see the treetops… you can't land, it's forested below… "

"Be silent and let me concentrate, Dummkopf, that's an order!"

With a sick heart, Peter watched the other FW 190 drop lower and lower, skimming and then entering the heart of the mist, thinner now, for he could see the trees, even make out their colours within the whitish-grey depths.

He could still see the 190 in the obscuring mist, a grey shape like a shark swimming in the depths of the ocean, and then there was the sudden bloom of yellow fire, silent and shocking, a dissipating bubble of flame ascending, burning a ragged hole in the thin blanket of mist as the burning remains floundered and scattered across the ground below, leaving behind a spray of incandescent sparks and a burning trail of fuel and broken debris in its wake.

"Herr Leutnant?"

Silence.

Despite his intense dislike of von Lutz, Peter felt churning in the pit of his stomach, and he took deep breaths, trying to overcome the nausea.

Don't be sick into your oxygen mask, Peter…

Feeling empty, he turned his fighter onto a heading for the coast. Von Lutz had sunk a ship, glory enough, why had he then risked it all for some empty gesture for a target he could hardly even see?

Ten miles further along he spotted another aircraft on a reciprocal heading, and he waited for it to draw nearer. Typical! He had had no luck so far on this mission, so being intercepted by what was probably the only RAF fighter to be aloft in this poor weather was only to be expected.

Um Gottes willen! What else could go wrong?

But as it drew closer, he saw the other aircraft was not an RAF machine but a Bf 109, and he breathed a sigh of relief as it rocked its wings when the other pilot recognised him.

It was Braun – but of Majork Schenk, there was no sign.

"Peter, thank God it's you. Where is von Lutz?"

"Flak, Herr Hauptmann."

"Did he… ?"

"I can't be sure, sir, but I don't think he survived."

"Himmel! I lost the Herr Major. We attacked a train and then an army camp, but the flak was heavy. He managed to parachute out, though, the old hound. Shrapnel peppered my fighter, and my compass is useless. I thought I was heading for home."

"No, sir, you were heading west."

"Then it is a very fortunate meeting indeed for me, then, Peter. I will be your Rottenfleiger, take the lead and get us home. I've had enough."

Chapter 16

The field telephone jangled discordantly in time with their nerves, which were on edge from the red Very light suddenly arcing up. The corporal hurriedly took the cigarette out of his mouth, picked it up and listened for a moment, frowning as he concentrated on the voice within. "Right, OK… thank you."

He stood up abruptly and leaned over the desk.

"Bandits angels 30, gathering over the Pas de Calais. Scramble, Toffee Red Section, scramble!"

Even as the words left his mouth, the Coffman cartridges coughed explosively in their engines, and in an expanding swell of curling blue-grey smoke, Rose's Sabre snarled into life as his rigger banged the door closed on his cockpit.

Caught first time, thank God.

As the chocks were pulled away, Rose checked his groundcrew were safely away and the runway confirmed as clear, and he pushed forward the throttle and began his take-off run, rudder counteracting torque hard, keeping the tail wheel down until he had picked up sufficient speed, pushed back into his seat from the sheer power of his new Tiffie, poor Tommy's replacement, S for Sugar.

As he did so, he was uncomfortably aware of a shock of thick smoke issuing from Cox's air intake and of the airman ducking forwards and desperately squirting the inside of the radiator with his extinguisher as Cox scrambled out of his cockpit, jumped down and raced away, his face turned towards Rose's take-off, shouting silently.

Toffee Red Section was the duty Immediate Readiness section, but with Cox's Typhoon unavailable, Rose took off alone.

Whatever threat was materialising, he would have to face it by himself until the fifteen-minute readiness boys could get airborne and follow him. As he climbed for the coast at full throttle, eyes looking in and out of the cockpit, anxiety feathered his spine.

"Toffee Red Leader to Blackgang, course please?"

The Ventnor CHL station, codenamed Blackgang after the famous chine on the Isle of Wight, responded immediately, "Blackgang to Toffee Red Leader, course zero-nine-five, patrol line fifteen miles east-south-east of Saint Catherine's Point."

The standing patrol would have been placed south of Saint Catherine's Point, and the Typhoons from Warmwell and Matslake would form the first line of defence at the coast itself and the eastern approaches to the Solent, whilst Rose's Red Section (such as it was) and Excalibur's standing patrol would act to intercept any raiders outbound south and south-west of the Isle of Wight following the raid.

Ten tense but dull minutes later, one eye on the sky and the other anxiously watching the distant smudge of the English coast on the horizon, Rose was beginning to hope there would be no action for him after all, and that the bandits had fled after the attack back the way they had come, to their bases in north-eastern France.

"Blackgang to Toffee Red Leader, five bandits at ten miles, steer two-eight-zero, angels zero."

An icy ball settled in his chest. "Received, Blackgang. Two-eight-zero, angels zero."

Turning to port, eyes searching. Five against one? What on earth am I supposed to do against odds like that?

But there was no choice. There was only one thing he could do, and that was fight. He looked at her picture, and the warmth of her smile steadied him.

Dear God, bring me safely through what is coming…

An attempt at levity in the face of bowel-loosening odds: "Wish me luck, Blackgang!"

Did they know he was alone?

And then, shame flooded through him. The odds had been hideously against them in the summer of 1940 when he and his friends had flown against the Luftwaffe to the point of exhaustion, often far worse than five to one. Some of them were dead now, others injured, but those left would continue the fight for the ones no longer able to.

Until the end, whether it be peace or death.

The voice on the other end of the radio transmitter was gentle, almost a whisper. "Good luck, Toffee Red Leader."

Like a wish, or perhaps even a prayer.

My Lord, give me the strength I need, please. Flick the safety off, check mirror and gunsight.

The smudge of the coastline grew darker as he drew nearer, and he strained to catch sight of his foe.

Where are you, where are you, you bastards? Oh, Hairy, if only you were here, with your phenomenal eyesight…

A tight-knit flock of seagulls floated above the waves, skimming over their own shadows, distant dots that grew larger as he raced onwards, gleaming and glowing in the light, and he could see that behind one of them flowed a thin ribbon of pale smoke, showing it had been damaged by the defences. His guts tightened as the seagulls grew into five Messerschmitt 109 G6 fighter bombers: slim, beautiful and very deadly fighters, which looked more like a hungry shoal of sharks as they drew closer to him.

He pulled back to balloon upwards – the heavy fighter powerfully zooming up like a thoroughbred smoothly cresting a fence – so that they would flash past beneath him, and he picked the fighter on the far right to him, even as the smoke from his companions' exhausts thickened and they began to scatter, three to their starboard and one to port. Oil-stained, pale blue under surfaces shining in the sunlight, thin white vortices whipping back from their wingtips as they struggled for altitude.

The damaged Messerschmitt, however, dipped closer to the waves and he corrected to target it.

For a split second he took in the grey-blue upper surfaces, over which a mottled pattern was painted, the spinner with a white spiral that swirled in a dizzying blur, the rudder beginning to push over as the enemy fighter responded to its pilot's wishes, turning in towards him, and as the distance shrank giddily, he aimed ahead of where the fighter would be, wing down to turn with it, and squeezed the trigger for a three-second burst, mindful of the formation coming apart and losing cohesion.

They'll be low on fuel and ammo, they won't hang around, this will be quick …

Please God.

The enemy fighter that had broken left passed safely above and in front of the wounded 109, but still it caught the damaged aircraft in the turbulence of its slipstream, and he saw the damaged aircraft wallow and almost crash as his cannon fire slammed into it, tearing great holes in its wings, puffs of smoke erupting on its cowling and canopy, the thin banner of smoke it pulled behind it wavering unevenly in the wan sunlight, his cannon shells brutally pushing down its nose so that its own machine gun and cannon response curved away beneath.

The single 109 which had broken left now reversed and tried to turn into him, hammering a speculative burst, the cannon in its spinner and the machine guns sparkling, but it had turned too late and, unable to draw enough deflection, it swept past Sugar uselessly.

Rose pulled up Sugar's nose, dropped a wing and pulled her around tight, turning after the one he had hammered, whilst that which had reversed its turn now sped away.

The wounded enemy fighter was low and slow against the water now, a thin tongue of flame leaking from beneath the torn cowling, the smoke behind thicker.

He punched his thumb against the firing button on his spade grip. His cannon thumped, and through the vibration he watched the smoky trails reaching out for the enemy fighter, the shells converging with it, snatching up waterspouts around his target. Tiny explosions flared along the length of the fuselage. Smoke and dust and small pieces of debris flicked off the

109 in the fleeting instant that was transfixed in the deadly web of his cannon fire, flame spreading, his shells ripping through the main spar, the wings slowly folding back along the fuselage, and the wreck passed below and behind him, the dark ribbon of smoke now dragging along behind a dark cloud, shot through with weeping incandescence and torn flame.

Rose pushed gently forward to full throttle, a fleeting touch of boost, open the distance for a few seconds, eyes on the mirror – where are they? Then, tightly back for another slashing attack on the retreating enemy.

Stick back and rudder over, turning hard now, the pressure pushing him back into his seat, keeping the speed up and one wary eye on the sea slicing just below his wingtip, the other in his mirror and casting in the sky for the others.

There! He caught sight of one disappearing into the distance.

I can't catch him, he's too far, it'll take forever to catch him… but where are the others? And where's the one I had a go at?

Away to starboard, the sea roiled as wreckage was flung up and outwards, an expanding white circle of disturbed water glittering beneath fragment impacts, from which grew a shining crystal pillar of water, glittering brightly in the glum light, the waterspout caught motionless for an instant in his eyes before the last drifting wisps of smoke dispersed and the shining column finally began to subside.

Of the pilot, there was no sign. No parachute, but at this minimal height there was little chance or time to bail out.

Got him! Triumph surged powerfully through him.

He felt sweat prickle his face as his eyes explored ceaselessly. One more of the swine who'll never raid again… but there's no time to celebrate, keep your eyes open…

He licked dry lips and smeared sweat from his goggles. Light glinted in the sky, and he saw them turning after him, and his heart juddered. The three 109s that had broken together, three-quarters of the way through their turn to chase after him.

Fight or flight? I got one of them, but he was damaged already. And I've got the advantage of speed; they can't catch me if I turn tail.

Turn tail. Oh, how awful it sounded! Not what was expected from a courageous warrior…

He turned into them, watching as the lead pair mirrored his manoeuvre, the third curving up a mile behind the first two, out into a wider climbing turn to starboard.

Yes, brave, stupid boy, be a warrior against odds of three to one, as two of them force you to face them whilst the third hammers you in a beam attack from the side or drops in behind you onto your tail, trickled the voice of caution into his mind.

But there was no time left to run for safety, they would catch him and finish him in short order if he fled, and now they closed with one another at a combined speed of more than 700mph at full throttle.

For an instant, the unwanted memory of the impact with a Bf 109 back in 1940 surfaced in his mind, the recollection of his Hurricane tumbling and breaking apart, and he hunched behind the deceptive safety of the huge Sabre at the half-expected awful rending impact of fighter against fighter.

At this height, no-one will survive a collision. Maybe I shouldn't have gone for the one that was damaged, they don't seem to appreciate me shooting him down…

The wings and noses of the 109s flickered brightly as they opened fire, smoke trails leaping at him, and he returned the favour, the aircraft shuddering as his cannon pumped out a slashing swathe of 20 mm death towards them, destructive messengers of hatred. He spat profanity as his deadly burst flashed uselessly past the onrushing enemy pair without connecting.

Tracer flashed bright past his starboard wing in turn, whipped closer, and suddenly the Typhoon jolted and yawed, throwing him hard against his straps as enemy metal flailed at his wingtip, the control column shaking jarringly against his tightened muscles as the shadows of his adversaries flashed dark over his cockpit like harbingers of death.

He fought with the controls to regain stability in the disturbed air of their slipstreams, heart pounding and temples throbbing with the effort, the damaged wingtip dragging the air as he pulled back to put some distance between the sea and S-Sugar, the acrid reek of cordite, hot oil, rubber and sweat overwhelming and sharp as he applied rudder and stabilised the control column.

His nerves still jangling from the near miss, he looked to the side. Where are you?

The oxygen mask was rubbing painfully at his face, and he yearned to pull it down, but with the risk of carbon monoxide in his cockpit, he dared not.

A flash of movement to starboard in the periphery of his sight, the third 109 barrelling in fast, already too close, Oh God, so close. Rose hurriedly turned into him as sharp as he could, but the 109 was on its approach for a front quarter attack, shit, no time, and he eased off, before violently ruddering over into a slewing skid to fox his attacker, his stomach muscles tensing at the expected impact, teeth clenched in expectation of sudden pain.

The move succeeded, and the solid stream of fiery tracer ripped past him close enough to make his nerves scream, but not quite close enough to physically shred them, as his attacker soared past.

Eyes racing from his mirror to the treacherous firmament and back, no time to see what that one is doing, more important – what are the other two doing?

Rose blinked the sweat from his eyes, the collar of his drenched shirt catching against the skin of his neck despite his silk scarf, control column hard back, rudder hard to starboard, cutting back again into a vicious turn, the damaged wingtip not affecting S-Sugar at all – or at least, not in any way that he could tell, for she was as responsive as ever.

The single 109 had not turned as he had, instead, it continued on towards the coastline of Brittany, already too far ahead to catch without a long chase.

That's it, you Nazi bastard, you keep going... please keep going... please...

The duo of 109s, however, had not turned for home, and his heart sank.

They had climbed to just below the low cloud a couple of miles away and were lining up already in a staggered line abreast formation, to come back down in a high speed slashing dive for another go. His own turn to starboard had placed S-Sugar facing north-east and he found himself pointing the nose at the English south coast and pushing the throttle through the gate, full boost with the stick pulled back a little.

He could have headed for the cloud, but climbing steeply would not open the distance between them as rapidly, and a lucky shot could still claim him. Better to run like mad and climb into cloud as they fall back.

He looked over his shoulder warily as they came down after him.

I should have the edge over them in speed, and with a spot of luck, I should be able to outrun them. Discretion is the better part of valour, and all that jazz, after all…

The Sabre was growling roughly like an enraged big cat, the power of the engine gradually opening the distance from the diving 109s, pulling S-Sugar away, and his eyes followed them anxiously as he began to gain altitude and the cloud drew closer.

In his mirror he could see the long trail of their exhausts at full power as they tried to close, the speed gained from their dive still giving them hope. He was rocking against his straps, willing her on, come on, Sugar, come on – when a glance ahead made his heart stop for an instant.

Another pair of dots had detached from the haze before him, and he felt like screaming at the unfairness.

Oh, dear God! Not two more! Oh God, no!

The shapes drew closer and he could see the glint from canopies and the heavy noses of the onrushing fighters.

Bloody FW 109s! Shit! Fuck, fuck, fuck!

If he climbed now they would pepper him into oblivion. Try and split them? Blast his way through and keep on going for home at full throttle? With two Bf 109s behind and two FW 190s ahead, it was his only chance.

Rose pressed down hard onto the firing button, hoping to make them break apart to clear a path between them, and once more his cannon spat defiance out at the approaching enemy. They were farther away than he had thought, and his burst fell short, creating a pattern of splashes, and the formation opened a little but continued on towards him.

"Cease fire, Red Leader!" Granny bellowed over the radio transmitter. "You're shooting at us!"

Rose pulled his thumb away from the firing button as if it was red hot. What had looked like 190s in his eyes were now clearly visible as Hawker

Typhoons. No wonder his burst had fallen short, they were further away than he had thought.

Oh no, I almost shot Granny and young Brat Morton down!

He sagged with relief as the two Typhoons spread apart and zoomed past him on either side, their combined slipstreams buffeting his fighter like a dinghy on the open ocean.

The remaining 109s, seeing the new arrivals, promptly decided it was time to head home, banked hard and turned tail to disappear rapidly into the haze.

"Head for home, Red Leader, we'll cover you."

"Received and understood, Excalibur Leader."

Eyes busy inside his cockpit and out, and grateful for his timely rescue, Rose allowed himself a sigh of relief.

Lucky once more, Moll, thanks be to God…

Chapter 17

Big Dave helped a shaky Rose from the cockpit, and Jimmy passed him the stained cloth.

Rose grinned weakly at their expectant looks, and his voice was hoarse. "One. A 109."

Big Dave bounced with his fists punching the air like a champion prize fighter celebrating a knockout, and Jimmy patted her fuselage. "Good girl! Dear ol' Sugar!".

"I'm not sure it'll be confirmed, though, lads," he continued apologetically.

Big Dave smiled at him. "It don't matter, Mr Rose, sir. Maybe we can't paint 'im on Sugar's side, but we'll know you got 'im." He nodded solemnly. "That's what matters."

Rose shook his head gently. "I didn't get him, Dave, *we* got 'im, er, him." He looked towards Cox's Tiffie, now looking bedraggled with an intake doused in foam. "Have you seen Mr Cox?"

"He tried getting into one of the readiness kites that were sent up later, but the pilot wouldn't let him. He was swearing like a trooper, but the adj calmed him down. The MO's checking him out, I think he got a lungful of smoke." He saw Rose's concern, and hurriedly added, "Think he's OK, though, sir, he was cursing summit chronic. Even I ain't heard some of them words before!"

Jimmy caught sight of Granny's approach, Morton tagging along behind hesitantly. "Uh-oh, 'ere comes the old man, stand by yer beds!"

While his groundcrew hurriedly found something important to do, Rose girded his wobbly loins and turned to face his friend.

Granny's face was stony. "Flash? Walk with me." Young Morton sheepishly nodded at him, looking embarrassed.

Young 'Brat' Morton, once a sergeant pilot and wingman to Rose in that last flight in 1940, was now a flying officer with a DFM, well earned in the final climactic weeks of the Battle of Britain. His hair was slick with sweat and his face marked by the oxygen mask, but he still looked like a schoolboy.

As they walked out of earshot of Rose's groundcrew, Granny stopped and faced him. "What the fuck is wrong with you?" His voice was low but shook with anger.

Rose tried, unsuccessfully, to stop the quivering of his exhausted body. "Pardon me?"

Granny glowered at him. "Don't come the innocent with me, Flash. You're not bad, but you ain't as good as me. However, you are one of my flight commanders, and I'm too busy to arrange a replacement if you're daft enough to take on a whole fucking Staffel because you've got nothing better to do."

"It wasn't actually a Staffel of—"

"Shurrup! I wasn't asking you anything." Granny pulled the wet rag that was his sodden collar away from his neck and twisted it one way, then the other.

Rose licked his dry lips and dumbly stared at his CO and dearest friend. His temples were throbbing, and he wanted desperately to sit down in a quiet and darkened room for a while.

And now Granny's young wingman spoke up. "Er, I think I'll go and get a cuppa from the NAAFI van if that's al…"

Granny silenced him with a searing look and spoke to Rose. "You silly tart! Trying to earn yourself a Victoria Cross, were you, you bloody dozy clot?"

Rose scratched the corner of his eye, feeling hot tears lurking treacherously. "What was I supposed to do, Granny?"

Oh dear, I did sound a wee bit truculent there…

"What you can do, you prune, is fight clever. I can see you've never boxed. Quick couple of punches then get the hell out of it, sharpish. You don't go toe to toe in a slugging match with the buggers if you can avoid it."

Granny's face purpled with rage as he noticed two faces peeking over the top of Rose's open Sabre. "And what the fuck do *you* think you're staring at, you idle beggars?" he roared, and the faces suddenly disappeared from view. "Get on with it, or I'll come over there and kick your sorry arses right into next week! What d'you think this is? A ruddy party? Fuck me!"

The ensuing silence was broken by the quiet, industrious scrape of metal on metal, and the faces did not reappear.

"Bloody nosy bastards," Granny grunted fondly. "Could at least pretend to be working while they eavesdrop."

He sighed, and his voice softened. "You did what I would have done, but you should have got out of it after the one pass. There was no need to mix it up with Jerry without a wingman — there were five of them, for goodness' sake! There's no future in that. It might have been a different story if you had Hairy covering your silly arse." He shook his head reprovingly. "But, fact is, you didn't."

Morton was grinning, and Granny rounded on him. "What the bloody hell do you think you're smirking about, you soft blighter? Isn't it bad enough that I have to give one of my flight commanders a rocket, without you stooging around like a bloody Cheshire cat, too?"

The grin didn't slip. "Yes, sir. Very sorry, sir."

Granny scowled. "Sorry my swollen scarlet arse! And why are you standing there like a spare part at a wedding? Why aren't you getting me a cup of char and a bun from the NAAFI van? What kind of squadron have I got here? Has a man got to shout himself hoarse before he's given a cuppa? Do I have to shout myself to death? D'you want my job, you cheeky tart?"

"No, sir. Yes, sir. Sorry, sir. I'll get you one right away." And with an encouraging wink at Rose, Morton trotted away.

Granny watched him go, fondly. "Awful lad. Got a decent sense of honour, keen as blinkin' mustard and daft as bloody bollocks. Silly sod. Reminds me of a silly bugger I flew with once." He looked at Rose slyly. "That ruddy gormless twit didn't know when to quit, either."

Rose gratefully grasped the proffered olive branch. "I didn't think they'd fight, Granny. I thought they'd scarper for home. I just meant to give 'em one last burst in parting." He pursed his lips in contrition. "I thought they'd be low in fuel and ammo and they wouldn't hang around."

"Well, it's a good thing we came to rescue you, you daft sausage. Molly would have castrated me with a bleedin' rolling pin and fried my tenderised goolies in beer batter if you got shot down after I asked you to come back to join me on Excalibur Squadron." He patted his pockets. "Well, at least you got one of them, didn't you? But what did you expect? They wouldn't just piss off after that, eh? They'd want blood, see?" Granny saw the surprise in Rose's tired eyes. "Yeah. Blackgang confirmed it, they noticed one of the bandits had dropped off their scopes after they vectored you onto them, and I thought, if I know my old mate Flash, silly flippin' sod that he is, he'll likely be the reason for one of the Jerries to suddenly disappear off their scopes."

He cleared his throat and spat the phlegm onto the grass. "Ulch. I need a fag." He sniffed. "Blackgang thought the 109s had got you, but when Jerry started rushing about and chasing you around, they realised you must be still there, else Jerry would have just carried on for France."

"I did get one, but I wasn't sure the camera caught it, and without confirmation, I wasn't going to make a claim."

"Well, you can, gormless lad. Tell those layabouts working on your Tiffie to get the old paint pot back out again, OK?" He coughed, spat again, and patted his pockets again absently. "Blimey. Flash, got a gasper?"

Oh, for goodness' sake! Rose rolled his eyes.

Dear God, thank you for sending this awful man to save me…

*

Rose took a sip from his cup. "So, before opening fire, you needed to make sure there was a healthy distance between you and the bandit, more than enough to take evading action should the need arise. Not up close like you can in a Hurricane, say. It was easy to get too close; distances are pretty deceptive at night. More than once Chalky and I landed back at base with dear old Doggie needing a new coat of paint and me a new pair of trousers."

He smiled at the memories of his faithful night fighter, D-Dog. She was a sweet kite, took good care of Chalky and I. We were a good team, the three of us. I wonder if she's up there now, hunting…

'Will' Scarlet, Excalibur's A Flight commander, snorted with derision and flapped a hand in ridicule. "That's a pretty tale, Christ! What a line shoot! I still think it's a piece of piss sneaking up on Jerry in the darkness."

Rose tried not to show his irritation and instead placed his hand solemnly over his heart and smiled. "God's honest, Will, not a word of a lie." The memory of it still made his stomach quiver. "We passed right through the fireball. Wouldn't want to do it again, I can tell you."

His fellow flight lieutenant was tall, suave and confident. A pre-war regular, Scarlet had fought in France and then in the Battle of Britain. He had eleven confirmed victories, a Distinguished Flying Cross and Bar, and an ego the size of the Milky Way. He was good – and unfortunately, he knew it.

And for some reason Rose could not fathom, Scarlet had developed a dislike of him.

"Aw, don't mind him, Flash, he's just jealous cuz it was you and Hairy who were the lucky ones the Heinkels blundered into," drawled the other flight lieutenant in the room. "Willy here would've liked three more on his scorecard. He's just sore you've got more than he has. What is it now, three Heinkels, a 190 and a 109?" He grinned easily at Scarlet.

The speaker was sitting on the WAAF's desk outside Granny's office, and he was a man on the run. Originally from Dexter, Penobscot County in Maine, he spoke with a phoney Texan accent because, as he said, "Everybody loves a cowboy." To Rose's uneducated ear, Hansen's accent was exactly like the ones from the westerns he'd seen as a child.

His aptitude with a six-shooter was unknown, but Jeb 'Cowboy' Hansen was a highly capable fighter pilot, dropping out of college to fly with the Republican forces in their support of the Second Spanish Republic. He'd continued his fight against fascism by joining the RCAF and earned himself a DFC.

Hansen was fleeing not justice, but the United States Army Air Force. The USAAF was rounding up all the RAF's Eagle Squadron personnel and US citizens serving in the RACF, to draft them straight into their own fighter squadrons.

Scarlet stared at him coldly. "I'd be obliged if you didn't call me Willy, Cowboy."

Hansen winked at Rose and shrugged. "Yeah, OK."

They sat in uncomfortable silence, the WAAF gazing adoringly at Hansen (it helped that he looked and talked like a Hollywood star), and when Rose could stand it no longer he asked, "So why are we here? And where's Granny been all day?"

Scarlet ignored him, but Hansen put up his hands. "All I know is that he had a meeting with the AOC."

The door slammed open, making them all jump, and the WAAF tsked-tsked in rebuke.

"I do wish you wouldn't do that, sir," the girl said reprovingly. "I keep expecting the door to come off its hinges and fly across the room at me!"

Granny grinned disarmingly at her as he slouched into the room, a cigarette hanging from his lower lip. "Bloody thing keeps sticking, Lizzie, be a dear and get someone to look at it for me, would you?" He clapped his hands enthusiastically and rubbed them together. "Evening, lads! Sorry to keep you waiting, come on into my office, would you?"

*

Once the door was closed, Granny sat them down and settled behind his desk, ash dropping from his cigarette onto his tie.

"Feel free to smoke, lads." He cast a baleful eye at Rose. "All 'cept for those of you who don't."

Scarlet got straight to the point. "So, Granny, may one ask why we've been called here?"

Granny leaned forward. "The scourge of the Atlantic!"

Rose blinked. The others were nonplussed. "Scourge of the Atlantic?"

Granny dropped his cigarette butt into the ashtray made from a 20 mm shell. "Will, give us a ciggie."

Scarlet frowned but dug around in his chest pocket and produced a packet of Pall Mall king size. Granny's eyes lit up and he grabbed several of the cigarettes.

"I'm talking, of course…" he lit the cigarette and puffed on it "…of the FW 200. Winston's a bit rattled about the way the Battle of The Atlantic is going, and the Jerry fleet air arm, or whatever it is they call themselves, is giving him headaches. The U-boats are giving our merchant marine a bloody hard time of it, but the Condors have also been playing a part. They've been finding our ships and convoys for the U-boats, and in addition to the recce role, as you know, they're bombing them. We've lost a lot of ships to Condors, directly and indirectly, so all of those based in France are an added risk to our convoys. They can push Condor patrols farther out into the Atlantic from there." He waved the glowing cigarette at them. "And now it seems that Jerry has stationed an additional Condor flight at a Luftwaffe base close to Brest, and it's got the Admiralty worried. That's where we come in."

With a flourish, he pulled an envelope from his pocket. "Orders for an attack. An hour before dinner this evening, Mata Hari is going to give us a briefing, he's got the gen, and we're going to plan a raid of our own just after dawn the day after tomorrow." He looked at their faces. "There'll be eight of us in total, including our number twos, a single strafing pass in line abreast, let 'em know that they aren't safe there."

"Why not a ramrod, Granny? Why us?" Scarlet wondered why an escorted short-range bomber mission was not being used to counter the threat.

Granny nodded, took a last pull on his cigarette and dropped it into his improvised ashtray. "OK, Will, good question. Thing is, we can get in there at low level, strafe and get out of it sharpish, so fast that fighters won't be able to catch us, whether we're together or we split up." He puffed out a stream of smoke at Scarlet. "And anyway, you cheeky tart, why *not* us? We're the best there is!"

Scarlet nodded thoughtfully and smiled. "That we are!"

Granny looked across at Rose. "There was some question of you not going, Flash, old bean. Because you've flown Beaufighters with hush-hush gear, there was a worry that Jerry might learn something useful from you. But, don't worry, I soon put 'em straight! I told 'em that you were useless when it came to all things technical and mechanical and that Jerry could torture you 'til they were blue in the face and not get anything useful out of you. I told 'em nothing you say ever makes any sense. I think some of them must've met you before because I didn't have to do much to convince them!"

Rose blushed at their amused faces. "Er, OK. Thanks… I think."

"Thing is, Jerry has already got a pretty effective night fighting system set up, as Butch's boys have found to their cost." Butch was the name given by his crews to Air Chief Marshal Harris, the C-in-C of Bomber Command.

Granny slapped the surface of his desk. "Right, lads, we'll meet up again tomorrow for the final details, but even if we don't get them, we want them to know that they're targets so long as they're there. What the Admiralty really wants is to get the Condors withdrawn from the Brest area. Of course, though, the aim is to get at least one of 'em!" He stared doubtfully at them. "You boys do know what a Condor looks like, don't you?"

Hansen nodded. "If it's big and got black crosses on its wings, I'll know." He shook his head. "Do we know what a Condor looks like? I ask you!" Then he looked sideways at Rose and stage whispered behind one hand, "Say, Flash, what's a Condor look like?"

Rose smirked and shrugged, and Scarlet obligingly piped up. "Well if memory serves, and I may be wrong, but I think it's made of rubber and goes over one's John Thomas!"

Granny glowered and waved his arms dismissively at them. "Bloody children! Think you're all funny, don't you? You bunch of clowns! Now go on, you dopey bastards, piss off out of my office!"

But he was grinning.

Chapter 18

'Mata Hari' ('Mati' for short) Mason, Excalibur Squadron's intelligence officer, blinked owlishly at the eight pilots and smiled shyly. "All settled and comfortable, chaps? Granny? Yes? Then I'll start." He turned to the blackboard and whipped off the covering cloth, exposing the chalked drawing underneath.

"So, this is your target for tomorrow, the Luftwaffe airbase of, um, Brest-Lanveoc, about nine miles south of the city of Brest, on the north shore of the Crozon Peninsula. There are a number of military units and formations based there or thereabouts."

"For Gawd's sake, Mati, speak up, will you? I can hardly hear a fucking word!" moaned Granny. He pulled out a cigarette pack cantankerously and lit one, the flame flaring brightly as if to punctuate his sentence.

"Right you are, sir, terribly sorry." Mason's voice seemed as quiet as before, and Rose scraped forward on his chair to hear better.

"The area is heavily defended and the Kriegsmarine has an extensive presence, primarily light coastal forces based at several locations, with large numbers of Wehrmacht units concentrated north and south in Brest and Douarnenez. Needless to say, your ideal approach would be from the west, coming in from the Atlantic at low level. They'll not expect an attack from that direction, I shouldn't think. In and out sharpish, before the fighters can take off and come after you."

His mouth turned down. "There is a risk that any vessels leaving or returning to the Morbihan, for example, E-boat patrols, may catch sight

155

of you and alert the defences." He looked up at them anxiously. "The best way out will probably be back the way you came."

Granny stood up and blew out a stream of cigarette smoke directly at Mason. "Blow that for a game of soldiers! The approaches to the Crozon Peninsula will be bristling with defences, bloody Jerry fish heads and all. We'll head in and back the way the crow flies. Straight in, straight out. If we see anything worth having a go at we'll stick a few cannon shells into it while we're at it!"

Granny looked hard at them. "Four pairs in line astern going in, spread out to line abreast when we hit the coast, one strafing pass, and split into separate pairs and steeplechase back across France and then home. Condors are the primary targets, but anything on the field is fair game, and feel free to give anything on the way back a cheery squirt, too, but don't hang about. I want us long gone by the time Jerry gets into the air. In, one pass, out sharpish. If the fighters get up there and catch one or more of us, turn back and support if you can, don't if there are about fifty of the bastards, but if we take off after the attack at full throttle, they shouldn't catch us. Any airborne patrols are unlikely to be in the right place at the right time to intercept, fingers crossed."

Mason seemed to droop a little, wilting beneath the smoky onslaught, but nodded thoughtfully. "Actually, that does seem a bit more sensible." He choked back a cough and smiled brightly.

Granny stared at the drawing on the blackboard. "Can you get me the latest gen on flak batteries in North Finisterre, Mati?" He peered closer. "Take a good long butchers at this, lads. I want you familiar with the airfield's arrangement."

Mason half raised his hand, then put it down again self-consciously. "Granny? There is a dummy airfield five or six miles south-west of the target. Much smaller though, different layout, so just learn where the hangars and main buildings are, relative to one another."

"Thanks, Mati, me old chum. Here." He gave Mason the chalk. "You forgot to mark north on the map. Tsk, tsk, you're slipping old lad."

Mason blushed. "Oops, sorry Granny."

Granny nodded with satisfaction. "Good man, oh, and while you're at it, could you tell me which building is the Jerry WAAF barracks? I'd much rather not blow up any totty, even if it is Teutonic totty. I don't make war on girls." He looked at Rose, momentarily sharing the seared memory of that summer day in 1940, the smell of fire and smoke and brick dust, the tears and the pain, the lines of dead WAAFs beneath dirty tarpaulin.

Rose nodded slightly, the prickling behind his eyeballs hot. Will I ever forget? Can I?

The answer was simple.

Never. Not for as long as I live.

Never forget.

"Come on, Flash! There's room for everyone! Come and take a gander!" Mason smiled at Rose, and the moment was broken.

*

Rose folded the letter and placed it back into the envelope, then looked at the picture of his friends from RAF Dimple Heath on the dresser beside his bed. Six crews standing before the dispersals hut, Chalky and himself grinning like a pair of idiots.

Billy Barr had seen success commanding a night fighting unit in North Africa and had recently received the DSO. Rose was delighted for his friend and one-time flight commander and suspected that he had played a significant part in Operation Torch.

Reading between the lines on the censored letter, it seemed that Billy would be taking a Beaufighter flight to Malta to bolster the night fighting forces there and increase their scope of night fighting operations in depth on the northern Mediterranean and over Nazi-occupied southern Europe.

After the Second Battle of El Alamein, Rommel's threat to Egypt and the Suez Canal was all but finished, and battles at El Alamein and Torch had turned the war in North Africa decisively in favour of the Allies.

Following the Axis domination of the Mediterranean and Europe, Rommel's desert campaign, the punishing war in the Atlantic, and the bitter loss of Singapore in early '42, it was a relief to know things seemed to be changing for the better.

At last, it seemed that there may be a real hope of defeating the madmen in Berlin.

In their tour of US factories and newly set up RAF Flying Training Schools during early 1942, Rose, Molly and their companions had found the American people extremely friendly and supportive and were impressed and heartened by the range and depth of America's industrial base. An ally like that would hopefully ensure victory over Hitler's 'thousand-year' Reich.

He looked across to the photograph of Molly and Daniel on his bedside cabinet. One day, my darlings, God willing, as Vera sang so sweetly, when the world is free…

He picked up his copy of Agatha Christie's *The Body in the Library* and tucked Billy's letter in the back. He would pop down to the mess for a cup of tea before dinner, after a couple of pages or so.

"Psst! Hey Flash, gotta moment? You wanna see somethin'?" Cowboy Hansen poked his head through the door, brandishing a shoebox.

Rose put down his book and smiled in welcome. "Hello Cowboy, come in. What have you got there?"

Hansen sat down on the floor by the window and beckoned Rose to join him. "Just some mementoes of my time in Spain, come and see, Flash."

Rose joined Hansen, easing his weaker leg into a comfortable position as he sat, and watched curiously as Hansen removed the lid.

His fellow pilot lifted out a handful of worn photographs, leaving behind a dried red carnation, a couple of medals and a metal flying badge incorporating a winged laurel wreath with an arrow pointing upwards, nestled on a neatly folded black silk shawl with a fringe and embroidery.

"What're those, Cowboy?"

Hansen put down the photos and handed the flying badge and medals to Rose. "Those are my Republican Air Force aviator's wings, the Yugoslav People's Hero neck medal, and the Russian Order of the Red Banner. The Russki one was from a Soviet tank colonel, big hairy bastard, thought he was Rasputin. He took it off his own chest and pinned it on to me with a big slobbering kiss. He said that Lenin himself had pinned it onto his chest. He said it made us brothers. Even pinched my bottom."

The photographs were of a much younger Hansen, standing beside a dark-painted and stubby Polikarpov I-16 monoplane fighter and gawping comically at the camera; Hansen with his arms around a couple of other pilots; with a group of Soviet pilots in which he was being hugged by a huge officer with bushy eyebrows and a metal punctuated smile; a formal set picture of a Spanish family; and the last one was a small passport-sized picture of a girl. A slim face, delicate lashes and dark eyes filled with mischief and a slight smile, a strand of hair falling rebelliously across her face.

Hansen spoke softly, his affected Texan accent gone. "Her name was Aniceta, and she was Basque. She didn't make it out of town when the Nationalist forces bombed Durango in '37." He cradled the photograph tenderly in his palm and sighed.

"She was such a sweet girl, Flash." He wiped his mouth. "It has been almost six years, but it still feels like yesterday." He placed the photo face down onto the embroidered shawl. "In that first year, I thought I'd be taking a Spanish bride home with me." He looked down, smiling sadly. "Not meant to be."

Rose shook his head in sympathy. "I don't think I could carry on if I lost..." He shied away from the awful thought. "She's everything..."

And then the warrior was back. "We must've killed hundreds strafing, and in the air, I got two Junkers, a Dornier and one of their Heinkel fighters, but we were pretty outclassed by then, cuz the Legion's new monoplane fighters had arrived on the scene. I was wounded and grounded, and then it all went to shit. I was drinking so much that I'd lost the edge. I got shot down twice, but then trying to tough it out with a 109 in a Mosca was no picnic, I can tell you. We had the edge in turns and fighting in the horizontal, pretty much as we did in Hurribags and Spits, but the Typhoon is an altogether different beast." He reached out and stroked the carnation with his forefinger. "Those 109's had us by the short hairs. I was evacuated via the Pyrenees and managed to get a ticket back home. Soon as I was able, I walked into an RCAF recruiting office, and so, here I am!"

He turned and looked at Rose then, and Rose shivered within at the expression in those eyes. "Once I had a decent plane to fight in, it was a different story. I've had eight 109s, so far, Flash. I don't count the others, though my lads do. It's the 109s that made us bleed, in Spain. I've got a few scores to settle, yet, buddy."

He paused. "There have been others, but my Aniceta, well." He swallowed dryly. "She was the one. You know what I mean, don't you?" Hansen gently stroked one dried petal with a finger.

Rose, who had only ever been with Molly, didn't have a clue what he meant. But he nodded, attempting to look worldly-wise.

He was struck by how similar Hansen's experiences were to those of his dear friend Stan Cynk, how their crushing hatred had been kindled and stoked to a raging fervour by the loss of those they loved dearly, their strengths in combat buttressed and enhanced by their hate.

How many times had that story been repeated over the past three years? How many hearts had been broken? How many had ceased to beat? How much suffering?

A handful of fascists had thrown the world into chaos – disruption, destruction, and death – and the effects would be felt by those who survived and the generations that followed. The rank cruelty would scar those yet to be born.

Hansen bleakly looked at him. "God, Flash, I really miss her."

Rose stood and lightly squeezed his shoulder. "Come on, Cowboy, let's have a cup of tea. You can tell me all about Aniceta, and we'll remember her together. I'd like to find out more about her. Tell me about her over a bun and a cuppa."

Hansen carefully replaced the lid on his precious box of treasured memories and lost hopes, and looked up gratefully. "Thanks, Flash, I'd like that a lot."

Chapter 19

The tea came boiling hot in a tin pail, strong and sweet, the sausages and slices of bread incongruously stacked in a soup tureen.

Granny whooped and slapped two of the plump and oily bangers between bread and took a bite, chewing ferociously. "Mm, just what the doctor ordered! Come on lads, tuck in!"

Rose's stomach roiled, and he took a small sip from his tin mug to try and settle it. The others gathered around the food and began to eat quietly, the rasping whisper and hiss of the hot stove loud in the near silence.

Outside a Sabre coughed a muffled bark and growled into vibrant and pulsating life as the mechanics ran it up a couple of times before cutting it again.

It's nearly time.

He checked his pockets again.

The revolver stuck into his left flying boot felt heavy and strange, but Granny had insisted they all carried one – "Don't even think of having a gun battle with Jerry, chaps, it's for handing over to Jerry if you are likely to be captured. If you give 'em something, they'll be happy that you didn't have a pop at them and that they got a souvenir. They get a story to tell over the sauerkraut and schnapps, and you're less likely to get a slap or have your balls whipped off!"

He had held up one finger. "But, if you are rescued by the Resistance, then use it to shoot rabbits and elks, or whatever it is they have in France, until you get sent back to us. Or give it to 'em, they'll be so grateful the Resistance popsies might give you a shag or two."

Molly's photograph and the little pink bear shared their pocket with an emergency pack, which was about the size of a paperback and packed tight with helpful goodies such as sweets and a fishing line, and he checked that nothing had slipped out in the thirty seconds since he had last checked.

Cox came up to him, sausage sandwich in one hand, and held out a fork on which had been impaled a glistening sausage, fried a dark brown and dripping with fat. "Flash?"

Rose made a face and shook his head, but his wingman frowned disapprovingly. "Don't sod about, mate. You'll be hungry later, so get it down your neck, will you?"

He sighed and took the fork, nodding his thanks to Cox, but wanting to be outside in the cool night air, amidst the comforting fragrant blend of rain and grass and fuel, the dark roof of cloud above.

The sausage was oily and fatty and tough, but he pushed it down with big mouthfuls of tea.

It was true what they said.

War is hell.

*

The Typhoons were lined up on the field, facing the coast already, and they took off at full throttle, the pairs of fighters rising into the first gloom of dawn, staying low in line astern until they reached the coast, the barrage balloons of Exeter a distant smudge in the still darkened sky to starboard, then dropping even lower to skim the sea, but not low enough to be buffeted badly or to raise a tell-tale plume spray behind them.

They opened out and settled into line abreast. The initial idea of a line astern pattern of Typhoon pairs would have created too much turbulence for the following pairs, and the loose formation allowed them to concentrate on their flying and on keeping a good lookout.

As Granny said, "We're more likely to look like a Staffel of Focke-Wulfs," and he had cast a meaningful glance at a furiously blushing Rose. "Easy mistake to make, I'm told."

I'll never hear the end of it…

But of course, If he had thought Granny and Morton were a couple of 190s, perhaps the Jerry squaddies might think so, too? A second's hesitation by the flak could make all the difference.

The sea blurred past as they raced across it in excess of 380 mph, a blurry dark grey stippled plain, thankfully empty of surface craft, mist and a squall in the distance confining their vision. The horizon was invisible, and the lightened sky to the east edged the brooding ceiling of cloud with grey-white lace.

Cox and Rose were on the starboard wing of the formation, and as he rotated and turned his head to scan the sea and the sky, Rose admired the shapely yet pugnacious profile of Cox's Tiffie, the light outlining it and turning the spinning blades into dancing radiance. Beyond his wingman's machine, the other fighters slipped in and out of view, wraiths over the sea, beautiful and deadly, and he wondered how many of them would make the return journey.

Will any of us make it back?

It would be the first time in his operational career that Rose would go above enemy-occupied territory, and his first time in France since that idyllic family holiday of 1932.

As usual after take-off, the excitement and heightened awareness subdued niggling apprehension, which always lurked at the back of his mind whilst he was on the ground.

In the air, he was too busy to take notice, and when he was with Molly, it faded enough that he became unaware of it. He looked down at her picture, just for a second, and her smile soothed the tension slightly. God, how I love you, Moll. How I miss you.

He crushed the sudden feeling of emptiness that her distance from him created. There was no time for melancholy reflection, for the sky was lighter and the faded smear of the Finistère coast emerged rapidly from the mist.

A rowing boat appeared and slid rapidly to starboard of Rose, the astonished figure of the fisherman merging with the boat as it disappeared behind the hurtling formation. A flock of seagulls startled into flight, but not close enough to cause them concern.

To port of them would be the city of Saint-Pol-de-Léon, famed for the twin spires of its cathedral and the island forts, but from his cockpit, there was nothing visible.

And no flak.

One last check of the instruments. All good, thank you, Lord God.

One last prayer, Keep us safe within your mercy, O Lord.

"Gesäß, mein Herren!" Granny's voice gave the instruction to close up and climb, using a prearranged codeword in German. If any enemy radio operators were listening in on the frequency, they would – hopefully – assume the broadcast was from a Luftwaffe unit.

Rose had been greatly impressed when he first heard Granny use the code words. "I didn't know you could speak German, Granny?"

His friend had shrugged nonchalantly. "Just the important words, dear boy, enough to get by if I ever have eine Zuordnung mit einem raulein!" (an assignment with a young lady).

Smoothly, they breasted the coastline, no higher than 50 feet above the picturesque countryside, bearing a little to starboard to clear the high ground, the thunder of their Sabres reflected back at them. Then, easing down again as the ground fell away, streams and woodlands and farmhouses and fields and little hamlets flashed past, only half sensed as Rose concentrated on staying low and keeping her there as the ground undulated beneath their speeding Typhoons.

Now they were sweeping past the Landerneau river, settling abreast above the rippling water, the outriders a little higher over the banks, eyes searching anxiously for electric power lines across their flightpath, even though Mati had assured them there were none, and out through the river mouth into the Morbihan, back down to 0 feet.

Stay low. Don't catch the water with the tips of your prop, fight the urge to climb…

Still no flak.

Dear heavens! They were over France – enemy-occupied territory. A fresh tide of adrenaline rinsed through him in a cold rush.

Rain began to smear the Perspex, the cloud had lowered. With a bit of luck, the Luftwaffe fighter patrols would still be sitting on their runways.

The port of Brest was away to starboard, invisible in the haze, and Rose strained to detect surface vessels as they crossed the Rade de Brest. The likelihood of coming across enemy naval units was high in this busy body of water, and surely the alarms must be ringing by now? But they were too low for a clear view of their surroundings.

Still luck favoured them, and nothing emerged from the haze of brooding mizzle.

Mata Hari's intelligence had revealed that the airfield defences included more than twenty flak posts within five miles of the Luftwaffe airbase. The early morning peace was about to be broken…

"Titten!" Granny gave the codeword order as they passed low over the north of the Crozon peninsula, heading south, the flat green expanse of the airfield now evident, the single runway a long concrete finger pointing north-east.

They dropped even lower and Rose flipped back the safety. Trees obscured the airfield as the Typhoons hugged the ground.

"Arschloch! One pass, Excalibur go!" The Typhoon pairs surged apart into four sections in line abreast.

"Excalibur Leader, large four motor aircraft taking off ahead, 10 o'clock level." Cox again with his incredible vision.

Still no flak!

"Candle section intercept and destroy, and beware the flak!" grated Granny, harsh over the radio transmitter.

Already the four-engine maritime reconnaissance aircraft, a slim and elegant shape clad in a dappled pattern of light and dark grey, was wobbling uncertainly away from them, as it dropped its nose in an effort to build up enough airspeed to allow it to bank away safely, seeking the safety perhaps of the airfield's AA guns.

The raiders of Excalibur had arrived with perfect timing, catching the maritime reconnaissance bomber just after take-off. Scarlet and his Free French wingman tore after it in a shallow climb, the clumsily turning Condor not much higher.

Flak flashed upwards from two positions, fiery red blobs tearing upwards, too high, and the remainder of the defences were still silent – fearful of hitting the Condor?

And then they were zooming, soaring like showjumpers over the trees and diving back down again as the airfield perimeter passed beneath, and the airfield lay wide open before them.

Rose had memorised 'his' part of the airfield, no hangars, fuel or munitions storage here, no road to the seaplane station. But targets enough for all of them.

They were so low he felt that he was almost taxiing on the grass, and he half expected the tips of his propeller blades to slice up grass or even clods of earth.

Instead, his eyes reached for and found the dispersals and the parked aircraft, adjusting his direction of flight with rudder slightly, even as a distant fireball bloomed brightly in the sparse rain, south of the airfield, perhaps on the water near the seaplane base?

Was it the Condor? Or one of the Excalibur boys?

Alongside him, Cox opened fire, and Rose reflexively pushed down on the firing button too, his cannon crashing death and ruin out, into the enemy.

They were so low that the gunners could not depress the guns sufficiently for fear of hitting the dispersals area, the bright orange-brown blossoms of flak bursting too high above them to do damage, inter-crossed by glowing lines of terrifying tracer, but their only effect being to buffet them, which made him twitch with fear but did no damage.

The crump-crump-crump of flak mingled with the distant, muted boom of explosions and the pattering of shrapnel and debris, audible even over the deafening growl of Sugar's Sabre.

A group of four or five Luftwaffe groundcrew, dressed in crumpled black coveralls, frozen and terror stricken with staring eyes and gaping mouths, were engraved for an instant into his memory as they passed untouched beneath his starboard wingtip.

Their 20 mm cannon shells churned the earth, spraying it high enough to patter against them, and then the explosive shells were playing across the open shelters of one of the field's three dispersal areas in a line of destruction.

Acrid stink from his cannon filled his cockpit, the view in front blurring with the shudder of recoil. He hunkered down in his cockpit as more earth and metal bespattered Sugar.

A pair of Heinkels and a Junkers tri-motor, glistening and wet from the rain, enveloped in a cloud of fragments and spurting smoke, rocked and shuddered beneath a stabbing, flaring storm of explosions, great holes blown through them and pieces ripped off. The Junkers 52 minesweeper aircraft collapsed tiredly as metal lanced through it, the wing root shattered and torn away in a smear of flame, the strange metallic ring arrangement it incorporated splintered, undercarriage shattered by over a second's worth of 20 mm devastation.

The air was filled with eddying banks and trails of smoke from their gunfire, damaged aircraft and flak.

A third Heinkel was parked on the perimeter road 100 yards further on, its propellers spinning, black crosses stark and ugly upon it, dorsal gun position empty, and Rose took a snapshot, his 20 mm shells tearing a ragged trench uselessly into the tarmac behind the bomber. But Cox was better placed and his cannon fire ripped away most of the bomber's rudder and the starboard tailplane, the spine of the aircraft breaking where the tail surfaces joined with the fuselage as the Typhoons flashed past.

Rain and smoke and fire, explosions blooming, tracer strobing and flashing, the sound of the Sabre and the cannon and his own stertorous breathing, loud and straining in his ears.

The heavy stench of smoke and cordite made his stomach roil and lurch, and he felt for an anxious moment that the early morning sausage might make an oily return into his oxygen mask.

It was like a scene from a nightmare, and he ruddered and aileroned alternately to adopt an irregular, slightly weaving path of flight.

A blur of movement to port attracted his attention, and he saw a drably-painted fuel bowser racing away, the unwound hose snaking and bouncing along behind like a tail. It was too far from him to bring his guns to bear, but

Cox eased rudder smoothly into a skidding sideslip and let fly, the bowser disappearing into an eye-searing and expanding balloon of yellow-white flame, and they felt the pressure and boiling heat of the concussive slap of the explosion jostle and wash over them, their fighters lifting and yawing, lurching sickeningly, righted quickly before they flew into the ground, by firm pressure on the stick against and into the pressure waves.

As they wobbled in the boiling, roiling air, shells chased after them – too high for they were so low – yet they pushed even lower and the edge of the field rushed towards them dizzyingly.

A yellow flash smeared the edge of Rose's vision, close to a Ju 87 Stuka sitting minus its engine cowling, and he wondered what it was, straining arms and legs fighting to keep S-Sugar stable, the ground effect and turbulent air mercilessly heaving against them, keeping her below the streaking multi-coloured lines of tracer.

The barracks complex appeared from the mist and smoke, nestled on the edge of the field, and received a quick squirt of cannon – poorly aimed, but nonetheless, a wall or two collapsed satisfyingly beneath the onslaught, the brownish-green tiled roof on one building crumpling completely, and then the airfield was behind them, just the forest before them, and they fled gratefully over the trees, flak ranging after them but failing to connect.

They were so low he dared not look back, lest he fly into the trees, but the irregular orange glow in his rear-view mirror suggested that their journey had not been wasted.

How on earth had they managed to fly so low over the airfield, in the chaotic midst of all that noise and light and rough air, without crashing? How was it possible?

His teeth were clenched tightly together, and he made an effort to relax his jaw, the joints tight and aching, his ears popping.

Rose had been holding his breath, and now he filled his lungs with oxygen and fidgeted to try and get comfortable, his sweat-soaked clothes sticking to him uncomfortably, his underpants tight across his groin, muscles aching.

He felt stunned yet triumphant at the destruction they had wrought in a mere handful of seconds, death coming out of the rain for goodness

168

knows how many. The poor weather and their low level approach had kept them safe.

Thank God!

Rose began to turn to starboard in a wide arc, keeping low, and looked across at the Typhoon still faithfully tucked in close alongside, stained from the smoke but otherwise looking undamaged. Cox held up a hand in acknowledgement.

"Jenny looks fine, Two, can't see any damage, how does she feel?"

Cox's voice was breathless but strong. "Feels good. You have a couple of bullet holes in your rudder, Leader, but otherwise Sugar looks OK."

"Thanks, Hairy."

Just a couple of bullet holes? After flying through that maelstrom? That would explain the strange little flutter I can feel.

Or is that my heart?

As they turned back onto a heading for home, skimming low, he kept his eyes on the view ahead, but his fingers reached out to touch her photograph.

Somehow, we survived. Thank you, Lord, but now... please help us to get back home safely.

Chapter 20

The journey back passed almost without incident.

Concerned about flying back the way they had come after losing touch with the others, Rose and Cox turned east, Morgat silent and grey to their port side, and flew out from the peninsula into the Atlantic for ten miles – which had made him feel more than a little queasy – then back to Britain, at low level for the first third of the way, then climbing above cloud.

Out there over the Atlantic, he wondered at the courage of the sailors, the little warships that braved not only the elements but also voracious attacks from U-boats, raiders and bombers. The survivors of a sinking ship seldom had much to be grateful for – the chances of being picked up were close to zero.

No, he would never have joined the navy for all the tea in China. He was not brave enough. They were a special breed all of their own. He looked longingly at the distant land and wished he were over it.

Finally, back at Little Sillo, he stood beside J-Jenny's fuselage and gently probed the silver-edged metal bloom that had flowered in her side, courtesy of a light flak battery situated on the Fort de Toulinguet.

The German Fliegerabwehrkanone personnel they had encountered at Fort de Toulinguet came not from regular Luftwaffe troop formations, but were reservists, having an easy war and slackened by the lack of enemy activity and plenty of good French food. Their reflexes were too slow to capitalise on the heaven-sent opportunity as the low flying Typhoons zipped past at full throttle.

Rose and Cox were fast and experienced, but luck had played its part, and he shivered involuntarily as he thought what might have been.

Cox nodded grimly and spat onto the grass. "There but for the grace…" He patted J-Jenny's side. "Thanks, doll." The skin of his face was tight across his skull, the lines appearing deeper in the morning light.

Mata Hari Mason trotted up to them. "Am I glad to see you back safely, chaps!" His eyes widened as he saw the hole in the side of J-Jenny. "Wow!"

Rose smiled, but to Mason, it looked like a rictus grin on the young pilot's weary face. "Yeah. I've a couple of little ones in Sugar's rudder. But this one takes the biscuit!"

He touched the torn edges of the metal petals. We made it back. Thanks be to the Almighty.

Mason smiled. "First of all, chaps, congratulations! Granny radioed the code word that the mission had been successful. I'm sorry for being a pain in the behind, but any chance of a quick account of events? We'll have a proper debrief later, but Granny needs to get a report back to Whitehall."

Cox lit a cigarette and asked, "How'd we do, Mati?" He hesitated, then, "Did we lose anybody? I can't see Will and Jackie Lucas' Tiffies."

Mason beamed. "No, you all got back safely! Will and Lucas managed to down a Condor in the air but didn't turn back for a pass as the airfield defences were alerted by then, and they're on their way back. Jacques wanted a quick look at his old stamping ground, so they'll not be long. Granny and Will's sections managed a successful attack, too. There was a second Condor parked outside the hangars at the eastern dispersals area, and they managed to destroy it as well as giving the hangars, the watch-tower and the officers' quarters a good squirt of 20 mm. Will reported a large explosion on the field as they were on their way out, so it's possible they got a good hit on one of the munitions dumps or ordnance of some sort. There'll be a photo-reconnaissance flight in the afternoon to assess the damage, but it looks like there will be smiles all round in Whitehall. Granny and Brat Morton were chased by 109s on the way back, but Fritz couldn't keep up with them. Cowboy's section hit a dispersal area then they strafed the seaplane base. Left one He 115 floatplane sinking and

171

another burning on the water. All I need is your report and I'll be able to give Granny an assessment of the damage done. But looks like you lads did an amazing job!"

Rose took a deep breath. Here goes. "OK, well, the journey out itself was pretty uneventful, didn't see Jerry until we got to the airfield. There was a Condor in the air already, must've been about to go on patrol, Will got him, and we were so low Jerry couldn't bring his flak guns to bear."

Cox stretched and they could hear the bones in his neck pop. "Yep, I was worried I was going to damage the tips of my prop on the ground, we were that low. I dunno what you felt, Flash, but it was like the ground was trying to keep pushing me upwards."

Rose nodded in agreement, remembering how he had to fight the ground effect from pushing him up into the flak. "Yeah, you're right. I felt I was always trying to keep the nose down, but I was concerned that if I kept it too far down that the prop might hit the ground! That was a dicey do, if there ever was one."

"Damage?" Mason sucked in his lips and looked at the hole in J-Jenny. "To the enemy, I mean." He poked in fascination at the torn metal with his pencil.

"We gave a couple of Heinkel 111s and a Ju 52 minesweeper a good belting." Rose looked at Cox. "I think the Junkers was pretty wrecked, eh, Hairy?"

"That Junkers'll never fly again, that's for sure, and I think that both the Heinkels were pretty badly damaged. We hit 'em pretty hard, and to be honest, I don't think Jerry will be able to make either of them airworthy again. We tore some pretty big holes into their airframes. With that much damage to the airframes, I'd say they'd be write-offs." He gave Mason a look of irritation. "Do you mind, Mati?"

The intelligence officer hastily withdrew his pencil from the hole in J-Jenny.

"Then Hairy and I had a go at another Heinkel 111 on the perimeter road. I missed him completely, but Hairy tore Jerry's tail right off, broke the Heinkel's back. Won't be worth repairing, I reckon. Not even sure it's repairable, to be honest. I'm pretty sure none of the four will fly again."

Alice's Cheshire cat could not have smiled wider, nor more ferociously. "Capital! I wish I had been able to help, chaps. And then?"

Cox flicked away the butt end of his cigarette and shrugged. "I gave one of their staff cars, a whatchamacallit, um, a Doodlewagen, a quick burst, and it blew up, must've hit the fuel tanks."

Ah, that explains the bright yellow flash near the knackered Stuka, thought Rose.

Mason interjected. "Doodlewagen? Do you mean a Kubelwagen?"

Cox glowered. "Yeah! Doodlewagen, Kubelwagen. One of them. Anyway, it went up like a ruddy bomb, flung bodies all over the shop." Mason chuckled and wrote it down. "After that, we stuck a couple of cannon shells into the barracks buildings and then got the out of it, fucking sharpish."

"Egress route?"

"We cut back across the north headland of Finistère, about four miles west of Brest."

Mason gaped. "Four miles?"

"I know. We came out super low and at full throttle, then climbed above cloud when we were safely out at sea, and we were very lucky, thank God."

"Goodness me! I'll say!"

Rose looked sheepish. "There was still a bit of mist and rain about, and I was counting on any scrambled fighters not expecting us to go back out close to their airbase, and hoping any Flak would be unable to draw a bead on us. I thought they'd expect us to head out to sea."

Mata Hari shook his head with wonder. "And no fighters?"

"We saw some, high up behind us, when we were above cloud, maybe from Rennes, but the distance was too great and we showed them a clean pair of heels. They tried, but they couldn't catch us, even from a dive. We got lucky. But if they had managed to get close, we'd have dived back into cloud."

Very lucky, thank God… he thought, remembering the dots trailing thick exhaust smoke in the mirror as the enemy fighters tried unsuccessfully to reach them.

"Glad to hear it! Wizard show! Wonderful! Well done! Thanks, lads, I'll be able to get a preliminary report together now. Now get yourselves inside. There's tea and bully sandwiches at dispersals. I believe Granny's not expecting you back on the roster until the first patrol the day after tomorrow, so have a rest. You've more than earned it!"

Cox grinned broadly. "Fantastic! I'll get to spend the next couple of days in bed with Lily!"

Lucky blighter! There's never enough time to get up north to see Moll…

Just as Rose picked up his parachute, Mason stopped and turned. "Oh, Flash, there was a phone call for you."

"Molly?" His heart missed a beat. They always talked in the evening, the sound of her voice a very special part of his day. Why had she called so early in the day?

Oh Lord, let my precious ones be alright.

"Oh, gosh, no! it was a WAAF, um, Flight Officer Charlotte something or other. Sorry, Flash, I didn't catch her last name, the line was a bit dodgy. She asked if you'd give her a tinkle? I've got her number here somewhere."

He searched his pockets for a moment, then triumphantly flourished a crumpled piece of paper. "Here we are!"

Conscious of Cox's knowing grin, Rose took it, his other hand flat against Molly's photograph. a feeling of guilt and misgiving mixing with one of pleasure.

Don't call her, said the little voice in his head.

Of course I won't, what am I, daft?

But he knew he would.

*

"Charlie?"

"Flash!" She spoke breathlessly, and her pleasure was tangible, despite the crackling line.

"How are you?"

174

Oh God! Can't you do better than that, you useless lump?

"I'm well, thank you. And you?"

"The same."

Aargh! He felt tongue tied, and fell silent, not knowing what to say. A few seconds passed.

"Hello? Are you still there, Flash? Hello?"

"Yes, sorry, Charlie, still here."

"OK, so, Flash, I wanted to pick your brains, and I promised that I would buy you dinner. So I was wondering… I'm off for today, and I know it's a bit short notice, actually very short notice, but I was wondering if you could come down to Bournemouth? There're some terrific places to eat. I'm staying at my parents' flat, and the Beach Café does a lovely Woolton pie, or there's the old faithful of cod and chips, lovely crisp batter, or even bangers and mash. The gravy is gorgeous!"

"Today, Charlie?" Rose felt exhausted, still feeling the vibration from the Sabre in his bones, and a little bit flat after the attack on Brest-Lanveoc, the post-op anti-climax bringing its usual feeling of melancholy.

"Please say you'll come. Please, Flash? An afternoon at the seaside? Do you a world of good. What more could you ask for?"

Don't be silly, say no.

What, and stay here with nothing to do except for nipping down to the Ramrod with the lads, or moping around the mess…?

Rose sighed, might as well be bored in Bournemouth as here. "OK, Charlie. I don't know Bournemouth all that well, and I'm not sure when the next train is, either."

I'd better get a bath right away, I'm not all that fragrant after that trip to Brest…

She laughed, the musical sound delightfully refreshing to his tired mind. "Don't worry, I'll drive up in my Dad's car and collect you. I'll drop you off later, too. I'll be there around lunchtime, all being well."

Oh God, what if she drives like Molly? After this morning's attack, I'm not sure the old ticker can take any more excitement.

"I'd rather you didn't have to drive around in the dark, Charlie. The roads can be pretty hazardous at night."

When my Molly was driving her little red motor car the blinking roads were hazardous all of the time, day or night! He considered. To be honest, though, she is a bloody good driver…

"It'll only be for a couple of hours. We can do dinner another time, I'll treat you to a nice cream tea. So don't worry! I'll have you back long before nightfall, Cinders! See you soon!"

As he put the telephone down, Sid walked in and called out to him. "Flash! Flash, I'm glad I caught you, pal! Are you free this evening?"

"Think so, Sid. Why?"

Provided Charlie can get me back in time and we don't end up with the car in a ditch or somewhere equally disastrous…

"Jacko and I are off to see the Amazing Ginger Ring in Poole tonight! Join us, it'll be a laugh!" Trailing in, Jacko nodded gloomily.

"The Amazing Ginger Ring? What on earth's that? Is it a magician's act or something?"

"It's magic, but just not quite the way you think!"

Rose was intrigued. "Oh? Do tell."

Sid warmed to his theme. "Well it's a cabaret act, but not one you usually see doing the circuit. Very specialist. It's performed by a contortionist, Zelda her name is. She starts off doing this thing with her head, then her arms and spine, and then she performs the splits. That's pretty special in itself, but it's just to get your blood pumping. Once she's doing the splits, she lays with her back down on the ground, up comes her tutu and lo and behold, the Amazing Ginger Ring appears. Never seen a girl's bits while she's doing the splits, but it's quite something, I can tell you."

"On stage? You mean she actually shows you her, erm…" asked Rose in disbelief, trying hard not to blush.

Sid beamed proudly. "Oh yes. You see, she's got these lovely ginger pubes, and they form the ring around the pink lips of her dolly doodad, and when she's doing the splits her legs are so far apart you can see right up

176

inside, but that's not all, because then she does some quite amazing things with fruit and veg, and, er, her other props."

Jacko nodded, his eyes shining.

Rose was aghast. What kind of act was that? It sounded rather sordid and appalling.

"*Props*? No, actually, don't tell me, Sid, please. I'm not sure I want to know; in fact, I rather think I really don't." The thought of it made Rose feel quite ill, yet strangely fascinated at the same time.

"Poor old Jacko's getting nowhere fast with Mavis, she's just not playing ball, or, at least, she's not playing with *his* balls." Jacko puckered his lips despondently. "And because he's got a bit of a thing for redheads, I thought I'd take him to see Zelda and the Amazing Ginger Ring. Even Granny was speechless when I took him last month, and he's been to the legendary fleshpots of Cairo. So, the Ginger Ring is something really special, see? Go on, pal, say you'll come?"

He couldn't get the mental image of Zelda and her ginger ring out of his head. "Uh, um, well, I don't really know…"

"Mate, you don't know what you're missing! You ain't *lived* 'til you've seen the Amazing Ginger Ring!" Sid leaned closer, conspiratorially. "We're all meeting up at seven tonight in the mess, don't be late!" And with a salacious wink from Sid and a lip-smacking leer from Jacko, they were gone.

Bloody hell… I'm not sure I want to see Zelda and the Amazing Ginger Ring – perhaps I should stay later for dinner with Charlie after all…

*

Good to her word, just as Rose had just polished off a light lunch – because it wouldn't do to have a hearty lunch if he was driven around at speeds approaching that of a Tiffie at full throttle with boost on narrow country roads by a bubbly and rather attractive WAAF – Charlie appeared at Little Sillo's front gate.

He took his walking stick with him, in case Charlie planned to show him the sights of Bournemouth by foot or intended to stride along sandy or rocky beaches, forgetting that the country's beaches were mined and barricaded in the event of an invasion – which nowadays was pretty unlikely.

As it turned out, Charlie arrived in a Sunbeam Talbot 10 saloon, informing him that, "Daddy told me I'd be for the high jump if I so much as let a pigeon do a plip-plop on it!" And, to his great pleasure, she drove more slowly and with greater care than Molly ever had.

The realisation made him feel guilty even for thinking it, for whilst motoring around the country with Molly was petrifying, just sitting beside her and listening as she chatted and laughed was also wonderful – and she had become a far more circumspect drive since Danny had appeared on the scene.

The drive to Bournemouth was fun, and Rose enjoyed it immensely. Charlie, clearly worried about damaging the car, drove at a speed that barely stressed his heart.

It was a trip with a friend who happened to be a girl. Charlie and Rose were both married, and very much in love with their spouses, so there was no need to feel guilty or uncomfortable.

And there was no need to impress the girl, it was an opportunity just to have a pleasant afternoon in the company of a vivacious woman without the deeper overtones that came with a relationship. And just to remind himself of this, he had slipped Molly's photo into his pocket.

When they reached Bournemouth, Charlie headed to the seafront, and finally parked up just off Saint Michaels Road.

"Here we are, Flash, come on, shake a leg, Mummy and Daddy have a flat here," she said, indicating the 1920s Art Deco building behind them.

Just as he thought with trepidation that she was going to make him meet her parents, she pointed downhill, towards the beach. "The café's just along there, Flash. Shall we have a cuppa and a sandwich?" She tilted her head quizzically. "Or would you like to walk along and see the pier? Can't walk on it with the mines and all, but we could go and see it? It has a wonderful history, extended twice, I could tell you all about it. It has a really fascinating story."

It was a bit breezy with low, patchy cloud and not very sunny, and the thought of bumbling along near the pier, no matter how wonderful it was from a historical perspective, attracted him not in the slightest.

This was perfect raider weather, and it would be just his luck to be close to an obvious target if the lads of the Luftwaffe decided to visit the seaside. That was something they would want to bomb, surely, even if only because the bloody place was, figuratively, giving them the finger.

"Tea and sandwiches, please, Charlie." He didn't care that he might seem an old stick in the mud, because it didn't matter.

She smiled. "Sounds perfect! I need to bounce some ideas off your brains!"

Wonderful.

Despite his cynicism, her presence had refreshed him, and if he were honest with himself, he was looking forward to hearing her ideas and having a pleasant afternoon beside the sea with an attentive new friend.

Chapter 21

The waitress smiled at them both. "What can I get you, dearies?"

Charlie placed her cap and gas mask on the chair. "Could we have a pot of tea for two, sandwiches and some of those wonderful looking scones, please?"

"Right you are, dear. Be back in a jiffy with your order."

Rose put his gas mask down next to Charlie's and looked around with interest. The windows would have shown a scenic view of Poole Bay and the Needles, had they not been steamed up. The café was filled with delicious smells, the wholesome warm depths of freshly-baked cakes, scones and pastries, the twang of vinegar on fish and chips, the meaty aroma of bangers and mash.

He sat down and turned to her. "So, tell me all about your ideas."

She looked around and moved to the chair closer to his, and lowered her voice, even though the café was more than half empty.

"I've been thinking about how it might be possible to use Typhoons in night fighting! I wanted to know what an ace Typhoon pilot thinks of that."

Ace pilot? Night fighting? In Tiffies? Oh, my Gawd...!

"Well...?"

She grabbed his sleeve. "Imagine this, Flash. You're at 5,000 feet at night, you know there's a bandit somewhere ahead of you." She gestured dramatically at the fogged window. "You can't see a thing, but you know he's out there, so... what do you do?"

What would I do? I'd clear off home, that's what I'd do...!

"You tell me, Charlie, I'm all ears. What should I do?"

She looked around again and leaned forward, lifting the coaster on the table in front of him. "You'd look down into the screen of the AI set fitted into your plane, see where the Hun is, and, abracadabra, you get after him and bang, bang, bang, shoot him down. Be a piece of cake for an ace like you."

Oh? Is that all? He was both pleased and embarrassed. "I wish you wouldn't call me an ace, Charlie. Everyone will think I'm the most awful line-shooter ever!"

"Line-shooter or not, Granny says you've shot down about 100 bandits, though David says it's closer to 200!" She giggled behind one small, shapely hand.

He tried to scowl but found he couldn't, so he smiled instead. "OK, have your little joke."

How do I let her down gently?

"Hm, interesting. Well, it sounds like a good idea on the face of it, but the reality is, operating a set is a full-time thing, that's why there're two people in the Beaufighter, and why you still need two in a Mossie." He could feel her breath caress his cheek and was discomfited by how nice it felt. "Flying a high-performance fighter requires all your attention, you know, Charlie. It would be awfully difficult if not impossible to use a set and fly at the same time. When you were directing me, I was able to carry out the interception successfully, I couldn't have done it without you. You were my operator that night, and, if truth be told, that Heinkel really belongs to you. That's your kill, Charlie, I couldn't see a blessed thing! You saved countless lives that night. If it were up to me, I'd award you an immediate DFC, because you certainly deserve it."

And he meant it, for it was true. Without Charlie, the Heinkel would have got through.

Her eyes were shining. "That's quite possibly one of the nicest things anyone's ever said to me, Flash. Thank you." She kissed him lightly on the cheek, her own cheeks flushed, and then she shifted closer as the waitress appeared with their tea.

Rose, uncomfortably aware of the effect that her closeness was having on his groin, thought about moving his chair.

181

But he didn't.

It would be rude to. We're just friends, he reassured himself piously.

"I'll be mother." She poured a little milk into the cups before adding the tea. "D'you think the idea might work, Flash?" She offered him the sugar, looking at him in the strangely intense way he had noticed at the Ramrod. But he didn't feel uncomfortable beneath her gaze this time, in fact, it was rather enjoyable.

"Technically it should, but it would be very hard to do, Charlie. I've already done a tour on night fighters, so with experience, maybe I'd be able to get the odd success, but can you imagine trying to find Jerry with one eye on the sky and one in the cockpit? And the screen image would likely affect the pilot's night vision. And can you imagine sending some youngster out of training up there into the night sky? They might be able to do it, but they might die trying. The current system works fine as it is, I think. The operators have earned their spurs in battle. I'd not become a night fighter again if it meant flying alone."

He finished the last of his sandwich. She looked crestfallen, and he didn't want to rubbish her ideas. "But if I had a chance, I would definitely fly an interception or two with you. We've been successful already once, so in a Beaufighter or a Mosquito, we could do it again! I bet you'd make a great operator!"

She gasped at the idea. "Oh my God, I never even thought of that! Do you think the powers that be would allow it, Flash?"

No chance. Never, ever, in a month of Sundays, although it isn't actually that bad an idea. In fact, it's a pretty good idea. He nodded. "You should suggest it, Charlie."

She put a scone onto his plate. "I'm going to write a proposal, Flash. If they use experienced RDF WAAFs, they'll be able to increase the numbers of night fighters, overnight." She giggled again. "If you'll excuse the expression!"

Rose smiled as he took a sip of his tea. Mmm, delicious. I wonder why tea always tastes so good beside the sea. Might it be something to do with the rather attractive popsie he was sitting so close to?

Of course not.

She tapped her ring finger against the rim of her saucer absent-mindedly, the tinkle barely audible. "How about a Typhoon and a Turbinlite instead?"

Perish the thought!

"Another great idea on paper, perhaps, Charlie."

No, the idea positively stinks!

"But trying to make it work at all would be the problem. Flying in formation in the dark is fraught with problems, and a collision is quite likely." Rose popped a crumb into his mouth. "Also, if the Turbinlite does actually manage to light up a bandit, they both have to follow its manoeuvres together – huge possibility of collision when two aircraft are flying close to one another whilst chasing and trying to get closer to a third."

She looked a little deflated. "Oh dear. I hadn't thought of that."

He saw the waitress was watching them from beside the steaming urn.

She'll look at poor Charlie and think I'm being beastly to her…

"Don't be disheartened, old girl," he added hurriedly. "Despite what David says, I don't know everything! If I were you, I would still write a proposal and submit it to the Air Ministry. Technology is moving along fast, there may already be solutions to the problems I suggested, in which case your ideas may be possible."

Think, think! Um…

"Why don't you suggest a GCI guided fighter with a powerful fitted searchlight? Perhaps synchronised with the cannon?"

Sounds a bit daft, but they seem to like daft ideas at the Air Ministry, and perhaps it's a project that might keep Charlie busy…

She picked up his half-eaten scone and nibbled it, thoughtfully.

Hey! Eat your own, you cheeky girl!

"Oh, Flash. That sounds like a great idea. You're a genius!" She tilted her head to look at him, and he marvelled at how young and innocent she looked, the way a strand of hair caught the corner of her mouth, the soft smoothness of her skin, the light glowing on her lips, the interest in her eyes, and he felt his penis stir.

Oops! Flipping heck! You mustn't look at her like that, or think the thoughts you're thinking, old chap. What would Molly say, if she could see you now?

But she can't, can she?

Daringly, he took the remains of his scone from her hand and popped it into his mouth, grinning at her outrage. "Plenty for everyone, ducks," he said with an appalling attempt at a cockney accent, and then, "But for the moment, may I have another cup of tea, please?"

Suddenly, as if from nowhere, the waitress was standing beside them. "Is everything alright, dear?"

Charlie smiled brightly. "It's wonderful, thank you."

"It's just that I noticed you seem a little preoccupied, or shy. If you want to kiss…" and she glanced at a table beside one of the windows where a matelot, tea forgotten, was enthusiastically smooching with his companion, "just go right ahead. I don't mind. We're not prudish in here. Young love's a wonderful thing, especially when there's a war on." The waitress' eyes held warm memories, and she looked at Rose's ribbons. "Looks like you've earned a kiss or two from your missus."

Meaning to correct the waitress's misapprehension, Rose opened his mouth, but Charlie spoke up.

"He's a lovely man, just a bit shy, that's all. But thank you, that's very considerate of you!" And she darted forward and clumsily kissed Rose on his mouth. "There, dearest, that's better, isn't it?"

Shocked, speechless and ashamed by his liking it, Rose blushed hard, face feeling hotter than the urn behind the counter, and the waitress tittered.

"Oh, I say! Not often you see a Brylcreem boy blush! I should've taken a picture!" She smirked. "Don't waste your leave being shy, lad, enjoy yourself… and your missus!" She winked, then tittered again.

The woman retired back behind the counter, cackling, and Rose stared at Charlie in disbelief. His lips were tingling, but he was filled with a strangely relaxing inner warmth.

She was blushing as hard as he was and laid her hand on his lightly. "Oh, Flash, I'm sorry! I don't know what came over me! I can't believe it!"

She looked away and poured him another tea. "Thank you for being such a lovely friend, I didn't mean to do anything that might upset you."

She tossed her hair. "I don't know what I was thinking! I'm very sorry." She sounded contrite.

He could still taste her mouth on his lips, and he muttered hoarsely, "Don't worry, Charlie, she sort of goaded us there." His head was spinning. It had felt rather nice, and part of him wanted her to do it again.

You dirty dog! Behave yourself, for goodness sake! You're a married man!

"Here, Flash, fresh cuppa." Her eyes were anxious. "Am I forgiven?"

"Thank you. Nothing to be forgiven for, dear girl."

He felt light headed as she dabbed at his lips with a napkin. "Oh dear, you're wearing my lipstick!"

"I bet it doesn't look half as good on me as it does you, Charlie," he said gallantly.

She reddened again, her lashes were wet. "I've missed being complimented by a lovely chap without ulterior motives. Thank you, Flash."

She looked at him hard for a moment, until he began to feel a little uncomfortable at that intensity in those beautiful glistening eyes, and opened his mouth to ask her what it was. Then, she reached up to rest one hand on his cheek, turning his face towards her, and kissed him on his mouth again, and he didn't pull away, instead finding to his horror that his lips responded to hers.

It was just a bit more than a fleeting kiss and they were both blushing furiously again when she sat back, and this time she didn't apologise. "There. That one's for the idea of the searchlight Typhoon. I think it's a wonderful idea, and I'm so glad you suggested it. I will write a proposal for it!"

She dropped her hand to rest it lightly on his chest. "And I'll suggest they put RDF-trained WAAFs in night fighters, I think it's a terrific proposal!"

"I'm glad," he croaked as she dabbed his lips again.

You're a married man, you oaf! What on earth are you thinking? You kissed her back! You better go before you make a fool of yourself…

"I had a lovely time, Charlie, really lovely."

Cor, not half!

"But I ought to think about getting back to Little Sillo. I don't want you to have to drive back in the dark."

She was disappointed and tried hard not to show it, the corners of her mouth dropping. "Oh, Flash, must you go already? I've had such a nice time! I was hoping we could walk along the Undercliff promenade. Or maybe go to the pier together? Can't go on it, of course, because of the mines, but we could go and look at it? I can't go for a walk alone without being propositioned all the time, even though I'm wearing a wedding ring!" She gasped. "And you have to see the Needles! You can't go without seeing the Needles!"

He could feel his resolve weakening. Oh Lor'! I'd rather go home before I say or do something wrong.

And that little voice in his head again: Oh no you wouldn't, you'd rather spend time with Charlie. That kiss felt too good, didn't it? You'd much rather go for a walk with her on the front, wouldn't you? You're enjoying this too much, and you're relishing her attention and admiration.

And maybe hoping for another lingering kiss…

Bloody hell! Shush…!

"Alright, Charlie, I surrender, let's go for a walk, but just a short one."

Just a short walk, then a comfortable drive home, and some very lovely memories of tea at the sea with a very sweet and spirited girl.

And really rather sexy…

Shush!

Chapter 22

It had still been bright at Little Sillo when they left in the early afternoon, so Rose, like an idiot, had decided against bringing his greatcoat.

Now, with a lovely girl on his arm and a delicious afternoon tea in his belly, Rose felt more relaxed than he had for weeks. The breeze had sharpened, the mizzle of Brittany had come and gone, and the puddles shone in the brightening light, and he fervently hoped the patchy grey clouds above were not going to add to the puddles.

Large, rough edged, light grey concrete blocks and sandbag walls lined the Promenade, running on into the streets leading off from it, whilst barbed wire crisscrossed the mined beach. But the plaintive sound of the gulls and the tang of the salty air awoke memories of his childhood.

It also awoke memories of his walks with Molly during their honeymoon, as she worked to strengthen his poor leg once more. The thought of her loving care brought a stab of guilt, but he remonstrated with himself.

You're not doing anything wrong, your heart still belongs to Molly. She is the mother of your child, and she and he are the dearest things in your life.

And these few hours spent in Charlie's company seemed to have replenished not just Rose, but the girl herself seemed more relaxed, her face bright in the occasional patches of sunlight, her eyes dancing and happy.

He felt the déjà vu of walking with a WAAF flight officer on his arm, the trim figure eye-catching in blue, her cap badge, buttons and belt buckle shining as brightly as her eyes, her short hair whipping in the gusting wind, slim legs clad in silk stockings, very non-regulation, and drawing the eyes of all the passing servicemen, for there were many training camps based in the area.

He half listened to the sound of her soft voice as she gave him a basic history of the pier as they walked, enjoying the peaceful surroundings, and now she led him onto the path that snaked from the beach up to the clifftop.

She looked at him beneath the brim of her cap and asked casually, "Can I treat you to fish and chips, Flash? They're terrific, or, if you like the crunchy bits, a portion of chips and scraps are only a penny. You can't visit Bournemouth without having had the local special."

He stopped, something catching his attention, but he couldn't tell what it was. She turned to look at him, the question in her eyes.

"Flash?" Disquiet and concern filled her voice as she saw him look back out to sea.

Something's wrong... what is it I'm feeling...?

"I'm not sure, Charlie, there's something..." he murmured, looking out to sea, and then he felt it before he heard the quiet bam-bam-bam-bam-bam, quickly increasing in cadence and volume as the explosions of the Bofors' defiant 40 mm tattoo grew closer, and his heart skipped a beat as the brown puffs appeared in the sky to the east, rapidly heading towards them.

He made out a small dark shape as it barrelled westwards along the promenade, no higher than 100 feet, trailing a carpet of ack-ack too slow to catch it, the flash of its guns as it cruelly strafed the promenade they had been walking on just minutes before.

He recognised with horror the grey and blue dappled paintwork of an FW 190A as it streaked low past them in a blur, the pilot's face visible through the canopy.

They could hear the cries now, of pain and of fear, the awful sight of the little egg-shaped object that dropped away and landed on the mined beach, exploding, Ba-BOOM, and showering sand everywhere, the pressure wave punching and clutching at them. She would have fallen if her arm was not tucked into his.

Already a second pattern of explosions appeared in the sky, the eruptions growing rapidly towards them but unable to catch a second raider which was already hurtling towards them, the thump of its cannons preceding it.

Beside him, Charlie cried out in terror, and the sound awoke him to their predicament. Shouting – quite unnecessarily – "It's a raid, Charlie, get down!" he grabbed her by the shoulders and pushed her beneath the parapet, her cap rolling from her head, before throwing himself down to cover her body with his own.

She moved against him and he pushed her down with his body, noticing the sensation of her buttocks firm against his groin, but his instinct to protect her from harm overriding any sense of propriety. "Get down, Charlie!"

As he felt the ground shake and the churning of the earth beneath the cannons of the raiders, he shoved his arm carefully beneath her head to support it on the ground and pressed his temple against the back of it, holding her in place and shielding her firmly. Her dark blonde tresses tickled his nostrils, and the lavender fragrance of her hair and her perfume merged with the cordite and smoke and dust, sand and seawater.

She pushed up against him, her buttocks pushing him upwards, her hand grabbing his tight as if in reflex, and he pressed her down once more, easing her body further into the sheltered area where the parapet rose from the floor. He yelled again, strands of her hair catching in his mouth and against his lips, "You can't get up, Charlie, stay down, for goodness' sake!"

Ba-BOOM! The explosion of another bomb, heavy and dull against the sharper bam-bam-bam of the Bofors guns, and the ground shook and shuddered, sand showering them, her gas mask container poking him roughly in the side, hot fragments of metal hissing and pattering around them.

At last, an air raid siren began to wail in the distance.

The movement of her bottom against him was arousing, and he realised to his horror that he was developing an erection and that it was pushing against her straining buttocks.

Oh no! Instinctively he pulled back from her, and her hips moved up with his, her bottom angling into the backwards curl of his body.

She's going to think I'm some sort of depraved pervert!

Ba-BOOM! Another bomb exploded, but further away, less sand spraying across the path.

Again, he pushed her down with his pelvis, and as something whirred past, a spinning fragment of peril, he tried to ease her further into the protective shelter offered by the parapet, pushing her further into the gap. "Charlie! For fuck's sake, keep down, do you want to die? Stay down! Don't move!"

His erection throbbed urgently against her and he tried to introduce some space between their hips again, but her hand gripped his convulsively, held it painfully tight, and her bottom pushed hard against him again, insistently, sliding and rubbing against his manhood. He gasped at the sensation, and he pushed her hips down again with his, his groin sliding hard against her, and he felt the tingle of impending doom, and he told his body to pull away from hers, yet it was as if he was no longer in control of it, for he remained pressed hard against those firm buttocks which continued to push against him, and he knew with disbelief and dismay that he had reached the point of no return.

"Oh, Charlie, don't…" he whispered, knowing it was too late.

There was a tearing, crashing sound and something slammed into the beach, the wave of pressure washing over them, secondary explosions marking the annihilation of some of the landmines planted there years earlier to resist the impending invasion.

Oh, my giddy aunt!

With a convulsive heave against her body, he ejaculated.

It had been some weeks since his last leave, and he emptied himself abundantly into his trousers, his body shuddering against hers, and her hand relaxed and the pressure from her buttocks finally eased, too late, against his pulsating manhood.

At last, it stopped and he lay atop her silent and trembling body, shocked and dismayed by his actions, incredulous and disbelieving that in the middle of a raid this could have happened.

Good grief… what have I done? We've just had a lovely tea together, a very enjoyable walk, and then I've come all over her like some bloody

Lothario! How will I ever be able to face her again… I can't… she'll think me the worst kind of man there is… look how scared she is of me…

She finally let go of his hand and wriggled beneath him, her voice hoarse to his ringing ears. "Let me up, Flash, I think it's over…"

She's not wrong there…. oh, cripes! What if Molly finds out? She'll bloody kill me!

He didn't want to face Charlie, didn't know *how* he could face her, but he shamefacedly got to his feet nonetheless.

But it only got worse. He noticed with fresh horror that his ejaculate had soaked through the front of his trousers and left a wet patch on the seat of her skirt.

Oh no, fuck me…

She got to her feet and patted herself down. The once neat uniform was looking much the worse for wear, and the damp patch over her buttocks did not help.

You bloody idiot!

On the beach beneath them was a large, smoking hole, caused by that last explosion, and from the hole protruded the broken remnants of an FW 190A. The sight of the wreckage would normally have cheered him immensely, but his mind still reeled instead from the enormity of his actions of the last few minutes, the dark patch on her bottom the awful, immutable evidence of his unbelievable and inexcusable behaviour.

He retrieved her cap from where it had rolled, pulled his own down over his eyes, and tried to cover the sticky front of his trousers with his gas mask container, just as he had done when he had been accompanied by the gaggle of walkers back down the mountain.

And the esteemed instantly turns into the despised. Thanks, Fritz… you've ruined everything…

You selfish bastard, there're people hurt or dead down there and all you can think about is what Charlie thinks of you?

"Charlie, I'm so sorry. I don't know what to say. I don't know what came over me." He cringed with mortification at the triteness of his words, looked anxiously at her beneath the peak of his battered cap.

191

Expecting Charlie to at least slap him for his scandalous behaviour, he was surprised when she didn't.

Below them the ammunition was cooking off, popping and crackling, and there were cries from the wounded. They ducked, even though nothing came close to them. Normally he would have rushed down to help, but how could he when he had just ejaculated what felt like a gallon or two of semen into his underpants?

Oh, goodness, what if she calls the police? He felt alternately hot and cold with dread at the thought.

She did not look at him, but her face was as flushed as his as she adjusted her cap, and she shook her head. "I can't take you back like that, Flash."

"I understand, Charlie, I'm so, so sorry, forgive me. Forgive me. Please forgive me. I'll take the train back. I'm so sorry to have behaved the way I did, it's inexcusable." His lips and throat were parched and thick with humiliation, and he dry swallowed, picking one of her hairs from his mouth. "You were wonderful today, you're very special and John's very lucky. I'm sorry to have ruined your day."

The cold wet fabric at his crotch stuck to him uncomfortably.

"No, I mean I can't take you back like *that*, you'll need to clean yourself up a little before I can let you sit in Daddy's car." She pulled at her skirt. "And I need to change."

Rose noticed that she was still trembling. Somewhere he could hear the approaching tinkle of a fire engine.

She began to walk purposefully up the path, bent over for protection, and he followed her.

What? "But, how…?"

"You'll have to come back to the flat and have a quick wash."

Dear heavens. He felt faint. The cherry on the cake. Mummy and Daddy will kill me when they see the stains on her skirt and my flies. I'm finished…

"Oh no, Charlie, I can't! What on earth will your parents say?"

She looked back at him with surprise, her small face pale and strained. "What do my parents have to do with it?"

192

"But… if we're going back to their flat?"

Realisation dawned, and for a moment a small smile came and went. "Oh, for goodness' sake, Flash!" She shook her head in exasperation. "They aren't here, they're in Oxford!"

Relief swept through him, and she continued. "Mummy and Daddy both teach there, physics and anatomy, respectively, and my little brother Timmy goes to school there. This is our home during the holidays because Mummy was born in Bournemouth and she loves the sea. As do I."

Charlie shook her head, her body still trembling from the experience, but still didn't look at him directly. "Do you really think I'd take you home if they were there? After what just happened?"

A fresh wave of mortification washed over him and he hung his head with shame, feeling the cold tackiness slowly slide down his leg, and his penis seemed somehow to have got caught in his sticky underwear, twisting his shaft uncomfortably with each awkward step.

Sheepishly he nodded. "I see. No, no, of course not."

"Well come on, then, Flash, don't dawdle. "Down to earth again, though neither of them could meet the other's eyes.

As he sheepishly followed her up the path, holding his gas mask self-consciously in front of his groin, they passed two policemen and their sergeant rushing the other way back down the path. The sergeant, after a double take, stopped to stare after them, wide-eyed and shaking his head in disbelief.

Blimey, looks like that pilot just pissed hisself, and that poor wee girl with him, I think she's shat herself, too. How in blue blazes did they get into the air force? It was a lot different in the last little lot. We must be scraping the bottom of the ruddy barrel. I thought we was winning, but things might be a lot worse than I thought…

Chapter 23

She threw her keys onto the hall sideboard, which in the half-light bore visible scratches deep on its polished surface, suggesting this had happened many times before, and disappeared into a doorway off the main hall.

The keys slid to a stop against an ornate picture frame on the sideboard, from which a gap-toothed ten-year-old Charlie, holding a baby, grinned shyly out at him, eyes squinting at the camera bashfully, evoking the tenderness that all pictures of children engendered in adults. He thought longingly of his son and imagined Molly's embrace.

Oh God, Moll, what have I done?

He heard her moving around inside, and the light first dimmed as she slid the blackout curtains together, and then brightened again as she switched on a lamp. He heard the soft pop as she lit a gas fire, and the light brightened further, taking on an orange glow.

So now you're thinking of Molly? After what you've just done? He could have kicked himself.

The voice that came from within the flat was anything but shy. "Don't lurk out there in the shadows, Flash, come on in."

Hesitantly, he stood in the doorway of the front room, half expecting to see her parents sitting grim faced and censorious in the armchairs on either side of the fireplace.

But mercifully she was alone.

She stood before the fire, hands on hips, face stern, in shadow with the gas fire hissing comfortably behind her.

"Right, Flash, get undressed, those need to come off, underpants too. I'll put them in the washing tub with mine." She turned away. "The bathroom's at the end of the corridor, last door on the right, OK? There's warm water, have a shower, you'll feel better." And then, "John's bathrobe is hanging on the door. You can use it."

He hesitated, and she said again, her eyes dark in the shadows, "Get undressed, Flash. I'm not coming over there to help you, I'm sure you're old enough to do it yourself. I'll make us a strong, sweet cup of tea; I think we both need it after the shock."

The shock of what? He wondered, do you mean the shock of the FW 190 raid or the shock of me ejaculating all over you during it?

She sighed and looked down. "And Molly's not here."

What on earth's *that* supposed to mean?

She removed her jacket and began to undress too, and he quickly did the same, glancing across at her, knowing he shouldn't but being unable to stop himself.

She was down to her singlet and blackout knickers when he was done, and, leaving his soiled underpants and trousers folded neatly atop his shirt, and knowing that he shouldn't be looking – but wanting desperately to – he fled, naked in this unfamiliar flat, to the sanctuary of the bathroom.

*

Greatly refreshed, Rose emerged from the bathroom ten minutes later, skin tingling and feeling delightfully clean, the roughness of the frayed linen bathrobe somehow comforting.

He found her in the front room. She had placed a little table beside one of the armchairs before the fire, a mug of tea and a saucer of sweet biscuits on it.

Charlie was still in her singlet, and he forced himself to look away, but not before he saw how the silk of fabric was raised by the twinned points of her nipples, the skin of her smooth slim legs edged pale orange by the subdued flame of the gas fire.

195

"The tea will perk you up, Flash, and there are some biscuits, too. Take a seat, I'll not be long."

He sat down and was relaxed by the warmth and lulled by the hush. There was no sound from outside, and he wondered why he could not hear the bustle that would normally be associated with the aftermath of a raid and the nearby shooting down of an enemy raider, and then he heard the water from the shower gushing, and draining the last of his tea from the mug, Rose sat back into the embrace of the armchair and closed his eyes.

"Flash?"

He sat up with a start. He must have slept, for the light which had lined the edges of the blackout curtains was gone, and Charlie sat cross-legged on the rug before him, her hair shining and brushed. Without make-up she looked young and fresh, lively eyes shining above soft lips.

"Charlie! What time is it?"

"Just after seven. When I came out of the shower you were dead to the world, and I hadn't the heart to wake you."

After seven? Good Lord! I have to give Molly a ring!

But then he remembered that he had already telephoned Molly in the morning to let her know that he was safe, that he had the day off and might go down to Bournemouth.

"Oh, Charlie, it's dark! I didn't want you to have to drive in the dark! It's much easier to get lost, and accidents are far more likely. I want you to be safe!"

"So, stay. I don't want to drive in the dark, either. And you do have until the day after tomorrow before you're supposed to be back on duty, remember? I could show you more of the town in the morning. Besides, your clothes are still drying from the wash, and you can't put them on yet. I'll drive you back tomorrow afternoon. You'll be at Little Sillo, safe and sound, before teatime. Enough time for an air test of your kite. I promise."

The mention of his laundered clothes reminded him of the reason that they had to be washed, and he flinched inwardly.

"Stay here?" he asked, voice gruff with embarrassment.

She shook her head reprovingly. "You could sleep on the promenade if you like, but it gets a bit cold and wet at night. It's better if you stay here with me. I'll make us a bite to eat, and we can listen to the radio later. You'd be doing me a favour, to be honest. I really could do with the company."

She turned her head to look at a photograph on the mantlepiece, and after surreptitiously admiring her profile for a moment, Rose moved his eyes to look.

"It's been quite some time since I felt as happy as I did then."

Charlie, standing outside the church with her husband on their wedding day. John was smiling boyishly; hope, expectation and the happiness of the day relaxing his young face. Like Rose, he had dark eyes and a dark thatch of hair, proud and self-conscious in his new pilot officer's uniform.

"We were married last year, just after he had completed training. It was a lovely spring day, Flash. I wish you had been there."

She turned her face to his. "It was the happiest day of my life. He's kind and sensitive, and like you, he's an honourable and thoughtful man. But God help us, a slave to duty and honour. You can probably see from the picture that you look quite alike. I was struck by that when we first met. I hope you didn't notice me staring."

So that's why Charlie's eyes had been so intent, her expressions strangely wistful…

"You can usually see a person's character from their face, by the way it changes and moves when they talk to you or the way they look at you when you talk to them. Words say a lot, but our face tells who we really are. I think I know who Harry Rose is, and can see why Molly loves you and why David adores you. And why such a cynical old boot like Granny thinks so highly of you. When we met at the Ramrod Inn, I didn't want to like you as much as I did. I just wanted to meet David's hero, get to know who it was he was always waxing lyrical about so much, and who I had been chatting to during the interception." She sighed. "But, sitting there with you over a drink soothed me in a way I can't explain, your whole manner was somehow calming. I felt content for the first time in ages."

197

Rose thought to make a humorous comment of how she must mean his manner was dulling and dreary, but recognised this was no time for levity, and, unwilling to destroy the moment, held his tongue. He nodded reassuringly.

"I was feeling miserable. Misery is my constant companion, day and night, since John was shot down, which is why dear Belinda invited me to the pub for a drink. Your being there was an unexpected bonus."

Charlie clasped her hands together. "After our little chat, I felt so much better. I felt hope, and I think that's why I wanted you to come to Bournemouth and spend some time with me. I miss John so very much, and I thought if I could have your company, just for a few hours, I could keep on going." She nodded to herself. "And it worked. It was the loveliest day I've had for months. I actually felt happy!"

"And I ruined it all with the way I behaved," said Rose bitterly. "I'm so very sorry, Charlie, sorrier than I can possibly say. I can't explain the way I behaved, but it was inexcusable and I'm terribly, terribly sorry."

She tilted her head to one side so that the rebellious strand of her hair, shining a dark orange-gold in the light, fell across her face again. She hooked it back with one finger.

Charlie smiled shyly, and he saw her cheeks had coloured. "You've nothing to be sorry for, Flash. You were trying to protect me – very gentlemanly of you, I might add, but when I felt your body pressing up against mine, despite everything that was going on around us, or maybe perhaps *because* of it, I felt something change in me. It was like a revelation, and it felt wonderful. I *enjoyed* having you on top of me, and I could feel your thing hard against my bottom… "

He groaned inwardly in humiliation, wanting to hold his head in his hands. "Um, yes, I'm so sorry about that…"

"As I said before, Flash, you've nothing to be sorry for. I liked it. A lot. Since John was shot down, I haven't…" She sighed. "What I'm trying to say is that when those bloody Nazis were shooting and blowing things up around us, all I could think about was how much I wanted you." She looked back into the hissing flames. "I was rubbing against you because

198

I liked how it felt. I didn't just want to feel you against me. I wanted more. You do understand what I'm saying, don't you? It's just that men can be a bit thick sometimes, especially the really nice ones, like you."

He swallowed, his throat feeling tight. He looked at the mug, but he'd drained it earlier, before falling asleep, and there was no help there.

"Ah, er, I see." He could feel an unwanted bulge beneath the linen bathrobe and crossed his legs discreetly to hide it.

For goodness sake, stop it! The ruddy thing had no sense of decorum!

"I don't want your heart, Flash, that belongs to Molly, she rightfully owns it, and if I'm any sort of a judge of character – and I think I am – it will always be hers. But I would like your friendship and companionship. I need someone who truly cares about me, someone who'll dry my tears and stop me from falling, a gentle and considerate man to help me through this time. Someone to hold me when I need to be held. I didn't think I needed anyone until I met you. I thought I could manage, but it's been so hard. As I told you before, I don't want to be untrue, but I can't carry on alone. It's killing me, and I know that after what John's been through, he'll be a changed man. All I can hope for is that our love endures beyond what has to come when he returns. I know things may be difficult, but I love him, and I want to be the rock for him that Molly is for you."

She bit her lip, and he saw her face sag with misery. "But I need someone now. Someone to support my soul at least until John's repatriated. I'll not love him any less, whatever happens, and I promise that I'll not destroy what there is between Molly and you."

Charlie paused and looked away. "I really like having your friendship, but when you were on top of me out there, I realised what it was I was denying myself. I don't want to deny myself any longer. I want more."

He licked his dry lips, heart beating frantically, and fruitlessly tried to think of something wise or clever to say. But he saw her loneliness and sincerity, and his heart wept at the sudden weariness in her lovely eyes.

She continued, her eyes moist now, voice quivering with emotion, hands clenched tightly in her lap. "It was the raid that made me realise what I needed, Flash. I liked the way you felt. I want to feel that again, and I don't want to have to wait for another raid. I could so easily have died today, and I would have missed all that it means to be alive. I would never be able to kiss anyone ever again, never be able to make love. I'm denying myself what it is to be alive when I don't know how much of my life I have left. You live with that knowledge every day, I know, and I want to be there for you too, give you what you need as well. You and I may be very happily married to other people, but with the lives we lead, the chance is that it might all suddenly come to an end. It's like some awful sword of Damocles."

She gazed carefully at him, wanting him to understand. "I don't want a man who just wants to get between my legs, they're two a penny. Even one of John's friends tried it on, can you believe that? I sent him on his way with a flea in his ear and a smarting cheek. No, I want someone who appreciates being with me, and understands who I am, thinks about how I feel and stops me falling. Someone who wants me to be happy. A true friend. One who will be with me completely, but cares enough to let me go when John comes back."

Charlie shifted onto her knees, hands still clasped in her lap. " I know you'll understand how I feel, because you're alone, too. I can see it in your eyes. We're both of us alone, trying to cope with it, and I know for sure that I can't, anymore. Flash, will you please help me? Will you let me help you? Will you be the friend I need, the man I need? I like you more than I can say, and I want to be the companion you need right now, too. I want to enjoy you, and I want you to enjoy me, and sod tomorrow. It can take care of itself."

A teardrop fell silently onto her cheek as he nodded with understanding and acceptance.

After the raid on Brest-Lanveoc, he could relate to what she felt, the anti-climax of the attack that morning, the repetitive tedium of patrolling with very little to show for those hundreds of hours, the need for something else.

With Molly so far away, he had no means of emotional release. Her voice on the end of the telephone only made him realise how much he missed her, and when he put the receiver down, the feeling of loneliness was overwhelming. The lads were amazing, their antics always welcome diversion, but they weren't enough. High spirited jinks were no replacement for compassion and understanding and emotion.

With disquiet, anxiety and stress his relentless companions, continually whispering during the hours of wakefulness, gradually chipping away at his masculinity and ego, he understood that Charlie was right, he needed someone to take comfort from, someone to refresh and strengthen his sense of self.

The thought of closeness and intimacy with this hurt and lovely girl seemed like an incredible dream, a fantasy found only in novels or films.

She stood up, and said wearily, "I'm not a tart, Flash, I'm just a very unhappy and lonely girl. I'm so very tired of being miserable and alone. I don't think I can bear it anymore. But I think you know that, now."

To his surprise, he found his eyes were heavy with tears, and he wondered if they were, in part, for himself. No one could understand and share the seclusion and loss caused by separation from loved ones, except for those unfortunates in the same situation. He would take comfort and release in her, and provide the same in return.

Rose held out his arms to her, whilst also trying to hide his erection by remaining seated. "Charlie, you're right, I need the same things you do. You're not alone anymore. I'm here now."

She wiped her cheeks and came to him, her lips soft against his, her hands on his shoulders, turning into his embrace to sit on his lap, and gasping as she felt his hardness caught beneath the softness of her buttocks.

She adjusted her position and reached down to grasp him tentatively through the folds of the bathrobe, bending forward to kiss him lingeringly, then deeper, her tongue running lightly over his teeth and into his mouth, the scent of her body and hair filling his nostrils.

His hands went around her body and he returned her kisses, lips answering the demand of hers, sliding down the smoothness of her back to cup her trim, rounded buttocks in the palms of his hands, and his manhood throbbed in her gentle fingers.

Her breath was hot and sweet against his face, her fringe brushing against his brow playfully, her mouth yearning.

He picked at the hem of her nightdress, one hand caressing, dewy soft petals against the tips of his fingers.

She moaned, and pulled away. "Not here, Flash." She kissed him again. "Come with me."

She still held him and pulled him with it as if it were his leash, leading him to a bedroom. "This is my parents' bedroom, but now it'll be ours, too."

The room was warm and shadowed, lit by two shaded lamps and by another glowing gas fire, and she drew him onto the large bed, sweeping the soft eiderdown aside, onto the floor. Rose noticed that the picture frames had been placed face down, so what was to come would not be witnessed. She had already decided this was going to happen, he realised, heart racing.

And then she pulled John's bathrobe from him, then stepped out of her nightdress, standing naked before him for a moment.

"I want you to see me, Flash. I want your eyes on me as well as your hands. I want every moment to be precious. There won't be anything you can't see, you can't touch – I want you to know that."

"Oh, Charlie, you are exquisite," he said in wonder, breathless at the sight of her, his chest and neck and mouth tight with desire.

How is this happening to me?

Her eyes, open and anxious, were on his. "It's been a long time, more than six months since I was with John last. Flash, will you be careful, please?"

He pulled her gently to him, clasping her protectively in his arms. "Of course I will, Charlie. I promise not to hurt you. I'll never hurt you. If you want to stop at any time, just tell me, alright?" He bent forward and kissed her, and repeated his promise: "I won't hurt you, I swear. I'll stop whenever you say."

She nuzzled his throat, and her voice whispered against it, "I don't want you to stop, Flash."

He leaned down to kiss the top of her head, and then pushed her gently backwards onto the bed. She looked so vulnerable, as sweet and fragile as a butterfly. Her eyes were on him, cheeks flushed as she lay back against the pillows, open and welcoming to him.

She smiled with shy pleasure as a gasp of wonder escaped from him.

His heart was beating like a kettle drum, but he asked again, "Charlie, are you sure?"

She reached out her arms. "Of course I am, Flash, you silly, dear man. If I wasn't, would I be like this before you?"

He crawled onto the warm sheets, leaning forward to kiss her again, rubbing her nose with his as she wriggled comfortably beneath him.

Rose eased himself carefully into her embrace, clumsy at first, and then they were joined, careful and gentle, resisting the sense of urgency in his heart, and then she whimpered and began to cry.

Alarmed, Rose immediately pulled back, but she gripped him tighter, pulling him further into their union, and she clutched his body tightly against hers, and her shaky, breathless voice was filled with delight. "Oh, Flash, just hold me like this, please, just for a minute?"

He held her for a moment, their mouths joined and her body encompassing him in unbelievably delicious unification.

He breathed her in, the girl cradled carefully in his arms, rejoicing in the moment at the incredibly exquisite sensations of her body.

And then they began to move together, quickly reaching a smooth and flowing tempo, the creaking of the bed and their gasps and murmurings the symphony of their lovemaking.

Suddenly, Charlie cried out and arched against him, and he stopped for a moment and held her, and as her shaking subsided, he began again, her breath hot against his cheek, and she called out again, and this time he felt the tingling spark and found himself sliding helplessly over the edge, and, as he tried to disentangle himself from her grip, he gasped, "Charlie, I'm going to come!"

Her only response to his warning was to clutch him even tighter to her trembling body, and by then, it was too late.

And for the second time that day, he quivered and shook in delicious rapture, flooding warm into her.

For a moment he felt a twinge of regret and guilt.

Oh, Moll, my love, I'm so sorry…

And then it was over, the overwhelming ecstasy progressively settling, changing now into a deeper feeling of inner tranquillity, his universe comprising in its entirety the girl

They lay like that for some time, two parts of what had become a single thing, her relaxed limbs entangled but now loosened around his, their breathing gradually slowing and their senses returning, sleepy and drowsing comfortably still entwined together, nestled within the cushion of la petite mort.

This was one trip to the seaside he would never, could never, forget.

And he'd had the local special, after all!

Chapter 24

Business as usual, just another couple of hours of incredibly mind numbing, eye wearying patrolling of the same grey-blue choppy sea as he had yesterday, and the day before that, and the day before that, etc., etc...

It was mid-afternoon, and the sun was halfway down to the horizon, adding to the heat of the cockpit, the sky clear and the deep drone of his Sabre simultaneously deafening and lulling him. But not enough to make him forget the mantra that ran wearily through his head.

Control, power, fuel, sky, mirror.

Molly's picture was tucked into its usual place, and he touched it for a moment, before checking the little bear and the pebble safely kept together in his pocket.

A fortnight earlier, Rose and Charlie had breakfasted together in the café before she dropped him back at Little Sillo. On the way back to the car, she had taken the pebble from her pocket and given it to him.

"I have seven special lucky pebbles, Flash, or at least I did. John has one of them. I'd like you to have one, too."

Poor sod, didn't help him much, thought Rose cynically, turning the pebble in his fingers, smoothed by who knew how many years or decades or centuries of friction on Bournemouth beach.

"I think that's why he survived. I think my lucky pebble kept him alive for me. Are you superstitious, Flash?"

Instantly he felt humiliated, thinking of Molly's little pink bear and how it had flown on every sortie with him. Alive with a couple of broken legs and an amputated foot may sound a bit unlucky, but it's way better than being a bit dead. Can't really come back from that. It might actually have helped, after all.

"Yes, Charlie, I suppose I am. Most aircrew are, I think. Anything to even up the odds, give us a better chance to get through this."

"Will you take my pebble, Flash? I'd like you to have it. With my love." She squeezed his arm. "I very much want you to see the end of the war. I want Molly to have you now, and when she's old." She giggled. "And all the years in between, of course!"

The new relationship between them, the intimacy, had changed Charlie, and he was surprised how she seemed softer and happier and somehow more lively.

Whatever she had been holding on to, locked inside her, had drained away overnight. They had made love again and again before collapsing, exhausted, and then twice more again on awakening from a solid sleep, free of nightmares or worries.

She seemed somehow invigorated. He, however, after the shock of the raid and her demands on him – although they were welcome and enjoyable – felt fit to sleep for at least another twelve hours.

He too felt calmer, as if he had shed something weighty yet intangible, his mind more relaxed, the lurking disquiet and sense of foreboding seemingly gone.

The pressures of being a flight commander and operational fighter pilot were still there, of course, but felt somehow lessened by the calm contentment he found in being with Charlie, even when it was just over the telephone. He rather liked the C Flight office phone, now, because sometimes Charlie was on the other end.

That next day, as they walked to her father's car, she had stopped and turned to him as he pocketed her 'special' pebble. "I would give you a memento of our time, Flash, like a photograph or a lock of my hair." She smirked playfully. "Or even a pair of my knickers, but if Molly were to find them, well…"

If Molly were to find them, I'd be for the high jump. But I'll never let her find out because I intend to do everything I can to enjoy my old age with her…

The air was cold, and he shivered. It did not do to dream of growing old in wartime.

Dear God, please bring me through this to see it…

Charlie looked concerned and pulling him to her, kissed him softly. "Let that warm you up, darling." A squad of gunners running past in their PT kit gave an ironic cheer, and the bombardier in charge screamed a profanity at them.

They stood at the clifftop for one last moment before finally getting back into the car, and she hugged him close, her eyes closed, and again he was surprised at her strength.

His eyes took in the Isle of Wight and the Needles, and he thought how much nicer they looked in the early afternoon sunlight, the lighthouse only just visible through the thin haze, but not the defending AA battery located nearby.

But then, everything looked quite a bit different today because of the soothing release he had experienced with the girl's company and intimacy. Each had given and received a gift of contentment.

Bournemouth would always be a very special place for him. Whenever he saw the Needles, he would think of their night together and of how much each had needed the other. Strangely, despite the lack of sleep, he felt new.

Her voice was muffled against his neck. "Flash, will you come again?"

"I would love to, very much. If I may, Charlie, yes, please."

"How about the coming weekend? Saturday afternoon to Sunday afternoon? I can pick you up if you can wangle a pass?"

"I'll be there, Charlie."

Charlie is right, all of us need a pressure release valve, a renewing confirmation of self and value, and we found it in each other, at least for now, for we have our own worlds to return to.

And he also wondered, all that had transpired between them – was it just delightful happenstance? Unlike her fingernails, which bore clear varnish in compliance with King's Regulations, and in clear defiance of aforesaid regulations, Charlie's toenails had been freshly painted scarlet. He could only have seen them, as he had, by Charlie removing her stockings, which she had. Had she, even subconsciously, somehow sensed that their relationship would quickly develop to one of physical intimacy? How had he missed the signs, which surely must have been there?

Or was it just, as Charlie said, that men can be a little slow in recognising that which is obvious? What mattered was that she had trusted him with herself.

They had loved and talked and loved some more, the girl reckless and unashamed with need, clutching him tightly to her before the sleep of total exhaustion overcame them, and then awakened in the diffuse bloom of dawn to each other again, slowly, quietly, and with a deeper understanding and wonder, leaving a pleasant ache and lightness between his legs.

He would accept with boundless gratitude the favour she had bestowed on him, even though it was an act of betrayal for those to whom each was joined.

He kissed the area beneath her ear tenderly and closed his eyes, content to hold her, knowing that Charlie had changed things for the better.

Whatever the truth of it, he had found an extraordinarily precious source of real peace from an unexpected quarter. The dissonant murmurings of fear and foreboding which had shadowed his mind for so many weeks had gone, and whilst they would more than likely return, at least for now, he was free of them.

And he was immeasurably thankful.

*

"Toffee Red Leader, please be advised, ten plus bandits, angels zero, currently at your two o'clock, course three-zero-zero, thirty miles south of St Catherine's point, turning to three-five-zero now, possible raid on Bournemouth or Swanage, can you intercept?"

Raiding Bournemouth? The bastards! For an instant, he remembered Charlie's cry of fear and the sight of the little FW 190s barrelling along the seafront, cannon and machine guns slashing dispassionately at military and civilian targets alike.

Red Section were currently about twenty miles west of the Needles. "Roger, Blackgang control."

He pushed the throttle lever through the gate, boosting the engine through 400 mph and praying that the Sabre would continue to growl smoothly, despite the sudden increased demand on it, already climbing to 200 feet, faithfully followed by Cox, the distance between them closing as they raced to reach the enemy.

Ten plus bandits, two of us. With a spot of luck, the Immediate Readiness sections from both Little Sillo and Warmwell should be on their way, and the duty patrol east of the Isle of Wight, too, he thought hopefully as he flicked off the gun safety.

Black oil spotted his windscreen as his engine raged fiercely before him, driving S-Sugar to a rendezvous with the German fighters.

There were patches of haze and mist before them, and he began to worry the bandits would slip through the net and evade their interception until it was too late.

Once more, unsurprisingly, Cox saw them first. "Two to Red Leader, bandits fine on the starboard quarter, two o'clock low, I count twelve." Cox sounded calm, whilst Rose's heart was racing ten to the dozen.

Thank God for Hairy…

"We'll hit them on the port quarter from out of the sun, Hairy, try and split them up, get them to jettison their bombs and mix it up."

The sun behind them to one side made him feel twitchy. At least at this speed, they would be difficult to catch and bounce from behind. And Jerry's rate of climb was poorer than theirs, wasn't it?

Beware the Hun in the sun…

"Roger, Flash."

They were visible to him now, a tight group of slim pale shapes catching the sunlight – Bf 109s? – skimming low across the darker sea glittering east of Toffee Red Section.

"Toffee Red Leader, second formation of bandits, ten plus, angels

209

zero, at your five o'clock, five miles." A pause, then, "Bandits climbing."

Damn it! Rose cursed their bad luck, eyes gauging the angle of interception with the 109s ahead of them.

With the second formation so close behind, they had little time to break up the first formation before the second would be on them.

We're the filling in the sandwich… but by accident or design? They had no way of knowing that we would be where we are, they've been lucky to catch us between them.

"OK, Hairy, we've only got one shot before we get that second lot up our backsides. One pass, scatter the first mob best we can, then round to face the second lot."

And hope and pray that all twenty plus of the bastards don't hang around to mix it up because then we'll have a real fight and a half on our hands…

"Roger, Leader."

They had dropped back down to 50 feet, skimming through a thin layer of haze, Rose and Cox taking care to modify their approach with reduced throttle so that they turned after the shoal of enemy fighters a little behind and in their eight o'clock position.

The enemy had also dropped down further, and a fine spray dotted the Typhoon's windscreens, smearing the dark blobs of oil that continued to spatter the Perspex thinly.

The enemy formation loomed out of the haze and mist, and at a range of 200 yards, Rose opened fire, straining to focus it on the smeared shapes in his gunsight whilst continuing to peek sideways and behind for the second formation of enemy fighters, Cox following his lead immediately, smoke trailing back from his wings.

Rose could not see the result of Cox's cannon fire, but his own shells chewed away the port wingtip of the trailing Bf 109G, and the bandit tilted away streaming smoke, his bomb suddenly curving away below and behind them.

Leave him, there are plenty more…

Already he was turning after the next one in line, hammering a two-second burst at the blurred shape, a necklace of coruscations flashing across the smeared shape as it wobbled under the spray of 20 mm destruction, bombs falling away from more of the enemy fighters now, the formation coming apart under their successful interception.

Smoke merged with the haze and Rose thought he saw a falling, burning silhouette smash into the water.

"Break, Flash, break, break!"

Out of time and unable to do more, Rose and Cox split up, ready to fight lonely and desperate combats against overwhelming odds, praying with dry lips that they would survive the next few seconds and minutes.

Rose glanced once into his rear-view mirror, the frantic warning from Cox still ringing in his ears, even as he hauled the control column back, hard back, into the pit of his stomach so that it hurt, kicking the rudder pedal as he did so.

S-Sugar immediately twisted around violently to starboard, the pressure pushing him hard to one side, his neck straining against the forces, the harness holding him tight, and he rammed the throttle forward with a jerk.

The hairs on the back of his neck stood up on end as he saw the stubby FW 190s swarming towards them, the boys from Rennes, most likely, less than a few hundred yards slightly above and behind, cannon already sparkling but no hits on the hard turning, skidding Tiffies.

His chest hard with tension and dread, making it hard for him to breathe, making him suck at the oxygen mask, hungrily, desperately, its discomfort on his sweating face forgotten.

As the Typhoon pair broke apart from one another, so too did the enemy formation.

The German fighters broke apart messily into singles and pairs, each trying to aim their guns at the two Typhoons, now turning into them, but confounded by jostling with each another, each one trying vainly to choose one of the two targets available and getting into one another's way.

"Keep turning, Hairy," Rose rasped over the radio as he continued to drag the Tiffie in its violent turn.

Damn it! If these 190s hadn't appeared we could have really created havoc amongst the 109s, and now I can't see them at all… any of them. Where did they go? What are they doing?

As he began to bank and ascend, he saw some of the enemy fighters begin to turn after him, whilst trying to avoid one another. The control surfaces glinted and caught the sun as they, too, manoeuvred desperately, slipping and skidding as they tried to follow him around, muzzle flashes from the eager ones, but the tracer falling away, far short of their mark.

One was close enough to draw ahead, turning so tight that vortices spiralled like thick streamers from its wingtips.

Despite the fact he was turning, a few of the 190s streaking past below in confusion, the image of one of those fighters was seared into his mind.

Even as he pulled harder into his turn, grunting and cursing to himself, his vision greying, praying S-Sugar did not fragment beneath the irregular stresses of the vicious turn, Rose appreciated the lethal loveliness of the trim little fighter; level curves and surfaces and streamlined, dappled green and blue paintwork and yellow panels, red and white whorls on the spinner.

His instinct yelled to immediately reverse his turn and hunt some of the others, but he knew that if he did so, the show would be over.

Forever.

His only chance now lay in trying to keep turning into the enemy. There were too many them, but he knew that he more than held the advantage in a low-level turning fight.

In his rear-view mirror, he could see the cowling of the 190 slipping in behind him.

Oh God! He could feel his insides quivering uncontrollably and his heart throbbed.

A flaming streak of tracer from the side and he braced himself, his insides turned to ice, but it flared past, glaring and terrifying.

Now the one behind fired his guns, but the fire curved out of the turn, and he could see the enemy fighter was already falling away, less of it visible in his mirror as it slipped slowly backwards in the punishing turn.

Thank goodness.

Keep an alert eye open for the others, slashing through the fight.

Those cannon shells were explosive, and just one could do a lot of damage to S-Sugar.

Rose kept the stick pulled rigidly back, hard back right into his stomach. Arms and legs moving without conscious thought, in harmony with the Typhoon.

Keep calm, keep a cool head...

Keep turning tight, tight as you can. Slight adjustments to hold her there.

Grey sea swirling and churning so close beneath the wingtip, more throttle, Oh, God, keep me safe!

Another Focke-Wulf 190 shot past, a blur so close that he flinched and pressed the firing button, the cannon shells spraying through empty space, the fighter long gone.

Steady pressure on the rudder. Reduce the throttle a smidgen, and careful, watch that angle of bank. Keep the nose pointing just above the horizon.

God! How much more?

He gulped oxygen into his lungs, mouth opening and closing as his muscles strained and sweat dripped down his face and inside his goggles, into his eyes to sting them painfully.

S-Sugar wobbled uncertainly for a moment as they passed through someone's slipstream, and his turn widened as he fought to control her, and he strained his neck and blinked his eyes to see where the pursuing FW 190 had gone, just in time to see it break away and flee, turning so tight it had gone into a bank of haze even as he straightened to fire at it.

Damn it!

And suddenly, even as his eyes were seeking another target, fire-bright meteors streaked past a pulsing stream of glowing balls so close over the wing it was incredible that he was not hit, the tracer and cannon shells closely followed by another FW 190, the slashing pass on his Tiffie from such an awkward angle mercifully unsuccessful, and he lurched through its slipstream.

Again, his salvation had been in the tightness of his turn, and again he fired, and again his cannon shells did not connect with the German aircraft, and it disappeared swiftly into a bank of mist.

Unbelievably, he was all alone, alone amongst the swirling mists below and the patches of haze above, and he peered at the airspace around his Typhoon anxiously, pulling his aircraft onto a heading for the Solway, grateful to have survived, almost playfully flying through the upper layer of the mist, like a speedboat skimming the waves, rocking his wings gently to check above and behind, although visibility had dropped alarmingly.

He was reminded of the mists swirling over the moors in *The Hound of the Baskervilles*. Certainly, being alone in this milky oblivion was more than a little disquieting.

On the radio transmitter, he heard Cox. "Red Two to Toffee Red Leader. Are you receiving?"

Hairy was OK! Rose breathed a sigh of relief, dashing the sweat from his cheeks. "Toffee Red Leader to Two, received. Any luck?"

"Got a Hun before he jettisoned his bombs. The sod blew up, damaged his wingman I think, then I played ring-a-roses with some 190s. I've lost 'em now, and I'm heading for home, the ol' Sabre's running a bit rough."

"OK, Hairy, I'll see you there, good luck, chum."

It was easy to believe he was all alone in this world of patchy haze and mist, and unbidden, he began to feel the hair on his neck begin to stand up.

It was almost as if he were being stalked, not by some four-legged slavering monster but by something far, far deadlier…

He shivered and keyed the transmitter. "Toffee Red Leader to Blackgang, a vector for bandits, please?"

"Stand by, Toffee Red Leader, please stand by…" The voice of the young WAAF at the RDF station was comforting.

"Toffee Red Leader to Blackgang, understood."

Not much future in stooging around at low level in this haze, he thought, be quite easy to fly into the drink, I'd better get up there out of this muck to where it's clearer…

To his surprise, as he pulled back the stick and eased S-Sugar up a little into the overhead haze, a shadow appeared around 400 yards ahead of him, and he gingerly eased forward the stick, to approach it from directly astern and slightly below.

As he drew closer, he could identify the silhouette as a Bf 109, and then one of its wingtips tipped slightly and the German fighter began to gently bank back towards France.

OK, my chance to do the stalking…

"Toffee Red Leader to Blackgang, one bandit, angels zero. Heading zero-two-five, erm, twelve miles south of… Worthing, I think, attacking now."

Oh God! Don't hang about, Jerry's chums may be close…

He closed the distance and pulled up until he was directly behind, the enemy fighter filling the gunsight.

Mirror, clear the space behind you…

With a last check of the translucent murk around him, carefully ensuring that another enemy aircraft wasn't doing to him what he was about to do to the 109, he centred his sight, no allowance needed for the fall of shot this close, and firmly pressed the button for a single one-second burst, eyes focussed unerringly on the target as if his concentration would help it connect.

Hits flashed and the enemy smoked, staggering violently as his shells clipped off the 109s' port tailplane, shattered fragments flailing into the hateful black swastika outlined in white on the vertical stabiliser.

Another, longer burst, and there was a sudden puff of smoke from his cannon strikes on the starboard wing root, a second and third, and more fragments of the enemy fighter broke off.

A little rudder to skew the swathe of destruction from one wingtip of the 109 to the other, the enemy fighter continuing to flounder under the impact of S-Sugar's deadly storm of projectiles as they tore ruinously into the enemy airframe.

Another short burst ripped into the fuselage and started the Daimler-Benz DB605 inverted V12 engine smoking, debris ripped away by the devastating impacts.

He's not even trying to get away or take evasive action. He might be injured, or dead…

But there would be no mercy for the enemy flyer, just as there would have been none for those on the receiving end the Nazi bombs.

The enemy fighter dropped into a shallow dive as Rose's shells battered and hacked at it mercilessly, the canopy shattering into a million spinning crystal splinters, the cloud of particulate glass whipping back towards him but expanding and dissipating in the howling slipstream, the shining disc of the propeller breaking up to windmill, the twinkling white stars of destruction rippling along both wings and the length of the once trim Luftwaffe fighter, enveloping the aircraft in a short-lived cloud of paint and flakes of metal and dirty smoke that plumed behind in its slipstream, an expanding exclamation mark of doom.

Mirror. Keep watching your tail. Where there's one…

One eye fixed on the 109 in front with the other feverishly scanning all around for others, head throbbing and eyes aching, and he remembered something Granny had said after one of the great air battles of 1940 – "I'll be able to check out the arse on three popsies at the same time after this!"

But he was too busy to smile at the reminiscence. The 109 was still flying, despite the punishment his Hispanos were inflicting.

His target swayed and rolled lazily to port, and he knocked another merciless two-second burst into it, turning to follow its gentle bank.

Like shooting fish in a barrel, but if the shoe had been on the other foot…

Mirror, still clear, thank the Lord.

Dazzling yellow flame, a banner of disaster shot through with vivid orange jetting back from the wing-root, and he could feel the heat from it wash over him, eyes narrowing in the blinding glare.

Pull back! Ease back on the throttle; he could blow up any moment.

Rolling further to port, the 109's port wing twisted and broke off, folding back before whirling away towards the sea beneath them.

Minus one wing and uncontrollable, the burning remnants of the enemy fighter snap rolled twice through the haze before exploding in a seething ball of fire on the undulating surface of the sea.

Rose breathed a prayer. There but for the grace of God…

Chapter 25

Tea at dispersals.

Granny grinned at Rose and Cox, his face streaked with sweat and oil, his missing front teeth giving him a piratical air. He usually flew without his denture in his mouth – "Almost swallowed the fucking thing over Beachy Head when I was playing 'chicken' with a 110!"

"Flash! You got back alright then, my old lad? Heard you and Hairy got there first, didn't see you. What happened? How was it? We caught up with a quartet of 190s over Cowes. Clobbered them hard! Brat got one and mine came down in the New Forest. The other two buggered off pdq! Lovely!" Granny slurped noisily from his mug, tea dripping unnoticed or ignored onto his Mae West.

Rose patted Cox. "Hairy got a 109, and a probable, and then chased off some 190s. I damaged two 109s, I think, didn't see them crash, though. I'm pretty sure I got another in the haze after I'd lost touch with everybody, but I don't know if my camera will actually show anything."

Not that Big Dave and Jimmy cared much about that; they were already gleefully painting another swastika on the side of his cockpit as the sun settled on the horizon.

Granny sniffed thoughtfully and stuck a crumpled, unlit cigarette in his mouth. "They weren't as bolshie as they usually are. Ours tried to leg it. I think a lot of their top lads are out east having a go at Ivan."

Rose nodded in agreement. "The 109 mob did seem a little hesitant, didn't push their attack. The 190s were aggressive, though, hung around and had a go, had one trying to chew my arse off, but the 109s… not quite like the press-on types in the bad old days."

"Aye, when you were a lad!"

Rose lightly punched Morton lightly on the arm. "Shut it, Brat, you cheeky sod!"

Mata Hari Mason trotted up to them. "Ah, Flash, there you are! I believe congratulations are in order? I've just been on the blower. An ASR launch saw you shoot a 109 into the sea; they caught your squadron letters. They managed to pick up the pilot."

Rose recalled with surprise the 109 exploding on the water and lighting up the hazy arena like a thunder flash. How on earth had the Jerry managed to get out? Rose hadn't even noticed an ASR launch.

"Well, they can ruddy well keep him, Mati."

"They won't need to, old chap, he died on the launch."

Before, Rose would have felt something. But now he found that he didn't care.

"That'll teach him, the stupid bastard. Should've stayed in Heidelberg, or wherever he came from," Rose replied coldly, knowing how lucky he was that it had not been him.

Waiting at dispersals, Scarlet scowled with envy. "We didn't even get a look in! We haven't even had the sniff of a raider for bloody ages. The last one we saw was too far away for us to catch, and was poached by a pair of Spits! You get all the luck, you jammy beggar!"

His wingman, Sous Lieutenant Jacques 'Jackie' Lucas of the Free French Air Force, nodded glumly and added, "Merde!"

Mason smiled good naturedly. "Mm, yes. Oh well, c'est la vie, eh, Jackie? Anyway, with your 109 included, Flash, Excalibur got four confirmed, four damaged and four probables, all for no loss. Good day for us, gentleman, bad day for Jerry."

Granny clinked his mug with Rose's. "Here's cheers to that!"

*

218

The next day.

Granny clapped his hands. "Right you 'orrible shower! Are you ready?"

There was much groaning and grumbling and Rose sighed. Why, oh why? Dear Lord, why?

"Get your flabby arses off those chairs and come outside, the boys are ready." Granny bowed slightly to Rose. "Thanks ever so much for the loan of your ground crew, Flash, my old pair of pants."

There was tittering amongst some of the new boys, and Rose sighed again and made his way out with the other pilots of A and C Flights, to where his S-Sugar had been towed in front of the main engineering hangar for demonstration.

Scarlet's B Flight were absent since they would be providing cover for the rest of them during Granny's engineering class that afternoon.

Granny had done some thinking following the raid on Brest-Lanveoc. "Since other Tiffie squadrons, particularly Bee Beamont's 609, are now carrying out more and more roadsteads and Rhubarbs, I thought it might come in handy if you chaps learnt the basics of your Sabre engines. You never know when you might need the knowledge. Say you're tootling along over France minding your own, and the elastic breaks so you can't get back, what do you do? Land and try and get back to Blighty by bicycle and fishing boat? Surrender and enjoy a nice long holiday in Germany, courtesy of dear old Auntie Adolf?" He glared at them. "But what if it's something simple, like a broken fuel line?"

"Oh, sir, sir? Please, sir?" Rose saw that Sid had his hand up.

"What?" asked his CO, eyeing him suspiciously.

"I'm really good with glue and a needle and thread!"

"No, that's not what I want to hear, Sid, you scatty halfwit!" Granny roared and rolled his eyes with sorrow as there was more tittering from those at the back. "Whatever did I do to get a dodgy mob like this?"

He scrutinised them. "We're going to discover the fundamentals of how a Sabre is put together and how you can get a Tiffie down unbroken and undetected onto Jerry territory." He turned to nod at the engineering officer, Flight Lieutenant Wilkins. His colleague, Evans, would lecture B Flight the next day.

Wilkins' voice was soft. "Hello there, chaps. As you know, what we have here is an H-Block power unit."

The inspection panels had been removed, and they stared in wonder at the sophisticated power unit exposed. Jimmy, standing on a pair of steps beside the engine, looked nervous.

"The Napier Sabre is a 24-cylinder, supercharged and liquid-cooled H-type piston engine. It comprises primarily the following: valve train, centrifugal two-speed supercharger and injection carburettor. There are an oil pump, fuel filter and three additional ancillary pumps. Liquid cooling is via a pressurised water/glycol combination, and it runs on 100/130 octane petrol." He looked around. "With me? OK so far?"

Rose stifled a yawn. Not really, old chap, haven't a clue what you're flapping about...

There were some half-hearted grunts, and Rose struggled to look interested, trying not to let his mind wander back to the night he had just spent with Charlie.

Managing to get time off together was difficult, but nonetheless, they somehow managed. Last night had been their eighth time together in Bournemouth, and now Rose felt quite at home in her parents' flat. Absentmindedly, he rubbed her special pebble between thumb and finger, remembering her soft, questing lips, the silkiness of her skin and the delightful taste of her vulva.

"Right, then, gentlemen, back to basics! So, the cylinders turn over the twin crankshafts. This is the supercharger, behind it are the engine starter and the generator, and that above is the fuel injector. The exhaust stack is set quite high..."

He could feel his mind glazing as Jimmy used a long spanner to point at the component parts of the Sabre in turn as Wilkins mentioned them.

Rose had driven down late the previous evening in a car borrowed from the Motor Pool, the journey stressful in the dark, but the reward at the end of it had been well worth it.

After some pleasantries and a cup of tea in the sitting room, they had remained in bed for the rest of the time, only getting up to have a relaxed dinner of bread, cheese and pickles, before listening to the radio, light music, the news with John Snagge and then the ITMA show, the sound of her laughter refreshing. He wondered what her father would think of them finishing off one of the bottles of wine from his collection.

The time spent was a delightful combination of sex – or as Charlie would insist on calling it, lovemaking – and relaxation whilst she lay in his arms and chatted about her life, thoughts and experiences. She was quite a philosopher, and Rose found their conversations both enjoyable and soothing.

He no longer felt any guilt, or at least, very little, for Molly was and always would be his true love. Charlie was certainly far more than just a friend, and much, much more than a pleasant diversion. She was a source of mental peace and healing – something unavailable to him with Molly so very far away.

He had begun to care for her more than he thought possible, and sometimes his mind would drift fondly to her, and he felt glad to be the catalyst for her renewed happiness. Yet his love for Molly remained strong, his dreams and longing undiminished, for they had shared so much, the sharpness of cruel pain and the joy of success and happiness.

He knew it must be the same for Charlie, given the way she spoke of John. Rose understood theirs to be a true union of souls, and he saw the effects of the pain that their separation had caused Charlie, how her world had collapsed and loneliness and worry had almost crushed her.

To those on the outside, she might have seemed bright and unchanged, but it had been a façade to hide the devastating impact of her husband being shot down and injured so cruelly.

Rose had proven a very necessary distraction for the girl. He supported and reassured her, was her confidante. Until John returned, he would sustain and encourage her, help her come to terms with the permanent changes in her life, and strengthen her for the challenges of the future. John would need all of her love and care when he returned – Charlie would be the medicine that restored him.

There were some rather wonderful benefits to being her confidante and her distraction, and this morning, before leaving, she had been particularly vigorous and demanding.

"That's the biggest smile I've seen all day. The oil system seems to have cheered you up, Mr Rose? Know it well do we, hm? I'm gratified by your interest. Care to remind us of the essential parts of it?" Wilkins raised his eyebrows enquiringly at Rose.

Rose blanched as they all turned to look at him, the younger ones seemingly relieved they hadn't been picked, while the older campaigners, Granny and the other Halton brats amongst them, looking smug in their understanding.

*

Charlie had had the daytime watch again, and after coming off duty at 8.00 pm, she sat down to dinner.

As she stared at the spam fritters and chips on the plate before her without enthusiasm, she thought how wonderful it would be to feel John in her arms again, the lovely thought smoothly transitioning to the experience of actually having been in Rose's arms just over twelve hours earlier.

Being able to share her darkest feelings and innermost thoughts and worries with a sympathetic, caring and gently encouraging audience, whether on the telephone or in person, and relishing the re-discovered delights found in the physical pleasure and release of their lovemaking, Charlie was thriving in their relationship, her whole demeanour more relaxed and far happier.

Charlie's friends and colleagues had noticed the change and wondered, but knowing the depth of her feelings for John, believed that the impending return of her husband had brought about her renewed vitality and optimism. And of course, that was the case, but Charlie also knew that Rose's presence in her life had changed it, and not for the poorer.

And she knew that whilst she loved John deeply, and that her husband would always be the one she admired the most and yearned for, Rose was here, Rose was the present – not the hope of tomorrow, but the comfort of today.

Furthermore, Charlie also appreciated that he was more than a friend, more than a lover. He was these and so much more besides. He had brought her peace of mind and quietude and contentment at the worst time of her life, when she had been the most alone, at her most helpless, when despair had locked her into a limbo of utter hopelessness.

She would regret nothing, her love for John remained undiminished, and she looked forward eagerly to his return so they could build their future together. But Charlie also knew that she would never forget Rose, that despite her best intentions, he would always mean to her more than she had intended.

Rose was special, an honourable and decent man, thoughtful and considerate of her happiness, and it would be so easy to fall in love with him, oh, so easy!

And she feared that part of her had already done so.

Her friend, Assistant Section Officer Anna Turnbull, sat down opposite her, unceremoniously setting down her plate of food and her 'irons' with a clatter that roused Charlie from her thoughts. "Penny for them, Charlie?"

Charlie shook her head. "Oh, they're worth quite a lot more than that, Annie!"

Anna laughed, grateful for the positive changes in her friend these last few weeks. But even as they laughed and chatted, Charlie's thoughts returned wistfully to Rose.

Chapter 26

With the drastic reduction in enemy attacks as more and more Luftwaffe units were funnelled east, and a reduced need for defensive operations, the opportunity had arisen to carry the fight to the Reich. This campaign was enthusiastically led by the leading proponent of the Hawker Typhoon, and the man probably most responsible for the aircraft being kept in service, Roland Beamont of 609 Squadron.

By now, the RAF's Typhoons were regularly engaging in Rhubarb operations into France and Belgium by day and night, proving not only their mettle in low-level fighter combat, but also their suitability and capability as fighter-bombers. Accordingly, to multiply the factor of destructive power available to them, Typhoons were to carry bombs on attacks against ground targets and shipping.

Excalibur Squadron were to learn the art of bombing, much to the annoyance of the pilots. Yet despite their very audible invective and misgivings, they were secretly quite excited at the thought of conducting their own Rhubarbs against the enemy.

They were to be instructed on the ground beforehand by a laconic and leathery squadron leader of indeterminate age, with a glass eye and the ribbons of a DFC and DFM beneath his wings.

His remaining eye regarded the men dispassionately.

"Morning, gentlemen, my name is Phipps, and I'm here today to teach you the basics of dive bombing. Your CO will let you try out what you learn in the afternoon. That right, Granny?" He received a nod in confirmation.

"Your CO is already somewhat familiar with the art, because he and I practised it quite a bit against Rommel's finest in the Blue, though I rather suspect it's a whole different kettle of fish bombing in a Hawker Typhoon as opposed to the ancient and clapped-out kites we were flying."

Cox gave Rose a questioning look. "Flash, what the crap is the Blue?"

"It's what the Western Desert Air Force pilots call the desert," Rose whispered smugly in explanation, and his wingman's confusion cleared.

"So, what do we know about bombing?" Phipps asked, but continued before any of them could say anything, "Sweet Fanny Adams, I'll bet." He smiled tightly. "Awright, then, hang on to your bollocks, gentlemen, here we go."

He pulled the cover from an easel bearing a series of diagrams drawn onto boards. "These pictures will help you to understand some of what I'm going to say. Right? OK. So, when you're flying straight and level out of range of the flak, and you drop a bomb, it describes a sort of parabola as a product of imparted airspeed and gravity. You can calculate where it'll land, so long as you fly straight and level, and if you know your airspeed, altitude, wind velocity and weight of the bomb. That's why Butch Harris' boys have got them fancy bombsights – to help them to at least get close enough to the target to damage it. No good to you, because you've got a ruddy great Sabre engine in front of you, there's bugger all visible. High-level bombing in a Tiffie? Hit and miss, but it'll be miss 99 times out of 100. The one time will be because you got lucky. So that's out.

"What's next? Low-level bombing, that's what. Problem is, if you drop them level and you've got delayed fuses, they're going so bloody fast they're going to bounce off the ground and carry on like bloody torpedoes until you can't see them no more. They might even fly over your wing on their way. They'll only stay where you drop them if they hit something that stops them dead or at least slows them right down.

"But low-level bombing also needs you to be spot on with your steering, because you get only one chance at a surprise approach before you've alerted old Boche that you've arrived. So, if you're a bit rubbish at navigation, just popping up for a quick shufti's gonna give you away, too."

He looked around at the assembled pilots ruefully. "And I should ruddy well know." He tapped his glass eye with a nicotine-stained finger. "I lost this poor little blighter when we were bombing armour at low level outside Tobruk, just before the Boche took it off us. Took a quick butcher's to see where the bastards were, and they found out where I was at the same time, and there we are. Lucky to get back with the crown jewels intact, so can't grumble."

He looked at Granny again. "Grim times, I can tell you, eh, Granny?"

Granny scratched his crotch and sighed. "Can't argue with you about that, old man."

Phipps shook his head sadly. "I wouldn't even bother with low-level horizontal bombing if I were you, lads, no good sticking a bomb under your arse and carting it over hundreds of miles to just chuck it away. Not worth the effort."

Will Scarlet snorted. "See? What's the point of us bombing? Total waste of time."

Phipps fixed him with a steely gaze, which, with only one eye, was quite impressive. "Oh dear, oh dear! You're not a very patient chap, are you, laddie? Don't worry, let me tell you about how it should be done! So, no horizontal bombing, unless of course, you're on a mission where you can see the enemy from miles off, like on an anti-shipping strike. Right? Or if you take 'em by surprise. Otherwise, I wouldn't bother, if I were you."

"Say, how about skip bombing?" drawled Cowboy.

Phipps shrugged. "OK, that is a good way of getting your bombs into a ship's guts, but you need to make sure you leapfrog without catching the masts or rigging. Beauty of it is that you can go in high speed and low, but you have to let go just right – so the bastards leap into the side of the enemy ship, otherwise it might just fly over the top of your target, leaving you feeling and looking like a right tit. Ever tried it?"

"No, sir."

"If you try it, release low and close and then get out of it quick as you like. OK? Alright so far? Grand! So, I'd recommend an angled approach. You want to stay in the flak envelope for as short a time as possible, see?

So, the best way would be coming in fast as fuck at an angle, the steeper the better."

He had the attention of all of them now, even Scarlet. "If you approach the target high enough that the heavy AA can't touch you – y'know, 8,000 plus or so – then you've got plenty of time, provided there aren't any enemy kites buzzing around, to check out the target and set up your attack carefully, make sure the fucking thing that's been jammed up your arse isn't wasted. I prefer a steep angle, like I said, the steeper the better, 60 plus degrees because then gravity's helping you too, makes the trajectory almost a straight line, better chance with a hit with a good approach, minimises the drift. Faster you get in and back out, less chance for the lighter AA to get you. And press home the attack as close as possible to minimise the effect of wind to make sure you stick your bombs as near as dammit on target. But I hear the Tiffie is a bugger to pull out of a dive in, so make sure you know the point at which you must pull out, OK? Don't follow the bomb in, for Christ's sake!

"Another thing, flak is scary as hell, but go in one at a time, keep the number of attacking aircraft from a particular trajectory to a minimum, and know this, AA gunners generally are either under deflecting or too slow, so your chances are better than even, but it doesn't hurt to pray!"

He placed the palms of his hands together in front of him as if he were about to pray. "Jerry usually lets fly as soon as you drift a bit close, so let 'em have a go, keep just out of range, until the fire lessens off, as their ammo clips empty and they switch. They won't all run dry at the same time, just as all you bastards don't all finish your pints off at exactly the same time, but you'll know they'll be changing their ammo clips because the fire will ease off after the first bit of excitement. Soon as you see it lessen, get in there quick as you can!

"One last thing. Sometimes you come across a target without warning. If you do, try and bomb the bastards while you have the element of surprise, saves you coming around when they've had a chance to wake up! I've also found that if they can't see who you are, and they challenge you, drop a flare or two. They'll be confused, even if it's the wrong colours of the day for them, and it'll give you a few seconds to get closer." He grinned tightly. "Every little helps, as the old lady said when she pissed in the sea!"

They smiled uncertainly, and he clapped his hands together and made them jump. "Righto, well it's up to you now, chaps. Spot of practice after lunch to give you an idea what it's really like. Practice, practice, practice, alright? Get the technique down pat. It'll make the whole job a bit easier when you come to do the real thing, and you'll have a better chance of being on target. Come and see me afterwards if you have any questions, and remember, it's not as easy as it looks."

*

They gathered around him as he jumped wearily down from P-Popsie. An angry red line showed where the oxygen mask had pushed into the skin of his face in the dives.

Granny was exhausted, and he looked at each of them in turn. "Stone me!" He pulled off his silk scarf and, wiping his perspiring and oil-stained face, he accepted a mug of water from Belle, who had been sick with worry as P-Popsie dived and climbed and cavorted wildly about the sky. "Got a mouth like a camel's rear end!" He emptied the mug in one and handed it back gratefully for a refill. "Phew! Thanks, Belle, needed that."

Her eyes told him there was to be a very serious talk when they were alone.

He took another sip from the mug and grinned at his pilots. "Things I do for love! Right, you cheeky blighters, I think I know how we need to do it. Main thing is, we need about 4,000 to 4,500 feet clearance to pull out safely at about 400 mph ASI. That means the kite levels out at about 1,000 feet diving from an altitude of about 5,000–5,500 feet. I'd suggest you practice by starting at around 12,000 feet, give yourself plenty of room to find out just how much you need, just in case, and it'll help you to see how much force you'll need to pull her out and how much rudder you need to hold her steady. I blacked out for a few seconds, three times, but with the trim set to climb, you're OK as soon as you pull out of the dive. Try four or five attempts to calculate how much altitude will be needed for your particular kite, but it'll be around 4,000 feet, and be aware the kite will shudder like buggery and the controls will be solid."

He looked at the broadsword painted beneath his cockpit. "Bit like trying to pull Excalibur from the stone! So, nothing new there, you scatty lot will already know how much altitude you need to recover safely. What I did find, though, is that in a 60 degree angle of descent, just pushing the nose down once you see the target disappear beneath the nose, the angle is much less steep, and it takes a lot longer to build up speed." He thirstily finished off the last of the water, and Belle refilled it again. "But, if you pull up the nose a little, then go over onto your back, you go straight down and get a chance to straighten your dive and line her up. Well, you were watching, you saw what I did. You lads will practice after lunch, then tomorrow we'll try it again with practice bombs. But get your technique right and find out exactly what altitude you need to pull out safely."

He looked at Belle, saw her anger, and nodded to them. "OK, lads, go on, clear off. And be careful, I need all of you – even you Jacko!"

Chapter 27

The day was miserable, low cloud blanketing the south of England and Wales, accompanied by a sullen light rain that seemed unwilling to stop. With visibility reduced, the defenders peered into the shadows but could see little.

The eight Bf 109Gs streaked in so low, at angels zero, that Blackgang and all her sister stations missed them completely.

They swept up the beach and over the little seaside town in tight line abreast, cannons hammering, their bombs erupting shockingly, unexpectedly amongst the sleepy buildings of the little seafront, battering at the historic Georgian and Regency architecture. Two were dropped early and only achieved the destruction of a short stretch of the beach, some barbed wire and ten land mines. Another failed to explode, creating a deep furrow in one of the rinks at the local bowling club, just missing the clubhouse.

A bomb disposal officer would spend a stressful two hours, later that same day, successfully removing a Type 17 fuse and making safe the UXB, winning for himself a very well earned mention in dispatches and a free pint at the clubhouse for his section.

Considered a low priority target by the mandarins of Whitehall, the town of Sidmouth had a been given a single platoon of soldiers, the entire defences comprising just two Bren gun positions and a QF three inch 20 cwt AA gun. All at the helm of the defences had been taken by surprise by the stealthy approach of the sleek Jabos, remaining silent for fear of hitting civilians and the buildings of the town in a crossfire until after the bombs had been dropped and the enemy fighters were streaking safely inland and out of sight.

The three-inch AA gun crew, unable to swing around fast enough after the disappearing raiders, fired a round into the sea so that honour was satisfied.

Unscathed and congratulating themselves on excellent navigation at such low level, the pillars of smoke that rose in their mirrors reflecting their good luck and the success of their raid, the 109 pilots headed for Sidmouth railway station, which was on the Southern Railway's line and would be essential to the movement of men and materials to and between the channel ports, should there be any Allied invasion.

The frequency of trains was much greater in wartime than the line was used to, at its peak reaching more than twenty trains a day, as opposed to two in peacetime.

But that day, the Luftwaffe pilots were unlucky, and the two platforms of the station were frustratingly empty.

Still elated by the success of their attack on the seafront, a true attack on the British establishment – had not Sidmouth been a coastal resort in Georgian and Victorian times? Had not Queen Victoria's father stayed nearby just before his death whilst she was still a baby? The fact that both monarchs were Hanoverian was neither here nor there, for they were British after all, weren't they? – the Bf 109Gs disappointedly strafed the station anyway and split quickly into three formations.

The first, a Schwarm of four aircraft, sought another target to attack – preferably a train – and headed westwards up the line.

If they managed to find a train, they would destroy it. If they did not, all well and good. They would follow the line and strafe the stations along it, starting with Tipton St James and then on to Feniton.

The second formation, a Rotte of like-minded pilots who were a little more prudent in their ambitions and conduct of war, hauled their fighters hard around in tight turns and sped back out to sea at an even less well-defended point as soon as their Staffelkameraden had disappeared into the distance.

They had done their bit for the Reich and it would be nice to survive the day so that they might enjoy the evening with their French girlfriends.

The final formation, another Rotte, headed due north, eager to use up their ammunition on a target they could brag about later over coffee and schnapps. A quick frei Jagd inland, followed by a rapid egress.

*

Rose was up with S-Sugar for an air test and was enjoying the clean and streamlined feel of his Tiffie as he snaked her between billowing pillars of light grey cloud at 10,000 feet, savouring the way she felt without bombs and bomb racks. But as he turned for a high-speed curving pass between two swollen mountainous columns, the voice of Blackgang came loud and clear in his headphones.

"Toffee Red Leader, raid in progress north of Sidmouth, can you help?"

"Toffee Red Leader to Blackgang, roger, please provide heading." As he answered, he pushed forward on Sugar's stick and throttle lever. She descended rapidly into the murky embrace of cloud, but he knew that they would emerge through the cloud base at about 800 feet and began to pull back as he passed through 1,200.

"Toffee Red Leader, two bandits, angels one, ten miles, heading zero-one-five." Spitfires from Exeter had already been scrambled to deal with the Schwarm terrorising the railway line to the west, but would not catch them before they climbed up to disappear into the low cloud as they turned for home.

"Toffee Red Leader, received."

S-Sugar blasted through the cloud at over 420 mph and out underneath, the world here so much darker and more miserable than that he had just left. Ripping through and into the drizzle, a quarter of a mile offshore and about a mile east of Sidmouth, levelling out 100 feet above the sea and heading inland at full tilt.

The three-inch gun crew, seeing the faint shape of his Typhoon and unable to recognise it, lobbed a couple of shells hopefully in his general direction, but they would have won no coconuts at the fair with their shooting, and Rose did not even notice the dirty bursts of flame erupting far behind him.

The morale of the little seaside town's defenders dropped further.

Had he come down a couple of minutes earlier, he might have just seen (but only on the clearest of days) the tiny receding dots that were the 109Gs of the 'prudent' Rotte, at very low level as they fled for safety and the promise of an evening with la belle mademoiselle. But even if he had turned after them, with his small speed advantage, they would have been impossible to catch until they were pretty much back over their own airfield in France.

With a burst of boosted power, S-Sugar zoomed over the cliff exhilaratingly, the Sabre purring roughly, and shot after the Rotte to Rose's north, the towering pillars and drifting banks of black smoke from the little seaside town faded by the rain. He was painfully aware of how close the enemy were to RAF Little Sillo.

He had been on the receiving end of airfield attacks more than once, and had the memories to prove it – of sun-blocking clouds of smoke and brick dust, the smell of blood and burning buildings, the rows of dead hidden beneath dirty tarpaulin, including girls clad in RAF blue with smudged lipstick and torn stockings, robbed of their exuberance and life, the lines of pain etched onto Molly's lovely face, tears for her dead girls, and her blood on his fingers so that he wanted to scream his anguish.

He glanced at her photo with yearning. What an extraordinary woman you are, my love. I love you.

And a little voice whispered: …but you'll still lay down with Charlie every chance you get…

Shut up. I love Molly and she is my future and forever, but Charlie is my now, and I need her as much as she needs me.

He had more important things to do than to listen to his damned conscience, for he knew what damage and pain a Luftwaffe attack could inflict.

Just as he himself had done at Brest-Lanveoc – and he thrust the thought from his mind.

It's not the same. They started this whole bloody thing in the first place, damn them…

Well, they weren't going to do it again if he had anything to do with it.

"Ops, air raid warning, there are bandits in the vicinity of Little Sillo, have airfield defence on alert, and tell them to mind their trigger fingers because I'll be buzzing around."

He peered through the overcast and the drizzle, and for a moment he thought he saw something, while away to starboard lay the little green square of RAF Little Sillo, pale amongst the patchwork of fields.

He looked more carefully, using the old trick beloved of all fighter pilots – and just as useful at day or night – to scan the land and sky without focussing on a particular point, and again he felt movement, and as he detected it, he thought he saw pale wisps of drifting smoke.

Alert to the dangers of this dirty grey sky, Rose pushed S-Sugar into a gentle turn to starboard and almost immediately saw the glow of flame.

As he drew closer, he saw what had been a horse and cart, but the horse was dead and the cart of hay was well alight, with no sign of the owner.

You rotten, cowardly bastards...

A little further along was a car toppled over into a ditch, but the driver managed a wave as Sugar powered past.

And then, for a fleeting moment, he caught sight of them before they disappeared against the background of fields again. But in that moment, he saw their direction of flight.

They had sighted Little Sillo and were heading straight for it.

"Toffee Red Leader to Ops, two bandits, unknown type, approaching from the west, I am half a mile behind."

"Received, Toffee Red Leader."

He pushed the nose down slightly, eyes straining to catch sight of the pale shapes that were hidden so well in the poor light and rain, the droplets of water streaming across his windscreen, and then he swallowed convulsively with excitement as he saw the enemy duo, realising with horror that he would not be able to intercept them in time, for they were lifting up over the airfield perimeter already and splitting formation, one continuing straight ahead and the other turning to port towards the hangars at the northern edge of the field.

"Ops, I will pass across the airfield behind the bandits, west to east."

"Received, Toffee Red Leader."

Stay low, they'll fire at you anyway, the word won't get to them fast enough, stay low…

But which one to follow?

Eeny, meeny… The one turning to port, he's slowed down and he'll be a mite easier to catch.

Safeties off? Mirror clear? Yes.

In his eagerness to catch up, he did not slow soon enough, being forced to drastically cut throttle and put the stick hard over, stomach protesting as Sugar dropped suddenly, losing more height in the turn than he had intended, teetering on the edge of stalling.

Careful!

Something bloomed eye-wateringly bright in the dispersals ahead, and he saw a Typhoon explode, mushrooming a hellish orange, livid in the grey light, the bandit, clearly visible now as a Bf 109F, avoiding the rising fireball and triumphantly soaring upwards in victory, winging over and swooping around to come back for another go. But the victory was short-lived, as arcs of bright tracer spat out and a crop of dark stains of AA followed behind it, closing the distance as the gunners corrected their aim, and then connecting, and it flared once, twice and three times before disintegrating, shedding tail and wings and becoming just a flaming ball that twisted unevenly downwards in a steep curve, leaving behind a messy spiral of oily black smoke.

He saw this in a fleeting moment, even as he sought to correct his slew across the airfield. Mercifully, the AA guns didn't come after him, and he pushed forward the throttle again as he raced in after the fleeing enemy.

The second 109 had attacked a couple of Typhoons parked outside the hangars, the long burst of bullets and shells stitching through the fuselage roundel of one, shredding formers, stringers and stressed skin to cut the big fighter in half, and leaving the front half pointing ridiculously upwards at the sky and its tail blown backwards by the force of the rounds – but fortunately, there was no fire.

The Tilly utility vehicle parked just behind it was reduced to crushed wreckage by the impact of the separated tail, but luckily its WAAF driver was inside the main hangar sharing a cup of tea with the fitters who should have been working on the Typhoon outside.

When she saw the remnants of her vehicle, she paled and then fainted dead away.

There would be no need to bring the Tiffie into the hangar and out of the drizzle now, but at least the Sabre engine had not been damaged, and with a bit of luck, it would be reusable, even if only for parts.

A second Typhoon received just a single cannon shell hit, but this had been a ricochet which, rebounding upwards from the hardstanding, had fragmented the spinner and shorn off one of the propeller blades, before embedding itself into the sandbags around the entrance of an air-raid shelter, leaving the WAAFs who had taken refuge behind it tremulous and shaking.

Above them, the RAF flag continued to flutter bravely.

Rose saw none of this as he streaked after the enemy aircraft, his airfield just a blur of brown and green as he fought to close the range, anger and guilt flaring painfully inside his chest as yet again an airfield that he should have been defending received a hammering from enemy guns. The destruction of at least one Typhoon was evidence of his failure.

Rows of dead girls... please, merciful God, let it not have happened again. I couldn't bear it...

And then: I can't let this one get away, I simply can't...

*

The enemy pilot, seeing the demise of his wingman to the AA and the nightmarish appearance of an RAF fighter close behind, also put his nose down and desperately tried to put some distance between them.

He hoped that in the less than ideal light his pursuer might yet lose sight of him against the misty patchwork of fields, at least until he had achieved some separation and could make for home. The choices available to him were poor.

As he dropped down, the Leutnant considered his next actions.

To turn into the enemy would leave him exposed to the cannon as he turned, to climb and seek sanctuary in cloud was more attractive, but highly risky – for the Typhoon was faster and with a greater rate of climb, and too close behind. Indeed, the more experienced members of his Gruppe had warned him: 'Never climb if you have a Typhoon behind you, aileron roll away.'

Which helped him not at all, for at almost zero feet there was no chance of flicking into an aileron roll. Unless he wanted to flick the 109 into the ground, which he did not.

*

As he decided that the only choice was to try and lose his hunter, S-Sugar drew ever closer with her 20 mph advantage.

The 109 was almost skimming the fields and meadows below, jinking and bobbing, but his eyes were locked on it even as it skipped over fences and hedgerows, even as it slipped around a copse of trees, even as its shadow danced and dithered beneath the sleek fuselage, as sheep and horses scattered to either side. He dared not look away, lest it fade unseen in this grey light.

And all the while he drew closer, and the mirror was empty.

Rose realised with a sudden shock that their chase was describing a wide circle, as the enemy pilot tried to curl around and get onto a heading that would take him back to the misty sanctuary of the Channel. And Rose saw the pillar of smoke from the Tiffie that had exploded beneath the guns of the enemy's wingman and he thought, What if he has another go at Little Sillo? I can't shoot at him over the airfield… then, Fuck this, take a bit of your own medicine, you swine!

He pushed down hard on the gun button and his Hispanos clattered and thundered, a flaring necklace of flashes erupting against the enemy fighter's tail and fuselage, and the 109 trembled beneath the impacts and the Leutnant realised that his only real chance of survival lay in the low cloud, and he pulled back and shot upwards like a startled grouse towards it.

Concentrating on the kill, Rose was taken by surprise and pulled back the stick to zoom up after him.

Oh Lord, the cloud's so low I might lose him! Quick, quick, quick! Hammer a burst into him.

As the thoughts ran through his head, he centred the gunsight and ripped off a two-second burst that clipped off one wingtip and ripped away panels from the wing.

Desperately, the young Leutnant half rolled to port and made to climb again, but another two-second burst from Rose's cannon tore ragged holes in his rudder and tailplane, and he pushed her down to dive to escape the punishing impacts, the controls soggy and unresponsive in his hands when they passed over Little Sillo again. One or two dirty puffs of orange-centred smoke erupted before the gunners saw the Typhoon closely harrying the 109 from astern, and ceased firing.

Nobody wanted the toe of Granny's flying boot bruising their buttocks on its way up their arse.

So, far beneath the twisting fighters, the personnel of Little Sillo had witnessed Rose's precise and merciless destruction of the 109, his cannon ripping away and shredding fragments of the enemy aircraft's wings and tail. Then, gouts of flame belched out of the burning and shattered Daimler Benz engine, and the canopy flicked back, only just missing the vengeful Typhoon which drew back to let the 109 turn over, the tiny shape of the pilot falling out, arms and legs windmilling frantically before the parachute opened and broke his fall.

Minus its pilot, the 109, belching flame and burning furiously like a fiery comet trailing a greasy black stripe of smoke behind it, fell out of the sky and into a field a mile away, the velocity of the incandescent mass burying the engine block and cockpit into the ground fifteen feet deep.

Rose circled the airfield, feeling anything but triumphant, for of the three pillars of filthy smoke roiled into the air, only two belonged to the enemy. He could see what looked like broken playthings from this altitude and knew that the 109s had hurt Little Sillo.

Whilst they had destroyed two Typhoons and a Tilly and damaged a third fighter, the casualties were remarkably light. The pen housing the fighter which blew up had been empty at the time, and the blast had deafened three members of groundcrew and blown a fourth from his bicycle, giving him a broken ankle, a dislocated shoulder and concussion. In addition, chips of concrete torn up by bullets and shells had caused a few minor abrasions and cuts, but nothing that a sticking plaster, a sticky bun and a twenty-four hour pass couldn't heal.

A piece of shrapnel landed, sizzling, in the station warrant officer's mug of tea, and he was most put out, but realised after due consideration that it was better in his favourite mug than in his head.

As the enemy's parachute sailed peacefully down, Rose looked into the sky and at the ground, squinting to catch sight of any more of the enemy.

"Toffee Red Leader to Blackgang, any more business?"

"Negative, Red Leader. Thank you for your assistance. Any luck?"

He felt drained and cheerless as airmen raced across the field to capture the enemy pilot and take him into custody. "Two 109s, I got one and AA got the other."

Blackgang was delighted, her congratulations effusive, but Rose wasn't listening, instead feeling sick. Two 109s for the loss of at least two Typhoons. What a rubbish exchange!

Chapter 28

"Flash, old chap, you're a bit boring, mate, you need a girlfriend."

Jacko nodded sagely at Sid's advice.

Rose had been sitting alone in the officers' mess, peacefully reflecting on that evening's call to Molly. There had been reports of the Luftwaffe dropping butterfly bombs again in the North East – in Yorkshire and Lincolnshire – and the thought of the bloody things had been giving him nightmares. Molly had been reassuring, but he worried for those he held dear.

I'd better warn Charlie to keep her eyes peeled, too.

He stuck up two fingers at his section leaders. "Sod off, you scatty buggers. I'm a married man."

"No, No, Flash, I'm only saying this cos I care. You're a mate. I'm worried about you."

Jacko nodded again. "Worried."

Rose raised his left hand and wiggled his wedding ring in Sid's face. "Happily married. And I've got a baby."

And a rather sweet and sexy young WAAF officer tucked away in Bournemouth, but the less said about that…

"Well there you go then, me old mate, that's what your missus is for. After all, someone needs to look after the baby, don't they?"

What? Rose was lost. "Sid, what is this nonsense?"

"Well, it's a recorded scientific fact, ain't it? If you don't get a bit of the other at least once every month, yer bits fall off."

Jacko looked sadly into the distance and sighed.

"What? Sid, what on earth are you talking about?"

"Well, apparently – and I'm only quoting the science people, you know, the boffins and that, and they ain't stupid, I can tell you that for naught. You're only allowed to be a boffin if you're brainy. You and I, Flash, we wouldn't cut the mustard."

"Speak for yourself, you daft beggar. Look, Sid, you're spouting a load of bollocks, chum. Where do you get your medical advice? *The Dandy*? *Schoolgirl's Own*, perhaps?"

"Don't talk tripe Flash, they don't print the *Schoolgirl's Own* anymore, it's just called the *Schoolgirl*, now, not that I'd read such soppy crap. No, mate, it's been written about in the doctor's books. In the, erm, the *Lunatic*."

Jacko tut-tutted. "Sid! *The Lancet*!"

"Oh, yeah. *The Lancet*. They dun tests, and they say that a lack of use of the old man means the blood vessels become thinner and thinner 'til they get blocked, and then you can't feel your todger. Then you've got, like, three days before it drops off."

Jacko sighed and closed his eyes.

Rose grinned, trying not to laugh, and shook his head.

"Sid, for a man who holds the King's Commission, you do talk a lot of cock!"

Sid pouted. "You'll see. I like you, bein' my flight commander an' all. Didn't want to see you get hurt, see? Not allowed to fly Typhoons any more if you ain't got no bollocks."

"Oh, behave! I don't know if you noticed, but the replacement Typhoons flown in after that Jerry raid were all piloted by some very feminine ATA pilots. I think I could quite safely say they didn't have a bollock between them!"

Jacko took an anxious sip of his beer and returned Rose's amused gaze.

"He's right, Flash." Cowboy lifted his glass of beer, gazing into its dark depths reflectively, then took a mouthful, swallowed, and sighed with appreciation. "Happened to a friend of mine."

Jacko's eyes opened wide with concern.

"Cowboy! I'm surprised at you!"

"I was surprised, too, when I heard about it, Flash. Couldn't believe it. Made me want to weep." He grinned broadly.

"Yeah, I can see how bleak it made you feel. Go on, then, I can tell you're waiting for me to ask. Go on, tell me if you must."

Cowboy took another appreciative sip, then put his glass back down. "It was back during the Battle of Britain. My buddy, Herbert, was a Hurricane pilot flying out of Manston. They were so busy fighting, day, and, er, night, there wasn't time for a quick kiss, let alone a proper shag."

The three of them stared at him like three wise monkeys, and he felt a mad urge to scream with laughter at their earnest expressions, but he kept a straight face and nodded.

"Go on."

"Well, there he was, 20,000 feet with his squadron, about to knock a Hun bomber right out of the park, and they get bounced by about 100 109s, and it all goes to shit."

"Wouldn't have been for the first time, nor the last," Sid said, and Jacko nodded thoughtfully.

"So, he's upside down in a sharp turn backwards, and something goes 'plip-plop' and next thing he knows, these three objects are flying around the cockpit with him. And he thinks first that they're spent bullets and he's been hit, his groin feels numb, but then he realises – to his absolute horror I can tell you – that his cock and balls have detached and they're bouncing around the cockpit, and he almost shits himself."

He took another sip. "But he doesn't, of course, cos he's regular RAF. Not allowed to shit yourself if you're a regular. It's in King's Regs. Look it up if you don't believe me. You're not a regular, are you, buddy? Else you'd have got the special issue pants. The sanforised ones. Don't shrink when you piss yourself. Works just as well if you shit yourself. So, anyway, he sees 'em sailing around, bouncing off his canopy and he's thinking, Thank goodness I kept the canopy closed, otherwise they'd have flown straight out! I mean, it's no wonder he shat himself. He's got 109s up his arse and his old man's about to take his eye out!"

Jacko sighed in amazement, "Ooh!", and Sid tried to hide his grin behind his glass.

"Oh dear, bad show, must've been absolutely bloody for him," said Rose sympathetically.

"Oh, there was no blood, Flash, old man, old boy, old chap." Cowboy's fake British accent in falsetto was execrable. "It's like Sid said, the blood supply gets cuts off."

Sid looked at Rose in triumph, and Jacko covered his eyes with supposed queasiness.

Rose shook his head in disbelief. "I've heard it all, now. So what happened next? Do we have a squadron with a WAAF pilot called Herbert?"

"God, no! He hid in cloud 'til Jerry had pissed off, then back to airfield for emergency treatment. This was an RAF regular, so he got priority for special surgery."

"Managed to get everything put back, did he? Not sewn on back to front or upside down?" Rose asked solicitously.

"He was bloody lucky; the surgeons were really good. Got everything reattached, but I dunno if it all works. Didn't like to ask. I mean, you don't, do you? Not nice to."

Jacko nodded. "Not nice."

"Probably needs to stick his finger in the mains to get the old man to stand to attention, I shouldn't wonder," pondered Sid thoughtfully.

Jacko sombrely wiped dry eyes and murmured in awe, "Like a poker."

Sid sniggered. "Like a poker! Poke her! Geddit?"

Rose groaned at the atrocious schoolboy joke. "Yeah, OK, well, um, thanks for your concern, chaps. I'll bear it in mind."

Granny sidled up to them. "What's happening, men?"

"We were telling Flash about Herbert, Granny."

Their CO sniffed and clenched teeth on the crumpled cigarette hanging from his lips. "Herbert?" He pondered for a moment. "Oh. Herbert!" He looked from the three monkeys to Rose. "Bit of a salutary tale, that Flash, my old son. Bear it in mind."

"Yeah, Flash, you need to spend more time with Jacko an' me. You don't know what you're missing!"

Jacko nodded enthusiastically. "Missing!" he echoed.

"I don't think I want one of my flight commanders adopting your habits, you daft beggars."

"Aw, Granny, we were going to take him to see the Ginger Ring, and he missed it! One of the wonders of the world, that is! I heard de Gaulle fainted when he saw the show!"

Jacko nodded enthusiastically. "De Gaulle fainted!"

Granny bared his teeth. "I'm not ruddy surprised! I still feel a bit queasy when I'm having a ham sandwich!"

Rose looked at him with surprise. The Ginger Ring made Granny queasy?

I'm glad I spent the time with Charlie!

Yet a part of him wondered…

Cowboy's eyes were distant. "I been around the world, seen a lot of strange shit, but damn! I ain't never seen anything like what she does in her show! I ain't even sure that the girl's human!" He took a deep breath and then: "I haven't been able to eat black pudding since!"

An assistant section officer whom Rose had never seen before walked into the mess and sat down at an empty table.

Jacko stood up abruptly, eyes hungry.

Rose followed his gaze to the girl. "I say, Jacko, old chap, what about Mavis? Not giving up on her, are you?"

Jacko looked back at him in surprise. "Mavis?"

With an apologetic smile, Sid followed him over to the WAAF.

Rose shook his head in bemusement. "Well, I'll be…"

Jacko, the man who always got the girl, had failed with Mavis?

Cowboy stared appraisingly at the WAAF. "Hmm. She's new… looks like she needs rescuing from Jacko. He'll probably ask her if she wants to see a show with him. The Lord alone knows what she'll make of the Ginger Ring!" He got up. "Excuse me, fellas."

Granny groped for a cigarette, eyes on Rose. "You're looking a bit cheerier nowadays, old lad."

"Am I?"

"Mm. These last couple of months or so, you seem a bit more relaxed. Don't get me wrong, I'm glad." He pulled a crumpled cigarette out. "Ah!

Senior service!" he looked at Rose hopefully. "Did you keep your fag issue for me, old chap?"

Rose shook his head in reproof. "I don't know how you smoke those bloody things, Granny, don't they taste a bit grim to you?"

Granny waggled his cigarette and blew a cloud of smoke at Rose, "Not these, my dear old bag. Sweeten my breath, these do. Popsie's always gagging for a smooch because of these."

Rose gagged as the cloud of smoke enveloped him, before scratching his chin doubtfully, "If you say so."

"I do, you tatty pair of drawers," Granny sniffed, "Got a light, Flash?"

"'Fraid not, Granny, but I do have a couple of tins of NAAFI issue cigarettes in my room for you, and Molly sent me a tin of Ogden's No. 6 mature tobacco. She knows you like it. Come and get 'em when you get a chance."

Granny's face lit up. "Two tins? And some Oggies? That's my boy! If you weren't so ugly I'd give you a kiss!"

Rose looked across the room as the new WAAF found herself besieged by Cowboy and Jacko. It was impossible to see who had the upper hand in gaining her favour. He chuckled.

Granny was looking, too. "Hm, nice bit of totty, but Belle would spatch-cock my poor old balls with a butter knife if I even tried doing anything saucy with someone else on her station. Very forgiving, is my Belle, but she draws the line when it comes to that."

Your Belle?

"Anyway, as I was saying before you started flapping your gums at me, you seem a lot happier."

"I just am, Granny, can't explain it." He nodded, remembering Charlie's sweet, slightly shy smile.

Granny looked at him slyly. "Yeah, OK. I was talking to Belle this morning, she was telling me about Charlie."

"Charlie?" Rose asked innocently.

Uh, oh.

"Hm. You remember Charlie. Very pretty girl; dark blonde, shoulder-length hair; slim and petite; stands straight like a dancer?"

245

"Uh…" Rose put a finger over his mouth and adopted a thoughtful expression.

Granny guffawed. "Oh, my Gawd! You're getting senile, Flash! You know, *Charlie*! Flight officer in the WAAF? Belle's friend? The girl I introduced you to in the Ramrod, y'know, the same evening you force-landed T-Tommy?"

"Oh, *that* Charlie!"

"Yes, old son, *that* Charlie, remember her?" Granny looked at him sceptically.

"Now that you mention it…"

"Thought you would, you silly sod. Anyway, Belle was chatting the usual girly stuff, I was only half listening, of course, but it turns out that Charlie's different."

Rose scratched his neck uncomfortably. "What do you mean, different?"

"Oh, Granny! Charlie's changed! She's like a new girl! She's ever so bubbly and happy," Granny gushed in falsetto.

"Oh! That's nice to hear, she had been a bit worried about her husband…"

His friend interrupted him. "So I got thinking, how strange! My old pal Flash is looking less strained these last few months, too. Still can't tell the difference between a sleeve valve and a connecting rod, let alone where the oil scavenge tanks are, daft beggar, but he's handling being a flight commander on a front line Typhoon squadron rather well."

Rose forced a smile. "Well, I was taught by the best, wasn't I?"

"Don't come it with me, you cheeky cove! You been giving the girl a seeing to, haven't you? I was wondering why you kept heading off to the blinkin' seaside every chance you got. I thought you just liked building sandcastles and ogling popsie on the beach!"

"Oh, Granny, you've got the wrong end of the stick," he protested weakly, feeling the treacherous bloom of scarlet on his cheeks and knowing his friend could see straight through him.

"I think I know who's been on the wrong end of *your* stick, you saucy sod!"

Rose gulped in dismay. "Look, Granny, it's not like that, Charlie's a really sweet girl, a nice girl. She isn't a—"

246

"It's *exactly* like that, you little fiend! And I know she isn't a tart. I don't know any tarts!" His voice became softer. "I just know girls who are a bit lonely and want to be treated with respect, treated like a woman, and have a bit of fun and forget about things, even if it's for just a few hours."

Anxiously, Rose looked around, but there was no-one within earshot.

On the other side of the room, Jacko was looking glummer than usual and it seemed Sid was trying to cheer him up – probably suggesting a trip to see the Ginger Ring or something similarly horrendous – whilst Cowboy and the pretty young WAAF had disappeared.

Ah! The novelty of that American accent!

He licked dried lips and swallowed. "I don't know how it happened, Granny. I didn't mean it to, honest I didn't, but it just did." He shrugged helplessly. "I know that she's married and all, and I didn't do anything caddish, but we just ended up, er…"

Granny nodded with satisfaction. "Thought so, you can't hide things from your old Auntie Granny." He looked across to Sid and Jacko. "Bloody hell, Jacko didn't get the totty? He must be slipping."

He turned back to Rose. "I'm glad, old cock. It was something you badly needed."

Rose gawped at him in surprise. "You'll not tell Molly? If she found out, she'd leave me. And I couldn't bear to lose her, Granny. I couldn't bear it."

"Don't be daft, you silly sod. I never told her about that little redhead nurse in London, what was her name, Anna?"

Rose smiled at the memory of the girl who had held him tenderly and comforted him when he had been at his lowest during The Battle of Britain, and with whom he had lost his virginity.

Granny shook his head, "Why would I tell Molly? You two have something very special. It's quite rare, having what you share. Why would I want to destroy it? I know what an honourable sod you are, I'll bet you didn't shag any of the totty while you were flying that bloody desk, and they'll have been gasping for it! Babs told me her girls were keen, but you never took advantage of them. No, mate, Molly means a lot to me, I'd not want her hurt, and even though you've got a face like a camel, are daft as

247

bollocks, a huge pain in the arse and you get on my ruddy tits, I've learned to live with you."

Rose smiled, still a little embarrassed at being found out, but grateful Granny wasn't going to lay into him. "That's the nicest thing you've ever said to me."

Granny sniffed disdainfully. "Don't get used to it, you tart, there ain't any more where that came from." He grinned broadly at Rose like a naughty schoolboy pleased with his witticism.

Rose felt like hugging him but didn't, because chaps don't.

"I didn't think you cared."

Granny snorted. "That's because I bloody don't."

"I didn't mean to, Granny. Molly is everything for me. I love her so much, and I know she feels the same. I don't know why it wasn't enough."

His friend sighed sadly. "Oh, Flash, you daft blighter. It is enough, old man. If she were here, it would never have happened. The thing is, she isn't, and she's got her hands full with your wee brat, so she can't come down here, anyway. Best place for them, they're safer where they are, but never, ever tell her about it, there's nothing to gain from it, and you'll only hurt her needlessly."

He put his feet up on the little table, ignoring the exasperated stare of the white-coated waiter, and scratched his chin.

"Thing is, matey, you need something else otherwise you'd go mad. Flying is a dangerous profession at the best of times, but in wartime, well! As you said before, Sir Isaac is always just there, hiding in the shadows, waiting for you to make a balls-up of it so he can scoop you up."

Sir Isaac was the not-so-affectionate name given by RAF night fighter crews to the forces of nature that apparently conspired to kill them each night. Rose and Chalky White had been close to being Sir Isaac's victims on at least twenty occasions during their night fighter tour at RAF Dimple Heath.

One thing about Sir Isaac, though, was that he didn't take sides, as several Luftwaffe bomber crews had discovered to their cost.

"And now you boys are skimming the sea at low level on the off chance that Jerry will pop by. Hours of flying so low and trying to stay alert, and in such a boring bloody environment, eyes peeled so you don't get bounced, trying not to end up in the drink, day in and day out. It's a fucking torment. And then when we come back, feeling like we've been baked in a ruddy sauna with our brains numb, muscles worn out and our eyes red raw, we can't even get blotto or have any high jinks in case we break something and can't take our place on the roster. And then the boredom and constant tension are broken when Jerry makes his occasional experience. Nobody knows how dangerous low flying is, mate, and then if there's combat chucked in, too… Well! I don't know why, but you and Hairy seem to have had most of the luck with successful interceptions and kills, but then I can always remember you yammering on about Lady Luck back in '40."

They watched as Sid left the room, trailed by a dejected Jacko.

"Flying anti-Rhubarb patrols makes for tortuous flying, Flash, my old fart. And on top of it all, you've got the stress of being a flight commander, whole new world, ain't it? So, you need something to take you away from it, call it a distraction, help you forget about it all for a while, otherwise you'd go crazy, pal. Knowing that there's someone else waiting, someone who cares deeply for you, it makes a difference. You know that whatever you have to face out there, there's someone you can find a bit of peace with, whether in person or over the blower. Fighting taxes the spirit and our levels of courage, old son, we can only manage so much. We need them to remind us we're men. A good shag overcomes a lot of ills. We need that tether, chum, else we'd go right around the bend and out the other side."

Granny looked at him thoughtfully for a moment and then blinked. "I saw the strain in you after you got those three Heinkels, and then Belle was chatting to me about Charlie, and I thought, why not? Molly would be your anchor if she were here, but she's right up north far away, and I know you'll downplay what's happening here when you're on the phone to her anyway, not tell her what you're facing because you'll never want to worry her, what with little Danny, too. And it's just so bloody difficult getting around the country, what with delays and whatnot, a twenty-four or forty-eight hour pass gets you bloody nowhere. And poor little Charlie needed someone to make her feel like a normal human being again, someone who actually gives a damn and treats her right, and makes her forget, even if only for a little while. You get on my nerves, you weird beggar, but despite that, you're an honourable and decent fella, and that's what that poor girl needed."

He sat back and surveyed his friend. "You're rubbish at everything else, but I knew you'd treat her right. And looks like I was right, which isn't really a surprise to me. And I must say, my old tart, I'm pleased."

He pulled out his pipe, contemplated it for a moment, then put it away again. "You two aren't hurting anyone, Flash, just so long as you keep it discreet and don't get too attached. I know what you're like, you soppy tart! So just enjoy her and treat her right, she's a nice girl who just needs looking after until her bloke gets back. And you're doing yourself a favour at the same time, giving yourself something outside of flying and Little Sillo. You both need company and release. An empty pair of balls and a sore cock help you forget about a lot of things."

His lips tightened. "And don't think it'll be over when he gets back. The poor sod will have gone through a fucking nightmare, I shouldn't wonder, it won't all be sweetness and light from the start, and it'll take them some time to find each other again, y'know, rekindle things. In the meantime, she'll still need you to be there. Sometimes, we need to have someone just to talk to. We're only flesh and blood, chum, not plastic and metal, like the Air Ministry seems to think!"

Granny looked scornfully at Rose, and he teased, "It ain't all about having a shag, so keep that filthy little todger of yours tucked away, and don't keep waving it around at the poor girl. Hasn't the poor thing got enough to put up with without having to look at that wizened thing of yours all the ruddy time? Makes me feel ill. Have some decorum, you dirty little monkey!"

Rose stared at him, surprised at Granny's insight and grateful for his words. "Well now, that's just impolite! I've bloody heard it all, now! Definitely a case of the pot calling the kettle black!"

Granny stood up. "Strewth! What a rude little perisher you are, I know when I'm not wanted, so I'm going to find Belle, see if she'd like a little, er, *companionship*."

"She's a bit different to the other girls, isn't she, Granny?"

His friend and CO smiled toothily back at him. "I should ruddy well think so. She's *really* special. We've been married almost eight years!"

And with a cheeky wink, he turned and left, leaving a stunned Rose gaping.

Chapter 29

Rose was late to their meeting, and he was feeling more than a little hot and bothered as he finally parked the Austin 8 saloon he had borrowed from the motor pool at Little Sillo.

He had intended to arrive early, but a Morris field artillery tractor had somehow detached from its limber and 25 pdr gun on the A3090, and it had seemed an eternity before the gunners finally reattached it.

With a sigh of relief, he parked outside the Royal Oak Inn and hurried inside. He saw the girl instantly, seated beside a window.

He had kept her waiting for half an hour, but as soon as he stepped in, she stood up and smiled, her face a picture of happiness, and warmth flooded through him.

"Oh, Flash! I thought you might not be coming!" And instantly he felt better. What is it about a smile on a pretty girl's face that makes a man feel so good?

He thought of Molly, and the bite of guilt was still there, but the edge had blunted in the intervening months since he had first slept with Charlie – or as she preferred, made love to her. They had done it again so many times subsequently, whenever they could be together, and he felt his pleasure mirrored in her eyes.

Her company was delightful, and the sex (er, sorry, lovemaking) incredible.

"Sorry, Charlie, there was an accident on the way here, a blasted gun tractor had dropped its gun in the middle of the road!"

She hugged him warmly and lifted her face to him so he could kiss her.

He did so with pleasure and then held her at arm's length. "Oh my gosh, Charlie, you look terrific!" And she felt and smelt pretty amazing, too.

"Mmm, that feels wonderful, I needed a big, strong hug."

She gave him one last squeeze and let go of him shyly, her eyes shining and face flushed, and he marvelled that despite everything they had done together, the deep intimacy, the forthright and rather candid person she had been with him at the beginning, she had somehow changed into this quieter, almost shy girl.

Was this the real Charlie?

It was quiet in the room, a muted conversation between two old men enjoying a game of dominoes was the only background noise, another was reading a newspaper beside the open fireplace, pipe clamped between uneven teeth. But he could feel their curiosity at this young pair of interlopers.

His voice was hushed. "Did you, Charlie? Why? Is everything alright?"

She took his hand and placed it gently against her cheek. "Oh, golly, yes! Everything's fine. Even better now that you're here!" She sighed. "It's just that I've missed you, Flash, I think having you in my life has spoiled me! Poor Molly must hate being alone, and she must worry so."

He took her hand from his cheek, kissed the palm and held it between his own hands. "I think it's worse for the ones at home, sometimes, Charlie. All the waiting, but you know all about that, of course."

"I want to fight them too, Flash. At least when I'm guiding an interception, I know I'm helping. But I'd love to do more."

"Good Lord! You're the most important part of the whole thing, dear girl. You and your chums are the ones who put us in the right place at the right time, Jerry is only having a really bloody time of it because of what you all do. You and your colleagues do more than enough, believe me!"

"Still, I'd love to be there to press the button."

He chuckled. "I do like a girl with spirit." He looked around and noticed the barman's interest. "I'd better get us something, Charlie. Drink? How about something to eat? Have you had any lunch?"

"Just some toast and jam when I came off at 8.00 am, so yes please. But only lemonade for me because I'm driving daddy's jalopy. But I could do with a bit of lunch, I'm famished."

"Good idea, I'll have lemonade too, and order us something. What do you fancy?"

She surreptitiously touched his hip, stroking it. "Well, I know what I fancy, but I can't have *that*! I wish we had longer. But seriously, I don't mind, Flash, you choose for us."

Ordering sausage, chips and beans for them both, Rose returned with their drinks.

"Here we are, ma'am! So tell me, how was your night?"

"Actually, Flash, it was quite quiet. We had a couple of traces on the scope, but they were both US Air Force bombers that had got lost, one on the way out, and one on the way in. There was a Hun heading our way after a raid on Southampton, but a Beaufighter got him before we could get involved. After that, it was back to my room for a little nap, so I could be here with you, suitably refreshed."

Her ankles moved to comfortably interlock with his.

"Doesn't your father need the car, Charlie?"

"Oh, no, he and Mum cycle everywhere."

He had previously been curious as to how Charlie managed to find petrol for her father's car. "Easy," she had replied. "As I'm often called on to provide reports about the RDF on the south coast, I've actually got a driver and my own Austin 8. I siphon off a gallon or two of fuel into a jerrycan when she's off to lunch. Quite a handy arrangement actually, and because I have a hush-hush job, the police look the other way when I'm driving around in Daddy's car."

Rose, who found the roads unnerving, shook his head with incomprehension. "Do you like driving, then?"

"I love driving, and I often stick Millie – she's my driver – in the back and drive myself!"

What is it about driving that girls love? Whatever it is, they can bloody well keep it!

Charlie drove her father's car carefully, but he resolved never to take a ride in her own Austin 8 if she was driving. Molly had terrified him enough with her little red motor car, although to be fair, she drove the family car in a way that did not strain his heart or his blood pressure.

"How was the air test this morning, was S-Sugar OK?"

He took a sip of his lemonade. "Lovely, she's a beautiful kite and she's ready for the pre-dusk patrol." He tapped the table. "Touch wood. I wish I could take you up in her. You'd love it."

"Me too." She leaned closer to whisper in his ear. "Sugar's a lucky girl. You spend more time in her than you do in me!"

Cripes! He could feel an expanding in his nether regions in response to both her words and nearness, and he suppressed a cough. "Oh, I say! If only…"

"If only…" she echoed regretfully. "I want to wake up with you again soon, Flash, can you get a twenty-four hour or forty-eight hour pass for next week?"

"I'll try, Charlie, I would love to." With the pre-dusk patrol, only lunch was possible with this lovely girl today, and he tried to cross his legs to hide the tumescence of his groin, banging his knee painfully on the underside of the table.

You daft, randy bugger, you should be ashamed of yourself!

He sighed, drew her closer and kissed the corner of her mouth. "Any more news about John?"

"Nothing new. I should get another letter tomorrow. He's using a walking stick now, but he says the wooden foot they've made for him rubs a bit, needs sanding down, poor thing. Once he's back, the RAF specialists will sort him out, I'm sure. And I can rub his poor ankle better."

He felt a twinge of irrational jealousy and crushed it.

She breathed in and, moving her cap and gas mask haversack out of the way, snuggled against him on the bench. "No more news about the repatriation yet. The Swiss Red Cross are still chatting to the Huns. Apparently, before the desert battles, they had more of ours than we had of theirs, so they were in no hurry. After all the desert battles, though, the Desert Rats have captured thousands, and now that Monty's about to push through the Mareth Line into Tunisia, they want to talk at last. Bastards."

She sat up straight as the food arrived. "Oh, yum! Looks absolutely scrumptious!"

They tucked into the food hungrily, Charlie depositing a huge blob of Daddies Sauce onto her chips before burying them under salt, pepper and vinegar.

He nudged her playfully in the side with his elbow. "Got enough salt on it, love?"

She stole a chip from his plate, scornfully ignoring his protestations. "If you're going to poke a lady, at least do it properly," she said and blushed.

His calming bulge began to reassert itself. "Why, Charlie! Is that an invitation?"

She brushed the rebellious strand of hair from her eyes. "I didn't think the Brylcreem boys needed an invitation!"

Rose, who had never used Brylcreem in his hair, simply nodded. "This one does."

"That's what makes you a bit special, Harry Rose." She offered him a chip on the end of her fork. "Here, darling, try one of mine."

Rose eyed the soaked object dubiously, noting the generous coating of salt, and pepper flecks on its surface. For a moment, chivalry fought with sense and won. He opened his mouth with a sense of impending doom and she popped it in. After a couple of valiant but grim chews of the awful thing, he swallowed it, washing the debris down with lemonade.

She had been watching him, and now her eyes softened, soft lips curving at his expression, then she giggled. "The age of gallantry is not dead! You are such a sweet man, Flash." She kissed him slowly, and he groaned inwardly as she covered his mouth with a pungent blend of lipstick and condiments.

Urgh! Can't wipe my lips – not very nice to do so after being kissed – but how on earth can I get this mixture off my chops?

Impaling a sausage on his fork, he gnawed a piece, in the process wiping his lips clean with it.

She frowned at him. "You messy boy – look at all that grease on your lips! Here, let me." She picked up her napkin and dabbed his lips, cleaning away the last of the condiments.

Oh, that's much better, ta very much!

As they ate, Charlie recounted her memories of a hilarious trip with her friends to watch a show in London, Rose content to eat and listen until, with a sigh of pleasure, Charlie sat back, her plate empty.

"That was wonderful!"

Rose wiped the last of his chips with the sauce from his beans, popped them in his mouth and nodded with satisfaction. "Mm. Just what the doctor ordered. Would you like to have some pudding? Or a cuppa? Or something a little stronger?"

"No, thank you, that was wonderful. What time do you need to get back?"

He sighed sadly. "Four o'clock. I need to be on the patrol line with Hairy by five."

She snuggled up to him. "Flash, could we…?"

His groin stirred, but he affected ignorance. "Could we what?"

She nestled against him. "Don't pretend to be dense! I want you, Flash, rather badly."

Oh, if only we could! But there's no time.

"There's nowhere we could go, Charlie …"

She pouted and touched his thigh softly where the others couldn't see. "I *need* you, Flash." She looked around furtively, then said more quietly, "I'm tingling down there something fierce. I want you to make love to me so much, and I think I'll die if you don't."

Good grief, that's a bit overdramatic!

"Err… " His penis throbbed urgently. Blast it! "OK, but where?"

"I don't really care, I know there isn't much time so it'll have to be a quick one, in a field perhaps, if you like. We're lucky today, it's quite nice out."

It was quite warm outside. "Right you are, wait for me outside, I'll settle up here and join you. Um, I didn't think we might be able to make love, and I didn't come prepared, shall I get a packet of, erm…"

"Don't worry, Flash, I put my cervical cap in before I left. I was hoping we might be able to…"

Then he remembered her things and pulled his gas mask container to him.

"I remembered you saying you liked peanut butter, Charlie. Granny has a friend working at the US stores depot in Camp Foxley in Herefordshire, and he managed to get these." He opened the haversack to show her.

The gas mask itself was in his Austin 8, but its container was currently packed with three large jars of Holsum peanut butter and some tins and sealed packets of instant coffee, condensed milk, butter, shortbread biscuits and vanilla caramel sweets.

Charlie gasped and hugged him. "Oh, Flash! Thank you, my darling! It's an absolute abundance of delight!"

Bless you, Granny…

"Bloody heavy," he grumbled gruffly, pleased by her reaction. "Think the damned container just about dislocated my shoulder."

On his way to Bere Regis earlier, Rose had stopped at the post office in Little Sillo and mailed a large parcel northwards to Molly, a similar collection of delicious purloined goodies, and he anticipated a response akin to Charlie's over the telephone the following day when it had arrived.

Charlie grabbed him by the lapels of his tunic and pulled him to his feet. "Flight Lieutenant Rose," she said formally, "don't dawdle! If you aren't between my legs in the next five minutes, I think I'm going to explode rather messily!"

Uh-oh, better hurry!

*

Leaving her father's car where it was, Charlie sat in the driver's seat of his Austin and, pulling out of the car park, she turned right onto West Street, straight along then left through the adjacent hamlet of Shitterton.

Shitterton? Better not make any jokes, otherwise she'll think me immature, keep a straight face, man, stay serious.

Once through the hamlet, Charlie carefully guided the car onto a track, until they arrived at a wood, bordering a field of gently swaying maize stalks half a mile from the hamlet.

She turned and smiled eagerly at Rose. "Come on, Flash, quick!"

Only stopping to snatch up his greatcoat from the back seat, she jumped out and scampered off.

His heart was punching his chest in excited anticipation, and he locked the car and followed her.

Charlie had already battered down a rectangle of the stalks about ten feet in from the border of the field, creating a swaying, rustling space about ten feet by five. She had laid down his greatcoat on the battered stalks, had already removed her shoes, skirt and tunic and was in the process of removing her 'blackout' knickers.

She looked up, gasping with anticipation and exertion, blackouts not being the easiest things to slide oneself out of. "Darling, give me a hand, will you? I'm all fingers and thumbs! I should've worn the white button-up ones!"

Help you? Oh yes, please! It's only a sign of good manners for a gentleman to assist a lady in the removal of her underwear.

He knelt at her feet, hooked his forefingers and middle fingers under the elastic above her knees and expertly pulled them off.

At least I've learnt how to do *something* during my time in uniform…

"Stockings, too, Charlie?"

She rolled her eyes. "How else are you going to get it into me, you naughty boy?"

He grinned and pulled at her ankles as she rolled the stockings down over her knees and slid them off.

She blushed beneath his staring eyes, "Come on, then, get 'em off! Quick! We haven't all day! Lickety-split!

"Yes, ma'am!" He eagerly removed his tunic and dropped his trousers and underpants.

Rose knelt forwards, to caress her softness gently with his lips and tongue.

She moaned and her back arched and at last, she could take no more. "Flash my darling, hold me?"

He climbed up and went to kiss her

"Oh, Flash, wipe your mouth!"

Rose wiped his mouth and nose quickly with his sleeve, and kissed her hard, feeling her welcoming mouth open and envelope his, her tongue pushing between his lips to enter, her arms around his neck.

Between kisses, she murmured, "I'm ready, my darling, please…?"

Her arms loosened their embrace and he and eased himself up

"Hard as you like, my love," she breathed, and he drove himself hard against her

Balanced carefully above her, the crushed stalks and his greatcoat a springy mattress beneath them, they moved together urgently, the soft sigh of the wind, the rustling of the stalks and the songs of the birds the only accompaniment to the sound of their desperate coupling, until even those sounds disappeared and their senses only knew the frenzied fusion and movement of their bodies together.

She cried out in rapture, clutching him tight to her trembling frame, and his body stilled in response as she shook, until she slowed and finally relaxed. Gently kissing her open mouth, he resumed driving himself into her, kissing her hair and her eyes and her neck, revelling in the delicious fragrant blend of the girl and nature, and then once more she cried out and locked herself against him, and as if in sympathy, he found he could hold himself back no longer and stiffened in her embrace, his body spasming in climax, burying his face into her hair and releasing himself into her, their involuntary and muted gasps and cries unheard by anyone but themselves.

After a while, they became aware of their surroundings once more, and at first, the girl would not disentangle herself, wanting only to feel his body against hers. But then she relented grudgingly, and Rose climbed off her with regret, his chest rising and falling and muscles trembling.

He lay down beside her and took her into his arms, one hand covering a pliant breast, her heart fluttering beneath it, and she nestled silently against him.

After a minute or two, he spoke. "We had better get dressed, Charlie."

Now their lovemaking was over, Rose had visions of them being surprised by the owner of the field, both only dressed in shirt and tie and naked from the waist down, but thank goodness at least they hadn't been caught *in flagrante delicto.*

She whispered against his chest, "Don't want to."

He sighed sorrowfully, stroked her damp hair. "Neither do I, sweetest girl, but…"

"*But.* Yes. I know." She looked up at him lovingly. "That was incredible, Flash, I wish we could do it again. Can we do it again, soon?" She kissed him, trapped his lower lip between her teeth and nibbled it playfully, her hand gently cupping his private parts.

He carefully detached his lip from her. "Yes, please. As soon as possible." Rose hesitated. "You are quite lovely, Charlie, like a diamond with so many perfect facets. I hope he realises how lucky he is. It must be simply wonderful to be married to you."

She looked away, her face in shadow. "I could easily say the same, Flash, darling. I hope Molly appreciates you, too. I bet she does." She sighed. "If I wasn't married to the man I love, I would love to be yours forever. Very much."

There seemed nothing else to say, and they dressed in silence, joyful in each other's company and enjoying the pleasure of their time together, still glowing from their shared intimacy, but also sorrowful that it was time to part once again.

Chapter 30

The light had diminished to a thin glowing ribbon on the horizon, a last memory of the day draining away with the onset of night, and, like the sky above, the runway was dark, but, as promised by the ops room, a green light flashed readiness, and the avenue of lights flickered on for their take-off.

Rose cursed quietly under his breath as he watched Granny's Typhoon, the tongues of bright blue exhaust flame disconcertingly long as P-Popsie belted along the grassy runway like a rocket.

As it rose into the remnants of the dusk, he glanced at the instruments one last time – the cockpit lights painted over with red dope to reduce their brightness sufficiently for night flying – checked that S-Sugar's trim was set, checked that Molly's photo and Charlie's pebble were secure, said a quick prayer (Take care of a pair of idiots who ought to know better this evening, Lord!) and, taking a deep breath of oxygen, he released S-Sugar's brakes.

S-Sugar surged forward at full throttle, pushing him back into his seat, full rudder to offset the pull to one side, and as his Sabre bellowed eagerly, the speeding and bombed-up Typhoon finally lifting, he raised her wheels quickly and applied full throttle, with the propeller in coarse to catch up with the rapidly receding shape of his CO's aircraft, now a blur in the approaching night.

The sky was clear, and already the moon was just rising over the Downs to the east. It was almost full, and there would be plenty of light to both guide them and expose their targets on the ground.

"Fancy going on a Rhubarb, old man? A little scenic trip to see France by night?" he muttered sarcastically to himself as he settled into position 50 yards from Granny's starboard wing.

The previous day, Granny had sidled up to Rose at dinner with *that* look in his eye. "Ever been on any Rhubarbs before, Flash, old pants?"

Shaking his head, he wondered with trepidation where this was going. "No. Um, apart from the raid on Brest-Lanveoc, that is."

"Ha! Thought so!" His CO's voice dropped to just above a whisper. "The thing is, my old trout, Mati's had a prime piece of gen about goings-on at a Luftwaffe airbase in Normandy. It's normally an interceptor and fighter-bomber base, 190s mainly, but they've had some paratroopers arrive today for special training, Gawd knows what for, so there'll be some Ju52s there, too. I've been thinking... d'you want to go and visit 'em? Leave 'em our very best wishes? Things've been a bit quiet recently with Jerry sending their best and brightest east, not that I'm complaining, but how's about us nipping over to see 'em? Nice little night trip? You're a bit of a dab hand at night, ain'tcha?"

He looked around conspiratorially as Rose rolled his eyes. "Just you an' me, old stick, just like the good old days! Be a laugh!"

There had been no enemy raids or interceptions for Excalibur Squadron in over a fortnight, not since a section from B Flight had caught two FW 190s after a raid on Poole, shooting one down into the sea. Enemy activity had dropped off significantly in the last few weeks, reflecting the reality of more and more of their opposite numbers in France being transferred to the meat grinder of the Eastern Front.

But at least it had meant a four-day pass to see Molly and little Danny. He still glowed with pleasure at the memories.

He had felt a curl of excitement growing in the pit of his stomach. "OK, Granny, let's do it, count me in. How about Hairy and Brat? Will they be flying on the do with us?"

"Nah, just a section, you and me. Too many of us buzzing around at night will complicate things something chronic. Can you imagine us all flitting round in the darkness, be more dangerous to each other than to

Jerry. Just the pair of us would be best, I reckon. We'll see if there's anyone in the circuit and give 'em a scare at the very least, then we'll clobber their dispersals. In and out, quick as you like. Up for it?"

"Rather! But Hairy will be pissed off with me."

"No he won't, I'll tell him to sod off if he has a moan, but I reckon we should let Jerry know there's a war on. Besides, Bee Beamont, Des Scott and all the other Tiffie boys are conducting Rhubarbs pretty regularly already, generally by night, and it looks like Fighter Command are going to use us more on intruders and Rhubarbs, so he'll get his chance soon enough. Why else d'you think they trained us to lob bombs?"

Hm. Rose hadn't enjoyed the effect that carrying bombs had on their Typhoons, the powerful beast less responsive; sluggish and heavy.

With a glance to confirm that Belle wasn't near enough to hear him, Granny winked. "Might just remind all the French popsie that the RAF is on the way, encourage the mademoiselles to buff up their soft pink bits on the bidet in readiness for us!"

Granny picked up Rose's dessert spoon and, holding it like a dagger, pointed it at him threateningly. "And don't repeat what I just said in front of Belle, or else I'll stick this up where the sun doesn't shine!"

So here he was with Granny at 10,000 feet, passing over the coast, the glittering diamonds of stars above and the English Channel below like a sheet of restless obsidian, the French coast a dark, irregular clump before them. They had plotted the route thoroughly, and Granny believed he had (with Mati's help) found a route that bypassed the heavy flak, allowing the two Typhoons to escape the lighter flak with sufficient altitude.

It took them just seven minutes from the friendly coast to the not so friendly one, and as they entered enemy airspace, Rose wondered if they had passed any enemy bombers going the other way.

If only we had been allowed to carry out intruder missions, we could have done this two years ago, cut a bloody swathe through the Dorniers and Heinkels and Junkers as they rose over their airfields before a raid on Britain.

But the loss of their hard-earned experience, as well as a priceless radar set, should they have been shot down, and the possibility of the enemy

264

prising out their knowledge of air intercept equipment, had been too much to risk for the disruption of Luftwaffe bombing operations.

The Luftwaffe intruders, though not without success, had achieved mere pinpricks relative to what might have happened had they been equipped with AI. The shoe would have been on the other foot if that had been the case. Even the thought of it made Rose shudder.

Two thin beams of intense light flicked on as searchlights probed for them, and a single, hopeful crop of AA bursts came from far below and soon ceased, but already the pair were diving, spread apart to level out at 200 feet for safety, before turning back onto the heading for the enemy airfield. Hopefully, they had spoofed the enemy into thinking they were heading further inland.

They skimmed the darkened landscape, hoping and praying their low altitude and high speed would carry them safely past any enemy guns before the crews had time to react.

They were about eight miles from the airfield, when: "We'll start our dummy run in from here, just fly past, see if you can make out the airfield… Blimey! Flash! I just passed through something's slipstream, can you see anything?"

There was something just ahead, a large shape, which quickly grew two pairs of glowing blue exhausts as Rose looked to one side of it. Once he knew where it was, he slowly shifted his gaze onto it, and, trying hard not to focus too much, could easily identify the other aircraft in front of them, its slipstream causing the disturbed air through which Granny now flew.

"Crikey, Ada! Throttle back a bit, Granny, you're behind a Junkers 52!"

"In front of me?" Granny sounded surprised.

"Yeah, a little above, and about 300 yards in front. Can you see it? It's flying on the same course as us. Should be dead ahead."

"Ahead, eh? Is the gunner's position manned?"

"I can't tell from here, but I found that they sometimes didn't notice us, even when we went right up behind them, never found out why. Can you remember what I said about trying to pick up an enemy aircraft at night?"

Defocus your eyes and try not to stare directly at any movement, look out for the glow of exhausts.

A set of navigation lights suddenly winked on the other aircraft. "Flash, my old pants, I can see it now. Ta for doing whatever it is you did."

"Stop being daft, Granny, what do we do now?"

"Do now? Why, we follow it in, my dear old plum! We'll descend with it, all one happy Luftwaffe family, and just as we're about to pass over the perimeter, I'll shoot this poor lamb down, then you drop down low as you can and knock seven bells out of everything you see on the port side of the 'drome. I'll take everything to starboard. Just one pass, though, blast through fast. We'll meet up ten miles west of here, uh, bearing zero-two-zero, at 10,000 feet."

"Got it." Rose could see a large flat rectangular grey area ahead of them now, and gradually a forest and clumps of buildings around the perimeter became visible.

Well, it's jolly decent of you to show us where to go, Jerry, old chap!

The Junkers' right wing dropped slightly as the pilot turned his lumbering trimotor a little to starboard, losing height further as he did so, and as Rose looked ahead trying to make out details on the airfield, he noticed a flashing light on the ground.

On drawing closer, he realised with a start that what he had initially thought was one light was in fact a pair of lights, set close together, and there was another aircraft on the ground with its navigation lights on.

They were a scant mile away now, the airfield stretched out before them, and it looked as if the aircraft on the ground was taxiing almost perpendicularly towards the southern end of the airfield, either to dispersals or to take off. He nudged left rudder and eased the stick forward, pushing S-Sugar into a shallow dive, trying to put himself in the best position to attack the taxiing aircraft, and felt the hairs on the back of his neck rise as he realised how close the flak battery situated in the forest west-south-west of the airfield was to his side, and the thought of the guns in those flak towers encouraged him to drop Sugar's nose even further.

Even as he did so, the runway lights flicked on for Granny's Junkers, and then suddenly there was a bright flash as Granny pulverised the Junkers with a burst of 20 mm, the cannon shells exploding in the fuel tanks of

266

the hapless aircraft, lighting up the airfield in sharp relief for an instant – in which Rose saw his target was an FW 190 Jabo fighter-bomber – and further away, light reflected back from glazed canopies in shelters among the trees and the large hangar. As he allowed for deflection, aiming just before the little fighter bomber with the tear-drop canopy, he was already planning his attack on them.

The light from the exploding Junkers behind diminished as the fireball faded but was not extinguished, as large fiery fragments of the aircraft fell onto the edge of the airfield, and, too late, a red warning flare shot into the sky, closely followed by a second and then a third, bathing the surroundings in a disconcerting shade of flickering crimson.

S-Sugar curved down, Sabre snarling throatily, and Rose pushed down on the firing button, 20 mm shells ripping out to ensnare the hapless Jabo in a diagonal swathe of exploding and ruinous cannon shells. Because of the effects of glare on his night vision, Rose had earlier arranged for the tracer to be removed from their belts of ammunition, allowing him to sight on the 190 whilst his cannon thundered – although the thunder flash-like explosion of Granny's Junkers had done his night vision no favours. The exhausts had been fitted with shields that protected their eyes from the glare.

The 190 disappeared within a bloom of smoke and flame, the winking flashes of his rounds tearing it asunder, the blazing wreckage leaving a streaming trail of glowing sparks and embers of debris scattered behind it on the battered runway, but there was no time to see more as another FW 190 appeared, parked in a dispersals bay directly before him.

Rose snapped off a quick burst, but it missed the parked enemy fighter completely, the shells whistling over it and disappearing into the night. He cursed, exhilarated by the destruction of the first 190, forgetting the flak towers as the first of the belated defensive fire arched up into the sky, snaking as if in search, and he knew the defences were shocked and confused and probably unsure of their targets.

Perhaps even these bloody idiots can't tell the difference between an FW 190s and a Typhoon!

And now he was levelling off, flying low towards the hangar, punching out a long, vengeful burst, ruddering gently to splatter his oncoming targets in a wide field of fire, flashes and explosions as his vision trembled from the wicked recoil. He saw the glittering clouds of glass and flying metal as his cannon shredded all that stood before it.

There were a number of dispersals pens with connecting roads forming a little knot together and, behind them, the large rectangular shape of a camouflaged hangar, nestled between smaller aircraft shelters beneath the trees. He would have missed it, had not the large hangar doors bizarrely had the shape of a four-engine aircraft – viewed from directly behind – painted onto them.

Rose didn't know it, but one of the airbase's resident FW190 Staffels was relocating to Upper Saxony as homeland defence against the USAAF raids of Germany, and the painting of a life-sized profile of a B-17 bomber was a useful training aid. It was intended to show the pilots of the Staffel some appreciation of the size of a large four-engine bomber as it should appear from their cockpits, helping them to understand how large it should appear to them at the point they needed to open fire and then break off their attacks.

Sparkling splinters of light from hits on a twin-engine aircraft, his fire slashing diagonally across it in one of the dispersals pens, and he pulled up and then down. He heard the patter of debris against Sugar as he leapfrogged the bomber, and was suddenly aware of a vivid line of tracer, glowing high above, but knew that if they dropped it to try and hit him most would arc down onto the crowded pens and bays.

He edged the stick to starboard and ruddered to slide his shells across the shelters and the painted doors, fighting to keep the nose up and his aim steady, tearing towards a huddled group of three or four Junkers Ju52 transports, parked nose to tail, and toggled the bomb release convulsively, please don't skip up and take off my wings, feeling the fighter lift and zoom upwards from the sudden lightening of his aircraft, the bombs going off in a pair of flashes so close together as to appear almost as one, and debris blurred past as he pushed down her nose again.

Even though he was end-on and fleeing fast, the expanding pressure wave from the explosions behind lifted Sugar's tail and he thought, for an instant of pure terror, that he would fly into the ground, and fought with a chest tight with fear to pull her nose back up as she tilted over, feeling her shaking beneath his straining hands, fighting to keep her level – and then she was back under his control, and his last cannon shells battered a single-engine fighter (small, an FW190?) hidden beneath a dark tarpaulin into smoking, twisted metal.

And then the airfield was gone, everything suddenly disappearing behind him as he raced low across the airfield's perimeter and out over the forest of dark trees to the south-west of St André de l'Eure, the latticework of tracer a meteoric storm of red and white and green in the growing clouds of smoke behind him, laughing madly at the destruction he had wrought and at the gunners who had come nowhere near throughout his vicious full-throttle run across their airfield.

He stayed low, speeding and weaving slightly across the trees – there should be no powerlines across a forest, should there? – knowing that after he had counted to thirty he should be out of range of those flak towers and any other defences.

Behind him, an occasional burst of tracer lanced desultorily into the sky, but the airfield itself was covered by an expanding pall of smoke, draped low over it like some sinister miasma, lit from within and flickering with a red glow cast by the fires burning beneath it.

Something, or a number of somethings, were intermittently exploding at the western end of the north-east to south-west-inclined runway, suffusing the cloud of smoke with abrupt flashes of light, as if a violent electrical storm had descended onto the airfield, and he wondered what damage Granny had left behind him.

Then that little voice in his mind. What if that *was* Granny?

His mind shied away from the awful possibility. God forbid!

Head west… He pulled back on the stick to climb at full boost (uh-oh, engine temperatures a little higher than normal…) hopefully to his rendez-vous with Granny, the pressure dragging at his body and pressing the oxygen mask almost painfully hard against his face, the adrenaline still coursing powerfully through his sweat-soaked and shaking body. He felt an insane urge to barrel roll his Tiffie, whether in defiance or celebration he could not say, and clamped down on it, reaching out instead to run a finger gently across her photo, safely tucked in as usual. He might be betraying her in his intimacy with another girl, but he loved her no less than before.

He feared dear old S-Sugar may have battle damage that could cause her wings, or something equally vital, to fall off if he didn't treat her gently, although he could not remember feeling anything punching into her during the attack, just the drumming of hail, which comprised pieces of his targets blown airborne, doubtless mixed in with shrapnel from the AA, pattering against her fuselage. But the blast of his bombs might have caused critical damage.

But it's the one you don't feel that does the damage… or something. Breathing hard, he reduced throttle and the angle of ascent. If he wasn't careful, he might find himself crashing into Granny…

Wouldn't hurt to be careful, he had two women and a baby to think about, after all.

And then he laughed at the thought, how strange to think that immediately after an attack on a well-defended enemy airbase on occupied territory!

His earlier mood of near madness had dulled to a deep feeling of gratitude at having survived.

Thank you, merciful God, for keeping these two idiots safe in the midst of that violence…

Climbing steadily upwards at 300mph, the countryside below a faded blur, St André de l'Eure a smoke-shrouded glow in the darkness, only the coastline distinct through a thin layer of mist beneath him as Sugar finally reached 10,000 feet. Levelling off, he called quietly, "Granny? I'm here…"

Silently, a set of navigation lights winked on and off three times, half a mile ahead and to starboard, and he hurried to take up position on P-Popsie's starboard side, checking as he did so that it was a Typhoon he was joining formation with.

Fervently he thought, Oh, Granny, thank God you're OK!

"Glad to see you, you tart! Now join up, so we can get the hell out of it! Is your kite OK?"

The engine temperature had settled nicely again and she felt wonderful. "Flying sweet as a nut, Leader."

Rose thought of the glowing stove and the sweet cocoa waiting for them and laid his palm onto the photograph. We made it, Moll, and we're on our way back…

Chapter 31

My Darling Flash,

I wish you were here. I want so very much to hold you and to be held by you.

I miss you. I love you.

The War Office telephoned me today. John is being repatriated ahead of his group because he needs special care for his leg, and the Germans are making an exception to allow his early return.

The Swiss Red Cross will fly him in to Dublin Airport tonight. The RAF will be waiting and will transfer him to London, then I shall bring him home.

I'm so happy, I could burst, yet it feels as if my heart has broken. It's strange because I want to laugh, but I want to cry, too.

And I'm terrified. I'm scared that things will be different, because I've changed, and John has gone through so much. I can only hope and pray that there remains enough of who we were before he left, for our love to endure.

I miss you, and I love you, Flash. I want to kiss you and feel you moving inside me.

You have been everything I needed, when I needed it, but in so being, you became so much more for me.

When I was lost, you carried me to safety. When I was desolate, you comforted me. When I was alone, you came to me. When I was weak, you braced me. Without John, my soul was fading, and you restored it.

Some, if they knew, would think that what we had and did was wrong. What do they know? How can one quantify the value of what we gave and received? How can I explain how you changed my life, and perhaps even saved it? How can they know the depth of my despair, how lost and alone I was?

In losing John, I was adrift in a limbo of hopelessness and misery and deepest loss. I was finished.

And then you came, and made the dry ashes of my existence into joy and life, mending my broken pieces and strengthening me such that I can now face my future and my task with renewed hope and fortitude.

I regret nothing, except that I am unable to love you more, for you have enriched me in so many ways. In parting from you my heart will break, yet it will be healed by the man I hope to heal in turn. In leaving one love, I shall return to the other.

Thank you for everything. You were my dearest friend and my precious lover, and have become far more than both.

But now I have to return to my life once more, away from the wonderful, incredible distraction of you.

I once heard someone say that it was possible to love more than one person at the same time, and I thought how foolish they were.

But now I know better.

Thank you for being there for me when I most needed it, for not taking what was not given freely, for being gentle, for the respect, dignity and the love you gave me. Thank you for sharing yourself, and for giving all that you could without demands or complaint, for your tenderness and for your humanity. I fell in love with you without meaning to, and I am glad.

I love you, my darling, and I love being in love with you.

I will miss you until the day my heart stops, and beyond.

I adore you, my dearest man. God keep you forever safe and loved, and may you enjoy a long, fruitful and joyful life in the peace to come.

Always,
Your Charlie ~ x

Rose was still for a moment, his eyes on the letter, but no longer seeing it. Then, he slowly folded it and put it to his nose, the drops of scent she had scattered across it being all that was left of their time together.

He sighed, and lay back against the pillow, switching off the lamp as he did so.

You ungrateful fool, you have a wonderful and loving family waiting for you. You had a wonderful time with the girl, but it's over now. Be glad of what you had, treasure the wonderful memories you made together.

You've had more than most.

So why do I feel so bloody unhappy?

He had no answer, just a crushing sense of emptiness heavy in his chest. His other hand reached out to rest his fingertips lightly against the frame containing Molly's photograph on his bedside cabinet.

Rose closed his eyes against the oppressive darkness of the room and felt a tear trickle down his cheek.

Chapter 32

"Come on, Flash, you old misery guts. It might never happen!"

Too late. It already has, thought Rose glumly, but he mustered a smile for Sid. "You're right, old chap." He looked closely at his friend. "My goodness, the face on you! I could say the same!"

"It's this blinking briefing after dinner, Flash. Jacko and I were going into town to check out a new act. It's a brand new show, we've never seen it before, the Yanks brought it over from someplace called, er, what was it? Um, cor, can't remember."

"Fancy that," he said sceptically.

"Hang on, hang on. Flipping heck, Flash, don't look at me like that... I need to think. Blimey, what was it? New Lyons? Fuck me. Jacko, what was it?"

Jacko looked as if he were going to cry. "*New Orleans.*"

"Well, why didn't you say so, instead of making me look like a right ninny? What a name. Flash, eh? Properly exotic, isn't it? New Orleans!" Sid spoke with awe.

Rose stared doubtfully at him. "An act from New Orleans?"

"Yeah! Two girls, an' all!"

Rose shivered involuntarily. "Two? Good grief. I don't think I want to know any more, Sid."

Where on earth do they find out about these shows?

"They say it's proper classy, Flash. Not tacky or anything."

"Really?"

Not tacky? I thought it was the tacky ones you two like?

"Two girls, Flash, two! And you won't guess what they do!"

Jacko interjected, "And a goat!" Then he looked startled, as if he couldn't believe his own words.

Dear Lord! Rose shuddered again – a goat! If it's anything remotely like the Ginger Ring, I really, really don't want to know!

He tried not to think about it. "Please, Sid, Jacko, I'm not interested. Honestly, I don't want to know, it'll be dinner soon, and I really don't want to lose my appetite!"

Sid chortled. "Sometimes, Flash, I wonder about you! You sure you weren't taking Holy Orders before all this started?" He poked the knot of Rose's tie. "You ain't a vicar, are you?"

Jacko stared at him suspiciously. "Ooh! Vicar?"

Despite his gloom, Rose couldn't help but smile. "Go on, get lost, you pair of daft beggars!"

Sid tut-tutted and stood up. "Come along, Jacko. He might be a vicar, but our sainted flight commander is an unkind man, lacking in the nuts and bolts of understanding of the simple sufferings and desires of his fellow man, or men, in our case. Let us pray the CO keeps it short and allows us to partake of our deserved entertainments."

Giving Rose a dirty look, Jacko shook his head, then grinned brightly and winked at him, before turning and shambling after Sid.

Granny stood before the empty grate in the officers' mess, a pint of beer half empty in his hand, Belle sitting beautiful and demure to one side, Mati slouched against the fireplace.

"Thanks for being here, boys, I know some of you had plans." He glanced at Sid and Jacko. "And don't look at me like that, Jacko, I'm not coming with you blokes to that bloody show!"

He nodded at the assembled pilots. "Because we're flying more and more Rhubarbs over occupied territory, there's a chance that if it all goes tits up, we might end up down doo-dah creek without a Tiffie. So I've arranged for some intelligence bods to come down, and then we'll have a little exercise in escape and evasion, C Flight first, then B two hours later and A two hours after that."

He noisily slurped from his beer glass, stuck his cigarette back into his mouth, and smiled lopsidedly. "Be like a holiday for you lads, be a laugh!"

*

Rose felt as if he couldn't move. His cheeks ached where the soldiers had slapped him, and his muscles quivered with exhaustion.

Bloody hell, if that's what it is to escape and evade, I've had quite enough. If I get shot down and survive, they can pick me up, I won't struggle.

It had seemed simple enough, to begin with. The demonstration was given by a couple of chaps from intelligence, one of whom had been an RAF flying officer wearing a Military Cross ribbon in front of his DFM and was a successful escapee, having been shot down over Belgium.

The other was a civilian in a simple suit, with a sardonic smile and sharp, unsmiling eyes that made Rose shudder without knowing why.

The RAF officer had been very intense and spoke at length – "Don't offer anyone a cigarette or chocolate, keep moving, never stop for a few days, try and get in contact with an evasion line, if you're on evading without assistance move only at night time, blah, blah… " – before handing out escape and evasion material, which included a variety of objects such as buttons, pipes and belt buckles, all of which contained tiny hidden compasses or magnetised metal parts that could be used as compasses.

There were a number of routing aids too, including some rather beautiful and detailed silk maps of France, Belgium and Germany. These were meant to be returned after every trip, but Rose purloined one – it would make a great gift for Molly!

They had then opened up an escape kit pack to check its contents. Whilst the boiled sweets, milk tablets and chewing gum were quite acceptable, the liver toffee tasted a great deal nicer than it sounded! They examined the other items – fishing line, morphine, needle and thread, collapsible water bottle and phrasebooks – cursorily, and were given an idea of the cost of some basic staples, the better to use their foreign currency allowance should they evade alone and have to buy their own food.

Rose would have been half asleep, had it not been for the roving eyes of the silent man in civvies. The chap didn't look a very nice sort at all, but at least the lecture would soon be over and they would be able to 'escape' to lunch.

Except they didn't, as Granny led them straight out to an army Bedford truck ("Be a great experience, chaps! Be a laugh!") and dropped them twenty miles away, scattered in various locations, with instructions to get back and not to be caught.

Hairy, the cheeky bugger, telephoned a 'friend' and spent the rest of the day with her, in her bed, whilst Sid managed to get to within five miles of Little Sillo before getting caught. Poor Jacko was found in a pub ten miles north of where he'd been dropped off, looking dazed – the large collection of empty beer glasses in front of him may have contributed to his befuddlement.

Rose had traipsed across endless fields and through a stream, run from hedge to hedge, and trodden in an amazing quantity and range of faeces. He was run to ground (or more accurately, up a tree) four miles from the start point by a slavering army dog. Rose, being terrified of dogs, only came down once the huge brute was muzzled, leashed and led away.

Sid and Jacko's wingmen had made it. The two boys met up and hitched a lift in a truckload of communications Wrens on their way to the Royal Naval Base at Portland. The two youngsters were thrilled to share the back of a truck with a load of attractive and rather bold girls, who in turn were ecstatic to have a couple of the RAF's glamour boys amongst them. Consequently, the boys had shamed their elders and (supposedly) betters by being the only members of the flight to successfully return to the airfield.

Thus, while Rose and the others who had been caught were having their cheeks reddened by slaps – for which they should have been grateful, because the normal treatment included some pretty hefty kicks and punches, but Granny didn't want his precious pilots dented, just humiliated – the two junior pilots of the flight, with dates arranged for the weekend, were having their cheeks reddened with lipstick kisses.

Rose rubbed his tender cheek gently. Bloody youngsters!

Chapter 33

The sky was ominously dark, with fitful bursts of light rain and the promise of more to come.

It was perfect weather for Rhubarbs.

But, with the gradual re-direction of Luftwaffe fighters (bomber and fighter-bombers, in short, anything that flew and could be spared) to the developing cataclysm for the Reich that was unfolding on the Eastern Front, it was very unlikely that the coastal towns of England would have regular visits from across the water now, despite the ideal conditions.

And with the fast-approaching summer, the Luftwaffe Jabo aerial campaign was tapering off with a whimper.

The enemy could not afford to throw away men and aeroplanes for so little return when they were needed so badly elsewhere – in the grim struggle with Stalin's forces over an extended front and against the relentless day and night bombing raids over Germany.

When Belle presented him with that morning's met report, Granny rubbed his hands with glee. The day promised cloud, with a base of between 800 and 1,000 feet, mist and episodic squalls.

He was going anti-shipping with Brat, west of the Channel Islands, whilst Rose would take Hairy and go hunting around the Cherbourg Peninsula. The duty sections would maintain the standard defensive patrols.

With a little judicious planning, Belle and Mason arranged the roster to allow all of the pilots the opportunity to carry out at least one Rhubarb in a ten-day period.

Today, they would each carry a pair of 500lb bombs, and hoped for enemy merchant vessels skulking close in to the French coast. Another target – less desirable, because of their better armament and support of one another when closed up – would be small warships, with groups of E-boats emerging from their lairs along the coast pre-dusk, to cast mischief amongst Allied coastal shipping, ports and harbours. E-boats fared poorly if bracketed by a pair, or even close to the explosion, of 500 pounders.

Rose hated the feel of the bombs, the heaviness of S-Sugar's airframe and the drag as she flew, as if she were drunk, but my, the damage they had already managed with the things!

The previous week, Toffee Red Section found a small convoy of six Wehrmacht Opel Blitz troop-carrying trucks on the main road west of Bayeux, just after dawn. They tore them to shreds with a well-placed quartet of 250 lb bombs and two bursts of Hispano. As soon as the soldiers of the convoy heard the snarl of S-Sugar diving down upon them, they leapt from their trucks and ran for their lives.

The bent and blackened metal skeletons of what had been, only seconds earlier, rather a neat little group of trucks, now lay jumbled, broken and ablaze beneath rising edifices of oily black smoke on the battered road. Those not quite fast enough to escape were now scattered red and field-grey bundles of torn fabric and flesh.

What followed the slaughter of the trucks was strangely more agreeable.

The little convoy was being led by a sleek black staff car. With its charges wrecked and burning behind it, the open-topped vehicle scurried down the road like a monstrous shiny black beetle chasing after a crevice to disappear into, half hidden by the dust being thrown into the air behind its racing wheels, smooth sides flashing with light as it passed between the areas of shade, thrown desperately by its driver along turns in the road, the man behind the wheel showing his skill, taking it around bends at what seemed like insane speeds, yet never quite crashing.

I wonder if Moll went to the same school of driving, Rose thought unkindly, then glanced at her photo.

Sorry, my love, didn't mean it!

Again and again, he swooped down after the car, but the trees bordering the road were a hazard. More than once, he felt thin branches clutch at the tip of his wings and propeller, and the fire flashed through him, the excitement of the chase lit by the frantic actions of the car driver below.

And all the while, Rose took an occasional and fleeting look ahead and around him, fearing hidden flak or alerted fighters, but comfortable in the knowledge that J-Jenny flew close behind in protection and support.

The soldier behind the wheel weaved unpredictably along straight stretches, slowing or accelerating into bends at random, and the squirts of cannon fire were always just too short. Time after time, he overshot, but this contest could have only one conclusion.

Had the man stopped and fled with his passengers, Rose would not have pursued them. As it was, his fifth burst caught the fuel tank and the car was lifted by the explosion, tipping end after end, black-uniformed figures being thrown from it like rag dolls to be smashed by the road surface as it met their plunging bodies, the car and its skilful driver a disintegrating mass of flames as the vehicle careened off a wooden fence, caught a glancing blow off a tree trunk and finally came to rest in a ditch, now just a guttering ball of fire.

He would always remember the sense of victory as his cannon shells hit it, the sight of the flashes striking the body of the car and its softer contents.

I wish I could have told her what I did, how it felt to kill a man as he was trying to get away, the fear making him drive like a racing champion even as I blew him to kingdom come, he thought to himself. But he was troubled by the elation he had felt at the deaths of the men in the car, the pillars of smoke from the trucks far behind marring the sky, and again he experienced the feeling of loss.

He felt her eyes on him and lightly touched the photograph. I love you Moll, and I always will – for you are the most important thing in my life, you and Danny.

But I don't regret what I did with Charlie…

It may have been wrong, but it was right for us at the time.

And, God help me, I do miss her.

*

Just before dusk, over the English Channel.

The French coast appeared through the mist and light rain before them, a hazy line faded into the sea, and as they drew closer he could see the darker stretch of Cherbourg and its harbour, but they would be going nowhere near it, thanks very much. Whilst it may contain some rather juicy targets, it was also very heavily defended, and Rose didn't fancy their chances if they attacked.

He had heard tales from the few survivors of the brave Blenheim, Hampden and Beaufort boys, who were ordered to attack targets inside heavily defended harbours and – mostly – never came back.

What courage! What an extraordinary breed of men they must be, to go in when they knew the chances of survival were so low. Their ranks thinned rapidly, yet still the survivors would go again, and again…

And what extraordinary fools were the ones who sent them to do such things, squandering precious men like that.

And now, they would turn to port, away from the harbour, away from the light and towards the grey of approaching night, and with a bit of luck, catch an enemy ship heading north-east, close inshore, whilst there was still light in the sky.

The two Typhoons stayed below 100 feet, flying roughly parallel to the coast, about five miles out. They would be difficult to track from the shore in these conditions, and coastal flak should pose no danger. A lovely large and slow, slab-sided ship should be far easier to catch sight of against the darker shore.

Rose kept glancing at the sky around them, worried they might be bounced, knowing that with cloud at around 1,000 feet there was little room for warning or manoeuvre, should 109s or 190s emerge suddenly from the cloud.

Yet there was little chance of such a bounce; the cloud was too low. The usual escorting fighters were probably sitting on their airfields at readiness; the fighter presence over a convoy this close to Britain would only have alerted the Chain Home Low system that something was being protected, and therefore worth investigating. Without a fighter escort, Axis shipping had a better chance of going undetected.

And of course, whilst it might hide a multitude of dangers, nearby low cloud provided a wonderful cover to disappear into if attacked.

The minutes stretched out as they flew in silence, knowing that German radar would probably have picked them up and that even now as his eyes searched, enemy fighters may be rising from their airfields.

Mid-way between Cherbourg and Le Havre: "Toffee Red Two to Leader, something to starboard, two o'clock."

Rose looked, could just make out a shape, more of a blotch, dark against the lighter coastline, the blemish of smoke dull against the half-light.

"I see it, arm your bombs, Hairy. Must be a Jerry this close to the coast, and it looks as if the fighter screen's pissed off home for the evening. We'll attack straight away, cloud's too low for dive bombing, besides, the light's going fast."

He banked gently, heading directly towards the shape, reducing altitude and throttle as he did so, but not too low, for the light was slowly fading and it wouldn't do to fly too close to the surface.

In the gloom, a light flashed from the ship, piercing and insistent.

Uh-oh, we're being challenged… What was it Phipps said…?

"Hairy, I'm dropping a flare."

The flare worked, for the enemy did not open fire, instead the light on the bridge of the cargo ship flashed more persistently.

As they drew closer, the dark blotch resolved into a ship, the hull lighter against the sea. As he thumbed off the cannon's safeties, he could see that their target was a cargo ship, just over 2,000 grt and about 250 feet long, two masts and derricks, a single funnel behind a squat superstructure closer towards the final third of her hull. The stern flew her colours, and the snapping red flag with a swastika confirmed who she was.

As they closed, the white moustache at her bows increased as she sped up, her wake and the smoke from her stack thickening, already curving in towards the coast, and suddenly another light flashed on her stern, a muzzle flash, and a puff of smoke with a fiery heart appeared before them.

With a sick feeling, he saw that there was another ship behind the first, dropping back to provide cover, its grey lines sleeker and set lower.

Rose wondered why the escort had been on the wrong side of the merchant vessel, but there was no time to wonder, only to be grateful and to attack while he was still shielded.

At first, he thought it was an E-boat, cringing as tracer and cannon fire drifted up to greet them, then realised it was actually an R-boat, for the pugnacious little minesweeper was more like a mini destroyer, being only about a third as long as an RN Tribal class, but she could still pack a fair punch, which was the reason why they were often used as convoy escorts for Axis shipping.

Searchlights flicked on, turning towards him.

They'll try and blind me with the light, don't look at it…

Easier said than done, he thought, and thumbed the radio transmitter. "Hairy, get the cargo ship, I'll take the warship."

There was no reply, but Cox's cannon flashed and cannon shells tore across the distance to churn the sea and flash brilliantly against the shapely hull of the cargo ship.

The space between the Typhoon and the warship burst asunder with the dirty brown and yellow blooms of AA – crump, crump, crump – and he hunched down in fear as tracer lanced out towards him. It came lethargically at first, almost as if it begrudged appearing, but became faster and faster as it drew closer, until it slashed past at an enormous rate.

He ruddered to one side desperately, and then he was firing back, the sea boiling as his shells tore into the water, before climbing up the side of the R-boat, fighting against the turmoil of air battered and torn by the explosions of AA, to keep S-Sugar level and hold his cannon fire onto the hull of the enemy warship.

One searchlight flickered and went out, the other sweeping swiftly to seize at him, and he squinted in the glare.

As soon as the upper works of the enemy had erupted with the flash from his Hispano kiss, he released his bombs and pulled up to clear the warship's masts and aerials, feeling the chunk, chunk, chunk of impacts against Sugar's port wing, and she lurched, but thankfully she still flew.

The R-boat disappeared beneath him, a radio aerial whipping with a crack against the wing, and then it was behind him, the searchlight beam twisting and twirling to try and capture him once more, the afterimage all that was left in his eyes and he rapidly blinked to clear it, trying desperately to catch sight of the water. He could still see the image of the little vessel's bridge with the two rubber ring lifesavers in their clips, the bridge crew staring, wide-eyed and mouths open, the captain with his white-topped cap.

There was an almighty BANG, the creak of tearing metal, and S-Sugar leapt up fifty feet and was thrown over onto its side, and with a wildly hammering heart and his mouth open in a silent scream of fear, he fought to bring her back level and down as she winged over into a shallow dive, his arms and back straining, vision greying, and he heard and felt at least one of his bombs strike the enemy vessel, for now behind him the sky lit up with an awful flash and the air around him boiled, the shockwave threatening to knock him down into the sea.

Got her! He had not expected to succeed because the warship was quite a small target, and his bombs could quite easily have simply skipped over her, fore and aft.

He struggled to pull back up as the sea rushed to meet him, leaning hard into his straps, and at the last moment, unbelievably, he somehow kept her in the air, muscles aching and battered, his mouth set in a rictus of strain and terror as S-Sugar climbed upwards again.

Elation surged within him even as he settled her back into level flight.

No tracer chased after him as he levelled out fifty feet above the waves, ruddering and aileroning her to skim to starboard.

Made it! He felt like crying with relief as he turned S-Sugar in a wide circle. "Hairy?" His voice sounded cracked and weak even to his own ears as he struggled to breathe.

The cargo ship was stopped and burning, one of her masts gone, and she settled lower in the water as he watched, listing onto her port side as the water rushed in through the gaping hole Cox had blown in her.

Above her, the low cloud glowed an angry cherry red, as if in sympathy with the fires raging through her, welcoming and mingling with the thick smoke.

Of the R-boat, there was no sign, just burning fragments rising and falling on the black swell below.

Breathlessly, faintly: "Flash? You OK? Fuck me!"

"Good job, Hairy, right on target! You got her! She's sinking!"

Cox's voice was strained. "Fuck me!" he repeated. "I thought I was a goner when the bombs went off. Tracer from your warship was about to slice through me when your bomb blew her to bits! I really thought I was for the chop!"

Rose stared at the cloud above anxiously, wary of what might descend at any moment. "Me too, I couldn't hold her, almost went straight in!"

Thank God. He swallowed shakily and took a deep breath. "Is your kite OK?"

"Engine's overheating a bit, and I think I took a hit on the tail, Flash. I've got a strange vibration in the airframe." Cox's voice, normally unruffled, was concerned.

A cold spike of fear lanced through him. "Crikey! OK, Hairy, I think it's high time we went home, flash your lights and I'll form up with you, I'll catch up, just turn straight for home, pal, but carefully. Just in case."

"Right you are, Flash. I'm going to reduce the throttle and gain a bit of height, get above the cloud and into smoother air."

It'll still be light higher up. "OK, Hairy. Lead the way, I'm a mile behind you, and I'll join up with you when we're both above cloud."

*

Calais-Marck, Luftwaffe airfield, twenty minutes earlier.

"Alarmstart! Peter! Peter! Alarmstart! Get up!"

Peter started and snuffled awake as his young Rottenflieger gently kicked at the frame of the deckchair in which he had been dozing.

"What the...?"

286

"Herr Oberfeldwebel! The old man says the navy are screaming about British fighter-bombers patrolling off Cherbourg!" The youngster was quickly walking towards the fighters already, looking back at Peter as he did so. "There's a convoy they want protecting."

"Scheisse!" Peter rubbed his face vigorously and frowned at the young Fahnrich's enthusiasm, before getting to his feet and stumbling after him. "Stick to my tail like glue, Franz. No chasing glory or chancing a quick victory, stay with me!"

"I know."

"Like fucking glue, you hear me?"

"I know!"

Peter looked down at his life jacket and equipment, automatically checking his supplies and survival gear. "I mean it, for fuck's sake!"

"*I know!*"

They clambered into the FW 190s, the engines already bellowing their impatience, the billowing clouds of blue smoke choking them.

He saw his Rottenfleiger wave enthusiastically as his Schwarze Manner strapped him in and sternly ignored it, dropping his eyes to check the controls instead.

He was a Krieger, damnit, not a bloody Schüler!

It was really easy to die up there, terrifyingly easy, and young Franz needed to curb his eagerness and knuckle down, otherwise some RAF pilot would gladly kill him soon enough. Peter would have been the first to admit that he had only made it this far because he had listened to his betters and done what they told him to do, but also because he had been lucky, very lucky, and he feared the day when the luck ran out.

Lucky today, but tomorrow, who knew?

He now proudly wore the Iron Cross First and Second Class on his tunic, as well as the Silver Front Flying Clasp, and knew that Franz hero-worshipped him, which was a bit of a laugh, really, considering that he himself had been an eager, naive and inexperienced youth like Franz just a few short months ago.

But then, eight months counted as an eternity here on the Channel Front.

They were high above the cloud, around 5,000 feet, where the sunlight still shone, Rose fretfully weaving behind J-Jenny to scan the sky around them.

"The engine temperature's over 104 degrees, Flash, but it's holding steady there. I've got the radiator flap open and the revs down…"

Rose glanced anxiously at his friend's Typhoon, smoke-stained, torn and battered, but at least it was flying. "Thank goodness, but keep an eye on it, chum."

S-Sugar had received a cannon strike, but it had ripped through her fuselage without exploding, and he could feel the column vibrating in his hands as he kept his throttle reduced to maintain position with Cox.

Uh-oh. "Hairy, there's a thin trail of white smoke…"

If it's coolant…

Behind the two Typhoons, the pillar of smoke was climbing high behind them through the cloud and into the darkening sky, marking their success and the destruction of the little convoy.

We need to get away fast, that smoke's going to attract attention, and they'll be buzzing like flies around here very soon.

"Keep an eye on it, Hairy, we'll head for Warmwell. It's closer." He found he was jiggling in his seat tensely, as if it might make them get home faster, and he forced himself to sit still.

"Sod that, Flash, there's too much high ground around Warmwell, at least Little Sillo's a lot less hilly. I'm going home."

Then: "Oh shit."

Rose's heart lurched painfully. "What?"

"Temperature's starting to go up again, 110 degrees…"

Damn it! It must be coolant! And was that trail of overheated coolant just that little bit thicker? Boiling away that little bit faster?

He could imagine the hive of activity in his friend's cockpit as he fought to adjust the settings to reach a good balance between speed and trying to minimise the Sabre heating any more than it already was.

As the temperature of the engine rose, there was a danger it would burst into flames, or at least grind to a stop. But with the less than ideal conditions, bailing out over the sea would be like a death sentence for Cox, and trying to ditch J-Jenny would be no better.

"Toffee Red Leader to Ops, please advise conditions at the coast?"

"Ops to Toffee Red Leader, it's just after dusk, still light, dry, south-easterly four knots, six-tenths patchy cloud with a cloud base of 2,000 feet. You are just under nine miles south of Poole. Home is heading three-five-two." The girl must have noticed their reduced speed, for her voice was concerned.

"Thanks, Ops."

And then her voice again, timidly. "Good luck…"

It's going to be dark down there soon. "Hairy, try and get back over land, then bail out, don't risk a landing, you won't be able to see a thing."

"I've been through a lot with Jenny, Flash, least I can do is try and get her back. If I can't, I can't, fair enough, but if I can…"

"Toffee Red Leader from Blackgang, two bandits at your six o'clock, angels six. Range five miles, speed 380."

Rose's already strained heart lurched again, and he groaned inwardly. What? That's the cherry on the bloody cake, that is! "Hairy start your descent now. I'll cover you…"

"Stay with me, Flash! They won't find us in the cloud."

"No mate, they might, the cloud is a bit on the patchy side. I'll just give 'em a quick burst, cool their ardour a touch, so to speak, and then I'll be right behind you."

You've no chance against a pair of bandits, Hairy, old son, I need to give you a fighting chance by making sure they don't follow you…

"Make sure that you do, Flash, I've got you trained just right now, can't be bothered to do it all again!"

"Just get back down safe, Hairy!" Rose kicked right rudder and pulled back hard on the stick, throwing S-Sugar into a tight turn, eyes already searching for the enemy in the dimming sky.

Almost immediately he picked them up, a pair flying just above the cloud, the two black dots easy to see against the lighter backdrop.

In this light the fight should only last a short while, we won't be able to see each other shortly…

Lord God, let me live, and let Hairy come through safely, please.

The distance closed quickly, and he aimed directly for them, pressing the firing button, his cannon shells tearing across towards the enemy, the corkscrewing smoke trails reaching outwards, and suddenly they were past, dark blurs that felt so close he could have touched them, his Typhoon shuddering and lurching in the turbulence of their passage, and he kicked rudder again and pulled hard after them, turning tightly to starboard, praying S-Sugar had not received serious damage in the shipping attack which would cause her to break up as he threw her around so violently.

Hold it together, baby.

He felt like shouting with glee, for whilst the leader had continued on and up to gain position, his wingman had turned, and Rose cut the throttle and rolled over after him.

The Focke-Wulf was trying to turn into him, but not tight or fast enough, and Rose cut inside him and brought his cannon to bear from the front port quarter, hammering at the 190 as it shot past beneath him, tiny explosions flaring across it. With a glance to check the other one, he twisted again after the battered little fighter, the forces pushing him hard into his seat.

It was no longer darting about, just flying straight and level, a thin, almost invisible streamer of smoke trailing behind it. Rose dropped down behind it and centred the 190 in his gunsight. For a moment he stared at it thoughtfully, the dark shape shedding smoke and wallowing in front of him. He lifted his finger from the gun button, and with a burst of throttle, uneasily pulled alongside the damaged Focke-Wulf.

The sun was below the horizon now, the light muted, but he was still able to see how the enemy pilot slouched in his straps, the shattered Perspex of the canopy, the rent fuselage, and the jerky way the German boy slowly turned his head to look at the Typhoon alongside, before painfully facing forwards again.

Rose stared at him for a moment, remembering the crimson face of a lost American boy in a ghost bomber helplessly staring back at him. But the other 190 was already coming down behind them for a slashing pass, and with a sigh, he turned away hard and dived down into the sanctuary of cloud.

*

Peter, disbelieving that the enemy fighter had not finished Franz off, cautiously took up position alongside the battered Focke-Wulf, where the Typhoon had been moments earlier.

"Franz, can you hear me?" He looked around him nervously for any sign of the Typhoon returning.

The boy's voice was weak and filled with pain. "Peter, I think my arm is broken, and my head is aching. I'm finished, leave me…"

Peter looked around at the night sky, fearful of the monsters that might be lurking, but he need not have worried, for Rose was long gone.

"Shut up, you silly boy! Listen, Franz, I'm going to get you home. I want you to do exactly as I say…"

Epilogue 1

"I've just heard, Peter. The young idiot has a spot of concussion, and they're giving him a transfusion and setting his arm at the moment. He won't fly again for at least six months, but he's going to live. If you hadn't stayed with him, he wouldn't have made it back. You saved his life, but his FW190 Anton is a total write-off."

Peter looked at Braun with wonder still on his face. "That Typhoon pilot could have shot him down, but he didn't. Why would he do that, Herr Hauptmann?"

Braun took off his cap and scratched his head, and Peter was shocked to see how much new grey there was in his Staffelkapitan's hair.

"Who knows, Peter? He'd just blown the hell out our ships, killed dozens of sailors, and yet he was merciful to young Franz. Even in the midst of the butchery I saw on the ground in Poland, there was still decency. Perhaps he saw that killing Franz wouldn't change anything in the long run. Whatever his reasons, I'm grateful. Franz's death would have been meaningless. Just another boy dead in this madness."

Peter lowered his voice. "Careful, sir. You don't know who might be listening."

Braun nodded tiredly. "Yes, you're right, of course." He took a deep breath and let it out. "You did a good job, lad. I'm recommending you for the Kriegsverdienstkreuz. For getting him back. Franz's life counts for that much, at least."

The War Merit Cross! Peter was surprised and thrilled. "Thank you, sir! I just wanted to save Franz, that's all."

"I know, Peter, I know, but you deserve it. The boy's life is worth a lot, but he wouldn't have it if it weren't for your actions. But for the moment, enjoy yourself, get yourself a bottle and a girl, because we won't be here next week."

"It's true, then, Herr Hauptmann?"

"Yes, lad, it is. How good's your Russian?"

*

"Right, chaps, settle down, quick announcement. As you already know, our beloved Cowboy has finally been tracked down by the USAAF, and the poor bloke's been conscripted straight in, at the rank of major, no less!" There were boos and jeers, and Cowboy clasped his hands over his head like a champion rodeo rider.

"In addition, the powers that be, in their eternal glory, have promoted me, and they've also appointed me wing leader of 44 Wing, RAF. Just goes to show – occasionally, they get it right!"

More boos and jeers, and Mati's brow wrinkled. "Not sure I've heard of 44 Wing RAF. Where are they based, then, Granny?"

"Here, you soft tart! Little Sillo! They want me to form a second Typhoon squadron to make a wing of two squadrons, based here. So as of this moment, we are non-operational, and there'll be some extended and well-earned leave."

"Who will be leading the squadrons, Granny, er, sir?" asked Sid. "Have they been appointed yet?"

Granny grimaced. "'Fraid so, nothing I could do about it, I'm afraid. Went over my head. Fought 'em tooth and nail, but to no avail, I fear."

Their faces fell, and Scarlet swore – "fucking hell!" – and they all turned to stare at him in surprise.

The new wing commander nodded solemnly. "I wouldn't have chosen who they picked, but there you go, when has the Air Ministry ever done anything that made sense?"

Jacko looked as if he would be sick, and he scratched at the scars on his wrists anxiously. "Bad, sir?"

Granny nodded. "An absolute pair of blithering idiots. Truly the worst. I'll do my best with them, of course I will, but there's only so much a chap can do with a pair of thick planks."

He grinned, waved his hand at Scarlet. "Will gets the new squadron, and I'm sorry, I can't believe it myself, it's madness, but Flash here is Excalibur's new CO!"

There was uproar, and Rose thought he would faint dead away.

Squadron leader? Me?

Granny beamed at his two new squadron leaders. "Quieten down, boys, I know it's fucking awful news, but you'll just have to grin and bear it. There's more. I've a list of decorations for the squadron's conduct over the last six months."

He coughed modestly. "There's a bar to my DSO, Cowboy. Will and Flash get bars to their DFCs, a DFC for Brat, about bloody time, and there are DFCs or DFMs for all the section leaders. So, bloody well done, lads, I'm proud of you all!"

Debagging is the traditional ritual for RAF aircrew during celebratory events, and this was no different. Before he could react, Sid and Jacko had relieved Rose of his trousers and disappeared, whooping wildly.

So long as that bloody goat from the show doesn't end up wearing them, he thought sourly, but not for long. Because whilst he might be sitting in his drawers, he was now Squadron Leader Harry Rose, RAF, complete with a second bar to his DFC.

Strewth!

*

So, Granny, Mr Wing Commander, sir, tell me about you and Belle. Molly would love to know, if I'm allowed to tell, of course."

Granny looked down at his sleeve, still bearing the rings of a squadron leader. "Mm, sounds rather grand, doesn't it? Wing Commander Smith RAF. Yes, I like the sound of that. Perhaps I'll get stores to stick some rings on my pyjamas…" He looked up at Rose. "Belle?" He traced a stick figure in the coffee slops on the table, placing crumbs of biscuit as eyes. "Fucking hell, will you look at that? I'm talented! I could have been an artist!"

"Yeah, it's really good, who's it meant to be?"

"Why you, of course, you daft berk! Can't you tell?"

Rose grinned. "Well, come to think of it…"

Granny wiggled his fingers at one of the waiters. "Coffee and biscuits, please, Ned."

As the waiter disappeared, Granny watched him go. "I met her in 1933. Her old man was a judge, still is, the old bastard. I was always pretty handy with a spanner, and the summer before I left to become a Trenchard brat, he noticed me tinkering at the local garage and asked me to keep an eye on his motors. He had a chauffeur who knew his onions about motor cars, but he thought as I had an apprenticeship at Halton, I might be something special." He grinned toothily at Rose. "How right he was!"

"I knew the moment I saw her that she was the girl for me. She could have had anyone, but she chose me. As soon as we could, in 1937, we married. The old boy hated it, but there was nothing he could do about it. We loved each other, were both twenty-one, and that was all there was to it. I was fresh out of Halton and she wanted to go with me to my first posting." He sighed, then pulled out a cigarette and lit it. As he did so the waiter returned with their coffee.

"Thanks, Ned."

The waiter arranged the cups and saucers, then swept away their empties in his tray, nodding respectfully. "Sir."

Rose took a sip. "So where did you two go?" Ouch, that coffee was hot!

Granny pursed his lips. "We didn't. The old goat begged her to go to university and promised she could join me afterwards. He might be an atrocious old fart, but he is her father and she loved him too, going against his wishes hurt her. I couldn't bear to see her cry, broke my heart, so we decided that I would take up my posting alone, and she would go to Oxford. While I was out there in India, I was recommended for pilot training, and ended up as a sergeant-pilot in Excalibur Squadron."

"She didn't join you, then, afterwards?"

Granny crushed his cigarette out on his saucer. "We hardly had time to settle in together. Auntie Adolf stuck his oar in and goose-stepped into the Sudetenland, there was all that nonsense about 'peace for our time' from Neville Chamberlain, then just a year later, war was declared. Belle's dear ol' Pa wouldn't let her anywhere near an RAF airfield, and then Excalibur squadron went out to France with dear old Donald, the balloon went up and it all kicked off." Granny sighed in refection. "He was a fine man, was old Donald, but I don't need to tell you that, you know it already. Anyway, the mademoiselles were very welcoming, and I was most grateful. When you've been three miles up fighting Jerry, four or five times a day, surviving certain death stokes the libido something fierce, and the first thing you want, well the first thing I wanted when I landed, was a damned good fuck. The trick cyclists yammer on that sex is an affirmation of life, and after being almost killed, blokes have a need to spread seed, or some such bollocks. Maybe it's true, but all I know is that drinking and shagging made life easier. I reckon you'll know now what I'm chatting about, pal. Anyway, Belle found out. And that was that. I broke her heart, and I found that hardest to bear, because she means so much to me, always has, always will. When I saw how much I had hurt her, my precious Belle, I loathed myself. She wouldn't meet with me, but she didn't ask for a divorce, either."

"You are still married, then?"

His friend smiled sadly at him. "Yup. Belle never stopped writing to me, even when I went out to the Blue. I was young and daft, too bloody proud to apologise and ask her to come back to me. So, because I didn't have her, I decided I'd enjoy my life with the girls at hand. Some of them meant more than just a good time, you could say that for some of them I felt something, but there's only one who can be your first love. Mine was – and is – Belle. They're always more special."

Rose patted his pocket, his photo of Molly safe there. "I know what you mean, Granny!"

"Belle joined up in '39 using her maiden name and gave her father's address, so I don't think anyone knows we're married. The Air Ministry would have a fucking fit if they knew my senior WAAF is also my missus, but they can go hang, I'm not going to lose her again. I'm going to see if I can keep her here when we become operational again."

Just then, Belle walked in, and catching sight of them, walked over. "Hello, Danny – sir. Hello, Flash, I have a letter for you." Belle smiled warmly at him and passed him an envelope before taking a seat opposite Granny. Rose saw the way she smiled at Granny the look in her eyes, and was glad.

Rose took it carefully, the faint fragrance of Charlie's scent eliciting both joy and sadness.

"Thanks, Belle. Is she well?" he swallowed and asked, "Is he?"

She saw the look on his face even though he tried to keep his expression neutral, and her voice was soft. "She's happy and well, Flash, and he will be, too, given time and care, poor love. And he'll not be flying again. So she'll be happy about that. She has her life back again."

His heart felt heavy, his smile wooden, and his eyes hot. "So long as she's happy. In the end, that's what matters."

Rose swallowed to clear the thickness in his throat.

She nodded and touched his shoulder gently. "That's what matters."

"Oi, Flash, you dirty dog, get yer paws off her, she's mine!"

She pulled back her hand. "What an utterly dreadful man you are! I can't think what I see in you!" But she was smiling as she said it, and he saw the happiness in her eyes, mirrored in those of his friend.

Thank God they had found each other again.

He finished his coffee and stood. "I'll see you around, folks."

Granny scowled at him. "Stores, first thing, you tart! You're improperly dressed! Put up your correct rank before I see you next, or else you'll be on a fizzer!"

Epilogue 2

My precious darling,

I'm looking after John, and it's like we have never been apart! I want you to know that I'm very happy, because I know my happiness matters so very much to you.

You are an incredible and very sweet man, and I love you.

Fate has brought him back to me after all, just as I wished and prayed, and there are no words to describe how grateful I am.

But I will miss you so very much, more than I can say.

I want you to know that I'll never, ever, stop loving you, and will always remember with great pleasure and gratitude the joy that we shared, for the rest of my life.

Yet how I wish that I were Molly!

I might not have mentioned it until now, but I love you.

I may have been a naughty girl when I was with you, but now I'm very good, and I pray to God every night that he keeps my men safe and happy and well.

Keep my special pebble safe, Flash, and hopefully it will return the favour.

In future times, peaceful times, I pray that an old man, sitting in the sunlight in his garden, will lovingly remember the wonderful times he spent in his youth with a girl he once knew, a girl called Charlie.

My life is once more what it was, and I am content because I know how lucky I am in what I have.

And so very lucky in what I had with my precious Tiffie pilot.

But if we should ever meet, and I pray that we do, I hope that we might share a little time together... ...

Flash, my darling, I love you.

May God bless you and keep you safe always,

Your Charlie ~ x

Epilogue 3

He could hear Danny shouting and laughing inside, and the soft, gentle, loving tones of his wife as she played with their child.

He stood there for a moment, eyes closed, enjoying the peace of the moment. How can a man ask for more, when he has the love of his family, birdsong and the sweet fragrance of the countryside?

The glass-panelled door opened to reveal Noreen, who was Molly's ayah and had been her mother's before. "Harry, sahib! Aap agay, badmash larkah!" (Mr Harry! You've returned, you cheeky rascal!)

Rose found himself in a tight bear hug before Noreen dragged him inside, shrieking like a banshee, "Molly, Molly, aap ka shohor aagyah!" (Molly, Molly, your hubby is here!)

Oh my God! He feared his eardrums would burst.

And then she was there, standing in the doorway, flushed and beautiful, eyes glistening, her raven tresses awry and lips in a smile of pure joy. "Harry! Oh my God, Harry!"

He looked thinner, his uniform seemed looser, like a boy dressed in his father's clothes, yet there were dark circles beneath this young man's eyes and new lines around his mouth.

But as soon as he caught sight of her, she saw his face relax with pleasure, and the fixed smile he had been favouring Noreen with now brightened into the real thing.

She rushed forward and hugged him, even tighter than Noreen had, kitbag, gasmask, bags of gifts and all, before she released him and grabbed his lapels to pull him to her lips, his arms encircling her waist.

After a moment she allowed him to take a breath. "Oh, Harry!"

His lips and penis were tingling. "Good Lord! That's what I call a welcome home!"

"If I knew you were coming, I'd have come to pick you up in Dad's car!"

"Didn't think my heart could take it, Moll!"

"His driver would have driven, you brute!" She lightly punched his arm, but tears of joy were streaming down her face. "Oh, Harry!" She looked at him again. "I say! Is that another rosette on your DFC? And a half-stripe, so you're a squadron leader now?"

"I wanted to tell you in person. I caught up with you at last, Molly! I don't have to call you ma'am anymore; at long last, we're of the same rank! And, you won't believe it, but I've been given Excalibur Squadron, I'm the new CO."

It still felt unreal: Harry Rose, Commanding Officer!

In the room behind, he could see Molly's mother, Deborah, holding their son in her arms. "Look, Danny, your Daddy's here!"

His son clasped his grandmother tightly, hiding his face in her hair, but as she put him down, he ran straight to his father.

"Daddy! Daddy! Daddy!"

Rose gathered him up and kissed his head gently. "Oh, my sweet Danny, my little man!" And he was crying.

Once the chaos of his homecoming had settled, Noreen and Molly's mother in the kitchen preparing him a welcome home cup of tea, and Danny busy playing with the new tin tank that Cox had managed to find, he sat on the settee, caught beneath Molly as she hugged him tightly.

"I've got so much to tell you, Harry. I've felt so very empty without you!"

"I felt so lonely without you when I was down in Dorset as well, my love."

She put her hand lightly onto his chest and smirked. "That's not what I meant, you silly man."

He grinned foolishly. "Oh, I see!"

She leaned forward to kiss him lingeringly on the lips, her hand straying down from his chest to gently grasp his crotch, squeezing, and her voice

301

dropped to a breathless whisper. "As soon as we decently can, I'm going to take you upstairs and get what I've been missing until you're begging for mercy!"

It was good to be home.

Author's Note

Defeated by the RAF during The Battle of Britain and then The Blitz, the Luftwaffe's campaign of bombing the UK switched primarily to daylight 'nuisance' raids by swift fighter-bombers.

The concerted operation of attack evolved to include that which came to be known as the 'Tip-and-Run' campaign of March 1942 to June 1943, and this devastating campaign was to primarily employ the ubiquitous Bf109, as well as the Luftwaffe's newest radial-engine fighter.

In August 1941, the Luftwaffe introduced the superlative FW190 'Würger' (Shrike) into operational service, a highly capable fighter-bomber that, in short order, wrestled aerial superiority from the RAF's Fighter Command, particularly in terms of mid and low-level combat.

Aptly named, Kurt Tank's 'Butcher Bird' outperformed the defending Spitfires and Hurricanes in almost every way, more than earning its grim nickname as it cut a bloody swathe of death and destruction through RAF fighter squadrons.

But just when it looked as if the balance had shifted in favour of new tactics and a resurgent Luftwaffe, the Hawker Typhoon was hurriedly brought into service.

The RAF's answer to the FW190 was not without problems; technical and structural issues in addition to problems with misidentification causing an unforgivable loss of pilots, and a rapid plummeting of morale amongst the men tasked to fly and fight in the Typhoon.

Yet even with this loss of confidence in the new fighter, and a real possibility of its withdrawal from the front-line, Squadron Leader Roland Beamont led the charge to keep it at the sharp end, understanding and appreciating the tactical superiority available in the Typhoon's stability, manoeuvrability, robustness, sheer power and speed.

This determined persistence against a sceptical establishment finally prevailed, and with determined efforts to resolve issues throughout 1942, the Typhoon proved itself the answer to the best the Luftwaffe had.

Defending the south coast against the 'Tip and Run' raids was an exhausting and frustrating task, often unrewarded, and being attacked by one's own side was the final insult.

Some pilots found solace in drink, some in the company of friends and loved ones, or more often in both.

With his beloved Molly and Danny far away and as safe as it is possible to be in a country at war, unable to seek regular solace in them from the drudgery of endless patrols and the nerve-shredding stress of combat, I hope that readers will forgive me for allowing Rose's wayward behaviour with Charlie.

For many of the defending Typhoon pilots, the frustration of a tour of endless patrolling without once actually engaging the enemy was a harsh reality, and so Rose has been lucky in having had more than his fair share of interceptions and engagements (sorry, Molly, those grey hairs on Harry's head are down to me).

And now Rose's tour of operations has come to an end.

In it he found danger, uncertainty and terror, leavened by comradeship, salvation and peace.

Excalibur has been withdrawn for a rest and alongside Scarlet's new squadron, becoming a part of Granny's 44 Wing RAF. And for Rose, the challenges of squadron command beckon.

Much desperate and dangerous fighting still lies ahead before the final victory against Nazi Germany, but for the moment, Squadron Leader Harry Rose can rest on his laurels and return to the serenity of his family.

Once more experience and bucketloads of luck have brought him through combat with success and increased esteem.

Typhoon Ace.